No Sweeter Heaven

"Unique, elegant, and sensitive ... a tribute to the strength and hope and the miracle of love. A powerful novel not to be missed."

—Connie Rinehold,
author of
More Than Just a Night

"A dazzling emotional masterpiece ... this is a remarkable book by a writer of infinite grace and exquisite perception. Ms. Kingsley lights up the windows of our souls with a simply glorious love story in which searing passion is radiantly transformed into ineffable joy."

—*Romantic Times*

No Greater Love

"Irresistible ... I couldn't turn the pages fast enough."

—Mary Jo Putney,
author of
Dancing on the Wind

"A rare delight ... writing with exquisite subtlety and a delicate insight into every hidden emotional corner, Ms. Kingsley creates a bevy of unforgettable characters ... don't miss this enchanting love story!"

—*Romantic Times*

ANNOUNCING THE

TOPAZ FREQUENT READERS CLUB
COMMEMORATING TOPAZ'S
1 YEAR ANNIVERSARY!

THE MORE YOU BUY, THE MORE YOU GET

Redeem coupons found here and in the back of all new Topaz titles for FREE Topaz gifts:

Send in:

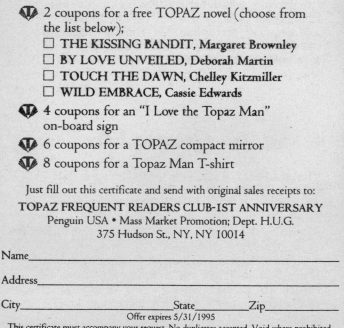

- 2 coupons for a free TOPAZ novel (choose from the list below);
  - ☐ THE KISSING BANDIT, Margaret Brownley
  - ☐ BY LOVE UNVEILED, Deborah Martin
  - ☐ TOUCH THE DAWN, Chelley Kitzmiller
  - ☐ WILD EMBRACE, Cassie Edwards

- 4 coupons for an "I Love the Topaz Man" on-board sign

- 6 coupons for a TOPAZ compact mirror

- 8 coupons for a Topaz Man T-shirt

Just fill out this certificate and send with original sales receipts to:

TOPAZ FREQUENT READERS CLUB-1ST ANNIVERSARY
Penguin USA • Mass Market Promotion; Dept. H.U.G.
375 Hudson St., NY, NY 10014

Name_____

Address_____

City_____ State_____ Zip_____

Offer expires 5/31/1995

This certificate must accompany your request. No duplicates accepted. Void where prohibited, taxed or restricted. Allow 4-6 weeks for receipt of merchandise. Offer good only in U.S., its territories, and Canada.

No Brighter Dream

by

Katherine Kingsley

A TOPAZ BOOK

TOPAZ
Published by the Penguin Group
Penguin Books USA Inc., 375 Hudson Street,
New York, New York 10014, U.S.A.
Penguin Books Ltd, 27 Wrights Lane,
London W8 5TZ, England
Penguin Books Australia Ltd, Ringwood,
Victoria, Australia
Penguin Books Canada Ltd, 10 Alcorn Avenue,
Toronto, Ontario, Canada M4V 3B2
Penguin Books (N.Z.) Ltd, 182–190 Wairau Road,
Auckland 10, New Zealand

Penguin Books Ltd, Registered Offices:
Harmondsworth, Middlesex, England

First published by Topaz,
an imprint of Dutton Signet,
a division of Penguin Books USA Inc.

First Printing, October, 1994
10 9 8 7 6 5 4 3 2 1

Topaz is a trademark of Dutton Signet,
a divison of Penguin Books USA Inc.

Printed in the United States of America

To all the Keepers ...
of the Flame, of the Dreams,
and of the Heavens

ACKNOWLEDGMENTS

I'd like to thank Rod and Margaret Evans who, aboard the spectacular *Nuku II*, introduced me to the magic and wonder of the Lycian Peninsula of Turkey. Thanks also go to Ümit İriş for good conversation and my kilim. Research has never been more fun—çok teşekkür ederim. And a big hug and thanks to Karen Pershing, who supplied me with a copy of Sir Charles Fellows's *Travels and Researches in Asia Minor*, without which I would have been lost.

I also don't know what I ever did without Robert Lee Whitmire or Carole Howey, both of whom nudged and prodded and generally encouraged me from start to finish.

Jan Hiland and Jan Jouflas patiently listened to my endless mutterings with great humor and never once told me to go away, an astonishing feat of patience and caring. And I owe Erica Winkler a five-course, five-star dinner and a *really* good bottle of wine for taking the time to read the final draft of the manuscript and bring her critical eye to it.

My husband, Bruce, and son, Alexander, did their best not to moan and groan when the door shut behind me for months on end, not an easy task. I love you both.

Finally, to the readers: your letters regarding the first two books of the trilogy, *No Sweeter Heaven* and *No Greater Love*, were a wonderful boost, pouring in when I was in the throes of this book, convinced that I had no business writing. The pleasure you take in reading makes the throes worthwhile. I hope you take as much pleasure in Andre and Ali's story. You can write me at P.O. Box 37, Wolcott, Colorado 81655.

Intreat me not to leave thee, or to return from following after thee: for whither thou goest, I will go; and where thou lodgest, I will lodge: thy people shall be my people, and thy God my God.

Ruth 1:16

Prologue

September 1854
Saint-Simon, France

"Andre! Andre, Jo-Jean, wait for me!"

Genevieve's shout floated across the meadow and Andre abruptly stopped and turned. "Genevieve!" he called, waving. "Come on, Jo-Jean and I are going to watch Alain Lascard open the beehives."

She ran toward them, beautiful Genevieve, her long blond braids flying behind her, a smile lifting the corners of her mouth, her porcelain cheeks lightly flushed with pleasure. Andre's heart turned over at the sight of her. He couldn't imagine a world without her in it. There *wasn't* a world without her—she was everything to him.

"You finished your lessons early," she said when she reached them, out of breath. "I went all the way up to the château and Monsieur Dumont said you'd already left."

"Sorry," Andre said with a smile. "We raced through Latin today, so old Dumont let us go. I'd have fetched you from the village, but you know how your mother is about letting you out with me, now that I'm old enough to be considered dangerous." He pulled a leer.

"Oh, you're dangerous all right," Joseph-Jean said. "About as dangerous as a fly."

Andre glared at him. "Just because you're a year older, you think you're—"

Genevieve punched Joseph-Jean's shoulder. "Stop it, both of you, before you end up rolling on the

ground. You might be a year older, but Andre is bigger than you are. You'll get hurt if you tease him."
She grinned.

Joseph-Jean playfully tugged one of his cousin's
braids. "Andre takes life too seriously. He needs a
good tease now and then. Come on, let's see if Monsieur Lascard manages to get stung."

"Don't be mean, Jo-Jean. Poor Monsieur Lascard
always swells up if the bees sting him. I can't understand why he insists on keeping them."

Andre took Genevieve's hand. "He enjoys himself.
Anyway, if he gets stung, Papa will fix him. Papa can
fix anything." His heart swelled with pride. Not all
sons had fathers who could work miracles.

"Well, I wish he would fix my mother's head," Genevieve said, entwining her fingers through Andre's.
"She says I spend much too much time with you."

"Wait until we're married," Andre said, lifting their
clasped hands and kissing the pale, fragile skin of her
wrist. "Then you can spend all your time with me,
and she won't be able to say a thing."

Genevieve's brow furrowed. "I don't know, Andre . . .
she knows that I love you more than anything in the
world, but still she says I'm not for you. I'm only a
simple village girl."

"Nonsense," Joseph-Jean said, giving Genevieve's
shoulder a squeeze. "Just because Andre is a duke's
son shouldn't be any reason to interrupt the course of
true love."

"Exactly," Andre said with satisfaction. "It comes
along once in a lifetime if you're lucky. We are luckier
than most, finding each other so early in life."

Joseph-Jean rolled his eyes. "I can see where this
is headed. I'm going on ahead. There's no point being
around the two of you when all you do is gawk at
each other." He hoisted his ever-present sketch pad
in a wave of departure.

"Go then," Andre said, sending him off with a
laugh. "We'll be with you in a moment." He turned
back to Genevieve and rested his hands on her
slight shoulders.

"I wish you wouldn't worry so. We have plenty of time to bring your mother around to the idea—I still have three more years of schooling here and then university to attend before we can be married, so that's seven years to convince your mother that you will make me a perfect wife."

He looked up at the château sitting above them, the vineyards running down the hillside heavy with fruit, laborers moving among the rows, preparing for the harvest as they had every autumn of the last fifteen years when his father had returned to the land and brought it back to life.

Oh, how he loved Saint-Simon. It was in his blood, as fixed a part of his existence as Genevieve. He couldn't wait until his school days were over and he could work at his father's side, helping him to manage the estate. He and Genevieve had such a bright future ahead.

He smiled down at her. "There are times I can't believe how blessed I am," he said. "To have you, two wonderful parents, Jo-Jean the best of friends, the land—what more could anyone ask?"

"And sometimes I think you live with your head in the clouds," Genevieve said. "You don't think about the realities of life, Andre. What do you think your parents are going to say when you tell them you want to marry me?"

"They'll be overjoyed," he said. "Why wouldn't they be?"

"I think you're wrong," she said, her eyes reflecting her worry. "They probably have already picked out someone for you to marry whose blood is as blue as yours."

"*My* parents? Are we speaking about the same people? They don't give a snap about that sort of thing, and you should know it." He grinned. "Anyway, look at them. I've never seen two people more in love. Don't you think they'll want the same for me?"

Genevieve slipped her arms around him and rested her cheek against his chest. "Andre, be sensible. You are already an English marquess, and one day you will be a duke in that country as well as this one. You will have many estates, and you have an important blood-line to continue."

"And you are saying that I cannot continue it with you?" He cupped her face in his hands. "Genevieve, I *love* you. No dukedom in the world is more important than that." He gazed at her intently, willing her to believe him. "You are my heart and soul, and that will never change. So please stop letting your mother fill your head with nonsense."

"You are only fourteen, very young to make such an important decision," she persisted.

"Don't be silly. I know my own mind, just as you do." He stroked her delicate cheek with his thumb. "It's no good trying to be sensible. I'll never love any-one but you, I swear that to you on everything I hold sacred."

"And you know that I feel the same," she said, gazing up at him, her eyes, the exact color of corn-flowers, filled with the love that had transformed them both that summer.

Andre's heart beat faster just looking at her. "Well, then," he said. He lowered his head and kissed her soft lips, and they trembled under his.

"You see," he said hoarsely, breaking off the kiss, his senses swimming. "God wouldn't have given us to each other to love if He didn't mean for us to grow old together."

"Oh, Andre ... Maybe you are right. Maybe it will all work out."

"Of course it will. I'd give you the moon and stars if I could, but you'll have to settle for a couple of dukedoms. Now put your worries behind you—fresh honey is waiting." He merrily pulled her off in the direction of the hives.

He had no way of knowing that in seven years time Genevieve would be dead, his world would be shat-tered, and he would turn his back on God, his parents, and France, vowing never to return.

Chapter 1

March 1864
Constantinople, Turkey

Joseph-Jean strode through the Great Bazaar of Stamboul, looking for Andre. He'd finally managed to collect the *firman* from the pasha that would be their passport for the next eight months of work—a trip he was not particularly looking forward to, given Andre's frame of mind.

"Make way, make way," he said, skirting a peddler shouting at the top of his lungs and waving his arms about in a dangerous fashion. A vendor nearly knocked his hat off with the tray of cakes he was carrying on his head, and he had to swerve to avoid the boy running past him with a hanging silver tray that held glasses of tea.

He could barely think above the cacophony of noise coming from every direction. Groups of veiled women bargained in the streets, men sat cross-legged on carpets in front of their shops, smoking narghiles, merchants haggled, and donkeys wandered down the streets, weaving around people clad in ornately woven vests, *chalvars,* red fezzes, and turbans. The variety of color and costume alone was enough to boggle the mind. It was a madhouse.

Still no sign of Andre, who had most likely concluded buying supplies. Joseph-Jean thought for a moment. Andre might like climbing about in the middle of nowhere for months on end, but he also relished cleanliness.

Joseph-Jean headed out of the bazaar and straight to

the hamam. Minutes later, draped in nothing but a sheet, he followed a Turk through a low stone door into the huge, domed main chamber. Shafts of light from small windows high above cut through the heavy mist like silvery ribbons, dimly illuminating the interior.

Sure enough, Andre was lying on the raised marble slab in the middle of the room, with a magnificently mustached Turk clad in a scanty loincloth busily scrubbing off layers of Andre's skin with a coarse mitt.

"I thought I'd find you here," Joseph-Jean said. "Not a bad idea, considering what we're in for." He started to wash in one of the stone basins against the wall, then sat down to steam while he waited his turn to be scrubbed and pummeled and pounded.

"Did you have any success?" Andre asked, turning his head.

"I got it," he said. "The pasha finally pulled himself together. We can leave at first light. I've alerted the dragoman, and the horses are ready."

Andre grunted. "It's about time. I suppose it was the set of silver plates that finally did it."

"Well, there was a lot of bowing and scraping and extremely flowery language that went on, so I'd assume so. There's nothing like handing around a little baksheesh to get what you want."

"I just love bribery," Andre said dryly as the Turk flipped him over and proceeded to de-breed his front side. "Now shut up, Jo-Jean, and leave me to my pleasure. As you say, there's going to be little enough of that where we're going."

Joseph-Jean cupped his fist on his chin and watched, since there was nothing better to do. Eventually the Turk rinsed Andre down, rolled him onto his front again, filled a chamois bag with soap suds, and then deluged Andre with it, slapping him rhythmically with a horsetail. He then settled into massaging what was now Andre's very clean, very smooth skin.

Yet even in a state of what should have been the utmost relaxation, Andre's face appeared taut and strained. Joseph-Jean worried for him.

It had been three years since Genevieve had died,

and nothing had changed. If anything, Andre had become more withdrawn with time. He had not recanted a single one of the terrible accusations he had made to his father that awful night. Nor had he ever spoken of his father or Genevieve again. He stayed at Saint-Simon only long enough to see her buried, and the next day he left for Constantinople, taking Joseph-Jean with him.

They returned briefly to England once a year, where Andre kept a house in London. He didn't visit his godparents, the Earl and Countess of Raven, with whom he had once been very close. He didn't visit his grandfather, the Duke of Montcrieff, with whom he had never been close, but whose title, lands, and fortune he would inherit. He only consulted with other scholars, mostly historians and archaeologists, handed over each year's work to the trustees of the British Museum, who funded his expeditions, and left again.

It was as if all the life had gone out of him when it went from Genevieve, leaving him nothing more than a shell. He concentrated on his work and he was brilliant at it. But people had taken to calling him "the black marquess," not only because of his coloring and his dress, but also because he never smiled.

He had transformed himself from the warm, generous person he was by nature into someone cold and curt, a man without emotions.

It was a tragic thing that a love that had burned so brightly and given Andre such happiness had equal power to destroy him. For no matter how good Andre was at concealing his feelings, Joseph-Jean knew the terrible depth of his pain.

He wondered how long Andre could continue like this.

April 1864
Cragus Mountains

"I'm going to have a wash before dinner," Andre said, putting away his journal and stretching. It had been a long, chilly day and the night was bound to be even colder, but he was determined to brave the freezing water of the stream nonetheless.

He knew he ought to have become accustomed to all manner of hardships by now, living outdoors from April through October, but the one thing his body refused to adjust to was the punishment of the cold. He was determined to force it to. Discipline was the key to survival—although there were times that he wondered why he bothered with survival at all.

"Don't hurry," Joseph-Jean replied. "Tonight's meal won't be any better than last night's. It's the same old goat." He stirred the foul-smelling stew, then clapped the lid back on the pot.

Andre regarded the pot with disgust. "God, I'm tired of slop."

"If you hadn't thrown Hamid out on his ear ten days ago, we wouldn't have had to worry about it. You'd think you'd know better after wandering all over Asia Minor. This is ridiculous, Andre. We really can't do without a dragoman."

"I couldn't stand another minute of his complaining," Andre said, pushing his camp chair back. "He behaved as if he'd never crossed a mountain pass before."

"I don't think he had, not one like this. The track's not safe for man or beast."

"I don't think that entitled him to call me a madman, the insolent devil." Andre rummaged in his pack, looking for his soap and towel. Privately, he had to agree with Jo-Jean. It was ridiculous trying to navigate the pass on their own, as well as inconvenient to be without a servant. But he wasn't about to admit to his own stupidity. Jo-Jean already had enough to berate him for without added ammunition in the form of Hamid's dismissal.

"You know, I do believe it was the appearance of the lions that finally did it to him," Joseph-Jean said, grinning. "And if I'm honest, they nearly did it to me as well."

"At least you kept your pants dry, unlike our friend. Damn! Where's the blasted soap gone?"

Joseph-Jean glanced down at him. "How should I know? I'm lucky if I can lay my hands on any of my own belongings."

Andre looked away, a stab of pain tearing at him as a trick of light turned Joseph-Jean's eyes the exact shade of Genevieve's cornflower blue.

It happened often, a sudden expression that crossed Jo-Jean's face or a familiar gesture that brought Genevieve acutely to mind. He sometimes wished Jo-Jean looked like someone else entirely, instead of sharing his cousin's fair hair and blue eyes, her wide smile. But it couldn't be helped, and he supposed in the end it made little difference. He lived with the pain every waking moment as it was.

He finally found his towel and tossed it onto the ground, still digging for the soap. "The things I do for England," he muttered.

"Never mind England. Look at the things I endure for you," Jo-Jean replied. "At the pace we're going, you're going to have the entire province mapped and every last ruin cataloged by autumn."

"I'll settle for having the Xanthian ruins finished by November," Andre said, pulling the soap out. "I suppose Charles Fellows made my work easier by sending so many of the sculptures to England, although this scholastic habit of removing artifacts from their original site is one I cannot abide. At least Frederick Lacey left things where they belonged."

"Except for himself," Joseph-Jean said dryly, referring to Lacey's unfortunate disappearance near Anatalya twelve years earlier. "And that's another reason we need a dragoman, Andre. We don't want to lose another fine scholar to bandits. I have to confess, I personally don't much like the idea of being set upon, especially with only one of us carrying a weapon."

"And you think that idiot Hamid would have been any good at chasing off bandits? Chances are high that he would have run screaming in the other direction and left us to our own devices." He slung his towel over his neck. "Put some tea on, would you? I'll be right back."

He walked down to the stream, stripping off his jacket and shirt and splashing water on his face and chest, shivering involuntarily. It was unbelievably icy, coming directly down from the snow-covered peak of Mount Massicytus.

He suddenly felt a prickling at the back of his neck, as if eyes were on him. Slowly straightening, he looked around. But there was nothing to be seen but sparse forest and the clearing in which their tents stood. Deciding he was imagining things, he bent back to the stream to finish his rudimentary and torturous bath, then dried himself and shrugged into his clothes, quickly returning to the warmth of the fire.

"Ready?" Joseph-Jean asked, pouring steaming black tea into cups and putting one directly into Andre's shaking hand. "You're looking a little blue around the gills, my friend."

"I'm frozen solid," Andre said, cautiously sipping from the cup, taking a moment to savor the warming effect of the tea. "I ought to have washed in the damned cup. Never mind, we'll be in Xanthos in about a week."

"And then it will be hotter than Hades. Here, sit down. The stew's ready." He ladled it out onto two plates and added sliced bread.

Andre dipped his fork into the mess and tasted it. "Christ," he said, making a face. "This is truly disgusting. You draw a great deal better than you cook."

"I warned you," Joseph-Jean said, forcing down a mouthful. "My God, what I'd give for a servant who could prepare decent food. Promise me, as soon as we reach civilization you will hire someone?"

"I swear it on my life," Andre said. "Just so long as it's not Hamid. Speaking of which . . ." He put his fork down and sat up straight, looking around the clearing again. "You don't suppose the fool followed us, do you?"

"Over the pass? Are you mad? He rode as fast as

he could in the opposite direction. Why?" He reached for his pistol.

"I thought . . . oh, never mind. I've had an uncanny feeling that someone's been watching us, but we haven't come across any sign of civilization for days."

"And I, for one, can't wait until we do," Joseph-Jean said, relaxing and shoving the pistol back in its holster. "And not just for the benefit of some decent food. I find it bleak up here."

"Cold, yes, but bleak? I hadn't noticed." Andre threw the rest of his bread toward the bushes and pushed his plate away, the stew half-uneaten. "Here, do you want any more of this? I can't bear another bite."

"You must be joking. Go on, get back to work. I'll wash up." Joseph-Jean cleared the table and started toward the stream with the plates.

Andre went back to writing, but he still couldn't shake the feeling that someone was nearby. His intuition had always served him well, even when logic spoke against it.

And then a movement caught the corner of his eye. Indeed, his intuition had proven correct. A small brown hand snaked out of the bushes at the edge of the clearing in the direction of the packs they had unloaded.

Furious at this attempt at thievery, he rose and softly skirted around the backside of the bushes. All to be seen was a bottom clad in baggy *chalvars,* thin little legs, and the worn soles of a pair of sandals.

Andre leaned down. With one hand he grabbed the *chalvars* and with the other the back of the boy's shirt. In one easy movement he hoisted him skyward.

"And just what do you think you're doing?" he asked in Turkish.

The boy uttered a strangled cry and struggled wildly, arms and legs flying everywhere. Andre abruptly dropped him, and he landed on his bottom, a whoosh of air exploding from his lungs.

He stared at Andre with wide eyes. "Effendi—I meant no harm!"

"Oh? And what were you intending on doing with my pack?"

"No, no—it was not your pack I wanted. Only what you had discarded." He stood shakily and pointed, his bony little body trembling with fear.

Andre looked. There on the far side of the bush was the hunk of bread that he'd tossed away.

"I am not a thief," the boy said, his chin going out. "I did not think you wanted it."

Andre's gaze raked the child. His clothes were ragged and he was far too thin, his dark eyes enormous in a small square face, his thick dark hair unevenly hacked. Andre thought him no more than twelve at the very most. "Your name?" he demanded.

"Ali, effendi."

"And your village?"

"My people are gone. The plague took them."

Joseph-Jean, alerted by the commotion, came quickly up from the stream, pistol at the ready. The boy gave him a look of alarm and put his hands out before him imploringly.

"Put it away," Andre said. "He's harmless, just a hungry child."

Ali swallowed with relief as Joseph-Jean lowered the pistol.

"What are you doing up here on your own?" Andre asked. "Surely you know it's dangerous?"

"I have walked from the plains of Dembre, effendi. I am going to Izmir."

Andre stared at Ali. "You have *walked* from Dembre?"

"Yes, how else? I have no animal. But I should have gone through the valleys instead. I thought it would be shorter to come this way."

"Good God," Andre said softly, amazed the boy had survived this far.

"Please, effendi, may I take the bread? I am very hungry." So saying, Ali fainted.

Andre sighed and scooped the child up in his arms, giving Joseph-Jean a look of resignation. "Why," he said, carrying Ali over to the fire, "do things like this always happen to me? Get the water jug, Jo-Jean, and a spare blanket."

He felt Ali's brow to see if it was feverish, relieved to find that it wasn't, since he didn't much like the idea of contracting plague. Then he dipped a cloth in water, wiped Ali's dirty face with it, and wrapped him in the blanket Joseph-Jean brought over.

"Damnation! What are we going to do with a malnourished infant?" he said. "We can't very well leave him here when we break camp tomorrow, can we?"

"No, I don't think so," Joseph-Jean replied. "We'll have to take him with us at least as far as Minara."

"I am in no frame of mind to act as nursemaid to a Turkish urchin," Andre said with annoyance.

"Naturally you are not, but I doubt he will survive much longer under these hellish conditions, not on his own and this far from any village."

"And what do you propose we do with him when we get to Minara?"

"Perhaps we can make arrangements for a family to take him in?"

Andre shook his head. "Well. He's suffering from exposure and starvation and certainly exhaustion. He probably won't live long enough to get to Minara, so it might well be a moot point. Still, I suppose I would rather know how many days it took for him to die rather than spend the rest of my life wondering about it."

Joseph-Jean nodded slowly. "Good. Apparently, despite your best efforts, you're not nearly as heartless as you like to make out. Can you get him to wake up and take some nourishment?"

"What do you want me to do, shake him till his brains rattle? Anyway, that stew would probably finish him off." He pushed a hand through his hair, thinking of what medicines he had in his pack. "I imagine he'll wake up in his own good time. He needs warmth and sleep more than food right now."

Andre looked down at the thin child, his face pale beneath the brown skin. He didn't look sturdy enough to have even contemplated the journey, let alone have made it this far.

"Amazing," he said. "He has to have been sustained by something to have come over the mountains from as far south as Dembre."

"A remarkable will, perhaps?"

"Perhaps. Or maybe his story is mere nonsense and he really was after the packs. In either case, we're stuck with him for the time being." He placed Ali on the ground by the fire. "He'll be better off close to the heat tonight. I'll watch over him. You get to bed."

"Are you sure?" Joseph-Jean said in obvious surprise.

"Yes, I'm sure," he replied, annoyed. "Don't worry, Jo-Jean, I won't roast him for breakfast. I may be heartless, but I do have a slight sense of ethics remaining."

"I didn't mean to imply—"

"Good night, Jo-Jean."

"As you wish. Good night."

An hour later Joseph-Jean lifted the flap of his tent and looked out. Andre sat by the fire, a blanket wrapped around his shoulders, his gaze fixed on the child. The firelight flickered over his strong features, so like his father's.

Take care of my son, Joseph-Jean. Stay with him, at least until he heals.

He'd never forget the devastated expression on the duke's face, the desolate look in his eyes as he had commended his only child into Joseph-Jean's care. "I will look after him, *Monsieur le Duc*," Joseph-Jean whispered. "For as long as he needs me."

Dear God, if only Genevieve had not succumbed to her last illness. If only she had grown stronger instead of becoming more fragile over those last months. Andre hadn't even realized, away at Oxford, completing his degree.

Perhaps if he had been in the room as the duke stroked Genevieve's brow at the end, speaking to her in his quiet voice, perhaps then he would have understood.

It is time, beloved. Look, Genevieve, the angels wait for you. Do you see? Go into their arms, dear one. Let them take you to God.

With her last breath Genevieve spoke Andre's name. And Andre arrived an hour too late to hear it.

Joseph-Jean squeezed his eyes shut. The scene that followed really didn't bear remembering. Andre had been like an animal mortally wounded, lashing out at anyone who came near him. The anguished rage had only been the beginning. Then had come the deathly cold.

He opened his eyes. Andre still watched the child, his face calm but his eyes intent. Well, Andre might not be able to heal himself, but he had some of his father's medical skill. He'd spent his childhood watching the duke treat people from near and far. If anyone could help young Ali, Andre could. What was amazing was that he would even bother to try.

But tonight Andre actually looked interested in something other than ancient history. Maybe the Turkish waif was a blessing in disguise. If Ali's problems could somehow remind Andre that life was worth living, Joseph-Jean would be eternally thankful. He would do anything to see Andre's pain eased, to see him turn his face to the future.

He lit a lamp and started a letter to the parents whose names Andre refused to speak.

And when he said his prayers that night, he added a fervent one for the child's life. They'd had enough of death.

Chapter 2

Ali stirred and sighed with contentment, unwilling to relinquish the dream. In the dream it was warm. In the dream it was safe. Nothing pursued her, nothing hid in the dark waiting to kill her while she slept. It had been too long since a dream like this had come along, easing the terror of the night, the fear of perishing. There was even a fire that crackled and the distinct smell of food.

A hand touched her cheek. For one awful moment she thought she had failed to escape her uncle's village, that Hadgi had come to hand her over to the Turkomen. Ali nearly screamed. But as her eyes shot open in sheer terror she remembered.

It was the foreigner who bent over her, the tall, dark-haired effendi with the strange gray-green eyes who had thrown his bread away, the one who had accused her of stealing. He held a cup out to her.

"Drink," he said in his rich voice. Ali tried to sit up, but her head spun. His arm came immediately around her.

"Drink," he said again. "It's sweet tea with some medicinal herbs mixed in. It will do you good."

Ali obeyed, grateful for the warm liquid. At the same time she realized she had a blanket wrapped about her and that for the first time in weeks she really was warm.

She blinked, wondering how this miracle had come to pass. The last thing she remembered was looking at the piece of bread on the ground, and then the ground rushing up toward her. The effendi must have carried her to the fire and wrapped her up.

Praise be to Allah, she thought. *He sent the effendi to save me.*

Or maybe not. "Am I dying?" she asked weakly, feeling most peculiar, wondering if Allah had perhaps sent the effendi not to save her life, but to bury her body. It was hard to tell.

"No, I think you're past that," he said. "You are weak, but you'll recover. What you need now is rest and food. How long has it been since you've eaten?"

"Many days," Ali said, lying down again. "Thank you, effendi," she thought to add.

"For what?" he asked, taking food from the pot and putting it into a bowl.

Ali thought that a very odd thing to say when he was busy trying to make her well. "For saving me. And for being kind," she added.

He looked over his shoulder, his eyes filled with irony. "You have no idea how many people would laugh if they heard you say that." He came back to her and knelt down, helping her to sit up and supporting her against his chest. "Here. Try to eat this."

He dipped a piece of bread in the sauce and held it out to her. Ali grabbed it and stuffed it in her mouth, chewing frantically.

"Slowly," he said. "You'll make yourself sick."

Ali nodded and swallowed. He poured her another cup of tea and helped her to sip it. Then he gave her some more soaked bread. Ali was amazed to find that she couldn't finish it.

He took it from her. "Sleep," he said.

She did.

For the next two days that was all she did, save to eat, wobble to the bushes to relieve herself, and wobble back again to sleep some more. She was vaguely aware that the foreigner stayed close by. Sometimes, when she wasn't really asleep but more in a dreamlike daze, she watched him. Handray, the other called him. It was an odd name, but she liked the way it sounded when she tried it on her tongue.

He liked to write in his book, his dark head bent,

his concentration absolute. She memorized the curve of his sculpted cheekbone above his beard, the high, arched bridge of his nose, the way he stared off into the distance, his odd light eyes slightly narrowed in thought.

She liked to watch him move too, his powerful body surprisingly graceful. And when he touched her his hands were gentle. She hadn't known that men could touch gently, but she liked it very much, the way he washed her face and hands with a cloth as if she were a small child.

She had heard terrible things about foreigners and their strange ways. Hadgi said that they did ungodly things. But then her uncle was not a good man himself, so maybe he was wrong. This foreigner was good, she was sure of it.

By dusk of the third day Ali felt very much better. She came out of her sleep with all her senses intact for the first time in a week. Sitting up, she looked around. Neither of the effendis was anywhere to be seen. She went to the stream and washed herself as best she could, delighted that she no longer felt too weak to do so. Then she returned to the camp.

It was time to take stock of the situation, since she was clearly going to survive. Ali settled herself back on her heels and gazed up at the sky as she always did when she consulted with the Almighty.

"So, Great Allah," she said, leaning forward and touching her forehead to the ground, before returning her gaze to the sky, "in Your divine wisdom You sent me to the Handray so that I might not die. You would not have saved my insignificant life unless You had a reason in mind. I am to give myself into the Handray's service, yes?"

Allah didn't answer, but then she didn't expect Him to.

"Yes," she answered for Him, "I can see that I am to devote myself to the Handray's service, but there is a problem. He thinks me a boy, which I can understand, given my clothes. But it was You, Allah, who put the idea in my head that I must dress like this to keep from harm."

Ali thought the situation over carefully. "Well," she said eventually. "If I tell the Handray the truth when he has gone to so much trouble to save me, he will probably be terribly disappointed and want my head on a pike and my body thrown to the lions. He will not wish a mere female to serve him, will he?"

No. The tall, powerful effendi was a leader, that was obvious, probably a pasha in his own country. He might even be a pasha here too, for his Turkish was splendid, and he spoke it with a clear, beautiful accent, different from the guttural speech of her own people.

"So I cannot tell the truth just yet, can I, O Mighty Allah? Still, it will be difficult to keep it from him, for many reasons."

Ali considered. She couldn't keep the truth from the Handray forever, obviously. She only needed to keep it from him long enough to make herself indispensable. And that shouldn't be *too* terribly long, not if this was what Allah intended her destiny to be.

Well, that made sense. A small deception to further the cause of eternal service? Yes, she could see that Allah had planned it all magnificently. And of course, there was the matter of educating the Handray. Everyone knew foreigners were infidels, and surely Allah would wish his conversion.

"So. It is ordered," she said with satisfaction. "I will obey Your every wish." She touched her forehead to the ground again, then sat up, pleased with the prospect of the future, which was infinitely brighter than the one she'd been facing four nights before.

And now to make herself indispensable. She looked around wondering where to begin. Yes, the cooking pot. Whatever the Handray had been feeding her had been most unpleasant once her initial hunger pangs had worn off enough to allow her to taste the food.

Ali took the top off the pot and dipped her finger

into the stew that was cooking inside. She made a face. "Oh, Allah, he really *does* need me."

There were packs heaped about, so she opened one. It contained books. That was no help. She opened another. Soaps, brushes, bathing things. But the third pack yielded precisely what she was looking for.

"Ali! What do you think you're doing?"

She spun around, only to see both the effendis standing there, glaring at her. "I—nothing!" she stammered.

"Feeling better, I see," the Handray said. "And is this how you show your gratitude, by stealing?" He folded his arms across his chest.

"No, effendi," she said, her heart about to stop in fright. "I have told you before that I do not steal. I was only looking for spices. You are a terrible cook." She held up a packet.

"True enough," the one called Jojan said.

Ali liked Jojan. He was tall, but not as massive of build as the Handray, and he had a warmth in his eyes that made her feel comfortable. She knew he wasn't going to kill her. The Handray she wasn't entirely sure about, especially at this moment.

"I tell you the truth," she said indignantly. "Why would I lie? You have saved my life. I wish only to help you. And why would I want to steal spices, when I have no food to put them in?"

The Handray's arms dropped to his sides. "All right, Ali," he said. "I believe you, although you shouldn't be going through things that don't belong to you. And you really should be resting."

"I am much better now," she insisted. "And since you cannot continue to eat this disgusting food, I shall try to make it better."

"Please," he said, waving his hand at the pot. "If you can fix that, I will be indebted to you for life."

Ali quickly turned back to the pack of spices, sending up a quick prayer of thanks to Allah for making it so easy for her to succeed. It was now only a matter of the Handray's honoring his words, for she was a superb cook. Even Hadgi, who hated her, said so.

*   *   *

"Good God, Ali!" Andre exclaimed in real surprise, taking a tentative bite. "How did you do this? Jo-Jean, taste this!"

Joseph-Jean, who was looking at his plate with misgiving, first smelled the meat on his fork, then cautiously put it into his mouth. "It's—it's good," he said, looking at Ali in amazement.

"Not good," Ali said. "It is only passable. It is hard to make anything good that has had such a bad beginning."

Andre stared down at his plate, trying to work out how a young child had been able to turn something inedible into a palatable meal. "But what did you do? This tastes of food—reasonable food."

"I used some of the spices in the pack, and I added other things that I found. Raisins, almonds, a little dried fruit. But still, it is not as it should be."

"Hire the boy instantly," Joseph-Jean demanded. "I cannot go on any longer eating our own cooking."

Andre flashed him an exasperated look. "He's hardly in any condition to be hired for anything."

"But I am very well now," Ali said quickly. "And after all, you have no guide, no cook, no bearer, no dragoman. In exchange for food I could do all these things for you."

"I think not," Andre replied, dead-set against the very idea. "We are traveling light and have no need of your services. I'm willing to take you as far as Minara, but you can make your own way from there."

"I eat very little," Ali persisted.

Andre shook his head. "You could eat an entire sheep every night and it would make no difference. I have work to do, Ali, and I haven't the time to look after a child."

Ali stared at him in disbelief. "You think you must look after me? It is you who needs looking after!"

Andre snorted. "I beg your pardon, but who just saved whom? You wouldn't have survived another night on your own." And by God, that was true enough. He considered it a minor miracle that Ali was standing here arguing with him at all.

"I cannot help it if I had no money to buy food and animals and warm clothing such as you have," Ali said indignantly. "It does not mean I am helpless." Ali's gaze lowered respectfully under the force of his glare. "I am not ungrateful to you, Handray Bey, I am not. I am fully mindful that you saved my life and that it is now yours. But you cannot cook for yourself, you cannot do all the small but important things that servants do."

"You are nevertheless a child. You have no idea how rough a life we lead." He turned, dismissing the subject, but Ali jumped up to face him, eyes flashing.

"You say this to me, knowing I came all the way from Dembre on my own through the mountains? You think I know nothing about this life?" Ali gestured at the tents. "You have shelter, Handray Bey, and blankets. You have food, and pack animals to carry all these things for you, and horses to ride upon. Your life is that of a rich man's compared to what mine has been these last eight weeks. And still I can look after you better than you can yourself."

Andre raised one eyebrow in question. "Oh? How?"

"It is simple. I can walk into any village and be accepted. Many people have never seen a foreigner before and will be afraid of you. I can reassure them on your behalf, I can bargain for you, make introductions. But most of all, I can look after all your needs as any good servant does."

The word "servant" once again rang temptingly in Andre's ear. Ali must have seen a brief hesitation in his face, for he was assaulted yet again with argument.

"You said you would be indebted to me for life if I could fix the meal, and I did," Ali said heatedly. "Would you go back on your word?"

Andre gazed at the child in fascination. He'd never come across such a determined, fiery little soul as this one. That determination partially explained Ali's remarkable recovery, but he was also intrigued. There was something in Ali's eyes, a fierce blazing light that spoke so intently of life. Maybe that was why he had gone to the trouble of seeing that the life didn't go out of them.

"All right," he said, thinking at the same time that he'd lost his mind. "I'll give you a try. All the food you can eat and two piastres a week. If you have failed me by Minara, I'll leave you there. If not, you may accompany us to Xanthos—but at Xanthos you will have to find other work, unless you have proved yourself so remarkable that I decide to keep you on." He crossed his arms. "And I warn you now, that is as likely as finding yourself drinking tea with the Queen of England."

He turned to walk off, but Ali dropped to the ground and took his hands, fervently kissing the backs. "Thank you, Handray Bey, *thank* you! May Allah bless you and your children, and your children's children."

"I thank you for the sentiment, but it's entirely unnecessary," Andre said curtly.

Ali looked up at him, sooty lashes blinking in confusion. "You do not wish to be blessed?"

"No, I don't wish to be blessed. Furthermore, I have no children, so there's no point in blessing them either. I am not married."

"Oh. I am sorry," Ali said, appearing astonished. "But a man of your age, with no wives, no children?"

"I'm not exactly in my dotage," he said dryly.

"Perhaps not, but you are still very old to be without a wife," Ali said reasonably. "Wives can do all sorts of things for you."

Andre stared down at Ali for a moment, ready to take the child's head off, then decided the remark was purely innocent. "I find my life easier without women to complicate it." He pulled his hands away. "For God's sake, will you get up? You're going to make a terrible servant if you insist on kneeling at my feet. And my name is Banes—never mind," he said, deciding not to complicate the issue. "Call me Andre. Just Andre."

Ali stood with alacrity. "As you wish, Handray. But

you really must not blaspheme so much. Allah does not like it."

Andre's eyes narrowed slightly. "Allah can like it or not. If you're to remain my servant for any length of time, you would be wise to keep Allah to yourself."

Ali in return regarded him gravely. "I cannot keep Allah to myself. He belongs to all. But I suppose as an infidel it is difficult for you to understand such things."

An *infidel?* Dear God, what had he taken on? On the other hand, he supposed it was true enough, so there was little point in objecting. And why bother? Ali could cook. That would save them at least to Minara.

He rubbed a finger over his forehead. "I believe it is time for bed," he said, dismissing the subject, Ali, and the entire situation. "Since you have volunteered yourself as my servant, you may clear up the remains of the meal."

Andre strode off to his tent, intending to restore a degree of order to his life, an order that had been badly disrupted since the appearance of the blasted brat.

But as he settled on his mattress to read by the light of his lamp, he found that his thoughts kept drifting back to dark, wide eyes that held an extraordinary innonence behind that fierce will.

He sighed and leaned his head back against the pillow. Innocence. Ah, well, there was little enough of that in the world. Ali's might as well be preserved for as long as possible.

It was a damned joke that he'd somehow volunteered for the job. Still, he supposed he hadn't saved Ali's life to throw it into the sewer. He'd see what he could do to arrange for a decent situation once they reached a village.

He put his book down and blew out the lamp, rolling over onto his side and pulling the blanket up over his shoulder. God, he hated the nights and the struggle for sleep, the constant fight against memory that he generally lost. He was so tired of the unending struggle, so tired of waking to yet another day of the same. Tired, period.

Andre closed his eyes. He might not be in his dotage, but he felt two hundred years old. Really, he considered, it would be a great deal easier just to ask Jo-Jean to put a bullet through his head.

Ali quickly fell into the routine, breaking camp early in the morning and riding for most of the day. It wasn't unlike the journey the Yourooks made once a year to the mountain pastures, although she was accustomed to traveling in a great caravan rather than in a tiny group. But she was thrilled to be traveling on a donkey rather than on her own blistered feet, even though the donkey was not as pleased with the arrangement as Ali was.

As they descended from the high mountain pass, the scenery became lusher, rich with fragrant fir trees and flowers in full blossom. Snipe, plovers, and quail grew plentiful, which Jojan shot and Ali happily cooked using whatever herbs and greens she found along the way.

She delighted in the pleasure the effendis took from her cooking, from their shared glances of approval and their praise—well, Jojan's praise, anyway. Handray was less forthcoming, but he didn't fool her, for she saw the way he devoured every last morsel.

She felt stronger every day, although her new master was very silly about not allowing her to carry heavy firewood or pack the donkeys by herself. "Perhaps next week," was all he said when she objected. Really, he could be very aggravating.

Ali shifted on the donkey. Her bony bottom ached from bouncing around so much, and she hoped they'd stop soon, for she was unaccustomed to riding without soft blankets beneath her.

As if he'd read her thoughts, her master pulled his horse up and took out his compass. Ali still couldn't believe a piece of metal and glass knew how to tell direction, but so far it had not led them wrong.

"We'll stop here," he called. "There's a river below

that will provide water, and we can pitch the tents on this terraced area."

When the tents were safely tethered, Ali went off to fill the water jugs. On the way to the river she stumbled across a grove of orange trees and after careful consideration of the matter she picked a handful of the young fruit. She didn't think there was anyone around to mind.

"Look, Handray," she said, tumbling the oranges to the ground from her shirt when she returned to the tiny camp. "I can cook with them tonight. There are lemon trees too—I think we must be close to the village of Minara, for I also saw the sure traces of goats."

"We're two or three miles away at the most," he said, settling at his writing table. "Tomorrow we'll be able to restock our supplies. Just think, Ali, fresh milk, butter, eggs, meat, all sorts of good things for you to cook with."

"I can make *kymac* for you," Ali said, her eyes shining with pleasure.

"Can you?" he said absently, flipping through the notes he'd made earlier in the afternoon at the tombs.

"Oh, yes, it's very easy to prepare. All I need is fresh cow's milk. Then I put it to simmer by the fire and leave it to sit overnight. The next day the scum has formed, and that is the cheese."

Andre glanced up at her. "Amazing, the things you know how to do."

"Oh, but I know hardly anything compared to you," she said earnestly. "You can read and write and speak two languages perfectly."

"Six, actually," he said even more absently, checking the nub of his pen.

Ali's eyes widened in awe. "Six? But I did not know there were so many! What are they?"

"What?" he asked, looking up.

"These languages—what are they called?" she repeated.

"Oh. Well, let's see. French, English, Italian, then Greek, Arabic, and Turkish, of course," he said as he unscrewed the top of his ink pot. "Oh, and classical Greek and Latin, but one doesn't really speak those."

Ali sighed. "I heard Arabic once, when the imam called prayers from the minaret in Dembre. How did you learn so many tongues?"

"I grew up speaking two of them at home and the others I studied at school." He rubbed a finger over his eyebrow. "Ali, must you chatter so much?"

"Yes, for how else am I to learn anything? Which is the language you speak with Jojan?" she asked, giddy with the thought that there were so many languages on the earth and her master spoke them all.

"French." He opened his book and found the page where he'd left off the night before.

"It is pretty," she said. "Like music. Is it the language of your birth? Where is this place, French?"

Andre sighed impatiently. "France. It's called France, and it's far away from here, in Europe."

"Where is Europe, Handray? Is it sit across the mountains?"

"No, farther than that. Here, look." He dipped his pen in the ink pot, tore a blank piece of paper from the back of his book, and quickly drew a rough sketch.

"What is that?" Ali asked with fascination, watching over his shoulder.

"This is a map of Europe and Asia Minor." He pointed. "Here, this is Turkey, this is the mainland of Greece over here, the boot is Italy, and way up here is France. And this," he said, adding an island on the top of the sheet, "is Great Britain, where I live when I'm not traveling."

Ali chewed on her lip. "There is much distance between your home and mine."

"Yes. Yes, there is," he agreed, trying to find his place again.

"Why did you come to this country, Handry?"

"Because it interests me," he said, not looking up. "I like to study very old things."

"Ah. Like the tombs cut into the cliffs that we stopped at today? You wrote down many things."

"Yes, like the cliff tombs and the old city below it."

"What is its name?" she asked, leaning her elbows on the table.

Andre finally closed his book altogether and devoted his full attention to her. "It used to be called Pinara by the Lycians, a people who lived here long before we came along. And Xanthos, where we go next, has many more old things, built by the same people."

"Lycians," she repeated, rolling the word around on her tongue. "Were they Turks?"

"No, Ali. They were here long before the Turks came. They were—look," he said abruptly. "If you promise to be a good servant and go away now so that I might work, I'll tell you all about the Lycians another time."

"You will?" Ali said joyfully. "Oh, thank you, Handray—I love stories above everything. Except Allah, of course. And I do like to learn," she thought to add. "Just think of all the things you can teach me." She smiled winningly. "You like to teach, do you not?"

"You are completely impossible," he said, handing Ali the sheet of paper. "Here. You keep this."

"For me? To keep? Oh! Oh, Handray, thank you!" She clutched it to her chest.

Andre smiled. "You're very welcome. Now off with you and let me get to work."

He watched as Ali flew away with the makeshift map, holding it as if it were the most precious of possessions. He shook his head, thinking he'd never get any work done with the child around, constantly pestering him. But he made a mental note to spend some time teaching Ali at least to read and write. If nothing else, studying might keep Ali out of his hair.

Andre turned his thoughts to pigeonhole tombs.

Ali lay looking up at the stars that night, the map carefully folded and tucked inside her bundle along with her book, the one with the strange writing she couldn't read that had belonged to her father. She sighed heavily. There was so much she wanted to learn. She knew so little about the world, about what was outside.

She began to whisper Turkish words to herself the way Handray pronounced them in his beautiful voice. She was going to have a beautiful voice too one day, if she practiced hard enough.

Maybe she would even learn to speak this new language, French, if she listened very carefully. She just had to make Handray speak more often. He was the most silent person she'd ever come across, although she felt she had made a little progress that evening.

Even better, it had been one whole week and she had not yet offended him. She hadn't even received a single beating. She didn't think she'd ever managed to go so long without one.

It was a good sign, she thought, turning on her side and propping her chin on her fist, wondering if Handray might not even like her, just a little. Only in the way one might like a dog one was not disposed to kick, of course, but he *had* made her a map of her very own and given it to her as a present.

And he'd actually smiled at her today too, something he never did. He had a beautiful smile, with a full set of lovely white teeth. It would be much nicer if his smile reached all the way into his eyes, though.

She rolled onto her back again and looked up at the moon that had just appeared over the crest of the snowcapped mountain, a lovely deep yellow. She loved the moon. It could be depended on to wax and wane, to rise and fall no matter what. She would have to remember to ask Handray if it did the same thing everywhere, or if it just happened in Turkey.

Handray knew just about everything. But there was one thing he didn't know much about at all.

Well, she would see what she could do. After all, Allah never did anything without a reason, and obviously He had sent her to Handray to teach him about happiness.

Chapter 3

Andre returned from his difficult hike up the south side of the perpendicular cliffs hot and tired and filthy, but satisfied. The pigeonhole tombs he'd examined yesterday were far better preserved, but this afternoon he'd come across some spectacular and unusual bas-reliefs.

He practically tripped over Ali, who lay comfortably curled beneath the tree where they'd eaten their lunch, sound asleep and oblivious to the world. He wasn't surprised. Ali still had a way to go before making a full recovery.

The breeze shifted dark strands of Ali's hair, and Andre reminded himself that he really did need to do something about a proper haircut. He'd never seen such an awful hack job. The clothes he'd bought in Minara that morning would help too. Ali was as ragged around the edges as could be. But useful. Surprisingly useful for one so young.

The excursion to Minara had been an enormous success, with Ali performing introductions that had him struggling to keep a straight face. A great English pasha, Ali had called him, and Jo-Jean had somehow become an *aga,* although of what, he wasn't sure. In any event, they came away with far more than he had hoped, and all for an astonishingly low price.

Yes, Ali was definitely useful.

He leaned down and poked a finger into one bony rib. "What kind of servant are you, sleeping away the day?"

"Handray!" Ali's eyes shot open. "You have not killed yourself! This is good."

"Why should I have killed myself?" he asked, dropping to his haunches and taking a bottle of water from the knapsack that held the remains of their lunch.

"Because you are very reckless," Ali said, stretching and sitting up. "It is not wise to climb up cliff faces. You might fall off."

"But I didn't, did I?" he said, tipping the bottle into his mouth.

"No, but you managed to make yourself very dirty. Look at your clothes! They are dirty, your face is dirty, everything is dirty."

"Then you'll just have to do some washing." He capped the bottle and put it away again.

Ali beamed. "Yes. Washing is a fine idea. A bath will feel very nice, very soothing after such a long climb and this way your muscles will not be stiff."

"I was talking about my clothes," he said, brushing some of the most obvious dirt off with both hands.

"Naturally I will wash them too, but first you must have a nice hot bath. And when you are clean and comfortable I will cook a very wonderful meal with the food that we have bought in the village. Yes? I have time for all of this."

"If preparing a bath will keep you busy and give me some peace, then very well," he said, thinking a hot bath would actually be very welcome. "Where is Jo-Jean?"

"Still down in the old city, busy with his pencils. He draws very nicely, although Allah says that it is not proper—"

"Ali," Andre said dangerously, stretched to the limit by Ali's ongoing campaign to convert him. Ali hadn't seemed to grasp the point that there was nothing to convert him from.

"Oh, very well," Ali said, shrugging. "You refuse to understand about Allah, but I refuse to understand why you spend all your time looking at things that are built by people long dead. Or looking at their tombs." Ali's nose wrinkled in distaste. "And then when you are not looking at them, you are writing about them.

How can you enjoy the present when you are so busy thinking about the past and dusty broken buildings?"

"What you don't seem to realize, my young philosopher, is that we can learn a great deal by studying how people lived and died a long time ago. For example, in Xanthos, the place we are headed, the women and children who lived in the dusty broken buildings I intend to study perished at the hands of their own husbands and fathers."

Ali stared at him in horror. "No."

"Yes. Rather than be conquered, the Xanthian men herded their slaves and their loved ones into the acropolis and set it on fire."

Ali swallowed hard. "They *burned* their families? On purpose?"

"Yes. And then they went to battle and died to a man. Furthermore, they committed mass suicide not once, but twice."

"But how?" Ali asked in confusion. "I thought they all died the first time."

"They did, but Xanthos was re-established by the few lucky Xanthians who had been away at the time. And then a man named Brutus laid seige to Xanthos hundreds of years later during the Roman civil wars, trying to force it to pay ridiculous taxes to raise money for a battle he was planning to wage. So the Xanthians did it again for the same reason as the first time, in a refusal to surrender. This time they set fire to everything, threw the women and children on the fire, and killed each other." He noticed with interest that Ali's eyes had misted over.

"But how terrible," Ali said in a cracked whisper.

"They were a fiercely independent people," he said. "Which is one of the things that makes them so interesting to study."

"Well, maybe so," Ali said, frowning. "I shall have to think this over. But I still wish you would be more like Jojan. At least he does other things than draw pictures for your book of buildings that have fallen down."

"That's because he has the time for other things. I,

on the other hand, have to have this book finished by November."

"And then you will take time for pleasant things?" Ali asked hopefully.

"And then I have to start working on another book," he said.

"Bah," Ali said with disgust, throwing the knapsack over one shoulder. "This is not living. My people work hard too, but we know the benefit of relaxing, of holding conversation, of listening to music, and dancing, and celebrating what Allah has given us. Allah says—"

"Ali—*enough!* Any more of your chatter and I shall dismiss you on the spot."

"Very well, Handray, I will go back to the camp," Ali said, as usual not looking the least concerned with his threat. "It will take me some time to make everything ready. You will not become involved in your crumbling buildings and forget?"

"No, I won't forget," Andre said.

"Do you promise me? I worry that you might think a bath is too much pleasure for you."

"Too much—" Andre raked his hands through his hair. "Go on, off with you, before I beat you for insolence."

Ali grinned and vanished from sight.

"Blasted little brat," he murmured, torn between frustration and laughter, and started toward the ruins of Pinara to consult with Joseph-Jean.

Ali beamed victoriously all the way back to camp. It wasn't easy getting her master to agree to anything he considered unnecessary, and a proper bath was a huge victory. She hurried about, carrying water, heating it, carrying more, heating that. It was a pity that she didn't have a vessel large enough to contain him, but that was all right. He would enjoy the bath anyway, and that was all that was important.

She'd chosen a beautiful setting, away from the camp in the middle of a clearing near the orange grove, and conveniently near the river. It was late afternoon, but still warm. The drone of bees in the grove and the gentle song of a flock of bee-eaters in the trees provided a musical backdrop, and the sweet scent of oranges mingling with the spice of fir and the tang of underwood added a sensual delight.

Ali looked around one last time. She had towels, oil, soap, fresh clothes all ready. The water was hot. Yes, everything was perfect. She hurried back to the camp and found Andre exactly where she had expected, at his writing table. He really was absurdly predictable.

"Handray?" she said, pulling at his sleeve. "Handray. You must come."

"Hmm? Why? Oh, yes, the blasted bath." Andre reluctantly put down his pen.

"Work, work, work," Ali said. "Come now. This will not kill you. You might even enjoy yourself." She took his hand and pulled him along the path.

"Ali, where *are* we going? I thought I was going to have a simple bath."

"You will see," she said, beaming up at him. "You are going to like this very much."

They reached the little clearing, and Ali released him. "Here we are. It is peaceful and soothing, no? Come and sit on this rock."

Andre went to the rock obligingly enough, where the water jugs still steamed nicely. "Thank you, Ali," he said. "This was very thoughtful. You may leave now."

"Leave? Oh, no. You must take off all your clothes."

"Why must I take off all my clothes?" Andre asked, pulling off his boots.

"So that I can wash you," Ali said, shoving her hands on her hips. "Why else?"

"*Wash* me?" Andre said, giving her a look of exasperation. "I think I am old enough to wash myself, thank you."

"But I would be failing you as a servant if I did not wash you. For a great pasha you do not know much about good servants, Handray. I come from a small village, and even I know how these things are done."

A flash of amusement crossed Andre's face, and Ali was pleased. "Come, come," she said coaxingly, holding out her hand. "Are you shy? A large man like you?"

"No, I'm not shy," Andre said, pulling off his shirt. "But it is not the custom of my people to sit stark naked in the middle of a forest while someone pours water over them. We have indoor bathtubs for that sort of thing."

"Oh. How silly. It is nice to sit outside and be bathed," Ali said, watching as Andre removed the rest of his clothing. She eyed him critically, pleased with what she saw.

"What are you looking at?" Andre asked.

"You. You are big and strong. This is good, how a man should be so that he can work hard and keep his family in food and livestock."

"Ah. Just what I had planned." Andre sat down on the rock. "And what about you? Are you planning on growing big and strong anytime in the future? How old are you anyway, Ali?"

She dipped a ladle in the bucket of water and poured it over his shoulders. "I do not know," she said honestly. She thought she must be about fourteen or fifteen, but then she didn't know how old she'd been when Uri had found her and taken her in, only that she'd been very young.

She finally now had body hair and the very beginnings of breasts, but nothing like the other girls in the village had. They all became women by twelve at the latest. But not her, and the girls had teased her unceasingly about it. She supposed it was what came of being an outsider.

"You don't know your age?" Andre asked with surprise. "How is that?"

Ali just shrugged. "No one ever said." That was true enough, but only because they didn't know either. Not that she was going to tell her master that and invite more questions.

"Well, by the look of you," Andre said, "you have a lot of growing to do."

Ali took the bar of soap and the cloth she'd laid out and made a thick lather, then rubbed his back in vigorous circles. It took some time since there was a large area to cover. "Yes," she agreed. "I hope I grow. It is annoying to be so small and scrawny."

She soaped his arms, then moved around to wash his chest. She liked the way he felt under her skilled fingers, the hard shape and planes of his musculature, the smooth texture of his skin. She liked the scent of his warm flesh too. For a foreigner he smelled surprisingly nice.

"You're not bad at this," Andre said, closing his eyes.

"I told you I make a very good servant. I can do all sorts of nice things. You will find out if you keep me with you long enough." Ali knelt, soaping his thighs and working her way down his legs to his feet. She was delighted when a contented sigh escaped his lips.

She rinsed him well, then took a towel and rubbed him dry. "There! Here, you must now wrap yourself in this blanket so that you do not take a chill."

Andre gave her a long look. "Don't think to treat me like an invalid just because I allowed you to bathe me."

"I would never think of such a thing!" she said. "My people are clearly more sensible than yours. When one is clean and relaxed, then one must remain warmly wrapped for a time. It is better for the body. I thought you, a great pasha, would know this."

She wrapped the blanket around him, then took out the almond oil scented with sandalwood that she'd bought in the village. "Now I will give you a nice rub." She started to knead his neck.

Andre obligingly dropped his head forward. "Tell me something," he said. "What makes you think I'm a great pasha? I certainly don't travel like a great pasha, nor do I dress like one. So what has put this idea in your head?"

"But of course you are a great pasha," Ali said with

astonishment. "You have the speech, the dignity, the bearing and command. What a foolish question!"

"I beg your pardon," Andre said dryly.

"I am sure if you told Jojan to take off my head he would do it in an instant," Ali said happily. "Of course, I hope you do not."

"It is not my whim at this moment, no."

"Oh, good," she said, smiling broadly. "So it is true, is it not, Handray?"

"That I am a great pasha? Well, yes and no. In England I am called a marquess."

Ali finished with his shoulders and came around to his front to massage his hands and arms. "How did you come to be this marquess? Did the vizier make you one?"

"No," he said. "We don't have viziers or even sultans. We have kings and queens, and a long, long time ago, a King of England gave one of my relatives the title Marquess of Banesbury. It is now my grandfather's lesser title, and so I have the use of it until he dies and I step into his shoes."

"What shoes are these?" Ali asked, imagining beautiful red leather boots with turned-up toes. "And how do you know they will fit your feet?"

"No, that's not what I meant," Andre said with a little smile. "I meant that I'll inherit his title, and then I'll be known as the Duke of Montcrieff."

"So many names," Ali said, very impressed. "But why are you called Handray, and not one of these other things?"

"Andre is my given name, just as your name is Ali."

"Ah!" she exclaimed. "So you are properly called Handray the Banesbury."

"Well, not exactly," he said patiently. "Banesbury is my courtesy title, as I explained. The name I was given at birth is Andre Nicholas Serge de Saint-Simon."

Ali sighed. "Ah, it is very beautiful, this name. It is a name with great dignity. It suits you, I think."

"Thank you," Andre said. "I am delighted that you approve."

"And your sons will also be marquesses?" Ali asked, imagining him in his palace, surrounded by beautiful wives and many children.

"No. Just my eldest son—if I have any at all. First I would have to marry, and that's the last thing in the world I wish to do."

"But why?" Ali said, shocked. "All great pashas have wives! Many, many wives. It is a sign of high position."

"In my country, it is the custom to only take one wife at a time," he said, then adroitly changed the subject. "Tell me, Ali, have you ever seen a great pasha? You seem to have a very fixed idea of what they do and don't do."

"Well ... one once came through the village near to us. It was a great procession." Ali sighed in fond memory. "The pasha himself, he was dressed in the most magnificent of colors, the silk beautifully worked. He wore the richest of jewels too. Even his horse wore jewels!" She began to knead Andre's thighs, not an easy task since the muscles were so hard. "His Zoorigees, they beat us all soundly as they passed to let us know we were vermin next to them."

"And in your eyes this beating made the pasha even grander?" he asked.

"Yes, of course," Ali said, looking up at him in surprise. "Do you not beat the peasants in your own country?"

"No, actually I don't. I give them stern looks instead, and they fall to the ground in mute terror."

Ali nodded, her expression thoughtful. "Yes, I have seen this look. You have given it to me, but I did not realize that I was meant to drop to the ground. I thought you would beat me if you wished me to do that."

Andre ruffled her hair. "I had no such thing in mind. If for some reason I wish you to drop to the ground, I'll let you know. Verbally. All right? I didn't mean it when I threatened to beat you earlier, you know. I was only teasing."

"Yes, I know you were teasing then," Ali said. "It

is at other times that I have wondered why you have not beaten me."

"Why do I get the feeling that I've just dropped a few notches in your estimation? I'm afraid I have no use for physical violence, Ali, but if you wish me to beat you in order to maintain my standing with you, I suppose I will have to summon up the stomach."

"Oh, no! It is only that I must learn to think differently about what you wish from me if I am to serve you correctly as my lord and master."

"You serve me very adequately as it is."

"Yes, but I only know the ways of my people, and some of these ways might not be correct for your happiness. Not," she said firmly, "that it will change the matter of your bath. This is good for you, and on matters involving your well-being I will not be turned aside." She finished rubbing his feet and held out his clean clothes.

"Very well," Andre said solemnly, dressing. "On matters that regard my well-being, I will not object. But if you wish to serve me well, then you must submit to my will when I command it. Agreed?"

"Agreed." Ali bowed, touching her fingers to her chest, then to her lips and forehead.

"Good. I'm glad we have that settled. Now what about a bath for you?" he said, running his fingers through his half-dried hair. "I am sure you want to put on your new clothes, and you don't want to be dirty, do you?"

"No. But this I will do for myself," Ali said quickly, fabricating an excuse. "It is not correct for servants to be seen bathing before their masters. It is not correct for servants to be seen in *any* state of undress, as it implies disrespect."

"What would I do without you to tell me how to be a pasha?" Andre said. "But very well. As you wish. Just be careful not to take a chill, and I am very serious about that. Oh, and Ali—thank you. It was a nice bath, and a nice massage. You are skilled indeed with your hands."

"I am pleased to have given you pleasure," Ali said shyly. "Your happiness is all I wish."

Andre lightly flicked her cheek. "I'm beginning to believe you mean it," he said. "But be careful, little one, about such unbridled devotion. I'm bound to disappoint you."

"You will never disappoint me. You cannot disappoint someone whose heart belongs to you," she said simply.

Andre drew in a sharp breath, and then he released it. "Ali," he said very softly. "Don't ever give your heart away. Ever. And certainly not to me."

"It is too late," she said cheerfully. "Allah has ordained it."

"Then your Allah is a fool, for I have no heart, and will only break yours," he replied harshly. "Remember it." He quickly walked away.

Ali watched him until he disappeared from sight, her brow knotted. Her master could be very silly sometimes. No heart indeed. Well, with an attitude like that, it was no wonder he was unhappy. She could see that she really did have her work cut out for her.

As she prepared her bath she set herself the task of looking for solutions. It didn't take her long to come up with one.

That night the skies opened and it poured with rain. Ali wrapped herself more tightly in her blanket and drifted back to sleep, but she woke with a start as she felt her blanket shifting off her face. Andre knelt over her, rain dripping in rivulets down his cheeks.

"Come, little one," he said, scooping her up in his arms. "It's wet out here. If you are to look after my well-being, then I must first look after yours."

He ducked his head and pushed aside the flap of the tent, settling her on the ground next to his mattress.

Ali curled up happily and tucked her cheek under her fist. "I have been thinking, Handray," she murmured. "I am going to find you a wife. Someone to give you sons."

Andre's voice emerged muffled from beneath the

towel he was using to dry his hair. "Oh? And how are you going to do that, may I ask?" He tossed the towel aside and regarded her curiously. "Do you think to find a wife for me in the bazaar?"

"No, no. You do not find wives in the bazaar, only slaves. Maybe in one of the villages." She sat up suddenly as a thought occurred. "Oh. But you probably need an English wife."

"Oh, and now you want to marry me to a cold fish?" he asked, settling back on his mattress and pulling his blanket up over his chest. "No thank you, Ali. There are few things more dreadful than an Englishwoman. But please, let us leave the subject alone. Lie down and go to sleep. We have a long day tomorrow." He rolled over onto his side and soon his breathing slowed into sleep.

With a little sigh of contentment Ali closed her eyes. But something woke her in the middle of the night, a sound as if someone was in pain. It took her a moment to orient herself, and then she realized where she was. She sat up.

Andre tossed and turned fitfully on his mattress, his forehead knotted as another moan escaped his lips.

Ali quickly moved over to him. She placed her hand on his forehead, smoothing it. "Shh," she whispered. "Shh. It is all right, Handray. I am here."

The tension on his brow gradually eased as she stroked it, and his body stilled. Ali pulled the blanket that he'd kicked off back over him, tucking it around him. "Sleep peacefully," she said, lightly laying her hand on his cheek. "You have me to look after you now."

Ali crawled back onto her blanket and turned on her side, watching him for a few moments. But he didn't stir again.

"Ah, Xanthos." Andre pulled his horse up and drank in the sight of the peaceful valley that stretched before them. "Finally. Look at that, Jo-Jean."

It was not their first visit, but Andre never failed to be stirred by the sight of the magnificent city sitting broken and abandoned in its valley, yet still exuding a sense of majesty. The history alone was enough to break the heart, and for Andre, the valley emanated echoes of a haunting past from every rock, every blade of grass.

Joseph-Jean glanced over at him. "Sometimes I think you would rather be here than any other place on earth."

"And in this instance you might be right," Andre replied. He looked over his shoulder.

"Ali. Ride ahead to Kooník. Tell the governor, Ahmed, that we come, and we seek his protection. These people know us, but it's only polite to give them warning—it's the tent city directly before us, perhaps two miles. Use my title."

Ali instantly kicked the protesting donkey and was soon no more than a dot surrounded by dust in the distance.

"You like Ali, don't you?" Joseph-Jean said conversationally as Andre watched until Ali had disappeared.

"Like him?" Andre said. "I suppose. I find Ali refreshing."

"Refreshing. That's an understatement, but yes, Ali is definitely refreshing. Do you intend to keep him on, now that we've reached our destination?"

Andre frowned. "Why wouldn't I? He's useful, far more useful than anyone we've had in the past. He doesn't complain, he gets things done, he's unobjectionable company. Why are you suddenly having questions now?"

"Only because you said you intended to let him go when we reached Xanthos," Joseph-Jean replied reasonably enough.

The thought of Ali's leaving gave Andre an unexpected shock. Ali was an odd, quixotic chatterbox with a mercurial nature and exceedingly strong opinions, but who was also endowed with a lively curiosity and a surprisingly quick mind.

He didn't even object to the constant ring of laughter that sounded around him. Odd. In the past that sort of thing had had the effect of making him feel even more isolated. But Ali was ... different. Comfortable.

He supposed it was because Ali gave without expectation of receiving anything in return, save for food, shelter, and an occasional pat on the head. God, it had been a long time since anything had been simple. And for some odd reason he seemed to sleep better with Ali in his tent.

He turned back to Joseph-Jean. "Ali stays."

"I'm delighted to hear it. Shall I track down another tent? He can't stay outdoors all summer."

"No need for the extra expense or baggage," Andre said. "He can share mine—he's small and unobtrusive enough. Just purchase another bedroll."

"Consider it done." Joseph-Jean kicked his horse into a trot and Andre followed him, thinking that the prospect of summer suddenly seemed more pleasant.

There was feasting that night in the tent city. Andre and Joseph-Jean rested against plush cushions on lavish carpets in front of the chief's black goat's-hair tent, as Ali watched from one side near the fire. Plate after plate of food appeared before them, and Ali was pleased to see that the chief had a clear idea of her master's importance.

"You are Ali?"

She looked up from her delicious pilaf of kid to see a boy, somewhere around fourteen or so, his dark eyes gleaming with curiosity. "I am," she said, gesturing for him to join her.

"I am Umar." He dropped down to the carpet upon which she sat. "You have come with Banesbury and Claubert—I know them from their journey here last year. You are their guide?"

"No, only their servant," Ali said. "I have never before been to this region."

"Ah," Umar said. "Where is your village then?"

"Farther south," Ali said. "My people are Yourooks, like yours."

"Ah," Umar said again. "This is good. But why are

you here with the foreigners and not with your people? You are young to be on your own."

Ali shrugged. "My people are gone, and so I came north to find work. The effendis are good to me, very generous and kind. It is a good life, full of adventure."

"They are very rich, the effendis?" Umar asked, pulling up one knee and leaning his elbow on it.

"Oh, yes," Ali said with enthusiasm, warming to her tale. "My master lives in a great castle with many coffers of jewels and servants dressed in the richest of materials. His camels even have ruby headdresses and his herds of stallions and mares all have cloths of gold and silver upon their backs." Oh, she did like the way that sounded.

"Ahhhh," Umar said, his eyes wide. "How many wives has he?"

Ali chewed her lip. She didn't want her master to lose face because he had no wives. It was a tricky matter. She couldn't exactly say that he found women inconvenient, or that the women of his country were like dead fish, smelly and cold.

And then she remembered the strange thing he'd said the day before about never giving away one's heart, and she seized upon that, improvising wildly as she went.

"He has no wife," she said sadly. "He had one once whom he loved more than life itself, the most beautiful woman who ever lived, but she died, leaving him distraught and heartbroken. He mourns her and honors her memory by not taking any more wives."

Umar let out a long, appreciative breath. "A great tragedy. A truly great tragedy. I thought there must be a story there, for your lord has the look of one who suffers in silence. He is to be praised for his forbearance and sense of loyalty."

"His honor is above all others," she said, her eyes shining with pride—and delight that her story had gone down so well.

"Indeed." Umar then launched into a hundred other questions, and soon they were joined by a number of others, all with questions of their own.

Ali was happy to answer. She explained how she'd been rescued by her master, how he had nursed her back to health and given her work, and the villagers were suitably impressed by his extraordinary kindness and his bravery in the face of his terrible loss, which Umar had been quick to relate even more tragically than Ali had—much to Ali's satisfaction.

But as happy as she was to indulge in talk, she was even happier when the music began and conversation stilled. Ali leaned back on her hands and listened, drinking in the soulful notes of the lute.

She hadn't realized how much she'd missed the sweet sound that poured like liquid into the dark, star-filled night. Music had always soothed her, assuaged her soul. It sang of things lost, things never to be again, but it transformed pain into something that could be borne. It sang of beauty too, all the things of the universe that couldn't be spoken but were perfectly evoked in the lyrical notes that drifted across the moonlit encampment.

Umar brought out a flute and played a simple, wild melody on it, and someone else got up and began to dance. Ali lay on her side and rested her cheek on her hand, watching, admiring the man's skill. It was nice being back in familiar surroundings, nice hearing familiar music, eating familiar food, holding conversation around a fire.

She regarded Umar carefully and decided that she liked him very much. He would make a good friend and ally. The very idea that she would be able to cultivate his friendship was particularly exciting, since it would have been forbidden had anyone known her true sex. Ali was beginning to get the first taste of a freedom she'd never known. Being a boy was very nice.

It was even nicer being with people who didn't shun her or make fun of her because she wasn't one of them.

But the very best of all was her master, Ali thought, looking over at him as he conversed with the chief and Jojan and a few other men gathered around.

The Yourooks wore the usual full costume, knives
and handsome silver-mounted pistols tucked in their
belts, but they could not compare in splendor to her
master, unarmed and unadorned in simple *chalvars,* a
white shirt and plain vest, and his European boots.
His very presence was more impressive than any show
of arms.

The firelight caught and ran like strands of filigree
through his dark hair and beard; it shifted the long
shadow of his figure against the side of the tent, making his great height appear even more imposing.

Ali's heart swelled with pride. He was magnificently
handsome in body, brilliant in mind, good in heart.
And she belonged to him.

Allah had been truly good to her at last.

Ali pulled her gaze away from Andre and stared up
at the moonlit mountains rising dramatically from the
valley floor, capped with great snow-washed peaks.
Their savage beauty served as an acute reminder that
sometimes Allah made one suffer greatly before giving
His reward.

She managed to offer up one quick prayer of thanks
before dozing off.

Chapter 4

"Ali, sit *still*. I'm going to make a terrible mess of this if you keep wiggling." Andre put his hand on top of her head and pressed down, then went back to snipping. "Whoever cut your hair in the past obviously put up with your leaping about, which explains the state your head was in when you appeared last April. I've never seen such tonsorial butchery."

Ali wasn't about to tell him that she had been responsible. It had pained her to take the scissors to her beautiful locks, her only vanity, but she hadn't had a choice. But she'd since discovered that there were certain advantages to looking like a boy, especially in the summer heat. The pleasures of behaving like one she'd discovered nearly immediately. It was proving to be the best summer of her life.

"Hurry up, Handray, I have things to do," she said impatiently, squirming on the chair. "And you must go to work."

"This from the person who constantly tells me I work too much?" He walked around the chair and started on the back of her head.

"You do. But there are so many ruins here that I do not think you can finish writing about all of them by November. It is already August and you are not even halfway done. You have to finish your book, you told me so yourself."

"Why does this argument come up whenever you want to go your own way?" Andre asked dryly.

Ali twisted around and grinned up at him. "Because it usually works."

Andre took one last snip. "You're right. Very well,

off you go. You look vaguely more respectable, I suppose.''

Ali leapt out of the chair with alacrity and brushed off her shirt. "I will see you at dinner," she said, rubbing her hands over her neatly cut hair. "I am cooking the brace of woodcocks Jojan brought.''

"Where are you going in such a hurry, anyway?'' he asked, putting the scissors and comb away. "Are you off with Umar again? I'm glad the two of you have become such good friends, and I'm sure the company is nice for him too, with most of the village in the higher pastures. But shouldn't you leave him to get on with his chores every now and again?''

"We only do things together when our chores are done," Ali said indignantly. "Anyway, Umar has gone to the mountains for a week to see his mother.'' She sighed sadly. "I'll miss Umar's dog almost as much as Umar.''

Andre gave her an incisive look. "If this is another blatant attempt at bringing a dog into the camp, you might as well wish for the moon. No pets, Ali. And that's final. Again.''

"It seems very silly," Ali said in a small voice.

"We move on in November.''

"A dog could come along. Why not, Handray? Oh, wouldn't a little dog be sweet? I could sleep with it at night as Umar does with Sherifay.''

"Ali. I have spoken. It's finished.''

Ali lowered her eyes. "As you say. I am going down to the river to do my lessons. It will be cooler there.''

"You are a devoted student, aren't you? What are you planning to do with all this education, anyway? Open a carpet shop in Constantinople and swindle Frenchmen out of their money, perhaps?''

"Much better than that. One day I will be a great pasha, you wait and see," she teased. "But to be a great pasha I need to learn all I can." She picked up her bundle, then flashed Andre a huge grin. "Do you think it is possible?''

"With you I believe almost anything is possible," he replied. "But in all truth you have an extraordinarily good ear for language. Your French is coming along beautifully and so is your reading. You make my efforts worthwhile."

Ali was ridiculously pleased with the rare compliment, but before Andre could see it, she dashed off.

He watched Ali go, a smile lingering on his mouth. He really did derive pleasure from their work together. Ali had a mind like a large thirsty sponge.

Even the whimsical stories he often spun at night for Ali's entertainment provided fodder. Last week the myth of Leda the swan and the egg that had hatched Helen of Troy had led to a thorough history of the Trojan war. He'd quickly learned that Ali's imagination was a useful tool to implement just about anything he cared to teach.

Ali was definitely a positive addition to their lives, he thought, picking up his knapsack and starting off to the ruins. It was hard at times to remember what life had been like before.

The breeze by the river was cooling, but it was a scorching day, and the heat, even in the shade, made it difficult to concentrate. Ali reread the same sentence three times, then gave up and put the book down. As much as she wanted to learn everything she could as quickly as possible, and as much as she wanted to make her master proud of her, her head had started to ache.

She gazed at the water longingly, then glanced carefully around. Nothing stirred. The herd of camels in the distance slept, the cows had disappeared into the wood, even the birds had hushed. Handray and Jojan were safely off excavating, the only people out in the heat of the day, as usual.

It was a risk, but one worth taking. She'd suffered the entire summer, laboring under the self-imposed but necessary fiction that she couldn't swim. But with Umar away and no one else about . . .

Ali hastily removed her clothes and climbed down the bank, wading into the shallows of the water. She breathed a sigh of immense satisfaction as cool little

ripples lapped against her calves, then cast her eye
around for the nearest safe pool, since she had no
intention of being swept away by a current.

Yes. There was a nice deep one, shaded too, and
even a convenient log to dive into it from. She waded
over toward the log, her toes relishing the feel of the
cold mud squeezing under them. In another moment
she was in the pool, shaking water from her freshly
trimmed hair.

She rolled onto her back and floated, taking pure
pleasure in the moment. It was a pity, she considered,
that she couldn't do this all the time. But discovery
would be disastrous.

Ali's brow furrowed. She wondered how much
longer she could keep up the fiction. It was difficult
as it was, attending to her bodily needs, bathing, dressing, the nuisance of her monthly bleeding, everything
done stealthily and out of sight.

Fortunately, her master and Jojan had drawn the
conclusion that she was modest about her body and
didn't question her need for privacy. But she couldn't
go on like this forever. One day something was bound
to happen.

And then what would Handray do?

She had planned to tell him the truth, she really
had, but the terrible fear that he would cast her aside
kept her mouth firmly shut. Her entire world revolved
around Handray as completely and unequivocally as
the moon revolved around the sun. Every breath she
drew, she drew in his service.

What would her life be if she were to be sent from
his side? It would be no life at all. No more wonderful
stories, no more sharing his tent, watching him as he
slept. No more hearing his laughter, or seeing the
smile that he produced more and more often these
days.

She might as well go straight to the Turkomen and
offer herself up, she decided. Better, she could find
the nearest cliff to jump from. It was a pity. If he were
a violent man, he would instantaneously have her head

severed from her shoulders, but there wasn't any chance of that.

No, she thought sadly, it would be far worse. He'd level that horrible cold look he had, the one that had turned her veins to ice on more than one occasion, and pronounce her gone, cast off, never to darken his days again.

"Oh, Allah," she said earnestly, gazing up at the sky beseechingly. "Please, please keep my secret safe. I couldn't bear it if Handray sent me away. I really couldn't."

The very thought made her heart pound in panic.

Ali stole a quick glance over at Andre. She'd been unable to shake the depression that had come over her that afternoon at the thought of her probable fate, the cruelty of her master who didn't care enough about her to keep her, all because she was a lowly female.

Dinner was over and he was busy cleaning his saddle leather, his dark head bent over his task, oblivious to her black thoughts.

Then she looked across at Jojan, whose fair head was equally bent, but in the worthwhile task of writing a letter to his mother. Ali knew, because she'd asked and he'd told her.

Handray never wrote letters. He only wrote in his book. She'd asked him why he didn't write to his family as Jojan did, and had her head taken off for her trouble.

"You are my servant," he said curtly. "Confine yourself to questions of a nonpersonal nature. Is that clear?"

It was more than clear.

She knew all about Jojan. He had a mother and a father and three sisters whom she missed very much, and who all lived in a little village in France. She knew that his father was a farmer, so they were not grand people like her master, but they were content.

It was a nice story about a happy family, and that contentment was reflected on Jojan's face.

Handray was another question altogether. One very big question. Maybe, like herself, he didn't have a family any longer ... but not ever to speak of them?

It occurred to her that he had never once asked about her family, either—not that she could have answered truthfully, but it hurt her that he didn't even care enough to want to know. He might think they were all dead of plague, but that shouldn't make any difference.

The fact was that Handray didn't care about much of anything but his old buildings. She was nothing more to him than the person who cooked and carried and cleaned, who gave him pleasant baths and massaged him when he was tired.

"Why are you glaring at me?" Andre asked, glancing up as if he'd felt her eyes on him. "Is your stomach indisposed, or are you merely indulging in a fit of bad temper?"

Ali scowled even more darkly. "You are very nasty. I have made you a brilliant meal and now you speak like this to me?"

Andre gazed at her with interest. "Let us ignore for the moment that it's your job to make brilliant meals, along with all the other duties you're paid to perform," he said. "Since when did scowling become part of your repertoire? Have I done something to offend you, said something unkind to cause you to look at me in such a manner?"

"No," Ali said, feeling ashamed.

"Then I'd thank you to keep your bad temper to yourself. You are treated extremely well for a servant."

He was right, of course. She was a servant and had no place expecting anything other than tolerance at best. Indeed, she ought to consider herself lucky that he didn't beat her. "I am sorry. I did not mean to offend."

He released a small sigh. "All right. Your apology is accepted. However, it occurs to me that you might be feeling neglected. I haven't told you a story in a good week. Maybe that would sweeten your mood?"

Ali nodded, although her heart wasn't really in it.

"Yes, please," she said, trying her best to sound enthusiastic.

"Which one would you like?" he asked, slinging the saddle over the post he'd made for that purpose.

Ali brought him soap and a basin of water. "The story of Xanthos?" she said. She was in the right sort of mood for a good tragedy.

"Surely not again?" he replied, washing his hands and drying them on the towel she provided.

Joseph-Jean glanced up. "I think our Ali has a real love for bloodthirsty drama," he said. "How many times have you heard the story? Five? Ten?"

"Stories only become better with many tellings," Ali informed him crisply, and instantly regretted her unintentionally curt tone as Joseph-Jean looked at her in surprise. "It is only that they grow in detail," she added contritely.

"Yes, I can see that they would," he replied, but she knew he was puzzled by her mood.

Andre pushed his chair back and stretched out his legs. "Oh, all right," he said. "Xanthos it is."

Ali settled herself at his feet, knowing that secretly he loved telling the story of the magnificent and honorable people who had once lived here. She usually loved just as much to hear the tale, especially the way he had of telling it in his deep, rich, melodic voice.

She tried to put herself in the correct frame of mind and closed her eyes for a moment, imagining herself thousands of years in the past.

"Xanthos was the capital city of Lycia," he began. "But to understand Xanthos, you have to understand the character of the Lycians—a strong and fiercely independent people, who are believed originally to have come from Crete."

"Probably Minoans, in around 1400 B.C.," Ali added, wishing he would skip the boring things, but knowing they would have to wade through them anyway. He always started the same way.

"Thank you," Andre said. "They were determined to remain separate from all of their neighbors and they fought to retain that independence. They did, however, fight alongside the Trojans during their war—"

"Told in the *Iliad*," Ali said, moving him along.

"How I am supposed to tell you a story if you keep interrupting?" he demanded.

"I was just helping you get to the good part," Ali said.

The corners of Andre's mouth curved up. "Naturally. You want to go straight to the catastrophe. Very well, I will oblige you."

Ali grinned victoriously. "Start with the king."

"Brat. When Croesus, King of Lydia, was no longer able to defend himself against Persia, Lydia fell. Lycia was next on the Persians' list and naturally the independent Lycians weren't very pleased about the prospect of being taken over."

"No, how could they be?" Ali said, warming to the tale. "It was very bad of the Persians to want to take all these places that did not belong to them."

"Yes, it was," he said, pausing a moment to light a cheroot from an ember he took from the cooking fire, now dying out. "But that didn't help the Lycians," he continued. "When they realized there was nothing they could do to defend themselves against domination, they decided that they would do anything rather than surrender."

Ali sighed heavily. "And so, being the very wonderful people they were, the men herded their brave women and children into the city. The women held their children in their arms to comfort them as their sad husbands set fire to the acropolis, where they had also placed all their possessions, including their loyal slaves. And then they marched out to meet the Persians and perished, every last one."

"Ali, perhaps you would prefer to tell me the story." Andre raised one eyebrow, which made Ali burst into laughter. It always made her laugh when he did that.

"No, no—you may tell it. It is only that sometimes you forget to talk about the magnificence of the women, who had to see the suffering of their poor children. At least the men were able to die in glory on the battlefield."

Joseph-Jean chuckled as he folded his letter and put it aside, then leaned back in his chair to devote his full attention to the story. "It *is* an important point, Andre."

"Of course it is," Ali said. "Men always want to die in glory. Go on, Handray."

"Yes, well, I think I had better skip over the years of distant Persian rule, and Alexander's conquest, and more Persian rule, since not much blood was spilled and you don't seem to care about the history," he said. "I'd hate to bore you."

"Thank you—but you may leave in the part about the League of Twenty-three Cities and all those nice rich people." Ali fiddled with her sash. She really liked this part.

"I wouldn't dare miss it for fear of my life," Andre said, puffing on his cheroot. "Let's see. Lycia grew prosperous, having formed a democracy of its own, despite all the warring going on around them. People grew rich—and yes, Ali," he said, forestalling her, "I'm sure they had jewels and servants and precious oils and handed them out all over the place. We do know that they were very generous with their own people."

"Well, of course they were," Ali retorted. "They were kind and brave and perfectly glorious in every way." She leaned toward him. "You may do all this studying and recording, but you forget that these were real people who lived good lives right here on this very soil. It was not all crumbled ruins then, you know."

Andre stared at her, then at Joseph-Jean, and they both burst into laughter.

"Well, it was not," she said uncertainly, wondering why they found that so amusing.

"No," Andre said, recovering his composure. "It wasn't. That's the point, little one, that's the point. Why do you think we're doing all this work, if not trying to make that period come alive?"

Ali, now annoyed, folded her arms across her chest. "And that is *my* point. Copying old inscriptions and making drawings and maps does not make something come alive. You talk about Xanthos as if you were giving a history lesson."

"And how else am I supposed to talk about it?" Andre asked curiously. "I can't change the facts to suit you."

"If I were you, I would tell a story, a good one, with people and families, speaking of the tragedies that happened to them, things everyone can understand." She looked up at the ruins for a moment. Dusk was drawing down and the silhouette of the old buildings and tombs stood dark against the deepening blue of the sky.

She tried to imagine how it would have been almost two thousand years before, a girl watching the night approach, the sounds of the city about her, wondering what she might have been doing—how she might have felt if she knew that war was encroaching on her city, for that was the next, most sorrowful part of the story.

"Ali?" Joseph-Jean asked. "What has made you suddenly so quiet?"

Ali turned to him. "If someone were to come along in another two thousand years, Jojan, and wonder about what my people were like, I would not want him to think of emptiness, of a mass of people without faces, the way we think of them."

She inclined her head toward the ruins. "I do not mean the big names, the important ones that you and Handray speak of, but people like me, like Umar, or Muzaffer and his wife," she said, looking back at Joseph-Jean. "I would want these people to know our names, to know about the details of our lives, in a way that would help them to understand what we were like."

"But we can't know," Joseph-Jean said. "We can only imagine."

"Exactly," Ali said triumphantly. "And if I were to imagine what it was like here in Xanthos all that time ago, I would make up a family."

"Oh?" Andre said, leaning his forearms on his thighs and looking down at her. "And what sort of family would you make up, Ali?"

She rested her cheek on her fist, thinking hard. "I would start with a family who had lived a simple life here."

"What, no riches?" Andre asked with a smile.

"Riches are not important to people like myself," Ali replied seriously. "They are only important to great lords like you, where they are necessary to maintain your standing. For others, riches are merely about greed. They do more harm than good, I think." She looked down at the ground for a moment, thinking of Hadgi. "The promise of riches," she added, "can be very bad. It can make people behave in a dishonorable fashion."

"Ali—I have rarely seen you so solemn," Joseph-Jean said. "Does something trouble you?"

"No," she said quickly, realizing that she'd nearly said too much. If Handray got even the slightest whiff that things were not as she'd told him, he would interrogate her until he'd dug out the entire truth.

"Ali?" Andre asked, his eyes sharp on her face. "What is it?"

"I was only thinking about that horrible man Brutus who wanted riches so much that he was happy to steal them from Xanthos, to make the people his slaves. And look what happened—they all died as a result of his greed."

"Yes, but that was their choice," Andre pointed out. "I don't think Brutus had any idea that they'd commit another mass suicide. It's not what people generally do when they're invaded. And they do say that Brutus wept when he heard their cries—so he wasn't entirely unfeeling."

"Well, when an entire city is burning and everyone is burning with it, I do not know what else he would expect to hear," Ali replied tightly. "All those poor dear children—and their mothers and fathers and aunts and uncles—"

"Don't forget the grandparents," Joseph-Jean supplied helpfully.

"And of course their grandparents, too. All suffering an agonizing death because someone else wanted money for his war," Ali said, tears starting to her eyes at the appalling image. "Now do you see what greed will do?"

"Yes, Ali, but don't forget that Brutus felt so terrible that he paid his soldiers a reward for every Xanthian they found alive. So a hundred and fifty of them did survive." Andre held out a handkerchief, but Ali pushed his hand away, suddenly filled with rage that Andre could be so callous, as if it didn't matter. He had no feelings at all, none.

"I don't need a handkerchief, and how could you defend that terrible man?" she asked furiously, jumping up and glaring at him. "Just because he was a great lord like you does not make what he did right."

"That's not what I—" Andre started to say.

"Bah!" Ali said in disgust. "All you care about is your stupid history. You and those clever effendis you are always talking about—Fellows, Beaufort, your great hero Lacey, you are all the same."

"Well, I can't object to being listed in that company," Andre said lightly. "So if you're trying to insult me you're doing a very poor job."

"None of it is real to you," she said heatedly. "It is all a big game, a puzzle you put together. You do not care about the people, how they must have felt. And this makes you a stupid man even if you are smart in your head."

"What in God's name—"

"Oh, never mind!" she said, knowing in another minute she would burst into tears, and she refused to cry in front of him. "You would not understand, anyway. You are right—you have no heart, none at all." She stormed off.

Andre looked at Joseph-Jean with astonishment. "What was that all about?"

"I have no idea," Joseph-Jean replied. "But something got to Ali. You've told that story countless times now and never had a reaction like that."

"I know. Oh, well. Whatever it was, Ali will get over it. I'm going to bed. Tomorrow I'm going to begin working on the necropolis and with the heat the way it's been, I want to make an early start."

He went to get his bedroll from the tent, for it had been too hot to sleep inside. He settled down but grew progressively more annoyed as he waited for Ali to return.

The night wore on, and he grew angrier by the hour, swearing that if Ali wanted to be eaten by wolves or whatever hungry predator was out there, it was no concern of his. And if Ali didn't wish to hear the story of the next constellation on the bedtime list, that was no concern of his either.

If there was one thing he could not abide, it was an ungrateful, temperamental child.

Ali barely spoke to Andre over the next three days, she was so annoyed with him. When she did have to speak, it was in short, curt phrases, but he didn't appear to notice, going about his business in his usual fashion and behaving as if she didn't exist, which only made her angrier.

He was an unfeeling monster like his friend Brutus, she told herself, stirring the superb soup she'd made for the evening meal with fish freshly caught in the nearby sea.

He was cold and insensitive, with not a drop of emotion in his smallest toe. He was ... Ali's head lifted as a commotion in the distance claimed her attention. Two horses rode hard toward the camp, kicking up a great cloud of dust. The camels and cows that had been peacefully grazing in the pasture scattered in alarm.

She stood, wondering who might be coming in such a fashion as not to respect the grazing rights of the Yourooks.

A man in European dress pulled up and abruptly dismounted. "Lord Banesbury," he demanded, and then followed it with something Ali couldn't understand.

She bowed respectfully. "I do not speak your language, effendi. I beg your pardon."

The second man, who wore white Arab robes, brought a crop down on her shoulders. "Your master, fool," he said in badly accented Turkish. "Where is he?"

"He is in the ruins," she said, fighting back the sudden sting of tears. It had been so long since anyone had beaten her that she'd forgotten how much it hurt. "I can summon him if you wish. Would you take refreshment?"

The Arab nodded. "Give it first to the lord. He is a very great Englishman, come from Rhodes on the queen's urgent business."

Ali looked at the Englishman. He didn't look like a great lord to her, certainly nothing like her master, whom one could mistake for nothing else. But she bowed obligingly enough.

"Effendi," she said, pouring him *ayran*, thinned yogurt with a little salt added. He took it without thanks. Ali poured some for the Arab. "Your names, effendi, that I might tell Banesbury?"

"Tell him Lord Weselley is here. My name is of no matter to you."

Ali bowed again and took off at lightning speed, racing past the acropolis, the basilica, making directly for the necropolis, where she knew Andre was working that day.

"Handray," she said, pulling up among the standing tombs and sarcophagi, breathing hard from having run all the way up the hill.

"So, brat. You are speaking to me again," Andre said, looking up from the inscriptions he was copying. "Now maybe you'd care to tell me what it is that set off your temper?"

"Never mind that," she said, still panting. "You have visitors—a great Englishman, his name is Lord Weselley. It is urgent, something about your queen."

He frowned. "Oh, God, not Thomas Weselley, of

all insufferable people. I suppose he has that damned Syrian with him too."

"His companion is an Arab of some sort, yes."

Andre swore fluently under his breath, and Ali sighed. She was beginning to think she was never going to break him of the habit.

"Well, I suppose there's nothing for it," Andre said. "Damn!"

"You do not like him, Handray? I am glad, for I do not like him, either."

"I loathe him," Andre replied, abandoning his task. "He, Ali, is precisely the sort of English person I cannot abide. But he's an historian too, and works with the same people I work with, so I'm forced on occasion to tolerate him."

"Is he a great lord?" she asked. "His servant says he is, but I do not think so, myself."

"He is what is known as a baron," Andre said, packing up his knapsack. "It's not a particularly prestigious title, but the measure of a man's worth is not in his title, it's in his actions." He shook his head. "If Weselley's are anything to go by, they put him on the lowest scale there is. He's one of the most unethical, dishonorable people I've ever had the misfortune to know."

Ali nodded in vigorous agreement, thinking of Weselley's disrespect for the animals. "Who is the Syrian?" she asked as Andre tossed his knapsack over his shoulder.

"Oh, him. His name is Abraham. He suits his master. And trust me, Ali, there's no lower form of humanity than a Syrian." He gave her a wry smile. "He'd sell you his mother if he thought he could make a profit, and stab you in the back if you were stupid enough to turn it."

Ali rubbed her burning shoulder, thinking Handray might be right about Syrians being the lowest form of humanity, with the possible exception of Hadgi, who also beat viciously and often without reason.

"Go find Jo-Jean, would you?" Andre said. "Tell

him what's happened. He's going to be equally displeased to hear of our visitors."

"Will they be staying?" Ali asked unhappily.

"I am sure they will. But not for long, if I have my way. Sadly, I have to be polite for the sake of my work. Weselley's the sort who takes offense at anything and will use it to make trouble." He started to leave, then suddenly turned back to her. "And Ali? Stay out of the way as much as you possibly can, all right? I mean it. Stay out of the way."

Andre cursed his bad luck as he started down the hill. He should have known Weselley would ferret him out on the pretense of research. But more than likely he was up to his old tricks.

The man had cheated his way through Oxford, and he was now cheating his way through his research, stealing right and left from other historians, Andre included.

He had no doubt come to sniff out what new theories Andre had come up with so that he could slip them into a paper before Andre's Lycian book came out.

And the damned Syrian—God, how he loathed him. Andre had once seen him cut the head off a dog for no reason other than the poor beast had the unfortunate judgment to lift its leg on Abraham's robe. Just looking at him sickened Andre. But there was nothing to do but put the best possible face on the matter.

"Hello, Weselley," he said curtly, seeing that Weselley had already made himself at home at his table. "Fancy seeing you here. What's all this about urgent business?"

"Well met, old fellow. I have a letter for you from the British Museum," Weselley said, lazily holding it out. "Offered to bring it out to you."

Andre took it, wondering if Weselley had already read it. More than likely. It was nothing urgent, only a letter from Lord Umbersville, updating him on a few developments. It was certainly nothing that couldn't have waited until he collected his mail in November. Weselley had no doubt bent over backward to convince Umberville to send it along with him. "Thank you," he said coolly.

"Ah, yes. Overflowing with warmth and gratitude as always," Weselley said, leaning back and crossing his arms. "So, Banesbury. Who is this new servant of yours? A little young, don't you think?"

Andre ignored him. "I suppose you're planning on staying?"

"For a few days, anyway. I might as well take advantage of the opportunity to rest the horses. If you don't mind, that is." He smiled. "I'd hate to disrupt your privacy. Speaking of which, where's your ever-present companion?"

"Working," Andre said as politely as he could manage. "And if you would excuse me, I think I should get back to the same. You can set up your tents nearby."

"Good of you, old boy," Weselley said, and nodded at Abraham, who smiled smugly.

Andre quickly left, thinking that the next few days were going to be sheer hell.

Ali watched from her place in the shadows. This Lord Weselley was not an unattractive man for a foreigner. His hair was fair and his eyes were pale. But they didn't reflect light like Handray's, which had a trick of changing shades with his mood and his surroundings, sometimes more smoke, sometimes more moss, sometimes almost silver.

Weselley's eyes were simply gray. He was neither tall nor short, broad nor slight. In fact, everything about him was medium. Weselley was like food without spice, she decided. Bland.

But there was something about him that made her uneasy. It was a feeling that there was something bad there, some sort of ill will he bore toward her master, even though he appeared on the surface to honor him. And she'd never seen her master behave in such a fashion. Oh—well, maybe when he'd very first found her, but that was different. This Weselley was one of his own. It was as if Handray were a completely different person, a man with ice in his eyes.

She didn't like the way Weselley looked at Jojan either, as if Weselley knew a secret he was keeping to himself.

If she'd been able to understand English, she'd have spent more time trying to listen to what he said to his servant when Handray and Jojan weren't there. She understood the sneering tone well enough.

But instead, she did as she'd been told and stayed out of sight as much as she could. It saved her a beating or two, since Abraham's crop descended on her shoulders and back every chance he found to use it—always when the others had gone up to the site and there was no one else to see.

She grew to loathe the sight of his turban-covered head, his white robes swirling around him as he commanded her to one task or another, the crop descending if she didn't fulfill his every wish instantaneously. Weselley she merely disliked. Abraham she hated.

They stayed only five days in the end. Ali breathed a sigh of relief when they finally thundered off again in the early morning, scattering the camels and cattle just as before.

It was Andre who declared a celebration the moment they'd vanished from sight. "Bring on a sheep, Ali!" he said, turning to her, a grin on his face. "We are free at last. God, what a miserable week."

Joseph-Jean nodded in wholehearted agreement. "You showed admirable restraint, my friend. There were a couple of times that I thought you were about to give him a tongue-lashing."

"I was," Andre said. "But what would have been the point?"

"I wouldn't have blamed you. The monumental arrogance of the man—imagine implying that the British Museum puts more value behind his work than yours."

Andre sighed and pushed a hand through his hair. "Ah, well, forget about him. He's gone and that miser-

able Syrian with him. What are you standing around
for, Ali? Get to it!"

Ali, delighted to see a smile back on her master's
face again and the warmth returned to his eyes,
hopped on her donkey and took off for the village to
find Umar. If her master wanted a celebration, he
would have one.

"Umar, quick," she said, riding into the village.
"The foreigners have left. We need a sheep for a
feast."

"A feast?" Umar said, his face lighting up. "What
a wonderful idea—we haven't feasted since my people
went up to the summer pastures." His brow furrowed.
"But there's hardly anyone here, just my father, my
brother—"

"And Muzaffer and Hatije and their five children,"
she said, dismissing his concern. "And the two of us
and the effendis. More than enough for a feast! And
we can have songs, and dancing, and—just have fun!"

Umar instantly caught Ali's enthusiasm. "Fun?
Well, come on then, we have to hurry. It will take
hours to roast the sheep."

By the time late afternoon had rolled around, they
were ready. Ali had helped grind wheat for *burghul*
while Hatije kneaded wheat flour into a dough. With
Umar lending a hand they prepared salads redolent
with spices that Ali had bought as a present for Hatije
on her last trip to the market.

The little village smelled wonderful with the mingled scents of roasting lamb, bread baking in the out-
door oven, spices, and *tulum*, the sharp cheese
fermented in goatskin.

Everyone left in the little village gathered around,
spreading carpets and pillows out for themselves and
their expected guests. Ali, satisfied that all was as it
should be, hopped on her donkey and rode back to
camp.

"Good God," Andre said as they approached the
tents, "you really did plan a celebration, Ali."

"Of course!" she said cheerfully. "Do you think I would disobey my master?"

He glanced at her skeptically. "I think you do precisely as you please and try to convince me that whatever you're doing is for my good."

Ali smiled happily. "As long as your needs are met, what difference does it make?" She pulled back on the donkey's reins and slipped off its bare back. "Come," she said, tugging on Andre's sleeve. "You and Jojan have the place of honor by the cooked sheep."

They ate and talked and laughed amid the gentle beauty of flat pastures and grazing land, the mountains rising up behind, the ruins of Xanthos just visible in the distance.

Andre looked around him, content. Ali was carrying on about something or other and had the group in tears of laughter, Jo-Jean included. But then Ali had the gift of bringing laughter to people, like an irresistible flame, a piece of the sun dancing about. One couldn't help basking in the warmth.

His gaze took in Ali's mischievous smile, those large, luminescent eyes, the funny, mobile face that twisted into a hundred different expressions, the skinny little body that wiggled about on the carpet in enthusiasm.

Andre smiled. He really had become exceedingly fond of the child. Indeed, he couldn't imagine life without Ali's high-spirited presence in it.

He realized that in the three years they had been traveling, never had they been so close to the local people. He and Jo-Jean had been considered oddities, to be looked up to and respected, but not treated as one of their own. But thanks to Ali, they had been accepted. Tonight, he almost felt one of their number.

He sat up a little straighter as another realization hit him. He was actually enjoying himself. Thoughts of Genevieve, of his father's betrayal and his mother's complicity, hadn't crossed his mind in some time—in fact, he couldn't remember when he'd last fallen into an uneasy sleep, curled up against the pain.

Andre slowly shook his head as if dazed. He had never believed it would happen. He thought he'd be forced to live a lifetime of unceasing agony, but somehow he was sitting here tonight, having a fine time.

He didn't know whether he ought to be disgusted with himself, or whether he ought to be elated that the anguish that had clawed at his insides for so long was no longer so acute. It had muted into a more distant ache, he discovered, carefully exploring the pain as one might probe a sore tooth.

Yes. It had muted, but how? And when? He was baffled. It was almost as if God—

He pushed that thought away abruptly, deciding to be grateful that time had eased the pain a little. It hadn't been easy living with a bloody wound where a heart normally resided.

But he didn't want to think about it anymore. It was a nice evening, and it was pleasant to be part of a festive gathering, especially one that held no reminder of the past—with the exception of Jo-Jean, of course, but he didn't count.

"Handray," Ali called. "You are looking too serious for a celebration. Come, dance for us! Umar will play for you on his flute."

"*Dance* for you? Ali, are you mad?"

"Certainly not! I am sure you are a fine dancer. Please?" Ali's shining eyes entreated.

"Oh, very well. Why not?" he heard himself say, as much to his own amazement as Joseph-Jean's, who stared at him, his mouth hanging open.

Andre grinned at Jo-Jean and stood, and hoots of approval broke out among the little group.

Umar began to play on his flute, a melody with which Andre was familiar. He put his arms out at his sides and began the slow, studied, traditional dance, his movements rhythmic and smooth. It was nice to feel the breeze in his hair, to feel his muscles shifting in time with the music. God, it had been a long time since he'd danced. He closed his eyes and let the music take him. That felt nice too.

He stopped as the music drew to a close only to be

replaced by more shouts of approval, and trills of delight. Jo-Jean applauded wildly and Ali's smile was so broad that it stretched practically from one ear to another.

He laughed, then gave a mock bow and sat down again, and Umar's brother took over, dancing fast and furiously to a wilder, more primitive song.

Only a moment later he sensed someone approaching, and he glanced up.

"You were very beautiful," Ali said, squatting down beside him. "Just as I knew you would be. Very magnificent. You danced with the heart you say you do not have."

Andre was silent for a long moment. "Perhaps I danced with the heart *you* say I don't have," he finally replied.

"Ah," Ali said softly. "So you heard me, then. It is good."

"Why is it good? Why do you even care, Ali? What difference could the state of my heart possibly make?" His eyes raked Ali's face as if he might actually find an answer there.

Ali considered. "A man's heart is the reflection of his soul. In it he carries everything he is made of, everything it is possible for him to give, and everything that is possible for him to become. He needs only to know his own heart to know all of this for himself." Ali lightly touched his arm. "It is not that you do not know these things. It is only that you do not wish to see them. Perhaps one day you will choose to look."

Chapter 5

Andre glanced up from his seat outside Gemil's carpet shop, sipping on his glass of apple tea as he checked on Ali's progress through the tented marketplace. He had to smile. Ali adored these monthly excursions, despite the three-hour journey each way, never failing to examine every last piece of produce, of clothing, the big buckets of spices, drinking in the colorful displays and the mingled scents while doing the necessary shopping.

He watched with amusement as Ali looked proudly down at the shopping list, reading his Arabic script, then grinned and tucked the list away.

A procession of camels made its way down the narrow street, their backs laden with merchandise, momentarily obscuring his vision. He returned to his conversation with Gemil. When he looked again, Ali had progressed to the fruit and vegetable stall and was in the process of squeezing a pomegranate, carefully checking it to see if it was ripe.

And then almost before he had a chance to register, a heavily bearded man dressed in the costume of the Yourooks appeared behind Ali and clamped his hand down hard on Ali's shoulder.

Ali turned, the pomegranate falling to the ground, crimson pulp and seeds splattering as the man brutally cuffed one ear.

"Hadgi, no!" Ali cried, dodging as he lifted his hand again. "No, do not!"

First shock, then rage surged through Andre. He leapt to his feet and tore across the street to the stall. Ali's head jerked up as he approached, fear sharp in the huge brown eyes that normally sparkled with laughter. His blood boiled even more furiously to see it.

No one—no one—would mistreat Ali. He didn't even stop to wonder who Hadgi was or what reason he had for his assault. The only thought in Andre's head was to stop him.

"Unhand my servant," he commanded, his voice cold as steel.

Hadgi spun around. He glared at Andre in disgust. "Your servant?" he said, his voice filled with contempt. "Your whore is more like it."

"My *whore*?" Andre's eyes snapped with anger. "I should kill you for that remark." He paused for a moment, struggling for composure. "However," he continued, "since I am a guest in your country I will let it pass. What is your business here, and what do you want with my servant?" he demanded as a crowd began to gather.

"My business belongs to me," Hadgi said. "As does your 'servant.' " He spat the word out.

"And how is that?" Andre asked, deliberately making his expression unreadable, but his heart tightened with apprehension at this unexpected piece of news.

"Ali ran away from me, depriving me of a great deal of money. She stole my son's clothes. She stole food from my household. If you want the little thief, you can pay for the privilege. Otherwise, she comes with me."

She? A cold sweat broke out on Andre's brow and his stomach felt as if Hadgi had just landed his fist in it, but he forced his face to remain expressionless. It would be a big mistake to show his shock. He glanced at Ali for one brief moment, then back at Hadgi. "Do you own her?" he asked.

"She is my niece," he said. "I was about to receive a bride-price for her when she ran off."

"A bride-price?" Ali cried. "Hadgi, you were going to sell me to the Turkomen to be put on the auction block as a slave!"

"You be silent," Hadgi shouted. "Not another word from your viper tongue, do you hear?"

"You will not speak to Ali like that," Andre said

in a voice of cold command he rarely used, and Hadgi fell silent.

Ali stared at him, admiration mingling with the dread on her pale face. If the situation hadn't been so potentially disastrous, he might have been amused. But there was no room for amusement when Ali's future hung in the balance.

"So, you were going to sell your niece to the Turkomen," Andre said after a moment. "And now you would sell her to me."

Hadgi nervously licked his lips. "I am owed something. I have supported her all of these years and have received nothing in return. Nothing. And all of this I did for an infidel out of the goodness of my heart."

"An infidel?" Andre asked coolly, even as another shock wave flashed through him, along with a sincere desire to wring Ali's neck. "How is it that your niece is an infidel?"

"Bah—Ali is not even of Turkish blood. Yet I fed her and provided shelter over her head because my brother was stupid enough to take her in."

Andre cast another quick look at Ali, whose gaze was fixed on the sticky mess of the pomegranate splattered on the ground. So. Ali had lied to him thoroughly and successfully, not only about her sex, but about her background. Well, there was only one thing for it, and that was a good offense. Ali he would take care of later.

He scratched his cheek. "The goodness of your heart. Yes. Of course. Well, since I find Ali's services useful, and since I would rot in hell before handing her back to you, I will buy her from you." A gasp of astonishment went through the assembled crowd.

He dug in his pocket for his purse and he pulled three gold coins out of the leather bag. "It's more than you would have extorted from the Turkomen," he said, throwing the coins at Hadgi's feet. "Consider the extra as payment for your son's clothes. Take it."

Hadgi scrambled to pick them up. He examined them, then quickly put the coins in his pocket. "Why do you keep Ali dressed as a boy, foreigner?"

"It amuses me," Andre said, doing his best to preserve the situation.

Hadgi sneered. "No wonder you paid so well."

Andre's brow drew down. "I paid to have you vanish. I suggest you do so. Immediately."

"I had heard that foreigners had perverted habits," Hadgi said as a parting remark. "But I had never imagined habits as perverted as whoring with female children dressed as boys. A little of both, is it?"

Andre moved so quickly that Hadgi didn't even register that he was in danger. Andre's fist connected with the side of Hadgi's jaw with a great crack, and Hadgi flew backward into the table laden with fruit and vegetables. Eggplants, cucumbers, and oranges scattered everywhere and Hadgi went down on top of them.

The merchant let out a great wail of dismay, but the crowd broke into loud shouts of approval.

Andre dug once more into his pocket and took out a handful of piastres. He put them into the merchant's hand, took one last look at Hadgi, who lay groaning amid the pile of multicolored produce, and turned his back.

He walked toward Ali. She dropped to her knees, her face white, and she took his hand, kissing the back. "Thank you, Handray. Thank you," she whispered.

"Get up," he snapped, barely able to speak at all. Now that the immediate crisis was over, reaction swept through him as furiously as if a dam wall had broken. He picked up the knapsack she'd filled with the shopping, slung it over his shoulder, and strode off, not looking right or left. She had to run to keep up with him.

They reached the horses and Andre strapped the knapsack to one of the bulging saddlebags. "Let's go," he said.

"But—but Handray, aren't you going to—"

"I don't wish to speak to you at the moment," he said, trying very hard to control himself. "In case you can't tell, I am very, very angry."

"Oh, please, Handray, beat me, shout at me, anything but this coldness. I can't bear it!"

"*Enough!*" he roared. "Enough," he said again a little more quietly when the veins no longer bulged at the side of his neck. "If I hear another word I will probably put my hands around your scrawny throat and throttle the life out of you. And I *hate* to waste good money."

He mounted his horse and set off at a fast pace, giving Ali no choice but to follow. He said not one word to her all the way back. He couldn't. He really couldn't. He was not just angry, he was deeply shaken. And he had absolutely no idea what to do next.

Joseph-Jean looked up from his sketchbook as he heard them approach. "You're back early," he said with surprise, walking toward the horses. "Did Ali not want to stay and listen to Gemil's stories after the market?"

"I thought it better to return directly," Andre replied tightly, swinging down. "There was a bit of a commotion, and I didn't want to have to answer any questions, since I didn't *have* any answers." He glared at Ali, who hung her head.

"Oh, dear," Joseph-Jean said, looking back and forth between them. "Trouble?"

"You might say that. Ali's uncle appeared." He undid the first of the saddlebags and handed it to Joseph-Jean.

"But I thought Ali had no family," Joseph-Jean said, frowning. "Didn't they all die of plague?"

"Oh, he wasn't really an uncle, since they share no blood. But apparently Ali ran away from his home. Ali said it was to avoid being sold into slavery."

Joseph-Jean threw a startled look in Ali's direction. "No ... how terrible. But why would he do such a thing?"

"Because, Jo-Jean, Ali is nothing to him but a worthless female."

Joseph-Jean stared at Andre in disbelief. "*What?*" he said when he'd recovered.

"You heard me. A worthless female infidel, who does not even have the honor of being a Turk. That is all I know. As Ali didn't deny it at the time, I assume it is true."

"Good God! What did you do?"

"I bought her." Andre stalked off, leaving Joseph-Jean holding the saddlebag.

Ali thought she might very well die. It had been bad enough in the marketplace when Hadgi had appeared out of nowhere. That had been merely horrible. And when Handray had discovered the truth about her, that had been truly devastating. Oh, she'd always known that the truth would eventually come out, that her life with Handray and Jojan was too good to be true. But despite all of her imaginings, nothing, but nothing, had prepared her for the force of Handray's anger. That had been worst of all.

She could see that Allah was going to punish her and punish her harshly for the brief happiness he'd allotted her.

"Ali ... is this true?" Joseph-Jean walked up to her, examining her tear-streaked face.

Ali nodded, her shame and fear threatening to overwhelm her.

"*All* of it?"

She nodded again and slid off her horse, rubbing her eyes with her fists. "What will he do to me, Jojan?" she whispered.

"I have no idea. Why don't you come sit over here—no, leave the supplies. We can unpack them later. I think we need to talk."

Ali reluctantly trailed after him. He sat her down at the table outside his tent and brought a bowl of water, dipping a cloth into it and handing it to her. She gratefully washed her hands and face.

"How did you ever get into a situation like this?" he asked, but his words weren't spoken harshly, as she had expected. Instead, he regarded her with sympathy.

"I did not mean to ... that is, not exactly," she said, faltering.

"It just happened by accident?"

Ali nodded vigorously, pleased that he grasped the point so quickly. "Yes. You see, when you found me, I was not strong enough to explain, and then later ...

well, I did so want to be Handray's servant as Allah
had willed, and I knew he would not take me on if
he knew the truth, so I—"

"Slow down, Ali, slow down. I can hardly make out
a word."

Ali took a deep breath. "I thought I would make
Handry happy with me first, and then I would tell him
the truth. But oh, Jojan, I found that I liked being a
boy!" Fresh tears of misery and shame poured down her
cheeks. "It was so nice, and Handray liked me as I was,
and I knew he wouldn't like me at all as I really am."

"There, there, don't cry," Joseph-Jean said, holding
out the washcloth. "I can see that there are going to
be some problems ahead, but nothing we can't
overcome."

Ali sniffed and wiped her nose. "I will clean the
cloth," she said, looking down at the mess she'd made
of it.

"Never mind the cloth," he said with a slight smile.
"I think we had better start at the beginning. I'm sure
we can straighten it out if we have all the facts."

"But it begins many years ago," Ali said reluctantly,
not certain that it was wise to divulge all the details.
"Are you sure it will help to tell you?"

"Yes. I'm sure." Joseph-Jean reached over and
squeezed her hand. "Please. Tell me everything."

"Well ... I was very young," Ali said, trying to put
herself into a storytelling frame of mind, for it was
the only way she could make Jojan understand. "I
had no mother, and my father lay dead, killed by the
Turkomen. I stayed huddled in the cave where he had
bid me hide."

Ali shivered. She never talked of the old memory,
only vague now, like a dream. It was not easy bringing
the words to her tongue, even now when she needed
them desperately. "Uri of the Yourooks was tending
to his sheep when he found me. He took me back to
his village and asked his wife Magda if she would foster me. She had no children of her own, you see."

Joseph-Jean nodded. "How nice for her that you
came along, then."

"Yes," Ali said, "I thought so, although Uri's brother Hadgi thought him a fool, and an even bigger fool to take in an orphan. And then Uri died a few years later, and Hadgi had to take both Magda and me in."

"Ah," Joseph-Jean said. "And Hadgi did not like the situation?"

"No. He did not," Ali said, her face darkening in memory. "He complained constantly, even though we both worked hard for him to pay our way in his household. Our lives were not easy, for he was not a kind man. And then my foster mother died."

"I see. And then you really had trouble."

"I did," Ali agreed. "Things became worse. One night Hadgi was very angry with me." Ali left out the reason why, not wanting Jojan to know anything about her humiliation. "He said he had found a way to be rid of me for good."

Joseph-Jean leaned forward. "And his plan was to sell you into slavery?"

She nodded. "Yes, the Turkomen were coming through in a few days time. He said they would take me to the city and put me up for auction. He would make much money. And so I decided that it would be better to run away." She looked away. "Even if I died in the attempt, at least I would not die as a coward who had let herself be meekly led away."

"You were brave, Ali. Very brave." Joseph-Jean wore a pained expression that she didn't know how to interpret. "And I am very glad we found you."

Ali swallowed hard. "Then do you understand why I had to cut my hair and take boy's clothing to wear? I would have been in even graver danger if I had tried to come all this distance as an unprotected female. Do you see? Please, oh, please try?"

"Yes, of course I do," he said.

"Really? But Handray does not, not at all." She looked at him imploringly, forcing herself to ask the question foremost on her mind. "Oh, Jojan, what is to become of me? He would not talk to me at all, he was so angry."

"Yes. But what else would you expect, Ali? You put him in a terrible position."

"I—I know. But I never thought Hadgi would suddenly appear like that. He has never come this far north before."

"That is neither here nor there. Ah, Ali. Can you not see? There are many things you must consider. All these months Andre thought nothing of your sleeping in his tent, of letting you attend to his personal needs . . ." He trailed off.

Ali was amazed to see Joseph-Jean's color heighten. "Do your people not let females do these things?" she asked.

"Our people let females do these things for other females. Men have manservants."

"Bah," Ali said. "How silly. In my village we do whatever is necessary for our family. The men come home tired from the fields, and the women have their baths ready and the oils, and—"

"But Andre is not a member of your family, Ali," Joseph-Jean pointed out. "He is your master."

"Even more reason that I should serve him," Ali said stubbornly. "If he is angry that I have seen him unclothed, I shall just tell him—"

"No!" Joseph-Jean said with alarm. "I think you would be wise to stay well away from that subject."

A tiny smile crept onto Ali's face. "He would be embarrassed?"

"He would be extremely annoyed, and you have enough trouble as it is."

Ali nodded thoughtfully. "Yes. You are right. It is bad enough that Handray doesn't like females to begin with."

Joseph-Jean rubbed the side of his mouth. "Ali," he said carefully. "There is something you need to understand. It isn't that Andre doesn't like females. It is just that he prefers the company of men."

"Ohhhh," Ali said, her eyes growing wide. "It is like that with him? No wonder he does not like me to speak of his taking a wife."

Joseph-Jean was silent for a long moment, his gaze

fixed on the ground. Then he rubbed his temples hard and looked up at her. "No ... no, Ali, I didn't mean it like that. The reason that Andre doesn't like for you to speak of his taking a wife is because once he nearly married, but his fiancée died shortly before they could be wed. Her death hurt him very deeply."

Ali clapped her hands together with glee. "I knew it! It is just what I told Umar!"

"It's just what you told—oh, God help us all," Joseph-Jean said, covering his eyes with his hand.

"You must not blaspheme," Ali said automatically. "Yes, I thought it must be something like that."

"But why did you feel the need to tell Umar anything at all?"

"Because the villagers were curious about why a strong handsome lord did not have many wives, let alone one. I had to think of something to preserve Handray's status, so I said he mourned a beloved wife."

"Well, do me a huge favor. Please do *not* bring it up to Andre."

"I promise. But surely she was not a dead fish?"

"I beg your pardon?" Joseph-Jean rubbed his temples again. "What on earth do you mean by that?"

"Handray says all Englishwomen are like dead fish," Ali explained.

"Ah," Joseph-Jean said. "You mean a cold fish. It's an expression that means someone is stiff, unemotional, lacking in passion. No, she wasn't like that at all."

"Oh," Ali said. "Then she was Turkish?" she asked hopefully.

"Genevieve was French, a girl from our village, very sweet, very pretty, with hair the color of corn silk, and eyes the color of the sky," he said softly. "She was like a moonbeam, fragile, the sort of person you wanted to protect, as if the world were too harsh a place for her."

"She sounds like a fairy-child in one of Handray's stories," Ali said wistfully, wondering what it would be like to be all golden and fragile, to be loved by Andre.

"A fairy-child? Yes, I suppose she was a little like that. She and Andre loved each other from the time they were very young—*why* am I telling you this?"

"I do not know," Ali said, sighing happily, "but I am glad someone is finally telling me what has made Handray so unhappy. Do not worry, Jojan. I will not speak of it. I have given you my word."

"Thank you," he said with real relief. "Because Andre would not thank either of us, believe me."

Ali bit her bottom lip contemplatively. "I think," she said after a moment, "that he is happier than he was. What do you think?"

Joseph-Jean reached across the table and took her hand, squeezing it. "I believe you're right. And if it helps, I think you've had something to do with that."

She beamed. "I think so too," she said. "I have worked very hard to make it so. When I first met him, Handray had forgotten about living life. Now he remembers a little more, although he is very stubborn about it."

"Yes. Yes, he's a stubborn, determined man, it's true. When he makes up his mind about something it's nearly impossible to change it."

"That is what I fear," Ali said, her face clouding over again. "But I shall have to be brave. Thank you for understanding—I have always thought you a very kind man. And I know that you love Handray too."

"Yes," Joseph-Jean said quietly, "I do. He is like a brother to me."

Ali nodded. "It is good. Come, Jojan. We should see to the horses and the supplies. It does not do to let either sit out in the sun."

Ali huddled against the rock face in a miserable ball, her arms crossed against her chest. Handray hadn't returned for dinner, which meant he was so angry he couldn't even eat. It was hard to be brave in the face of such a silent, distant rage. At least Hadgi had beaten her and then it was over with until the next time. This in its own way was far more terrifying.

The moon waxed nearly full and the air hung very still with little breeze. Light from the lantern shimmered from inside his tent. She supposed he was in there reading. She'd probably never be allowed inside again. Ali put her face in her hands, despair overcoming her.

"Oh, Handray," she sobbed, her entire body shaking with grief. "I am sorry. I am so, so sorry. And now you will hate me forever and ever."

"Perhaps not forever and ever."

Ali's head snapped up in alarm. He stood looking down at her, and his face wasn't the thundercloud it had been before.

"Handray! Oh, Handray ... I thought you would cut me up into hundreds of pieces and feed me to the lions," she cried. "And I would deserve it, I know that I would."

"As I said to you earlier, I hate to waste money."

"But why—why did you bother to buy me even after you knew the truth?"

"Why do you think, Ali?" Andre dropped down next to her and wiped her streaming face with his handkerchief. "Here. Blow your nose."

She did, resoundingly. "I thought that maybe it was because you once saved my life and did not want to waste that, either."

"Listen to me," he said, his voice gentle. "I paid your uncle the money because it was the only way to be rid of him. He would have been within his rights to take you away, and he would have either beaten you to death, or been paid handsomely for someone else eventually to do it. Do you think I would let that happen to you?"

"But I am only a girl," she said, staring down at the ground.

"Yes, I know," he replied with the glimmer of a smile. "But I can't suddenly stop liking you because you turned into a female, can I? I confess I'm extremely annoyed about it, and it's very inconvenient, but there we are."

"Then why were you so angry with me?"

"Because you didn't trust me enough to tell me the truth. It came as quite a shock to hear it in the middle of the market, in front of a crowd of people, from a relative you weren't supposed to have." He regarded her intently. "Can you understand that?"

"Yes," she said, sniffling. "It hurt your pride."

Andre thought about that. "Yes, I suppose it did. It also scared the devil out of me. I had no idea what might happen, or what other surprises might be in store. I would have much preferred to be prepared."

"But if I had told you in the beginning, you would have sent me away. And then what would have become of me?"

Andre sighed and ran a finger over the dry earth. "I honestly don't know what I would have done. I don't even know what to do now, Ali."

Her heart lurched. "Oh—but I belong to you," she said quickly. "You cannot send me away! You paid much money for me." Her eyes narrowed suspiciously. "You are not thinking about selling me to someone else, are you?"

"No, of course not, although I ought to, just to teach you a lesson. But right now, you and I need to have a talk." He settled himself on the ground in front of her and rested his arms on his knees. "Ali. What your uncle said. Was it the truth?"

"About the bride-price? No. I told you how it was. Hadgi was going to sell me." She hunched a shoulder miserably. "He did not want to keep me any longer."

"Yes, I know. Jo-Jean has already told me the full story. But I meant about the other things, about how you came to the village. Today Hadgi called you an infidel, an odd thing to say since you're always spouting off about Allah."

"I do not know why I am an infidel. Maybe Hadgi just made that up. He hates infidels and he hates me and the two go together in his mind."

"Maybe," Andre said, not looking very convinced. "But he also said you weren't Turkish. And yet you look Turkish enough to me with your dark hair and eyes."

"Do you suppose I am one of those awful Syrians?" she asked. "Oh, I do hope not. I would never stab anyone in the back, I swear it, Handray."

Andre frowned. "Do you mean to tell me that you really don't know where you come from originally?"

Ali shook her head. "I have no idea. I only know I am from the outside."

He took one of her slim hands and looked down at it. "I don't know why I never noticed before. You have such small bones. How old are you, Ali? Eleven? Twelve?"

"Older, though I do not know by how much."

"Well then, how long were you in the village?" he asked, turning her hand over and running his thumb over her palm as if he might find an answer there.

"I was in the village for ten years, and when I arrived I was not a baby, although I had not yet lost my first tooth. But you cannot count from that, either, since I did not do anything else as early as the other girls either." Ali blushed beet-red when she realized what she'd said, but Andre was unperturbed.

"Have you started your monthly bleeding yet?" he asked.

"Handray . . ." Ali said uncertainly. "I do not know if we should speak of such things."

"Oh, it's all right for you to strip me naked and pummel me on a regular basis, but not acceptable for me to ask you a perfectly logical question?"

Ali looked at him sideways. "Jojan said I was not to mention seeing you without your clothes on, that you would be annoyed."

"Did he?" Andre said with a grin. "He must think I have delicate sensibilities. I'm afraid that it doesn't bother me in the least. Nor does discussing your monthly courses. So? Have they started?"

"Yes," Ali replied, looking him straight in the eye, determined not to behave like a silly female. "Last year."

"Hmm," he said. "Well, you certainly haven't developed in any other way."

"I have too!" Ali said indignantly, forgetting for a moment that she hated being female. "You just never noticed."

"Begging your most humble pardon, but there

hasn't been anything to notice," Andre said. "I'm not *that* unobservant."

Ali thwacked his arm. "I am just skinny," she said. "You wait and see, one day I will impress you with my magnificent breasts."

"Oh, really?" Andre said with a laugh. "Well, we shall see about that. In the meantime, I don't think you can be above thirteen or so." He idly picked up a small rock from the ground and toyed with it. "Which brings me back to the original question. What do you remember, if anything, about your arrival in your village? Could you understand the language?"

"I think so . . ." she said, straining to remember. "It was so long ago."

Andre rubbed his eyebrow. "Unfortunately, none of this is much to go on. I don't suppose . . . no, never mind. This is probably too difficult for you."

"What, Handray?" she asked anxiously. "I will try to remember, I will."

He nodded. "All right. Do you happen to remember your father's name?"

"Oh, yes," Ali said, brightening. "His name was Pappah."

Andre dropped the stone. *"Papa?"* he repeated. "Are you sure?" He looked hard at her. "That isn't a name that maybe you heard somewhere else, from Jo-Jean, perhaps?"

She shook her head. "No. It is the only thing I really do remember. I—I remember crying out for him, over and over again. But he could not come." The shadow of those half-remembered but terrifying days alone in the little cave hovered dark in her mind. She shivered and looked away.

"Ali," Andre said softly, cupping her small chin in his large hand. He turned her face toward his. "I'm sorry," he said. "I'm so sorry. It must have been a very dreadful time for you. But let me help you? Let me do what I can to make it better."

Ali met his eyes, those lovely gray eyes that reflected genuine concern. She touched his hand, curling her fingers into it. "Thank you," she whispered. "Thank you for caring."

"Of course I care," he said, lightly brushing her hair off her forehead with his fingers. "Now let's get back to business. You say you called your father 'Papa.' Do you remember anything else about him, anything at all?"

Ali strained. She had imagined all sorts of things, but the real image of her father was lost in the mists of time. "No," she said sadly. "I wish I did. I only know he loved me."

"I'm sure he did, very much. It's a pity he didn't leave you anything to remember him by, but I suppose the Turkomen took it all."

Ali stiffened. "Wait," she said. "Handray—he did leave something. I have a book. Uri said he found it in my father's coat pocket—it is the one thing the Turkomen did not take."

Andre took her by the shoulders. "A book? Here? With you?"

"Yes. I cannot read it, but I have always kept it with me. It is in my bundle. Do you think you might be able to understand it?" She was pleased by the sudden excitement she saw in his eyes.

Andre jumped up. "I have an odd feeling I will. If I can't, I'm not much use, am I? Come. Take me to this book of yours."

Ali fetched her bundle from under her bedroll and untied it, drawing out the little square book. She gave it with both hands to Andre, who carefully opened the crumbling leather cover.

He held it close to the lantern. "Good God. No wonder Hadgi called you an infidel," he said, glancing up at her briefly. "He must have recognized the Cross on the inside cover. This is a copy of the Holy Bible, Ali. It's the Christian version of the Qur'an."

"Oh," Ali said, her expectant smile fading. Allah was going to be very angry. She probably wouldn't be allowed into heaven at all now.

Andre turned the fly leaf and she heard the long exhale of his breath. "I don't believe it," he whispered. "I don't damned well believe it."

He sat very still for a number of minutes, staring at the page, then lifted his dark head, his eyes filled with something she didn't understand at all. Tears.

"Handray?" she said uncertainly, touching his knee. "What is it? Please, what is it? Am I a Greek infidel, perhaps? That is not so bad. You *like* the Greeks."

He shook his head. "No," he said tightly, putting the Bible down on his mattress. "No, Ali, you are not a Greek." He took both her hands gently between his own and looked into her eyes for a long moment, his gaze searching.

Ali swallowed, wondering what he saw there. "If it is not too dreadful," she said in a small voice, "will you tell me who I am?"

"Your name is Alexis Minerva Lacey," he said, his voice ragged. "You are sixteen years old. And you have been missing and presumed dead for the last twelve of them."

Ali stared at him. "What?" she whispered. "What are you saying?"

"That you are the daughter of Sir Frederick Lacey, who died in a presumed ambush near Myra twelve years ago."

"No," she said in flat denial. "No."

Andre took her cold face between his hands. "Listen well, Ali, for this is going to be difficult for you to believe. Damn, it's next to impossible for me to believe."

Ali had never seen him like this before, so clearly shaken, not even trying to disguise it. "Tell me, Handray," she said firmly, moving away from him and sitting up very straight. "Tell me everything."

"All right," he said, his voice still rough. "I will tell you everything, at least as much as I can."

"Please. Do not leave anything out. Not anything." She felt most peculiar, as if she were two people in one. But surely she was still Ali, not this strange Alexis?

He drew in a deep breath. "Twelve years ago Sir Frederick Lacey was working in a remote area of Anatalya. Lady Lacey was an adventurer as well as a devoted wife, and refused to leave her husband's side, even after the birth of their daughter."

Ali absorbed this. She liked the sound of Lady Lacey. "Was she Turkish?"

"Lady Lacey? No, Ali, she was English."

"Oh," Ali said, disappointed.

Andre smiled. "In any case, they lived much as I do, spending their winters in Italy, or Constantinople, and traveling in the summer months. Sadly, Lady Lacey contracted cholera and died in the little village near Anatalya where they had made their summer home."

"Cholera?" Ali echoed, her head swimming.

"Yes. It's an unfortunate illness that affects the intestines. In any case, Sir Frederick was grief-stricken and took his daughter away, intending to bring her to England himself. He had booked passage for both of them from Myra—what you know as Dembre."

"Yes ... my village is not so far from there," she said, her mouth dry. All the pieces were falling into place with a nasty thud of finality.

"That's right, for you said you lived on the Dembre plain, which Sir Frederick and his daughter would have had to cross to get to Myra."

"But they never arrived," Ali said.

"No, they didn't. There was a search, of course, but nothing came of it, and eventually it was called off." Andre paused. "Now we know for certain that Sir Frederick didn't survive his journey. But now we also know that you did."

Ali stared at her hands. She didn't want to be Alexis Minerva Lacey. She didn't want to be Alexis Minerva Lacey at all. She wanted to be just plain Ali, who loved her master with all her heart and served him with devotion.

Ali felt sick.

"My God, Ali, do you understand what this means?" he asked, taking her by the arms.

Crushed, Ali forgot to tell him not to blaspheme. "Yes," she said despondently. "It means that I am a dreadful Englishwoman. And that is almost as bad as being a Syrian."

The tent rang with Andre's laughter, but for the first time Ali was not pleased with it.

Chapter 6

"Ali, listen," Andre said impatiently, trying to teach her English as quickly as possible, which she was equally determined not to learn. "Try again. This is a pencil. Please. At least make an effort to say it correctly?"

"Why?" Ali shot back. "You will only send me away to your horrible country sooner."

"You are going whether you damn well like it or not. And if you think your resistance is going to make the slightest difference in my decision to send you, then you have lost your mind."

"I have not," Ali said, pounding her fist on the carpet. "It is *your* mind that has gone crazy. Can you not see that I do not want to go? Why will you not listen to me?"

"Because I have an obligation to return you to your family. I realize it will be a big adjustment, but this is how it must be."

Ali scowled. "It is how *you* think it must be. It is not how it is. I see no reason why I cannot stay here with you, just as things have been." She folded her arms across her chest.

Andre fought for patience. "Look here. I have explained this to you a ridiculous number of times over the last month. You are going to England to be reunited with your family. I am staying here to do my work. If you don't learn English, fine. It won't affect me, only you." He tapped his finger on the page for emphasis. "Either way, you are going."

"The only reason you do this is because you admired my father. I am happy you admired him. I am

sure his work was very fine, and I am pleased it prepared you for your own studies. But it is nothing to
do with me."

"Indeed, your father was a very fine scholar and a
fine man, and yes, I admired his work tremendously,
as I've told you many times. As a result I feel a responsibility to his only daughter. That has everything
to do with you."

"And as I have told you many, many times, I do
not care."

Andre threw the pencil down. "I am not the villain
here. It's not my fault that your father was killed trying to get you back to England, any more than it is
my fault that no one found you before this!"

"How do I know you have not invented this story?"
she demanded.

"Oh, for the love of God, why would I bother to
invent something so farfetched? How many renowned
historians who mysteriously disappear with young
daughters in the wilds of Turkey do you think there
are?"

"I don't know. I don't care," she said stubbornly.
"You could have made a mistake."

"There is no mistake, and as God is my witness, if
your father wanted you in England badly enough to
risk the journey across treacherous territory, then
that's where you'll go. Why can't you understand the
point?"

"There is no point," Ali said, wishing it was raining
so that she could escape the confines of the tent, the
lesson, and his stupid argument.

It had been a miserable month. No more bathing
Handray, no more giving him the massages he so enjoyed. No more sharing the tent with him. Now he
insisted on sleeping either outdoors or in Jojan's tent
when the weather was bad.

No more of anything except these ridiculous lessons
in the hideous language called English. She hated
every minute of it. But worst of all was the gnawing
fear of being sent away from her beloved master.

"No, I don't suppose there is a point," Andre said, standing. "Not if you refuse to see it."

Ali grabbed his hand. "But it is so simple. You bought me. I am yours. No one ever has to know about this other problem. Oh, *please,* can you not just forget?"

"Ali," he said, pulling his captured hand away and rubbing it over his eyes, "there is nothing simple about this situation, and no, I can't just forget. I realize this is difficult for you—"

"Difficult?" she said with a snort. "It is not difficult, it is impossible! You wish to turn me into something I am not, something I have no wish to be."

"Only because you have no idea of what that is."

"You loathe Englishwomen!" Ali howled. "Why do you want to make me into one?"

Andre leaned his forehead on his palm. This was proving to be the most thankless task in the world, and the hell of it was that he agreed with Ali.

Yet he didn't feel he had a choice—not that he thought he was going to be able to manage the job, not while she was still here in Turkey, not while she stayed with him. If he could turn history around, move it back to how their lives had been before that fateful day in the market a month ago, he would have done it in an instant.

He looked at Ali slumped on the carpet, her small face turned away in misery, her little chin set defiantly. He understood, oh, how he understood her fears, far better than she realized. But then she had no idea of the emptiness he was going to be left with once she'd gone, and he had no intention of telling her.

He pushed the thought away for the hundredth time.

"Ali," he said in English, sitting down again. "Let us return to our lesson. This is a pencil. This is paper. Please, if you won't say the words, at least write out the alphabet ..."

All he got for his trouble was Ali's back.

Andre swore fluently and stormed out of the tent into the full force of the storm. The howling wind and shearing rain were a great deal easier to bear than the force of Ali's temper. Or the thought of sending her away.

October 1864
Izmir

"I will not go in there. I will not." Ali planted her feet and crossed her arms, her heart pounding with panic.

"Ali," Andre said dangerously, "you will do as you are told, and you will do it immediately. Mr. Ponesby is expecting you. He has gone to a great deal of trouble to arrange a passport, passage, and a traveling companion for you."

"I do not want a passport," she said, willing herself not to cry. "I do not want passage, and I do *not* want a traveling companion!"

Andre glared at her. "At this moment I could care less what you want. I've had enough of your infantile, impossible behavior. You will come inside now, and you will stop giving me trouble."

"I will not!" Ali knew that the moment she stepped inside the building her life was over.

Andre's thunderous expression suddenly sweetened. "Are you not my servant?" he said, his tone cajoling. "Did you not swear to obey me, to submit to my will when I commanded it?"

"Oh, you are cruel," she cried. "It was different then—that was before you wanted to send me away from you."

"It makes no difference. You gave your word."

Ali turned her face away.

"You gave your word," he repeated.

Ali's word was everything to her, and he knew it. She squared her shoulders and met his steely, determined gaze full on. "You are unfair," she said, a chill in her voice. "You invoke the oath I swore you, knowing I cannot refuse. You invoke it knowing that it will break my spirit."

"I can't imagine anything breaking your spirit. So let us give up the melodrama and go inside." He walked through the door without bothering to look back at her. Of course he knew she'd be forced to follow him now. Oh, he was insufferable.

Ali didn't miss Mr. Ponesby's alarmed reaction when she came into the room, quickly suppressed but not quickly enough.

She imagined it was due to the female clothes Handray had bought for her the moment they approached Izmir and insisted she wear. Ali thought she looked ridiculous in the all-enveloping *thcarchaf*. At least he had stopped short of a veil, but still the only thing to be seen of her were her eyes.

"So, Miss Lacey," Mr. Ponesby said in painful, halting Turkish after the introductions had been performed, "Banesbury Bey, he explain to me your trouble. I am sorry. You will tell your story now? I need to hear in your words."

Ali, who couldn't see how they were going to get through the conversation in her own language, answered him in French instead. "I thought Lord Banesbury had told you everything. I remember almost nothing of my early life." She took a deep breath and began to recite. "The Yourooks took me in when my father was killed. I ran away when my uncle was going to sell me, and my master—Lord Banesbury," she amended, "found me. He discovered the truth of my birth in my father's book. He has been very kind to me."

Mr. Ponesby smoothed a hand over his bald scalp. "I see," he said, looking even more alarmed. "Yes. Yes, that will do." He regarded Andre accusingly. "How is it that the girl speaks French? I thought she had been brought up in a tribe."

"Naturally she speaks French," Andre said, privately thinking that he was talking to a moron. "I taught it to her. That is beside the point. Miss Lacey has answered your questions and I trust you to keep the matter confidential until her family decides how they would like to handle the situation." He glanced around impatiently. "Please, let us get on with this process. Where is the Herringer woman? And mind you, I want her to know nothing—nothing at all about who Ali is."

"I understand. I will summon her."

Andre, who felt his forbearance had been extreme to this point, nearly changed his mind when Mrs. Herringer came through the door. She was short and fat. Well, that was no problem. It was the look of horror on the fool's face when she saw her charge. Her little eyes bulged and she took a step backward.

Andre stiffened. He could just imagine how Ali felt.

"Oh! Oh . . ." Mrs. Herringer said, faltering. "Good day, your lordship, Mr. Ponesby. And this is the—the girl?"

"This is Ali," Andre said. "As you can see I have not yet had an opportunity to attire her in European clothing. That is being arranged."

"But I—but who *is* she? Why am I to take her to England?"

"That is no concern of yours. Your duty is to see that she arrives safely in Sussex. You need know nothing more than that. Do you understand, Mrs. Herringer?"

"Oh, naturally, my lord," she said, still looking appalled.

"Ali doesn't speak English. I don't suppose by some lucky chance you speak Turkish?"

"That heathen language? Good heavens, my lord, our dear queen's tongue is enough for me."

"Is it? I see. So you have no French either. Well, I suppose there's nothing for it. If I don't send her with you now, it might be months before someone else is available to take her."

"Oh—I am sure we will get along famously, my lord. No need to worry over the matter of the language. The little poppet and I will find other ways to communicate."

Andre nodded. "Very well," he said. "Ali will be delivered into your care on board the ship. Here are your instructions." He handed her a packet. "In there you will also find the ticket to which I agreed and a bank draft which you may draw upon once you have delivered Ali safely to Ravenswalk."

Mrs. Herringer opened the packet and drew out the draft. Her eyes nearly jumped out of her head when she saw the sum he had written out.

"Treat her kindly," Andre said.

"Oh! Oh, yes, your lordship, as you say, your lordship! The girl will have everything she needs, every last thing." Mrs. Herringer practically curtsied her way out of the room.

Andre nodded to the consul, took Ali by the arm, and left without another word.

Absorbed in writing the difficult letter to his godparents explaining about Ali, Andre ignored the knock on his door until it became a bang.

"Andre, are you in there?"

He threw his pen down in frustration. "Come in Jo-Jean, and stop making such a racket!"

Joseph-Jean opened the door, his arms full of packages, which he dumped on the bed. "I have the materials for Ali's dresses, although personally, I think they're ugly as sin. How did it go with the consul?"

"Ponesby is as big a fool as ever. But Ali has a companion, at least, although she's an even bigger fool than Ponesby. Some widow who wanted to return to England but couldn't afford the passage."

"The steamstress will be here in a half hour, although I don't know what sort of job she'll be able to do."

"It doesn't matter. Anything is better than that damned envelope. You should have seen how those two bloody English snobs looked at her—I ought to have brought her in her *chalvars* and really given them a shock," he said, rubbing a hand over his aching forehead. "But never mind, the Herringer woman is being paid a small fortune to forfeit her opinion." He picked up his pen and returned to his letter.

"Andre—"

"Hmm?" He looked up again, wishing Joseph-Jean would vanish. He knew exactly what was coming.

"Are you sure you don't wish to reconsider your decision? There's still time to change the arrangements."

"I've heard enough of this from both you and Ali," he snapped. "She leaves for England in three days time and that's my final word."

Jo-Jean scratched the tip of his nose. "You don't even know that your godparents will take her. It's not as if they're expecting her."

"I'm writing them now. In any case, they don't have to keep her for very long. All they have to do is find her relatives."

"You don't even know if there *are* any relatives!" Joseph-Jean said desperately. "And even if there are, who's to say they'll agree to take her in?"

"Of course they'll take her," Andre said irritably. "Why wouldn't they?"

"Because," Joseph-Jean said impatiently, "Ali does not remotely resemble a well-brought-up English girl, and she's not likely to turn into one overnight. It's going to take very tolerant, open-minded people to help her through the adjustment."

Andre shoved both hands through his hair in frustration. "Do you think I don't know that? What would you have me do? I can't continue to drag Ali around with me for the next few years. She's a young woman, for the love of God, even though she doesn't look or behave like one."

He pushed back his chair and strode to the window, gazing out across the rooftops, his hands shoved on his hips. "The way you and Ali are carrying on, you'd think I was a hardened criminal!

"Tell me," he asked, turning around abruptly. "Suppose I kept Ali here with me as she wants. What do you think would happen when my grandfather dies and I'm forced to return to England?" He raised an eyebrow. "Can you see me explaining that I found Miss Alexis Minerva Lacey on a mountaintop and decided that she made a convenient servant? She deserves better than that, Jo-Jean."

"Of course she does. I'm only saying that she needs more time. Why can't you write ahead and ask your godparents to look into the matter of her relatives before you send her all the way to England?"

"No. In this case the element of surprise works well. Nicholas and Georgia aren't likely to refuse her once she's on the doorstep."

"That seems a little unfair to me," Joseph-Jean said. "They're not exactly in the first bloom of youth."

"I can't see what difference that makes. They like taking in strays."

Joseph-Jean skirted that issue, which Andre knew he would, since they both knew Andre was referring to the matter of his father's adoption.

"I only wish you'd be reasonable," Joseph-Jean said with frustration.

"That is precisely what I'm being. Ali has been away from home too long as it is. If she needs brushing up, Nicholas and Georgia can see to it before they send her off."

"Brushing up?" Joseph-Jean said, staring at Andre incredulously. "The girl can barely speak English!"

"Only because she's too damned stubborn. She had four years of it, so it must be in her head somewhere, just as I suspect French was in her head. Look how quickly she learned that when she wanted to."

"That was different. She didn't have to depend on it."

"Exactly. Ali will learn English in no time, once she realizes it's the only way to get food in her mouth. Don't worry, Jo-Jean. Frederick Lacey was a linguist, and Ali's obviously inherited his talent. She'll be fine."

Joseph-Jean shook his head in disgust. "I'm sorry, but I think what you're doing is unspeakably cruel. I hope you don't later regret it."

"Why should I regret it?" Andre said. "I'm doing her a favor. Now if you don't mind, I need to finish this letter." He waved his hand at Jo-Jean in dismissal.

"See to the seamstress, will you? And tell Ali she's not to give the woman any trouble."

Joseph-Jean picked up the packages. "As if she's going to listen. Lord, between the two of you my life is a living hell at the moment."

"My sentiments exactly," Andre said, glowering.

"You know, the worst thing is that I'm going to miss Ali nearly as much as you are," Joseph-Jean said, yanking the door open. "But at least I'm prepared to admit it." He slammed it behind him.

"Damnation!" Andre cried in complete frustration. He walked back to the window and pressed his hands on the frame, leaning his forehead against the cool pane.

"If you realize that, my clever friend," he whispered hoarsely, "then why can't you bloody well understand why I'm getting her out of here as quickly as possible?"

Ali stood motionless in the middle of her room, waiting for the summons that would take her away from everything and everyone she loved. Handray was casting her off, sending her back to a country he didn't even like himself. He was really going to go through with his cold-blooded plan with not a thought to what she might wish.

She steeled herself against the feelings of helplessness and misery that had threatened to overwhelm her for days. No matter how much she had argued, had cried, had pleaded, it had done no good against his implacable will. He was washing his hands of her, all because she'd had the bad fortune to be born female and English.

The dreaded knock finally came. She forced herself to cross the room and wrapped her fingers around the door handle, turning it as slowly as possible as if to delay the inevitable.

Andre stood there. She lifted her gaze to his familiar, beloved face, hoping to see some sign of a reprieve. But his expression was unreadable, his eyes the color of steel, which meant he had locked his feelings away. Ali's gaze dropped to the floor, her eyes stinging with tears.

"It's time, Ali," he said. "The ship awaits."

Ali avoided his eyes. "I expect you wish me to walk out now without a fuss, like a proper English girl." Her arms hung limply at her sides, the bulk of her unaccustomed skirts awkward to her after a lifetime of freedom in baggy trousers and overtunics. She felt ugly and stupid and very, very frightened.

"That's precisely what I expect. After all, that is what you are. Please, let us avoid another scene?"

She turned away.

"You'll be fine," Andre said. "As I told you, the journey should take no more than two weeks if the weather holds. England is beautiful in the autumn."

Ali spun around, her eyes flashing. "Do you think I care what England looks like? Do you think I care about any of the arrangements you have made? They are your arrangements, not mine." She bit back a sob, refusing to let him see how hurt she was. "If I were a Xanthian I'd burn myself rather than submit to your will!"

"But you're not a Xanthian," Andre said with infuriating calm. "You are the daughter of Sir Frederick Lacey, and you are going home to where you belong. Just think how it will be to have a family of your very own."

"My families do not seem to want me," she said tightly. "First my uncle sold me for three gold pieces, and now you are selling me for the price of a ship's ticket."

"Ali—" Andre took one step forward and then stopped abruptly. "It's time."

"Will your heart always be so cold?" she said, her voice breaking. "Oh, Handray, I hope not. This is not how Allah meant you to be."

"That's enough," he said tersely, but she saw that she had made her point from the sudden pain that marked his face.

"You are right," she replied. "It is enough. There is nothing left to say." She picked up the small bag that held her most precious possessions—her father's Bible, the map Handray had made her and the string of blue beads he'd bought her in the marketplace, and a little wooden tortoise that Umar had carved and given her as a farewell present.

"I am ready." She walked out of the room, her head held high.

Joseph-Jean waited for them at the blustery pier, his fair hair blowing about in the wind. He looked so sad, she thought, her chest tightening with the grief of parting.

"Ali," he said gently, taking her cold hands, his eyes filled with compassion. "I will miss you greatly."

"I will miss you too," she said, her voice choked.

"Don't be afraid. All will be well."

Ali reached up on tiptoe and kissed his cheek. "Thank you for all your kindnesses, Jojan. Look after Handray for me?"

"You know I will."

"Will I ever see you again? Will I ever see Handray again?" She barely managed to get the words out.

"I honestly don't know, Ali," he said very softly. "I doubt it. It's best if you settle into your new life with your new family and forget about us." He squeezed her hands. "But know we will always remember you. Thank you for everything you have given us these last few months."

Ali nodded, tears brimming over and running down her cheeks. She wiped them away before turning to Andre.

Her skirts whipped in the wind, stinging at her legs. She held out her hand. "Good-bye."

There seemed nothing else to say, nothing that would have been right.

"Have a safe journey." He took her hand and held it between both of his own for a long moment, then released it. "Good-bye, Ali." He looked away.

Her heart hurting so badly she thought it might rupture, Ali turned to face the ship. She took a deep breath and walked up the gangplank where the fat

Herringer woman waited for her, making disgusting clucking noises while her pudgy hand patted her shoulder.

The ropes were loosed and the ship's horn sounded loud and hollow as it started to chug away from the pier.

Ali watched as the gap of water widened between herself and the pier where her beloved master still stood, Jojan by his side. In a fit of panic she ripped violently away from the horrible Herringer's restraining grip and tore to the railing.

"Even though you send me away," she cried, "I will always belong to you, Handray Banesbury. Allah has ordained this!"

Her last memory of Andre, burned against the backdrop of the white houses of ancient Smyrna, was the sight of his stricken face as her words reached him through the howling of the wind.

Chapter 7

The moment that land disappeared, Mrs. Herringer's solicitous clucking turned into harsh scolding. "Get below to your cabin and stay there, you nasty little savage," she said, moving away from Ali. "You are not fit to be around decent people."

Ali's face fell at the sudden change of tone, the disgust on Mrs. Herringer's face. "I—I do not understand," she said.

Mrs. Herringer gave Ali's shoulder a push. "Go on with you. I'm a good Christian woman and I'll not associate with dirty foreign doxies, no I won't. The nerve of the man! And dressing you up like this—it's disgusting, that's what it is."

Ali didn't need much English to tell that it was going to be a terrible journey.

She was right. Mrs. Herringer did nothing but call her unfathomable names and insist that she stay confined to her cabin, even taking her meals there as if she weren't fit for human company.

But fortunately the sea began to pitch as they traveled north, and Mrs. Herringer became intermittently seasick as did the other passengers on board. Ali took advantage of their weak stomachs to sneak out on deck.

It took her no time to find an ally in Caleb, the Turkish deckhand, who at least was disposed to be kind to her. *He* didn't think her a dirty little savage. He was sympathetic to her plight.

Three interminable weeks later the packet finally pulled into the port of Southampton. Ali came up onto the drenched deck, the salt spray stinging at her face, determined to see just how awful England was. A thick yellow fog lay over everything, obscuring buildings and streets. The air felt cold and damp and smelled of must and the smoke that curled up from chimneys into a heavy gray sky.

"What do you think of your new country, young Ali?" Caleb came up beside her and folded his arms across his chest, looking out onto the streets of Southampton.

"It is very ugly," she said.

"Yes," he agreed. "No brilliant blue sky, no nice bright sun, not a single camel to be found." He grinned at her, his teeth gleaming beneath his mustache.

"It is no time to make jokes," she said miserably. "I have to live here. You can go back home."

"Yes," he said sympathetically. "It is true. I do not envy you the fate Allah has delivered you into."

"I think He is very cross that I was born an infidel," she said. "This is His punishment—to separate me from my beloved master and the country of my heart for all time."

"Yes, it is a true misfortune," Caleb said sadly.

Ali saw her fat companion struggling across the deck, pasty-faced, but still managing to shout and wave to her.

"Oh, no—here comes the horrible Herringer," she said. "I must go." She quickly took Caleb's hand. "Thank you for being a good friend to me. I commend you to Allah," she said in the traditional farewell.

"Go with a smile," he replied, completing the phrase. "And good luck."

"If Allah be willing," she said, pulling her cloak more tightly around her and starting down the gangplank after Mrs. Herringer.

Even the noise of the streets was ugly, a constant low rumble instead of the sharp cacophony of shouts and staccato exchanges she was accustomed to. Her head turned constantly trying to take in all the strange sights and sounds.

A carriage clattered past, the horses wearing odd

patches on the sides of their eyes. Ali turned to watch it go by—she'd never seen horses tied up in such a fashion.

"Come along, girl, come along. The sooner I'm rid of you the better." Mrs. Herringer grabbed her by the arm and pulled her across the street where the porter waited with their luggage. The next thing Ali knew she was sitting inside one of these enclosed conveyances, barreling away from the city.

Mrs. Herringer sat as far away from her as she could get, behaving as if she were afraid she was going to catch a disease. If Ali had had one, she'd gladly have given it to her.

Instead, she turned her attention to the outside and watched the countryside pass. Of all the things she saw, the trees most astonished her. They were multi-colored, shades of red and yellow and orange, and some were without leaves altogether. She imagined they had died of the cold, poor things. She would probably die of the cold too. It was no wonder that Englishwomen were cold fish. Their blood probably ran like ice water in their veins to match the climate.

She closed her eyes and thought of the valley of Xanthos, of high green mountains and the warm turquoise sea, of lush pastures and markets overflowing with produce and colorful carpets hanging on every wall.

And she thought about her master and Jojan, imagined sitting around the fire after dinner, listening to them converse in their comfortable, easy fashion, their hands busy with one thing or another.

Ali felt her shoulder being shaken hard and Mrs. Herringer's voice grated in her ear. "Wake up, you lazy girl. You've been sleeping for hours. We have arrived."

Ali sat up straight and shoved her knuckles into her eyes. She blinked and tried to orient herself. She certainly wasn't in Turkey.

On the other side of the carriage window was the largest house she had ever seen, built all of stone with hundreds upon hundreds of glass windows and a great many doors. It was the castle of a great lord, she was sure of it.

"Stop gawking and come out," Mrs. Herringer said in her grating voice.

Ali, who by now knew every nasty expression the Herringer possessed, climbed out of the carriage, staring at the man dressed in white stockings and skinny blue and gold *chalvars* with a matching coat.

Mrs. Herringer impatiently took her by the arm and dragged her along to the massive front door, which was opened by another man, older, this one dressed mostly in black.

"Mrs. Archibald Herringer to see Lord or Lady Raven on behalf of Lord Banesbury," she announced, handing him a card. "It is a matter of the utmost urgency."

The man disappeared, then reappeared within moments. Ali hung back as Mrs. Herringer marched through the door, but then the woman turned around and grabbed Ali's arm again, tugging her across a great hall laid in marble and down a wide corridor covered with lush carpeting.

Another door opened into a large room where a fire burned in a big fireplace. Standing by the window was a pretty woman, older, but her hair still fair, and her eyes a bright blue.

"I am Lady Raven," she said, coming forward, her expression puzzled. "What urgent business do you come on regarding Lord Banesbury?"

Mrs. Herringer held out an envelope. "He has sent you this letter along with the girl," she said, sniffing. "I am sure I do not know what wicked business he has importing a Turkish savage to England, but here she is. I have done my job, my lady, and I wash my hands of her. I only hope for your sake that she is not with child."

Ali looked back and forth between them, wishing she could understand. From the expression on Lady Raven's face, she was mightily displeased. Ali's heart fell. Did she think her a dirty little savage too?

Lady Raven frowned again. "If you will allow me

to read Lord Banesbury's missive, I am sure I will understand better." She tore open the envelope, and quickly scanned the pages, twice looking up at Ali and then returning to reading.

Ali shifted nervously, wondering what Handray had written.

"I see," Lady Raven said, folding the letter and replacing it in the envelope. "Well, Mrs. Herringer. You have done your job, although from your comments and the manner in which you pulled the girl in here, you have clearly not behaved toward her as Lord Banesbury intended."

"You surely would not expect me to treat his heathen whore as if she were respectable?"

Ali watched as Lady Raven walked over to the wall and pulled the bell rope. A moment later the door opened. "My lady?"

"James, you will please escort Mrs. Herringer off the premises immediately." She turned to Mrs. Herringer, her eyes snapping with anger. "It is a very lucky thing for you that the child does not understand English. It is also fortunate for you that Lord Banesbury is an ocean and two seas away, for I can assure you that your life would not be worth much if he heard your comments. Good day, Mrs. Herringer."

"Well!" Mrs. Herringer said, sniffing indignantly. "Well!" She stalked out without giving Ali another look, her nose in the air.

Ali was delighted to see her go.

Lady Raven waited until the door shut behind James. Then she turned and smiled at Ali. "There's no need to be frightened," she said gently, taking Ali's hands and drawing her over to the sofa. "Sit here with me, Alexis. My name is Georgia, and you're going to be staying with us for a time."

Ali's face lit up at the familiar words. "You—you speak French!" She couldn't believe it.

Georgia laughed, a lovely throaty sound. "Did you think Andre would send you to people you couldn't understand? He wouldn't be so thoughtless. He explained everything in his letter, all about your poor father's death, and how he found you, and how nicely you looked after him and Joseph-Jean."

"He did?" Ali said suspiciously. "I thought he did not want anyone to know about that."

"I don't think he thought it wise to speak to people outside of the family about it, no. But only to protect you."

"To protect me from what?" Ali asked in confusion.

"From the sort of silly ideas people might get, people like Mrs. Herringer, for example. I can imagine the last few weeks have been very trying, especially having to deal with that awful woman. Never mind, she's gone now, and you won't have to see her ever again."

Ali sighed with relief. "Praise be to Allah. She was truly horrible."

"Yes, so I gathered. I don't know what Andre could have been thinking to send you away with her."

"Handray thought she would be nice to me," Ali said loyally. "He did not know she would change once we had left Turkey."

Georgia nodded. "People can be deceiving. But it's all over and you are here. I must say, this is a surprise."

"What is to become of me now?" Ali asked, twisting the material of her cloak in her fingers. It was a question that weighed heavily on her mind.

"Well . . . I think the first thing to do is to get you settled in here. And then we will do everything we can to sort things out and to find your family."

"But how?" Ali asked, even more deeply confused. "And what happens if these people Handray calls my family do not want me?"

"Why don't we take things one at a time? I imagine you are tired and hungry, and you would probably like to go to your room. Maybe a hot bath would be nice, and then a little supper on a tray?"

Ali nodded, wanting to cry. It was almost more difficult being treated with kindness than with cruelty. "I would like that," she said, blinking back tears. Suddenly she felt unaccountably exhausted. "I am sorry. It is all very new."

"Of course it is. I am sure I should feel the same way if I had just arrived in your country."

Ali nodded. "Yes," she said solemnly. "It would be very different for you. But at least my country is warm and beautiful."

"You must tell us all about it. Tomorrow, perhaps, when you're rested. And of course, you must tell us all about Andre. We have heard very little about him these last few years." She took Ali's hand. "Come, Alexis. Let me show you to your room."

Ali followed, so overwhelmed that it all passed in a blur.

"Nicholas, it is all well and fine laughing," Georgia said after dinner that night, "but you must admit, that impossible boy has really gone too far."

Nicholas grinned. "I think it's splendid. Imagine, Andre falls off the face of the earth for three years without a word to anyone but his business associates, and now he sends us an English orphan he found in Turkey as if she were a piece of lost baggage."

"He might as well have pinned a note to her cloak: 'Please return to rightful owner.'" Georgia lowered her needlework into her lap and sighed heavily. "You didn't see her, Nicholas, her dear little face all pale and pinched, her eyes hollow with exhaustion and misery. She's a frightened, displaced child, whom Andre picked up like a stray and then abandoned."

"If you'd hop off your high horse for a moment, sweetheart, Andre didn't precisely abandon her. He sent her to us, knowing that if anyone can track down her relatives, I can. And I will start first thing tomorrow morning."

Georgia regarded her husband with affection. At seventy-five he was still a vital, striking man, his hair completely white but his winged eyebrows still black over his gray eyes. He was also as kind and generous as he had been the day she'd married him, and she knew he was as good as his word. If the child had relatives, he would move heaven and earth to find them. "Thank you," she said simply.

"I know you're annoyed with Andre for the way he's behaved the last few years, and I understand. But he's young and he's been badly hurt. He'll come around, I'm certain of it."

Nicholas poured himself a small glass of port and crossed the room to the window, looking out onto the night. "It can't be easy for him, having inherited his father's deep sensitivity and his mother's volatile temper, not to mention both their incredibly stubborn natures. It's a difficult combination."

"It's an impossible combination," Georgia said with exasperation.

"Not impossible, no," he said, turning around, "although thank God none of our children has chosen to turn his back on us. I don't know how Pascal and Lily manage to be so patient, especially since he's their only child."

"I wouldn't say they're patient in the least. I think they're heartbroken, but they're wise enough to know there's nothing they can do."

Nicholas rubbed the back of his neck. "That this should happen to Pascal of all people ..."

"Oh, it just infuriates me, the way Andre's behaved!" She abandoned her needlework altogether, too agitated to concentrate. "First he cuts us all out of his life, and we don't hear a word from him for years, and now he drops a child on our doorstep and expects us to deal with the situation," she said hotly. "The least he could have done was to bring her to us himself instead of sending her with that dreadful woman."

"Andre is obviously not ready for that. It's enough that he sent her to us at all. Let's be grateful for small blessings."

"Yes," Georgia said, her tone dry. "Just think. He might have sent her to the British Museum."

Nicholas burst into laughter. "I hadn't thought of that. Well, he didn't, which shows he had a thread of feeling for her welfare." He crossed over to the desk and picked up Andre's letter again, putting on his spectacles and scanning the pages. "Hmm. Something tells me there's a great deal more to this than meets the eye."

Georgia tilted her head. "What do you mean?"

"I'm not exactly sure. It seems to me that Andre has gone to a great deal of trouble to make us think he is doing his civic duty and that is all there is to it. Yet if you read between the lines, you can see that there is a certain amount of concern for Alexis—or Ali, as he calls her in this one paragraph, which is telling by itself."

"Ali? I suppose it makes sense that the Turks would have called her that. Maybe we should call her the same to make her feel more comfortable."

"Yes, fine idea, sweetheart. But listen to this." He read aloud.

" 'Although I expect that Ali will experience a certain amount of distress at being removed from her native surroundings, she is highly adaptable. Still, it might ease her arrival if you knew some of the things she enjoys. She is very fond of animals of any kind, but dogs especially. She loves listening to stories, the more improbable the better, and I found this to be an effective tool in teaching her language. Her mind is quick, her imagination staggering. Since she is extremely stubborn, the use of your own imagination will prove useful . . .' "

"These are not the words of a disinterested man," he said, pulling off his spectacles and looking across at her. "He clearly cares about her."

Georgia blew out a breath. "Possibly. Or maybe he's just feeling guilty."

"No. He must care about her very much to let his pride down to the point that he was willing to reopen communication with us."

"Yes . . . yes, perhaps you're right," Georgia said thoughtfully. "I hadn't looked at it like that."

"Whichever, this could transpire to be very interesting. As Andre points out, we can't turn Ali over to her family until she's presentable." He tossed his spectacles onto the desk. "We have a job ahead of us, Georgia my sweet. I suggest we get started immediately. There are lessons to be taught, clothes to be made, manners to instill—oh, all sorts of stimulating challenges." He grinned. "We haven't had an adventure for some time."

"And I thought this sort of adventure was behind us when the last of the children married and left home," Georgia said with a mock frown, although in truth she was pleased by Nicholas's enthusiasm.

"Nonsense. So—where is this little Turk?" he asked, rubbing his hands together. "Maybe we should begin her education tonight."

"Nicholas! You will leave her soundly sleeping in her bed. She's exhausted. Tomorrow is soon enough."

"Oh, very well. But it will do me good to have some fun. Life has become so dull since Charlie and Willy took over most of the business. India suddenly seems very far away with the two of them over there."

"Perhaps you're right. It will give you something to think about other than work. Not that you have ever been any example of propriety."

She pressed her fingers against her temples at the very idea of trying to turn Alexis Lacey into a lady. She could see she had her work cut out for her.

Ali woke up the next morning to light suddenly flooding the room and the sound of someone moving about. She cautiously poked her head out from under the bed.

"Who are you?" she said to the woman making a fire in the fireplace.

"Lord Almighty!" the woman screeched, her hands flying up in the air in alarm. "And here I was thinking you was in the water closet! What are you doing under there, miss?"

Ali, who didn't understand more than a word or two, climbed out on her hands and knees only to see Georgia standing in the doorway regarding her curiously. Her heart sank.

"Good morning, Ali," she said. "Did you not approve of your bed?"

"It is nice . . ." Ali said, getting to her feet. "But it is very high off the ground. I was afraid I might fall off in my sleep."

"I see." Georgia cocked her head. "Tell me. Are you accustomed to sleeping on the ground?"

Ali nodded. "Is this not correct in England?"

"Well, England is not as warm a place as Turkey, and tends to be drafty," Georgia improvised. "So the beds are raised up high to let the wind go under them. You'll be warmer if you sleep on top instead of underneath."

"Ahh," Ali said. "Yes, it was cold on the floor, even though I put many blankets down." She scowled at the woman in the white apron and silly puffed hat who still stared at her, mouth hanging open.

"Jeanette, who is French, will help you to dress," Georgia said, "and then you may join us for breakfast. My husband is looking forward to meeting you."

Ali looked at the gawking woman again in alarm. "She will help me to dress? But why? I can dress myself."

"Perhaps, but it is Jeanette's job, and her feelings would be very hurt if you did not let her do it. But that is not Jeanette, that is Mabel."

"Mabel," Ali repeated, dazed.

"Yes. Mabel is a chambermaid, which means that she looks after things in your bedroom. Jeanette is a lady's maid, and she looks after your clothes, your hair, and your baths, personal things."

Ali was dumbstruck. She closed her eyes for a moment, thinking that she had to be dreaming. She opened them again, but Mabel was still there, and she was still standing in the huge room with the enormous bed and the place behind the door that made a terrifying noise when one pulled the chain and water came roaring down.

"I know it is all a little bewildering, but you'll become adjusted in no time," Georgia said, patting her shoulder reassuringly. "A footman will show you down to the breakfast room when you're ready."

Ali swallowed as Georgia left. Now she was to meet the great lord himself. He would most likely banish her from his castle the moment he laid eyes on her.

In no time a gray-haired little woman appeared, and before Ali knew it, she had been divested of her night shift.

"Oh!" Jeanette gasped. "Why you poor, poor child—what on earth happened to you?"

Ali had no idea what she was talking about. "What do you mean?" she asked.

"But your back—it is covered in scars. And so red, so raw-looking. Oh, what a terrible thing!"

Ali colored fiercely. She hadn't realized that the scars looked so awful, never having seen them for herself, only having felt their raised surfaces with her fingertips. But she had no intention of discussing what had happened to her. "They are nothing," she said, dismissing the subject. "Please. I would like to dress."

"Yes, yes of course you would, poor lamb," Jeanette clucked. "Never you mind. But before I can dress you, first I must wash you. Here, child, over here."

Within minutes Ali found herself washed and attired in a hideous hooped petticoat and a dress she'd never seen before.

"It is Lady Raven's," Jeanette explained with a twinkle as she did up the buttons. "She is taller than you, but I took up the hem this morning. The bodice I could do nothing about at such short notice," she said sadly, plucking at the sagging material.

Then she sat Ali at a table with a mirror standing on it and started to brush her short cap of hair. "I am afraid there is not much I can do with this until it grows," she said, producing a ribbon and tying it around Ali's head.

"Have you been a servant here for a long time?" Ali asked, staring in horror at her reflection, the large bow on top of her head making her look like a monkey she'd once seen in the Dembre market. She wasn't sure how much more of this she could bear.

"Goodness, yes," Jeanette said. "I came shortly before the birth of Lord Brabourne—he's a grown man with children of his own now, of course. His eldest, Master Matthew, often visits us, now that he is over here on his studies."

She prattled on while Ali fidgeted, then she gave one last tug on Ali's dress. "There you are, Miss Alexis," she said, opening the bedroom door. "Now Walter will show you downstairs."

Ali nervously followed a man with powdered hair along the wide hallway, and down the immense stairs, her head turning back and forth and craning up as she gazed at the huge paintings that took up most of the walls. They were strange pictures of people dressed in strange clothing with even stranger hair.

But as she arrived at the bottom step she stifled a scream of horror. A man stood sideways in the hall, dressed all in metal, his face covered with a metal hood, a big double-headed hatchet in his gloved hand.

Ali took one look at Walter's retreating back, then at the big front door where freedom lay. Without another moment's hesitation, she bolted.

"I am sorry, your lordship," the footman said in bewilderment. "One moment she was there behind me, the next she was gone. I searched the entire downstairs but could not locate her, and no one else has seen her."

"Never mind," Nicholas said, throwing his napkin down on the table and rising. "It's not your fault. Miss Lacey probably took a wrong turn. I'll find her."

He waited for Walter to leave before addressing Georgia, who had paled. "Don't worry, darling, she can't have gone far."

"Oh, Nicholas, I should never have left her, not for a moment! Something must have upset her. Poor child, it's all so different for her."

"There's no point chastising yourself. We're bound to have a problem or two, especially in the beginning."

He dropped a kiss on top of Georgia's hair. "She's probably outside somewhere. I'll bring her back safe and sound, don't worry."

He walked outside into the wintry sunshine, considering where he might head if he were a young, frightened Turk. It was an interesting speculation for an old English earl.

One of the mares whinnied from the paddock, and a smile slowly spread across Nicholas's face. He followed the path that led toward the stables, picking up a discarded hair ribbon along the way. Sure enough, huddled in the feed room against a hay bale was a young girl with cropped dark hair, the tabby barn cat held tightly in her arms, her face buried in its fur.

"Hello," he said in French, his posture relaxed.

Her head shot up and a little tear-streaked face with two large dark eyes gazed at him in fright. Nicholas had to suppress a bark of laughter. Ali wore nothing but a pair of drawers and a chemise, a saddle blanket draped around her shoulders, her discarded dress and crinoline in a heap in the corner.

"I see you've met Martha." He moved into the room and took a seat on a hay bale opposite her. "She is the finest mouser we have in the stables, next to the dogs, of course."

"Dogs?" Ali said, the fear fading from her eyes. She wiped her nose on the back of her hand. "I did not know dogs could catch mice."

"Oh, yes, terriers can. They're very adept—I'll have to show you. I take it that you like animals?"

Ali nodded. "I am good with animals. Are you the keeper of the horses?" she asked. "I—I don't suppose you need someone to help you in your work? You are not a young man, and I am strong."

"Well ... I must say, although I don't feel particularly infirm, I wouldn't mind having someone to help me exercise the dogs. They need to be run at least once a day."

"Oh—oh I can do that," Ali said, her eyes lighting up. "And I can look after horses, and brush them and feed them and exercise them too."

"In that case, I would be happy to have your company on my morning ride. But as I am too old to ride on an empty stomach, I must eat first. Would you like to join me?"

"You are very kind to offer to share your food," she said, drying her eyes with her other hand.

"Not at all. I enjoy sharing my food. Maybe you would also like to help me check on the puppies?"

"Puppies?" Ali said, jumping to her feet, the cat spilling out of her arms. "Where?"

"They're on the other side of the stable yard. But I think you might want to put your dress back on. It's cold outside and you don't want to catch a chill."

Ali eyed the heap in the corner with distaste. "It is ugly," she said. "And I do not like the cage."

"Oh, the crinoline? Dreadful things, I know. Imagine how nice it would be to be a dog and never have to worry about one's dress."

Ali's mercurial smile transformed her face. "I had not thought of that," she said. "I would like to be a dog. Then I would not have to worry about learning to speak English, either. I am from Turkey," she explained.

"I am sure it is a very beautiful country. I've heard that the horses in that part of the world are particularly fine."

"Oh, yes," Ali said proudly. "They are the finest in the entire world, strong and brave. The stallions can gallop for hundreds and hundreds of miles without ever stopping."

"Really?" Nicholas said, hoping he looked suitably impressed with this gross exaggeration. "Goodness, they are indeed superior to European horses."

"And the camels can go for months without water," Ali supplied.

"Can they indeed? That is a feat."

Ali nodded. "There are all kinds of wondrous things in my country."

"I am sure. Sadly, the only wondrous thing I can think of to show you is that litter of three-day-old pups. They might not be Turkish, but I'm pleased with the way they turned out." He glanced over at Ali's clothes as if only waiting for her to dress.

His strategy worked like a charm. Ali instantly struggled back into her clothes, only asking for help with the buttons, which he obligingly fastened.

"Do you live here at the stable?" she asked, following him outside.

"No, I live up at the house," he said, waving at one of the stable boys as they started across the yard.

"Oh. I have just run away from there. I think I will probably be in terrible trouble, but I could not stay another moment."

"Why?" he asked.

"Because the great lord keeps an executioner in the hall! I think he orders his slave to chop off the heads of all who displease him. He must be very powerful."

It took every ounce of control Nicholas had to keep a straight face. "And you were worried that you might displease him, is that it?"

"How can I not? I am a stranger to his country and his customs. I am bound to make some terrible mistake, and that will be an end to me. My head will be stuck on a pike outside the gates that guard his castle as a warning to all."

"Good heavens," Nicholas said. "I would have run away too, if I thought my head might end up on a pike. But where were you planning on running to?"

"I was not sure. I would like to return to my country, where I could wear my *chalvars* and serve my master in every capacity that a servant should." She shrugged sadly. "But this is no longer possible. I have no money and no place to go, for my master does not want me anymore. So I suppose I must stay here."

"Well," Nicholas said, "although I don't have it in my power to give you back your *chalvars* or your master, I can certainly see to it that you have a decent pair of breeches in which to ride—but only if you agree to wear dresses the rest of the time."

"But why?" she asked. "They are nasty and uncomfortable."

"Out of respect for the servants. Unfortunately their

sensibilities are easily offended. It's a constant struggle not to outrage them, but I do my best."

Ali's step slowed and she eyed Nicholas with growing suspicion. "Who are you?"

"Why, I'm, um ... the great lord," he said.

Ali stared at him in horror. "*You* are Lord Raven?"

"I'm afraid so, although I'd prefer it if you called me Nicholas. I hope I don't come as too much of a disappointment."

"But—but I thought ... am I in very bad trouble?" she asked miserably.

"Certainly not. And I hate to disappoint you, but I don't possess a single executioner. What you saw was an empty suit of armor that belonged to an ancestor of mine. He used it for fighting in battles." He smiled at her. "Your head is safe."

"Ah," Ali said with relief. "Yes, now that I look at you I can see that you do not appear to be a violent man. Perhaps you will lock me in my room with only bread and water for endless days."

"And if you were locked in your room, how would you keep me company on my morning rides, or help me with the dogs?" he asked reasonably. "No, Ali. The only punishment you will receive is to be forced to spend endless hours in my company, entertaining me."

"Truly?" Ali asked, her little face lighting up.

"Truly. Now let's look at the puppies." He pushed open a door and showed her inside. A soft bark welcomed them along with the mewing of puppies. "This is Beulah," he said, leading Ali over to a large box. "This is her fourth litter. What do you think?"

Ali peered inside where five tiny bundles of fur wiggled at their mother's side. "Oh," she breathed. "Oh, they are wonderful ... look how small and new they are."

"It's all right to pick them up if you like. Beulah is very relaxed about her offspring."

Ali carefully reached into the box and picked up one of the puppies. It had three black spots on its back and one at the base of its tail, and both ears and one side of its face were brown. "Hello, tiny pup," she said, nuzzling it against her neck as it pressed its nose into her flesh, rooting around. "Oh, you are sweet."

"That one's a little girl," Nicholas said, checking the other pups to be sure all was well.

"I think she is the prettiest of them all," Ali said, planting a kiss on the minute nose.

"She is pretty," Nicholas said. "Would you like to have her for your very own?"

Ali's eyes opened wide. "Really? Do you mean it? Are you sure?"

"Of course I am. There's no point in being a great lord if one can't go about handing out largess when one feels like it. She's yours, although you'll have to wait another eight weeks or so before you can bring her up to the house."

"I may take her into the house?"

"You may take her anywhere you please, Ali."

Ali gently put the puppy back next to her mother. "I shall name her Sherifay," she announced.

"And a fine name it is," Nicholas said, scratching Beulah's ears. "Ali," he said more seriously, "I understand why you became frightened and ran off. But I want you to know that all Georgia and I wish is for you to be happy and comfortable for as long as you are with us. We only want the best for you. Will you try to believe that?"

Ali lowered her eyes. "That is what Handray said. But he still sent me away."

"I believe that he sent you away because he wished for you to have a better life than he could give you in Turkey, not because he had tired of you. But never mind that now. I'm very hungry, and you must be also. Georgia is waiting for us at the house. We don't want her to worry, do we?"

Ali attempted a smile. "No. She was nice to me."

"Naturally she was. My wife has a heart of gold. Tell me, Ali," he said, leading her out into the sunshine, "how was life with the Yourooks? Andre said in his letter that you had grown up among them, that they are a pastoral people. I don't know anything about them, but I would like to learn . . ."

Ali, forgetting her fears, started in on an enthusiastic description.

"All right, Ali," Nicholas said from his vantage point on the ballroom steps. "I think that's enough for today. If you attempt a curtsy one more time I think I'm going to be unable to eat my lunch."

Ali put her hands on her hips and looked up at him. "You are mean and horrible."

Nicholas smiled happily. "It's my job to be mean and horrible. Another month and we'll safely be able to present you to your relatives, be they the highest royalty in the land."

Ali slumped into a chair. "I might not *have* any relatives," she pointed out. "You have not turned up a single one yet, and it has been nearly six months."

"A slight hiccup in the matter," Nicholas said reassuringly. "Look at it like this—we have more time to concentrate on your education. Your English is as good as your French now, you can play the piano a little, you've learned all sorts of useful things." He started down the stairs. "When Matthew was home from school at Christmas, he said that he was impressed at how quickly you picked things up. It can only get better from here."

Ali slumped farther down in her chair, her arms folded across her chest. "I am sure that it was very kind of your grandson to say so, but I am tired of learning useful things. I would like my own tent, my own carpets, and my own cooking utensils. And I would like clothes that I can move comfortably in!" She plucked at her skirts. "These are impossible. Why must I have a huge bundle of useless cloth bunched on my backside which only makes it hard to sit, hard to fit through doors, hard to do anything? How would you feel if you suddenly had your trousers taken away and had to wear this?"

"Very foolish," Nicholas said agreeably. "But by the grace of God, it's not something I have to worry about. You, however, do. How in heaven's name do you think we're going to make you presentable to your family if we don't keep working at this? I know you're tired. I'm tired."

"You do not have to be tired," she said, smiling winningly. "You can give it all up right now and leave me in peace." She stuck her stocking-clad legs out in front of her and wiggled her half boots back and forth. "I will go and live in the stables and look after the horses. No one will ever know I was supposed to be a lady."

"No one would know you were supposed to be a lady at this particular moment," he said, fingering his brow as if it pained him. "Ali, we all love you dearly, but you can be a trial."

"That is what Handray always said."

"Andre," he corrected automatically.

"Handray," she repeated equally automatically. "Not the part about loving me dearly, which he didn't, just the part about being a trial." She sighed heavily. "I suppose it is my nature to be difficult."

She sat up straight, her brow furrowing. "If my family does not like me, do you think they will send me to the workhouse? I heard Billy Mott speaking about this the other day when he was blacking the boots. He said that he was lucky he found a job at Ravenswalk or he would have been sent to the workhouse, where many poor souls breathed their last."

"No, Ali," Nicholas said, putting an arm around her shoulders. "I don't think there is any likelihood of your ending up in the workhouse. But if you wish to make the correct initial impression on your relatives, then we must work a little harder." He steered her toward the door. "Now why don't we join Georgia for lunch? She's bound to be wondering what's become of us."

"Do you think I will ever know the correct fork for the quail, and the correct knife for the fish? I am so much better at eating with my fingers."

"I've seen you eat with your fingers. You do it very

prettily indeed. The only problem is that other people might not think so."

"You do not understand. I was not meant for such things. You try and try, you and Georgia, even the servants try to make me like yourselves, but I fear it will never be. I will always be a savage, just as Mrs. Herringer said."

"It seems to me that you only bring the ghastly Mrs. Herringer up whenever you wish to make us feel sorry for you and wiggle out of your lessons. I'm terribly sorry, but it won't work. This afternoon we will practice the waltz."

She groaned.

"Fortification is in order. Let's eat. And then before your afternoon lesson we will ride, all right? We can take Sherifay with the others today. I think she is finally ready to go the distance."

Ali grinned. "Let us go!"

But that evening when Ali came down for dinner, she knew something was different, that something had changed. Nicholas and Georgia appeared very solemn, very grave as she entered the library.

"Is something wrong? Has something happened?" she asked, her hand going to her throat in sudden fear. "It is not news of Handray, is it?"

"No, nothing like that," Nicholas said. "Come, sit here next to us."

Ali's face clouded over. This was it, she knew it. She was about to be sent away from the safe haven she had grown to love, despite the tedious lessons. She drew in a deep breath, her blood turning to ice.

"You found my relatives, and I am to leave," she said, standing very straight. "Very well. I will not make a fuss. But please," she added in a rush, "may I take little Sherifay with me? You gave her to me as a present, and I think she would be lonely if I left her. She is still very young."

"There is no need to take Sherifay anywhere, Ali," Georgia said gently. "Please, sit down."

Ali, her heart pounding with trepidation, sat opposite them in one of the armchairs. "It is about my relatives?" she asked in a small voice.

"It is," Georgia said. "You know that Nicholas has been working very hard to find them."

She nodded.

"You remember that we told you that your mother had no brothers or sisters, and both of her parents died some time ago? Well, we haven't been able to find any other relations on that side of the family. You see, it turns out that your grandparents came from Italy."

"Italy?" Ali said, her hand creeping to her mouth. "Is that bad?"

"Why should it be bad?" Nicholas asked. "Italy is a country like any other, although an Italian heritage does explain your dark coloring. In any event, there is no record of what might have happened to anyone else in the original family—it seems that they left Florence some years ago and there is no trace of them."

Ali licked her bottom lip. "And you told me that the parents of my father are also dead."

"Yes. That's right."

"But what about the sister of my father? You said you were searching for her."

"Yes, I was searching for her. But you see, I have just had a letter from Canada. Your aunt went there twenty years ago, and although she married, she had no children. Apparently she died last year, and her husband is not receptive to having you live with him."

"Is it because I am a Turkish savage?" Ali asked unhappily.

"No, Ali," Georgia said. "It is because he is newly remarried, and his wife has children of her own."

"Ah," Ali said. "So there is no one who wants me." She looked down at her hands. It was as she had expected all along. Just like Hadgi. Just like Handray. Now what would become of her?

Images of the workhouse danced before her eyes.

Nicholas placed the tips of his fingers together, making a steeple out of them. "That's not true," he said, fixing her with his gaze. "Georgia and I talked it over, and we thought it would be very nice if you became our ward, so I am going to London to have papers drawn up."

"What—what does that mean?" Ali asked suspiciously. "Is a ward like a chambermaid?"

Nicholas grinned. "No. It means that you will now be an official part of our family, and as such you must treat us with kindness and affection, as doddering grandparents deserve."

Ali stared at them in disbelief. Never, ever had she considered this a possibility, despite how many times she had imagined living at Ravenswalk with Georgia and Nicholas forever and ever, never having to brave the rest of cold, cruel England and unkind relatives.

"Would you like that, Ali?" Georgia asked, her eyes merry.

Ali could hardly speak. "I ... it was my dream," she said, blinking away tears. "But I never thought it could come true. Never. Are you sure you want me?"

"Yes, of course we're sure," Nicholas said. "Surely you can't think us so addlepated that we don't know our own minds? It's very simple. You will live here until you grow so tired of us that you decide to marry and move elsewhere."

"Never!" she gasped. "Never will I leave you. No one will wish to marry me anyway, and it is my duty to look after you in your old age."

"We are already in our old age," Nicholas said, his eyes crinkling with laughter at the corners. "But as you wish. Just remember when the time comes that we won't hold you to that particular vow."

"Then this is wonderful, for all dutiful children must look after their grandparents, and I shall be the most dutiful grandchild of all! Oh—oh, thank you!" She jumped up from her seat and ran to the sofa, throwing her arms around Nicholas, and then hugged Georgia equally hard.

"I have never had grandparents," she said happily, flinging herself back into her chair. "But are you sure you wish to take in one not of your blood? You might change your mind."

"We are truly sure, and no, we won't change our minds," Nicholas said firmly.

"If it reassures you, we do have some experience in loving children whose blood is not our own," Georgia added. "We took in Andre's father many, many years ago when he was just a boy, and he is still a very important part of our family. So you see, we are not fickle."

"*My* Handray's father?" Ali asked with strong confusion.

"Yes, your Andre's father. We think of him as our eldest son."

"But I thought Charlie was the eldest, and after Charlie there was Ghislane and Willy and Kate." She counted them off on her fingers.

"And there's Pascal in France," Nicholas said. "I'm sorry—I assumed Andre would have explained the connection to you before he sent you to us."

"He did not explain anything except that I was to go away and learn to be a dreadful Englishwoman. And anyway, I—I thought his parents were dead," she said. "He never wrote to them or even mentioned them, not as Jojan did his. He refused to speak of his family at all. Why, Nicholas?"

"It's an old story, Ali, and a painful one. We all hope one day it will be resolved, but it's best to leave it alone, all right?"

She nodded. "This is why Handray stays in my country?"

Nicholas scratched his cheek. "I think there is a combination of reasons why he chooses to spend most of his time in that part of the world. But as I say, let's leave it. It's very complicated."

"Yes," she said. "Just like Handray." She suddenly jumped to her feet, her face alight with joy as the most extraordinary idea occured to her. "But—but this means that when Handray *does* finally come home, I will be here, not lost somewhere else. Oh—oh!" She twirled around, hugging her arms around herself. "I *knew* Allah would not take him away forever. And now He has given me a nice family too."

She looked around at the familiar room with its large windows, its comfortable furniture, the desk that Nicholas used for his work. She'd never dared to think of it as home, afraid that her heart would be broken once again when she was forced to leave. But now . . .

"You have no idea what this means to me," she said, her throat suddenly tight. "I was very sad when I thought I would have to leave you. But now I promise to work very hard to please you so that you will not ever want to send me away."

"You needn't try to please us," Georgia said. "All we wish is for you to be happy. To tell you the truth, I was beginning to worry that we'd find one of your relatives after all, and then we'd be forced to let you go. But now we can keep you all to ourselves, and we're very pleased that you think enough of us to want to stay."

"You are very silly," Ali said, struggling against a fresh onslaught of tears. "I do not suppose I may take my crinoline off now that I do not have to be a good English girl for my relatives?"

"No," Nicholas said, his face wreathed in a broad smile. "And you still have to practice the waltz."

Ali danced over to him. "Poor, poor Nicholas. You are stuck with me forever." She threw her arms around his neck again, laughing with sheer joy. "You will be trying to teach me the waltz until the end of your days."

He regarded her with a gleam in his eyes. "Oh, but just think, Ali, if you practice very, very hard, you can waltz with Andre when he returns. Won't he be surprised? He probably thinks you'll never manage to become a lady."

Ali caught her lip between her teeth. This aspect of learning all these silly English things hadn't occurred to her, since she thought she was learning them only to be sent away. But now everything had changed.

A diabolic idea entered her mind. Handray would come home, and she, the little Turkish savage he had discarded, would be waiting for him. Oh, yes. She would be waiting. Wouldn't he be sorry?

"Now that it's all settled, shall we go in for dinner?" Georgia said.

Realizing that she was starving, Ali started her usual dash toward the dining room. She stopped abruptly as she reached the doorway. Turning around, she went to Nicholas and curtsied. It was lopsided, but still a curtsy.

She lightly placed the tips of her fingers on his arm. "Lord Raven, would you care to escort me into dinner?" she asked in dulcet tones, her English accent nearly impeccable.

"Good God," Nicholas murmured. "So you can do it when you want to."

"I can do anything I put my mind to," Ali said happily. "Wait and see."

Andre lay awake under the stars, his gaze tracing the outline of Perseus. How many times had he told Ali the stories of the constellations, lying under this very sky, pointing out the heavenly bodies? Countless. He'd talked her to sleep with his idiotic stories.

God, he missed her. He missed her silly little songs, her even sillier pronouncements on everything from her precious Allah to the next day's weather report. He even missed arguing with her. Odd. She had driven him mad with her constant chatter, and now the silence was deafening.

There were times he forgot, when he returned to camp absorbed in the day's work, expecting to see her shining face. What met him now was the wrinkled face of Hussan, not the same thing at all. It never failed to depress him.

He hoped to God she was safe and well, not too unhappy. It had torn him to pieces to put her on the steamer, to see her heartbroken face as the boat had pulled away. But it had nearly killed him when he'd heard her last anguished words cast as if she'd been trying to throw a lifeline between them.

I will always belong to you . . . Allah has ordained it.

Andre pushed his forearm over his face, blotting out the stars. "No, Ali," he whispered. "You belong to yourself. Only to yourself. Forget about me, little one. Forget all about me."

Chapter 8

Her lessons finally finished for the day, Ali flew out the back door of the library and across the lawn to her favorite spot by the big lake, Sherifay bounding along in front of her.

She liked summer, when the trees were in full leaf and flowers grew everywhere, although she could have done without Matthew following her around, now that he was out of school for the summer.

She supposed he had nothing better to do, but it really did grow tedious having him constantly hanging about.

It wasn't that she didn't like him, for she did, very much. And she had to sympathize with his gawkiness for she suffered from the same complaint. They both resembled overgrown foals, he a large and lanky colt, she a smaller, slighter filly, both of them equally knobby of knee and awkward. That in itself gave them a bond, plus the fact that they were closely matched in age, being only a year apart.

It was just that he wasn't Umar. Or Jo-Jean. Or Andre. Matthew treated her like a girl. An English girl. He didn't like it when she threw her shoes and dress off and went wading into the water to fish in only her shift. His ears went red. That, of course, only made her laugh, which made his ears go redder still.

And he didn't like it when she talked about Turkey. She could tell—it made him uncomfortable, as if he resented her belonging to someone else's country. But he liked it least of all when she spoke of Andre.

Oh, his ears really went red then, along with his face and neck. She didn't really understand why, other than he said that Andre was a terrible person who only knew how to hurt people, although he'd never say why.

That only made her own face go red, and they'd had some terrible arguments. In the end, they'd agreed not to speak of it at all. And that suited Ali well. She much preferred to keep her other life to herself.

England still wasn't anywhere near as beautiful as Turkey, she thought for the thousandth time, flopping down onto the grass. Turkey had no crinolines, or white gloves, and you never had to curtsy.

She splayed her arms over her head as she drank in the warmth of the sun, then closed her eyes and wished a camel or two into the background, and Andre, of course, while she breathed in the familiar tangy scent of wild thyme.

She drifted off on the wings of her imagination, weaving a long involved story about Andre and herself chasing across the desert on camels after retreating Turkomen whom they'd frightened away with guns. Ali backtracked in the interest of correctness and removed the pistol from Andre's hand, since he never carried one. She gave herself two lovely ornamented pistols instead, smoking from her brilliant aim.

Now. Where were they going to put their tents, and what were they going to have for dinner . . .

Little Sherifay's insistent barking interrupted her just as she'd decided to cook a savory kid.

"That's enough," Ali called, but the yapping continued, coming from farther away now. Ali finally sat up to see what the puppy was making a fuss about, shading her eyes with one hand and squinting against the sun.

Andre. It was Andre walking toward her, Sherifay leaping about at his heels. But that was impossible. Andre was in Turkey. And this man had no beard. She rubbed her eyes and looked harder, thinking her daydreaming had finally scrambled her brains, as Hadgi had always said it would, for the man was still there.

She shakily got to her feet. And then as the glare

of the sun left her eyes she realized it was not Andre at all, but someone whose dark hair, height, and high-bridged nose had created the illusion.

"You must be Ali," he said, approaching her, the richness of his voice nearly identical to Andre's.

Ali could only stare. The man that stood before her might have been Andre in another twenty years or so. It was only his eyes that were different. They were dark, very clear and dark, and they were peaceful.

"Yes, I am Ali," she said, collecting herself, knowing now without any shadow of a doubt that this was Andre's father, the duke.

"I have been most anxious to meet you," he said, taking both her hands and smiling down at her. "I am Pascal de Saint-Simon."

"But I did not know you were coming," she cried. She knew she looked like precisely what she was, a half-tamed Turkish girl with twigs in her hair and her hem hanging unevenly. "Oh," she wailed, completely flustered. "I wanted to look so *civilized* when I finally met you!"

His face broke into a broad smile. "Ali. You are exactly as Joseph-Jean described you, but even better, I think. I wasn't sure what was going to happen when Andre sent you here, although I trust Nicholas and Georgia implicitly. I see they have kept you entirely intact."

"But—but how did you know . . . you know Jojan?" she finished even more foolishly.

"Yes," he said. "I do. I've known him all of his life, and I owe him a great debt. He wrote me many letters about you. He also told me what you did for my son, about how you looked after him. It seems I owe you a great debt as well."

"Oh! Oh, no. It is I who owes your son a debt. He saved my life, you see," she said earnestly, feeling strangely comfortable with this man. She wondered if it was because he reminded her so strongly of Andre.

"Yes, I know. I'm delighted that he did, just as I'm delighted that you are now here with us. Tell me, how was my son when you last saw him, Ali? Was he well? Happy?"

"He was well," she said. "I would not say he was happy. He was improving, or at least I thought he was until he decided to send me away. Then his heart turned back to ice."

"I am sorry to hear that," Pascal said.

"I suppose he cannot help it," Ali said. "It is all because of his fairy-child, I think."

"His fairy-child?" Pascal asked, puzzled.

"Yes—oh, you do not know? I'm not supposed to know, either, but Jojan told me by mistake. Handray loved her more than anything in the entire world, and then she died."

That sounded rather flat to her ear and didn't nearly make the point, so she decided to embellish. "You see, she was one of those creatures not entirely of this world. Allah only gave her to Handray for a brief time, to shed the beautiful light of her love on his life, and then He called her back to Him. Poor Handray was left to wander the four corners of the earth, calling to her spirit to return to him, but of course it could not." She stopped, terribly pleased with the ring of her story. Now *that* sounded like a tragedy.

"I see ..." Pascal said, his mouth twitching at the corners. "Is that what Joseph-Jean told you?"

"Well ... not exactly," she admitted. "It was just how I thought it must have been."

"Do you know, Ali, oddly enough you're not so far from the truth?"

"I am not?" she said, her face falling in dismay. "Oh. Oh, how dreadful for poor Handray."

"Yes, it was," he said. "It was. And it was equally tragic that there was nothing any of us could do for him. But from what Joseph-Jean tells me, you somehow managed to put the light back in his eyes."

"He is very stubborn, your son. He had made up his mind never to smile again, and it was not easy to make him change it."

"No, I can imagine," Pascal said, kneeling down to scratch the puppy's ears. "And who is this?"

"This is Sherifay," she said proudly. "Nicholas gave her to me for my very own. She sleeps on my bed."

"Yes, I know how that is," Pascal said with a laugh. "I've shared my bed with a terrier for all of my married life. Nicholas gave Lily and myself our first as a wedding present, and little Bean moved right under the covers as if she had every right to be there." He shook his head. "Every terrier we've had since has asserted the same privilege as if it were a divine right." Sherifay put her paws on Pascal's knees and vigorously washed his face.

"Is Handray's mother here too?" Ali asked hopefully.

"Indeed she is. We would have come sooner to meet you, but we had business in America that couldn't wait. We came the very first chance we had, though. I wanted to welcome you to the family personally."

"Thank you," Ali said solemnly. "It is a very fine thing to have a family."

"I know just what you mean," Pascal replied. "Lily is up at the house, waiting impatiently to meet you."

Ali flushed with pleasure, but looked at him uncertainly. "Are you sure she will want to? Last Sunday the wife of the vicar came for tea, and she was not pleased to meet me at all."

"Oh?" Pascal asked. "And why was that?"

Ali looked down at the grass. "I probably should not say."

Pascal regarded her with interest. "Really? This sounds interesting. Here, sit on the bank with me and tell me about it. I know Mrs. Eliot, and personally I think her a very silly woman."

"You do? Well, then maybe you will not think me as evil as she did. She—that is I . . ." Ali wasn't sure how to phrase it. "She asked me why she had not seen me at the church, and I said that I could not listen to the prayers of infidels, for Allah would be very angry."

To Ali's surprise, Pascal roared with laughter. "Oh," he said, when he'd finally regained control.

"Oh, I do wish I'd been there." He wiped the tears from his eyes. "What did Mrs. Eliot say?"

"She said that I was a godless little heathen, and she hoped that Georgia would take me in hand before I disgraced them. Georgia was very nice about it, but I could see she was upset."

"Well . . . if she was, it was probably because you'd forgotten the story she and Nicholas created about your background to protect you from just this sort of thing. If I'm correct, they don't have too many Muslims in Switzerland."

"I forgot," she said miserably. "It is very difficult to adjust to being a Christian infidel. I was baptized a Catholic, Nicholas said, which means I belong to the Christian church, but if I go to it, I am sure to offend Allah. It is a terrible dilemma."

Pascal nodded sympathetically. "Yes, I can see that it would be. But I don't believe that Allah is quite as easy to offend as you might believe."

Ali frowned. "How would you know? You do not know anything about Him."

"Well, I know about the five pillars of Islam, and I can tell you something about Mohammed's teachings." Pascal launched into a brief but detailed description of the Muslim religion.

Ali gazed at him in wonder. "But how is it possible that you know these things? Are you Muslim?"

Pascal took one of her hands in his own. "Look, Ali. This is your hand that Allah made, yes?"

She nodded and he held up his free hand. "And this is my hand that Allah also made, yes?"

She nodded again.

"They look the same, don't they? Aside from the fact that yours is small and smooth and younger than mine, which is large and has hair growing on the back."

Ali grinned. "But it is not unattractive."

"Thank you. But the point is that Allah made us all essentially the same, no matter what the small differences are, and no matter where in the world we were born, for Allah is everywhere, even though He goes by many different names."

Ali's eyes narrowed. "I do not understand how you can say this when you know that Allah alone is God without second."

"Yes. And all over the world people acknowledge His presence and offer Him prayers of gratitude and love. The Hebrew religion calls him Yahweh, the Christians call him God, or sometimes Christ—"

"But this is not the same as worshiping Allah," she protested.

"Why not? Are you any different if I call you Alexis instead of Ali? Are you any different here in England following the English customs of eating and dressing and bathing than when you were in Turkey and followed the customs there? I don't mean on the outside, but on the inside where it counts."

She slowly shook her head. "No. But I was more comfortable being Ali. I liked being Ali. I do not like being Alexis."

"Because you are not yet accustomed to being Alexis. Trust me, Ali, I do know what it's like to be forced to go through a metamorphosis or two. It's very difficult, but one learns to adjust."

Ali plucked at the grass. "I do not mind so much being asked to change the way I dress, even if I do not like it. But I do not see how I can change the way I think of Allah, even if I was born an infidel."

"But why must you change the way you think?"

"How else am I to be a correct Englishwoman? Look at what Mrs. Eliot thought of me." She threw her handful of grass away in disgust. "But if I become a Christian, Allah will never speak to me again. And that I could not bear."

Pascal looked away for a long moment, and Ali had the distinct impression that he was trying not to laugh.

"What is so funny?" she asked with annoyance.

"Only the notion that Allah would be so judgmental." Pascal picked up a pebble and turned it around in his fingers. "Look, Ali." He threw the pebble into the lake, and it sank with a little plop, leaving only a spreading circle of ripples on the surface to show its passage.

"When a great teacher or prophet comes to earth to pass along God's word," Pascal said, "his message is like those ripples that spread and spread. The teacher is the messenger who, like the pebble, makes an impact and then disappears. But the message stays." He looked over at her. "There have been many messengers, not to mention the archangels God has sent with his word. And there's a point. I don't think God can be overly concerned with people practicing different faiths if He sent his archangels to the Christians, the Jews, and the Muslims."

"Jibril visited the infidels?" Ali asked breathlessly, her head spinning with wonder that it might be so.

"Yes. Although in the Christian religion he is known as Gabriel. Just as he appeared to give Mohammed the Qur'an, Gabriel also appeared to Mary, the mother of Jesus Christ, to tell her she was going to have a child who was to be the Son of God."

Ali shook her head, dazed. "But these two things are very different."

"On the outside, maybe. It all goes back to what I was saying earlier. I, like you, was baptised a Catholic, Ali." He smiled at her look of surprise. "But you see, it's never made any real difference to me what religion I practiced. In all the places I have been in the world, in all the different temples and mosques and churches I have visited, I have worshiped Allah, or God, or whatever He happened to be called. I may have followed the local customs regarding prayer, but whever I was, I was still the same man worshiping the same Almighty." He paused for a moment. "Does that make sense?"

Ali gazed at him solemnly. "Then if this is true, why is it so terrible to be an infidel? Why have people had Holy Wars for years beyond counting?"

Pascal sighed. "Because unfortunately, people tend to be more inclined to see their differences rather than their similarities. We are all cut from the same cloth; it is only the cut of the cloth that varies. It makes as much sense to kill someone for what he wears as it does for what he believes."

He threw another pebble into the lake. "Can you imagine how surprised those same people must be when they all end up in heaven together, after arguing to the death over whose God was the true one?"

Ali's eyes lit up with delight at the image that conjured up. "The angels must have a hard time explaining," she said.

He stood and held out his hand at her. "I doubt much explanation is necessary. Shall we go back to the house now? My wife is going to beat me if I don't produce you soon."

Ali nodded and took his hand, and he helped her to her feet. They walked along in companionable silence, Ali turning their conversation over in her mind.

As different as these ideas were from everything she'd ever been taught, in an odd way they made perfect sense, even though it was all still too new for her to accept just like that. And yet Pascal seemed as comfortable with Allah as she was, but also as comfortable with his Christian God . . .

She suddenly stopped. "Pascal?"

He glanced over at her with a smile that was so like his son's that it made her heart ache. "What is it, Ali?"

"Why does Handray not know about Allah?" she asked. "You must have explained this to him as you have to me?"

Pascal took a moment before he answered. "Andre once knew Him very well," he said quietly.

"Then why does he refuse to speak of Him?" she asked, truly confused. "It cannot be easy to know Allah and then lose Him. It would be like cutting off one's arms and legs."

"I don't think Andre has lost Him, exactly. I think he has merely misplaced his faith in Him, as he has in many things."

Ali's eyes filled with tears. "Poor, poor Handray," she whispered. "No wonder he is so sad."

Pascal released a heavy sigh. "We are all tested in

one way or another during our lifetime, Ali. I have to trust that Andre will survive his period of solitude and come back to us."

Ali flashed a huge smile at Pascal. "Oh, yes," she said with confidence. "Handray will come back. Allah will only let him wander in the desert for so long before returning him to his proper place, whether Handray wishes it or not."

Pascal gazed at her for a long moment and Ali had the oddest sensation that he was looking straight into her soul.

"You are wise for one so young," he finally said. "I am truly grateful that God has brought you to us."

She beamed. "I think I might be grateful too. And I do feel better about being born a Christian, if you are sure Allah does not mind. Thank you for explaining."

"It was my pleasure."

"Pascal . . . would you tell me some of these stories you spoke of? Maybe the one about Gabriel and the woman called Mary and the baby?"

"I'd be happy to. Why don't I tell it to you now, while we walk back?"

Ali nodded happily and listened carefully as Pascal began.

"A very long time ago in Galilee," he said, "there was a young woman named Mary, who lived in the city of Nazareth . . ."

All during dinner Ali's gaze kept slipping back to Andre's parents. His mother was one of the most beautiful women she'd ever seen. Ali had never known that hair could be the color of copper, but it was the duchess's eyes that held her, for they were the exact shade of Andre's, that strange but compelling color somewhere between gray and green. She had a beautiful smile too, warm and kind like her husband's.

But what Ali liked most of all about Andre's parents was the way that they looked at each other, as if

there were a silent language passing between them
that only they could hear.

It made her think of music, sweet and resonant, of
the sound that the waves made as they washed back
and forth on the shores off Xanthos. She had spent
many hours sitting on the sand, doing nothing but listening. Andre thought her very silly when she tried to
explain it was the music of Allah playing.

"Ali?" Lily asked. "You look very far away."

"Oh. I suppose I was," she said. "I was thinking of
Xanthos, where I lived with Handray."

Lily smiled encouragingly. "Would you mind de-
scribing it to us? I would so like to hear about your
time with our son."

Ali hesitated. She didn't want to upset Andre's
mother, who so obviously missed her son, by drawing
too sharp a reminder of his time away from them. But
the expression on Lily's face was so imploring that she
didn't see how she could refuse. After all, they had
nothing else but Jo-Jean's letters.

"Xanthos sits in the most beautiful valley in all of
Turkey," she began, trying to set the scene for her
story. "It is lush and filled with many forms of wild
animals, birds, trees, and flowers. Handray taught me
all their names in Latin," she said proudly. "And he
taught me to gather plants to make good medicines,
like the one he gave me to make me better when I
was dying."

Pascal's gaze dropped for a moment, and Ali wondered why he suddenly looked sad. "Did I say something wrong?" she asked.

"No, Ali," Pascal replied, looking back at her. "It
is good to hear that Andre is using his knowledge. It
is only that it reminded me of a time when we used
to do that together. Go on, won't you? Where is
Xanthos, exactly?"

"To reach the ancient city," she said, "one must
cross a broad plain which on one side has many banks
of sand, and on the other side are tall mountains."

She closed her eyes for a moment, seeing it exactly.
"Water falls from these mountains into the deep ra-

vines below," she said, "feeding the streams and rivers, and from the waters of Massicytus, the highest mountain of all, rises the great river of Xanthos which runs to the sea . . ."

A surge of homesickness came over her as she spoke of Umar and his village, described the tents where she and Andre and Joseph-Jean had lived, recounted the rhythm of their days. But as she spun her stories into the hushed, attentive silence, she began to enjoy herself, warming to her narrative.

". . . And there Umar and I were," she said, "our camels neck to neck. I knew I was going to win, for I had bet an entire piastre on the race, my camel being the fastest." She grimaced in memory. "But then the silly beast missed his step at the very last, and I went tumbling off his back and hit my forehead on the ground with a great crack. I thought Handray was going to murder me, he was so angry."

"What did he do?" Matthew asked wtih alacrity. "Nothing too dreadful, I hope?"

Ali looked at Matthew with exasperation. "Of course he was dreadful, as he should have been," she said. "He had told me I was not to race camels with Umar and I disobeyed him."

"Did he beat you?" Matthew asked, frowning.

"Handray does not beat people," she said. "Except for one time, when he knocked my wicked uncle Hadgi to the ground."

"*Did* he?" Pascal asked with interest.

"Yes, and it was very pleasing, since Hadgi used to knock me down all the time. You should have heard the crack—just like a pistol shot, and Hadgi went straight back into the vegetable stand and took it to the ground with him."

"Goodness," Pascal said. "Andre must have been very annoyed indeed."

"He was. His face looked like a thundercloud. And that is just how it looked when I fell off the camel, so I should be grateful he did not do anything worse than shout at me very loudly." Ali rubbed the place on her forehead where the huge lump had been. "That made my head ache even more than it already did."

"I'll bet he left you lying there too," Matthew said.

"No, he did not," Ali retorted. "He picked me up in his arms and carried me all the way to his tent. Then he wrapped my head in a big bandage with a smelly paste on it," she said, pretending she was winding a turban over her head. "He told me I deserved every moment of the stench."

Pascal smiled down at his plate.

"And then he sat there and glared at me for the next few hours and would not allow me to close my eyes or go to sleep, which was the meanest thing of all, since there were two of everything in front of me."

"Actually," Pascal said mildly, "I believe he was trying to save you from the results of a concussion. Sometimes people who go to sleep when they've had a bad knock on the head don't wake up again."

"Really?" Ali said, fascinated. "Then Handray was not punishing me?"

"No . . . I think you probably frightened the daylights out of him, and this is why he was so angry."

Ali considered this. "Maybe. It is not easy to frighten Handray, but he did look very upset, it is true."

"Can't you imagine how he must have felt, Ali?" Pascal refused the footman's offer of more wine. "You were under his care, after all. He was responsible for you."

"Yes," she said indignantly, "and look what he did with his responsibility. He knew Allah had given me to him, but he still sent me away the first chance he had. But I have a plan to get back at him when he returns."

"And what is that?" Lily asked, a smile hovering on her lips.

"I am going to be a perfect English lady. It will make Handray very, very cross because he despises perfect English ladies."

"Oh?" Lily said. "It's the first I've heard of that."

"Well, it is true. And he will be very sorry to see

what became of me, all because he banished me. Of course, first I must grow breasts and my hair must be long enough to fall down my back again," she hastened to add. "But when all of that has happened, which Georgia has promised me it will, Handray will see me and ask, 'Who is that horribly civilized creature?'"

She picked up her napkin and fanned herself with it, batting her eyelashes. "And I shall turn to him and say, 'But it is Miss Alexis Minerva Lacey. Do you not recognize me?' And then when he has recovered from his shock, I might forgive him and allow him to dance with me. What do you think?"

Ali looked around the table, wondering why Matthew's ears and neck had turned bright red, and Andre's parents were gazing at each other with mutually unfathomable expressions. She stole a glance at Georgia, who was watching Nicholas with a broad smile.

Ali turned her head and looked down at the other end of the table only to see Nicholas's shoulders shaking, one hand covering his eyes, which didn't come close to disguising the tears of laughter streaming down his cheeks.

"What is so amusing?" she asked indignantly. "Do you think I cannot become a fine lady?"

"Not at all," Pascal said quickly, his voice slightly unsteady. "I think you will make a very fine lady and give Andre a well-deserved shock. You must let us know how it turns out."

"Oh, I will," she said. "By the time Handray comes home I also plan to be educated. I will be able to converse on every topic he can think of in six separate languages." She nodded decisively. "All of that learning should give my breasts plenty of time to develop. Ha! I will show him."

She happily dug into her pudding.

Later, when the house was still, Ali crept down the stairs, careful not to make a sound. The huge house felt oddly still around her, but in a nice, comfortable sort of way. It was hard to believe that it had been nine months since the first time she had entered it, her arm practically pulled out of its socket by Mrs. Herringer.

She let herself out the door and started toward the lake, an important mission on her mind. The waxing moon bathed the damp grass in silvery light, and as she crossed the expanse, a solitary hoot of an owl sounded loud in the hushed night.

The water of the lake lapped soothingly against the bank as she reached it. She wore nothing but her night shift, and it only took her a moment to slip it off. She wanted Allah to see her exactly as He had made her, with no embellishments of any kind, no clothing to confuse the issue.

Instead of kneeling she stood straight and raised her face to the star-clustered sky.

"Allah, I have heard many strange and miraculous things today," she said gravely. "But I need to know directly from You if they are true. If they are, and You do not make any difference between Muslims and infidels, and if You really do not mind my being born a Christian, please would You let me know?"

Ali waited. At first there was nothing. But then the wind picked up, causing goose pimples to stand out on her skin and her legs to start trembling with the sudden cold.

"Oh," she said, unsure. "Is this a sign, mighty Allah?" She wrapped her arms around herself, trying to still the shaking of her body.

A cloud scudded across the sky, obscuring the moon, and Ali nervously bit her lip—first the cold wind, and now the moon going out? Allah's answer was not looking favorable.

"Allah," she whispered despairingly. "You put me on earth to love Handray, did You not? And You sent me to England where his home is, to wait for him to return. Why would You go to all this trouble for me if You were not the One Great God for all people?"

It was a good question, she thought. Andre's father had made such a convincing argument, and he'd done it without any of the shouting or screaming or frenzied waving of his hands that Hadgi and the others always used when speaking of Allah.

Instead, he had spoken quietly of God and angels and a holy baby born in a stable in a country not so far from Turkey.

She thought yet again about the wonderful story he'd told her, about the shepherds that the angels had summoned from their field, and the animals who had gathered with them to praise the tiny infant who lay in the manger.

But best of all to her mind were the three great kings who had come to the stable, bearing gifts of precious incense and perfumes, and jewels too, if she knew anything about it. Sheep, shepherds, bejeweled kings. Oh, and a great eastern star.

Yes, it sounded to her like just the sort of thing Allah might arrange. And He'd had the good sense not to arrange it in England where the dear baby might have died of the winter cold.

Allah was all-wise.

With that thought a rush of warmth and love suffused her, filling her being with peace and joy, as always happened when she addressed Allah, and Ali knew she had her answer.

She lifted her face to the stars, a smile of deep satisfaction on her face. "Thank you, Allah," she said solemnly. "Thank you."

The only reply was the sighing of the wind. But she needed nothing more.

She bent down and picked up her shift, and was about to slip it on when another thought occurred to her. She looked down at her skinny little body and lanky arms and legs, the chest with two little beestings for breasts.

"Allah," she said, putting her hands on her nonexistent hips, "do You think that since You have gone to all this trouble to give me to Handray, You might make me just a little more appealing?"

A sudden flash of lightning lit up the sky, followed by a deep rumble of thunder.

"I am sorry," Ali said contritely. "I should have realized I was asking too much."

The rain began to pelt down, and Ali, who had a healthy respect for inclement weather, pulled on her shift and dashed back to the house.

But as she dried herself off and slipped under the covers with Sherifay she rejoiced, knowing that Allah had not deserted her, nor did He object to being called by a different name. She supposed she ought to start learning about being a Christian, so that when Andre came home she would have that memorized too.

Oh, he was going to be surprised. And she supposed she really was going to have to learn to be a lady. Of sorts.

Ali sighed with happiness and tucked her hand under her cheek. She would be eternally patient. Andre was worth waiting a hundred years for, although she hoped he wouldn't be quite that long, now that Allah's plan had finally become clear.

Her destiny was not to be Andre's servant. She was to be his wife and give him many sons.

Chapter 9

Andre buckled the last strap on the final bag, then looked around the camp. He straightened, wondering how long it would be before he'd be back in this part of the world. God, he was going to miss it—the particular blue of the sky that could be found nowhere else, the startling contrast of the snowcapped mountains against the sandy beaches and the indigo of the sea at this time of year.

For the last five years he and Joseph-Jean had traveled around Syria, Lebanon, Palestine, and Egypt, but Andre always felt compelled to return to Turkey, and especially Xanthos, his favorite of all places.

He didn't even know why, since his work here had been completed long before. But he seemed to find a small measure of peace among the Xanthian ruins. And then there were his friends the Yourooks, who never failed to give them both a warm welcome.

He released a heavy sigh, knowing that in five days time he'd be in Rhodes, boarding one of Her Majesty's ships bound for bloody England. He wasn't even sure he remembered how to be a European. He and Joseph-Jean had long before adopted the local clothing, finding that not only was it more comfortable in the hot climate, but it often made their passage easier in unfriendly territories.

Andre smiled grimly, remembering Thomas Weselley's horror when they'd coincidentally crossed paths in the Lebanon. Weselley had found it inconceivable that a British aristocrt would so far forget himself as to be wearing desert garb and an Arab headdress. Still, he'd said nothing, only giving Andre and Joseph-Jean a sly, insulting look.

Oh, he had no illusions about Weselley's assumption that he and Jo-Jean shared more than a close friendship. But although Andre's general attitude in life leaned toward the creed of "to each his own," he didn't much care for Weselley's mistaken conclusion.

Typical. God, how he loathed the man and his petty mind.

And thank God Joseph-Jean hadn't put that together, or there would have been sure hell to pay. Jo-Jean could take down any man in a matter of moments. Weselley wouldn't stand a chance against Jo-Jean's rage.

Joseph-Jean rode up, a broad smile on his face. "Ahmed has invited us to a great feast tonight. It is in honor of our final departure from his land. I suspect it will be a late night affair—the entire village is in an uproar."

"Somehow it seems fitting," Andre said. "I will miss these people, Jo-Jean. I will miss them greatly. They give the phrase 'the salt of the earth' real meaning. The company of Englishmen is going to pale next to the Yourooks."

"I don't envy you," Joseph-Jean said sympathetically. "I would hate to be walking into your shoes. It will be nice for me to return to my simple family, but you? A dukedom after all this freedom?"

Andre shrugged. "It was bound to happen. My grandfather couldn't live forever. God, I'm inclined to turn my back on the whole damned thing, and don't think I haven't seriously considered it, but then there are too many people who are dependent on the duchy. So. Back to freezing, eh?"

"I suppose so. It's going to take something on both our parts to adjust to the northern climate."

"Mmm. To adjust in general," Andre said absently. The thought had brought Ali to mind. He often wondered what had become of her, how she'd adjusted to a new life in the outback of Canada with her aunt, for that was the last he'd heard. He imagined she was probably content living a life in the wild, which she was accustomed to. If he knew Ali, she was probably still running around in britches, behaving like a banshee.

God, he still missed her after all this time.

It seemed like only yesterday, that summer he and Jo-Jean and Ali had spent here. Nothing had been quite the same since she'd left, but then what could replace Ali's sparkle, her zest for life, the mad adventures she regularly dragged them into? He shook his head with a soft smile.

Ah, well. He hoped she was happy.

He, on the other hand, had to return to a life he loathed and an estate he despised even more. Sutherby might be beautiful, architecturally speaking, but it was a cold, dismal place reflective of his cold, dismal maternal grandfather, a place that had produced very little happiness and a great deal of misery over a number of generations.

He glanced over at Jo-Jean, envying him his return to Saint-Simon. That door was shut to him forever, although sometimes he ached unbearably for it, for the sight of ripe vineyards running down hillsides, for the sight of the château caught in the shimmering light of early morning, or bathed in the deep golden glow of evening, the sounds of the village drifting up the hilltop, the village fêtes, the general rhythm of life, the comfort of family.

But that didn't bear thinking about. He pushed the thought from his mind, knowing that by necessity his future lay elsewhere. But how he was going to miss his friend.

Andre gazed at Jo-Jean, the companion who had seen him through the last eight years of his own private hell and never once complained. Andre owed Jo-Jean his sanity, perhaps even his life, for there had been times in the early days that his will to go on had nearly failed him. Jo-Jean had been there always, and he could only be thankful for that unswerving loyalty when he had needed it most.

It wasn't going to be easy going into his new situation, but it was time that they each went their separate ways into the lives that had been ordained them, as much as it pained him.

"Jo-Jean . . ." he said hesitantly.

Joseph-Jean turned from unbuckling the girth on his horse. "Yes?"

"Thank you. Thank you for everything," he said, his voice tight. "I can never repay the debt I owe you."

"You make it sound like good-bye, Andre."

"I suppose I'm feeling sentimental." Andre ran a hand over his bearded chin. "This will have to go too, won't it? I won't know my own face after not seeing it for so long. I'll probably cut my throat from lack of practice the first time I shave."

"We'll have a contest to see who bleeds to death first," Joseph-Jean replied. "In the meantime, put an end to these morose thoughts and prepare to celebrate. You don't want to let the village down."

Since Andre wanted this to be a happy leave-taking for Jo-Jean, who had come to love this part of the world nearly as much as he, he forced a smile. "A celebration it will be," he said. "Give me an hour to walk the ruins one last time, and then we shall have a magnificent evening."

"Done," Joseph-Jean said. "I'll see you at sundown."

The feasting, the speeches, the stories that night ran for hours unchecked. Andre basked in the warmth of camaraderie, knowing it would be the last time. He danced, knowing it would be the last time for that too. And then, when the firelight had died down and the revelry had quieted, Umar, who had now grown to manhood, brought out his flute one last time.

"I play for you, Banesbury. It is a song I have made in your honor, a song that will be played after you have gone, and for many years into future generations."

He raised the flute to his mouth and began. The notes flowed slow, clear, and piercing, a haunting melody that cut straight through Andre.

It represented everything of the Middle East in its soulful tune, the vastness of the desert, the strength of the mountains, the steady ebb and flow of the precious water in the rivers and streams. And yet there was an ineffable sadness to it, for it was a song of loss. He wondered if Umar was expressing sorrow at their leaving.

Umar lowered his flute, his expression grave. "May Allah bless you in all your goings, effendi," he said.

"Thank you, Umar. And may He bless you and all of yours," Andre replied. "That was a beautiful piece of music. But what gave you the inspiration?"

"As I said, it was about you," Umar replied. "It was the tragic story Ali told us of you and the wife you loved more than life who died. It depicts your struggle, your journey through our lands to forget, to take the strength from our soil, to be uplifted by our people, so that you might learn to live again." Umar smiled happily, his teeth flashing white against his dark complexion.

"What?" Andre cried, half rising to his feet. He shot a ferocious glare at Joseph-Jean who appeared equally appalled, which suggested his innocence. But Ali? How is God's name had Ali known—or at least guessed?

"Ali," he said, dropping back down to his carpet. "Ali told you this story?"

"Yes," Umar said. "We were much moved when we heard it the night you arrived that second summer. It was a very grand story of your terrible loss. We have all been in awe of your heroic sacrifice ever since." He placed a hand over his chest. "It is not many a man who would not take other wives. And so I thought I must make a song about it to commemorate your departure."

Andre looked at Umar for a long moment. He looked at Joseph-Jean. He looked at all the other expectant faces around the campfire, wanting to leap down their collective throats for intruding on his private domain.

And then suddenly an incredibly clear image of Ali weaving one of her impossible stories came blasting full-sprung into his mind. Typical Ali. She had, as usual, no idea of what she'd been talking about but had, as usual, somehow managed to hit the mark.

He threw back his head and roared with laughter.

July 1869
London, England

Ali turned and looked over her shoulder at the bustle of her skirt. "I don't know, Hattie," she said, her forehead knotting. "You don't think the bow is too large?"

"Oh, no," Hattie said, gazing at Ali with admiration. "It is perfectly lovely. I wish I were as beautiful as you are."

Ali wrinkled her nose. "You are far more lovely than I, Hattie," she said, trying to cheer up her dear friend, who really was a lovely person, even if she wasn't particularly pretty.

"Don't be ridiculous," Hattie said. "Anyway, if you don't believe me, look at all the men who are forever hovering about you."

"The only reason that men hover is because they find me comfortable," Ali said reassuringly. "They know I'm not going to bat my eyelashes at them, or have a fit of the vapors when they say something improper, or try to lure them into marriage."

"Sometimes I don't understand you, Alexis. You've been out three seasons now and you've had many opportunities to marry, but you refuse to take any of your suitors seriously." She sneezed into her handkerchief and rubbed her nose hard.

Ali grinned. "I have yet to meet anyone whom I *can* take seriously. They're fun, but they're all overgrown schoolboys."

Hattie turned and gave her an injured look. "Don't

you think you're being a little harsh? I wouldn't mind having all those overgrown schoolboys crowding around me."

"I beg your pardon," Ali said contritely. "I know that you long to find a husband, and you will, when the right man comes along. And just like you, I'm waiting for someone very special. But until I find him, I just want to enjoy myself."

"What's the matter with Matthew?" Hattie asked yet again. "He's terribly attractive, and he's clever, and he's the heir to the earldom."

"The eventual heir," Ali reminded her. "His father comes first. And that's the point, Hattie. There's no hurry for him to marry, and I make a convenient foil. If I disappeared tomorrow, I think he'd pine for all of a week."

Hattie's frown deepened. "I think you are blind to what is right under your nose, Alexis. Matthew adores you, and he'd make a fine husband."

"For someone else," Ali said. "How many times do I have to tell you that he's a good friend and nothing more?"

"You're going to break his heart," Hattie warned, picking up her shawl and arranging it around her shoulders.

"Matthew? Bah. Don't you worry about Matthew. I'm nothing more than an old habit to him. He doesn't take me seriously. He knows me too well."

"Maybe, but I don't think that reassures any of the women who would like to be in your position. They're all horribly jealous of you."

Ali snorted. "Jealous of a girl who looks and behaves like a gypsy? I don't think so. If anyone is jealous, it should be me. You don't know what I would give to have lovely blond hair and blue eyes and—and to look fragile."

Hattie burst into laughter. "I am sorry, Alexis, but there is nothing the least bit fragile about you, despite your slight figure. And the only resemblance you have to a gypsy is your ability to charm animals. I've never known anyone who can sit a horse as well as you."

She regarded Ali with resignation. "I suppose that's why you're always asked to ride in Hyde Park."

"Gentlemen need to be exercised," Ali said with a mischievous gleam in her eyes. "I do my best to oblige by galloping like a maniac. Anyway, you can't help being allergic to horses."

"I'm allergic to everything," Hattie moaned, rubbing her watery eyes. "It's no wonder I don't have any suitors. What sort of man wants to marry a woman who sniffles her way through life?"

"One who loves you," Ali said firmly. "Come on, Hattie, your parents will be waiting downstairs. We don't want to be late for the Umbersville ball."

Ali fervently wished that her closest friend wasn't so eternally persistent on the subject of men and marriage. There was no way to explain why she treated all the men she knew like amusing older brothers. As much as she enjoyed their company, she found it inconceivable to view any one of them in a romantic light.

She knew it was unfair that she, who could care less, did have so many suitors, and Hattie, who cared deeply, had few. Yet it spoke to Hattie's sweet nature that she didn't hold it against her, that she had been kind enough to invite Ali to stay with her family during the last two seasons and didn't begrudge the gentlemen who called not to see her, but her guest. But at least Hattie enjoyed herself, for Ali was always careful to see she was included.

It would have been nice to confide in Hattie, to tell her about Andre, but she couldn't. She wasn't even supposed to know him, let alone speak of him—Nicholas and Georgia had been adamant, and she understood their concern, for a scandal would surely ensue if any of their past ever came out. Not that she cared anything about that, but she didn't want to jeopardize Andre's reputation in any way.

But she did wish he would come home. It had been nearly five years since she'd left him. None of his family had heard anything from him, which surprised nobody. Nicholas had said in his dry fashion that since

Andre's papers were regularly published, at least they knew he was alive.

Well, of course he was. She would have known if something had happened to him. Anyway, she liked reading his papers, and his books too. They made her feel as if she were with him. And Jo-Jean's illustrations brought everything vividly to life. Too vividly sometimes. They only made her miss Andre and Turkey more.

"Alexis? What are you dreaming about now?" Hattie asked, moving toward the door.

"Nothing," Ali said, hastily pulling on her gloves. "Nothing at all."

Andre looked one last time at the engraved invitation, then flicked the corner with his thumb. Well, why not? He had to announce his presence in London at some time, and now that his most pressing business was done, it was as good as time as any.

Umbersville had promised that his wife would not make a fuss if he arrived. There would be few people he knew, and that was all to the good. Maybe another trustee or two of the British Museum would be there and he could talk of business matters. He had little else to discuss.

Running a finger under his uncomfortable stiff collar, Andre took a swallow of cognac and placed the glass on the mantelpiece. He hated crowds, at least of this sort. He loathed British society and its affectations. God, he hated being a damned duke.

He walked into the hallway, allowed the butler to hand him his cloak and cane, and entered the carriage bearing the despised ducal crest.

The crush was exactly what he had expected, of course, the usual mix of pomposity and overstatement. There was a murmur as he entered, the sort of confused but excited whispering that came when speculation ran rife and people were not exactly sure whom they were regarding, and what level of importance that person had, if any. But it only took as long as it took him to cross the hallway before he heard the first gasp. He ignored it.

"Your name, sir?" the footman asked at the top of the ballroom steps, prepared to bellow it out to all and sundry as custom demanded.

Andre was damned if he was going to follow custom.

"Saint-Simon," he said, not entirely falsely.

"Mr. Saint-Simon," the man cried, giving it the English pronunciation. To Andre's relief, not a soul looked up.

It gave him time to peruse the room. He saw a handful of familiar faces, but mercifully few, considering the throng. But as he descended the steps his eye was caught by a slender woman, her delicate profile turned away from him, dark hair arranged above a swanlike neck. There was something familiar about her, but he couldn't put his finger on it, couldn't even imagine where he might have seen her before . . .

He felt his arm being grabbed from behind, and he spun around, years of ingrained reaction instantly coming into play.

"Good God—it *is* you!" Jack Clifford stared into his face, his eyes popping out of his head. "Good God. And here we were thinking you must have permanently vanished into the bowels of Asia after all this time. Ah, Banesbury, my man, this is a fine day indeed. Although I suppose we ought to be calling you Montcrieff these days, eh?"

"Hello, Jack," Andre said, thinking that he was never going to make the adjustment back to so-called civilization. "How are you?"

"Never better," Jack said, pulling on his ear. "I say, are you all right? Looking a bit queer just then, you were."

"I'm fine, Jack. Just fine. I've only been home a few days. I haven't quite adjusted, I suppose."

"No—no, naturally not. Too many years out there with the savages, I expect."

"Savages?" Andre asked silkily. "Well, maybe. Or

maybe not enough time with the savages in here. Hard to tell."

Jack swallowed. "Um ... your grandfather's death a bit rough on you, old boy?"

"Mmm," Andre agreed. "Very rough. But I'll manage, thanks. So. Who are these people?" He surveyed the crowd, thinking that nothing at all had changed in the eight years he had managed to avoid their unpleasant company.

"Ah, yes," Jack said. "You will be out of touch and needing to look for a wife, now that your situation has changed. Well, let's see. Over there is the widowed Marchioness of Stratton. Don't want to get too close to her—bit of a spitter, she is, and looking for a husband. Spat the last one to death, I suspect." He chortled at his own wit.

Andre gave him a withering look.

"Um, ah ... Well. Let's see. The gaggle of women directly ahead with their backs to us aren't worth your time. The blonde is the elder of the Charleton sisters, affianced to Hornesby, and the ginger-haired vision is ... well. You can see for yourself."

"Do you have an aversion to the dark-haired one in the middle as well?" Andre asked dryly of the women Clifford hadn't even bothered to mention.

Jack gave a bark of laughter. "Now you really are wasting your time."

"Why?" Andre asked, his curiosity piqued.

"Because she's entirely unavailable unless you want to ride with her, or share a picnic, or do any of the other countless mundane things that lead up to precisely nothing." He shrugged. "Anyway, the word is that she will marry Matthew Daventry. There's some family connection."

"Matthew Daventry? Brabourne's eldest son?" Andre asked with surprise. "I hadn't realized he'd come of age."

"Came back from India to complete his schooling— what, seven years ago? Know him, do you?"

"Slightly," Andre said, thinking that must be the

connection. She was some remote Daventry cousin
he'd met at one family gathering or another.

"Well, Daventry hasn't taken his eyes off her since
she first came out, y'know. Don't really see it myself.
She's from some deuced place on the Continent." He
made a face. "Can't abide foreigners myself, especially
ones that are too clever by half."

"Somehow I'm not surprised," Andre said, but his
sarcasm went straight over the idiot's head.

"She's good with horseflesh, though—speaking of
which, I've put together the most marvelous team.
You've never seen such a pair of high-steppers as
these."

"How nice for you," Andre said, hopelessly bored
and dismissing the entire subject before they got into
an interminable discussion of horses. "Excuse me."

He started across the room intending to get a decent
breath of air outside when he was stopped in his tracks
by the sound of laughter. Pure, rolling, unmistakable
laughter that he'd only ever heard emanate from one
person in his entire life.

He slowly turned, wondering if his ears were playing
tricks on him. His gaze swept the room, tracing the
laughter to its source. It was the same woman he'd
been asking about only minutes before. He frowned,
thinking that maybe he'd finally lost his mind.

And then she turned to greet a friend, her dark eyes
bright with welcome, her smile as warm as sunshine.
It was a sight he thought he'd never see again.

"Dear, dear God," he whispered. "Dear God
above."

It was Ali.

"Caroline! I'm so pleased you decided to come after
all," Ali said with delight. "Has your husband returned from Essex, then?"

"No," Caroline said sadly. "I miss him dreadfully.
But I grew tired of spending my evenings alone."

"Well, of course you did," Ali said, catching her
hands up. "And I'm thrilled that you decided to
have fun."

"Well, I knew you'd be here, and I always have fun around you," Caroline said. "Hello, Hattie, hello, Sabrina. How nice to see you both."

Her voice was full of genuine pleasure and Ali smiled with satisfaction. Caroline had been married only four months and was besotted with her new husband. She'd been utterly miserable since he'd left town on business and persistently refused to leave the house, despite Ali's urging.

Well, here she finally was and Ali was going to make sure that Caroline enjoyed herself this evening. She looked up to see Matthew rapidly making a beeline toward them, and immediately decided where to begin.

"Matthew, I can't possibly dance with you again," Ali said adamantly the moment he asked. "What would people think?"

"This is only the third time I've asked," he said, his tone injured. "And since when do you care what people think?"

"I suppose that's true enough," Ali said with a laugh. "But I don't really feel like dancing. Why don't you ask Caroline, since her husband is out of town and she needs to be cheered up?" Since Caroline was standing right next to her, she knew he could hardly refuse.

Matthew inclined her fair head and invited Caroline politely enough, but his eyes snapped with frustration. Ali watched him lead Caroline onto the dance floor, highly amused as heads turned to watch him.

Matthew had indeed grown handsome over the years, his gawkiness turning into the breadth and height that ran in the Daventry family. She had met them all now, become fond of them, although she was fondest of all of Andre's parents, who treated her like a daughter and visited when they could.

But Matthew. What was she to do about him? It was a sticky problem, especially since he refused to understand about Andre.

"If you see my point?" Hattie said, shooting Ali a

telling look as Matthew glanced back over his shoulder as if to admonish Ali.

"Oh, all right, he's stubborn and persistent and refuses to acknowledge that I'm not suddenly going to change my mind and topple over at the sight of him."

"I'll topple for you," Hattie offered. "I wouldn't mind him looking at me like that. As a matter of fact . . ." She trailed off, her mouth dropping open. "Good heavens. And just when one thinks there aren't enough dukes to go around."

Ali smothered a laugh, for Hattie might have been the recorder for Burke's Peerage. She knew every last title and detail of lineage in all of Great Britain.

"Which one is it now?" she asked, trying to be obliging.

"The Duke of Montcrieff of all people. Everyone thought he was lost out in Asia somewhere."

Ali's back went stiff and her knees felt as if they might collapse underneath her.

Andre. He was home. He was finally home. She concentrated on slowly inhaling and exhaling as a cold sweat covered her body.

"Don't you remember, he inherited the title last year, but no one heard a word from him." Hattie shook her arm. "Alexis? Why are you forever going off into a daydream when the most exciting things are happening around you? You haven't taken ill, have you? You're looking a bit pale."

"I'm fine, Hattie. Please. Stop shaking me. I just felt warm for a moment. It's a tremendous crush."

"I've never known you to be affected by anything so silly as a crush," Hattie said, peering into her face with concern. "Are you sure I shouldn't take you home?"

"No!" Ali said. "No," she repeated more quietly. "I—I'm perfectly well now."

She'd been waiting for this moment for five years, five long years, and she wasn't going to let a small matter like severe shock get in her way.

Chapter 10

Ali closed her eyes for a brief moment, struggling to regain her composure. Allah, she prayed fervently, help me. Please help me. Her heart pounded so painfully hard that it felt as if it might explode. But she willed it to slow, willed herself to remember everything she had worked so hard to learn for just this moment.

"Did I tell you I met him when I was a child?" she heard Hattie saying. "He was the Marquess of Banesbury then, and I thought him splendid, but he is even more spectacular than I remember. They called him the black marquess because he was so aloof and cold to everyone, and I remember thinking so myself at the time. Funny, he doesn't look the least bit aloof to me now."

"And where is this spectacular duke of yours?" Ali asked Hattie as casually as she could manage.

"Behind you, over to the left," Hattie said breathlessly. "You can't miss him. He is standing by himself—the tall one with the dark hair. I don't think people have realized." She frowned. "Odd, I didn't hear him announced ..."

Ali tuned out the rest of Hattie's prattle. Steadying herself, she took a deep breath and turned around, thinking a quick peek wouldn't hurt.

But to her horror Andre's gaze was fixed directly on her, and the shock that ran through her system as their eyes connected nearly undid her.

Everything came flooding back. Turkey, the noise of the streets, the brightness of the sun, the colors and tastes and smells ...

Andre standing on the dock that last day as the boat pulled away, looking as stricken then as he looked now, except that now he was in formal evening dress, the black of his long-tailed jacket and trousers contrasting sharply with the brilliant white of his neck-cloth and waistcoat.

And now he was clean-shaven. Without his beard he was even more beautiful, his cheekbones lean, his mouth appearing fuller yet finely sculpted.

She forced herself to drop her gaze, forced herself to turn around again, to pretend indifference even though her mouth had gone dry and her knees felt even weaker than before.

"Well?" Hattie asked. "Did you see him? He was looking right this way."

"Yes, I saw him," Ali said, grateful that Matthew and Caroline returned from the dance floor at that very moment. She badly needed a diversion, time to collect herself, to think what to do. She knew Andre would never leave it there.

"Well?" Hattie persisted. "What did you think?"

"He is attractive enough, I suppose," she replied, dismissing the subject and smiling with such welcome at Matthew that his eyes widened in surprise.

"Are you so gratified that I danced with your friend?" he asked her. "If so, I would happily dance with every last one of them."

"I am delighted that you gave Caroline pleasure," she replied, wondering if her voice sounded as shaky to him as it did to her. "I—I think I am going to go outside for some air."

"Alexis, what's wrong?" he said in an undertone. "You look upset."

"I—nothing. It is warm." He would find out soon enough on his own, she thought. There was no point in forewarning him.

But it happened even sooner than she had antici-pated. At that very moment Andre appeared directly in front of them, and Ali's heart started to hammer uncontrollably.

He ignored her, his attention fully on Matthew.

"Good evening," he said. "You must be Matthew Daventry—you have even more a look of your father about you since the last time we met. I am Andre de Saint-Simon. Perhaps you don't remember. You were only about ten at the time."

The sound of his familiar deep, rich voice cut straight through Ali like a knife. He was real. He was really here, standing in front of her. She wanted to reach out her hand and touch him, feel that reality transmitted through her fingertips, know him for solid flesh and blood instead of the figment of her imagination she'd lived with for so long.

Instead, she gripped Matthew's arm and felt it stiffen under her fingers.

"Good God," he murmured. "So you did come back after all."

"As you can see, I did," Andre agreed. "Well met, cousin."

"That depends," Matthew said curtly. "What brought you home? Surely not something as mundane as your responsibility?"

Ali's stomach, already twisted inside out, developed one more knot. Matthew retained an irrational dislike when it came to Andre, and it was showing.

"Actually, yes," Andre said, ignoring the insult. "It took some time for the news of my grandfather's death to reach me, and even more time to disentangle myself. But here I am, feeling a bit out of touch after being away so long." He looked around. "Won't you introduce me to your friends?"

Matthew paused, and Ali's eyes pleaded with him to keep his temper and his tongue in check.

"I beg your pardon," Matthew said, relenting, and Ali released a silent breath of relief, knowing what the civility must have cost him. He couldn't be happy with Andre's return, knowing how she felt.

"Alexis, allow me to present the Duke of Montcrieff," he said. "Montcrieff, Miss Alexis Lacey, my grandfather's ward."

Andre took her hand and bowed over it. "Miss

Lacey, it is an honor. It seems we have a connection, as Lord Raven is my godfather."

The simple touch of his hand sent a rush of love through her. She longed to hold it tight, to press her lips to it, to throw her arms around him and tell him how much she had missed him, how hard she had worked at growing up. But instead she slipped her fingers from his light grasp.

He lifted his head and she met his gaze full on. "Your Grace," she said, playing out the game from sheer necessity. "May I welcome you home?"

"Thank you," he said coolly, but his eyes expressed something else entirely. He looked startled more than anything else, and Ali was well pleased.

"I gather you have been away from England for many years," she said, her nervousness melting away. She almost felt as if the five intervening years had never been. Almost. But not quite. Something important had shifted and she sensed it acutely, although she didn't know what it was.

"Yes, I have been away a long time," he answered. "I find my return to be filled with surprises. Things do not appear the same to me as when I left them."

"How could they be, Your Grace?" Ali said. "Nothing ever stays the same."

"Apparently not," he agreed. "Where are you originally from, Miss Lacey? I detect a slight accent."

"I am originally from Switzerland," she said, wondering what he'd make of that bald-faced piece of fiction, and wondering why he was pushing her into dangerous territory.

"Switzerland?" He paused for a moment, and Ali saw a brief flash of amusement in his eyes. "I see. The Alps, perhaps? I have a particular fondness for mountains."

"No, we lived in a valley," she said mischievously, "but we did summer in the mountains, with the exception of one. I have many fond memories of that time."

Andre's mouth twitched, but before he could respond, Matthew jumped in.

"Allow me to introduce you to Lady Langley. You might remember her husband . . ."

Ali kept her eyes glued to the floor while Matthew performed the rest of the introductions. Andre replied graciously enough, but she'd seen him in situations like this before, when he gave every indication of attentiveness but his focus was elsewhere.

It was the first time that sidelong focus had been directed in such a way at her, though, and she wondered what was going through his head. Was he appalled by her impeccable English and manners? Had he noticed the swell of her breasts yet?

That happy speculation was interrupted by Hattie's nervous and uncharacteristic stutter upon her introduction to Andre.

"Your—Your Grace. We have met. That is, my f-father introduced us. Once. A long time ago. At our house on Berkeley Square. You w-won't remember, naturally . . ."

Ali had to bite the insides of her cheek to keep from bursting into laughter when Andre glanced over at her, one eyebrow raised in the old, familiar gesture. Poor Hattie. Ali had never seen her so upended. But then Hattie was faced with probably the most eligible bachelor in England, and he was very handsome too, Ali thought proudly. Too bad Hattie didn't know how Andre felt about Englishwomen.

"I am sorry to say that I do not remember, Miss Charleton," Andre answered. "But then it has been a long time, and there is much I do not remember." He turned to Ali. "Tell me, Miss Lacey, do you waltz?"

"Naturally," she said. "I suppose you also wish to know if I can play the piano, paint lovely watercolors, and do fine embroidery? I assure you that I am proficient in all the feminine arts."

Hattie gasped with horror, and Ali turned to her. "You see, Hattie, some people assume that when one is raised in a foreign country, one is ignorant of the social graces."

"Actually," Andre replied smoothly, "I was less concerned with your mastery of social graces than in your ability to refresh my memory. I am not certain I recall how the waltz goes, having spent the last eight years in places where it is not generally performed."

"Are you asking me to dance?" Ali said with a little smile, trying to imagine Yourooks waltzing around a campfire. "Or would you prefer that I describe the movements to you?"

"I think," Andre said, "that it would be better to go through the actual motions."

"Oh, all right," Ali said. "But please be considerate of my toes."

"Naturally," he replied, taking her by the arm and leading her onto the dance floor. The moment they were out of earshot, he dropped the pretense.

"What in the name of God are you doing here?" he demanded. "You're supposed to be in the outback of Canada!"

"I don't know what gave you that idea," she replied tartly. "I haven't left the shores of England since you sent me here. In fact, I've done precisely what you wished me to do." She rested a hand on his shoulder. "Now pay attention. One, two, three, one, two, three."

"I know how to do the damned waltz," he said, pulling her into his arms as the music began. "I needed an excuse to get you alone for a few minutes. I gather no one knows anything about us, about Turkey?"

"No, and you did a good job of covering up," she said, a most peculiar, heavy sensation taking hold in her lower abdomen as he swept her around in graceful circles, his hand firm on her back.

She had an overwhelming desire to press herself more closely to him, to rest her cheek on his chest. And wouldn't that look interesting to London society? There were already enough people watching curiously.

She satisfied herself by moving the hand resting on his shoulder a little closer to his neck, longing to run her finger down the skin just below where the hair curled behind his ear, knowing exactly how it would feel, how he would smell—warm, fresh, masculine. Like no one else in the entire world.

"I learned the art of covering up from spending time around you," he said from above her head. "You have a habit of delivering one shock after another, and you haven't let up. Now please explain what you are doing here?" He looked down at her.

"Why shouldn't I be here? I have as much right as anyone else," Ali said, enjoying herself tremendously.

It was extraordinarily nice dancing with Andre—nice being held in his arms and twirled around the floor, which he did far more skillfully than her usual partners, but then he always had been surprisingly graceful for a man of his size.

And oh, it was nice teasing him. She'd forgotten how much fun that was.

"Ali, cease trying to behave like some sort of highborn miss and answer my questions," he said. "The last letter I had from my godfather said that he'd found some relative or other in Canada." He lowered his voice as another couple came close. "And then I heard not another word, so naturally I assumed you had gone. But to find you here? Why? What happened?"

"Not 'How lovely to see you, Ali? How are you, Ali? Goodness, you're looking civilized, Ali.' All you want to know is why I'm not yet another continent away? I ought to step on your toes and make you howl."

He swept her around in another circle. "Don't be a little idiot. I asked you a perfectly simple question. All I require is an equally simple answer, not a show of your blasted temper, which obviously hasn't improved." He glanced around the room. "And people are watching us like hawks."

"Of course they are. By now word has spread that the stranger in their midst is the great Duke of Montcrieff, previously styled as the black marquess."

"The black marquess?" he said, puzzled. "Where did you hear that?"

"Oh, didn't you know? That's what they used to call you. I suppose now they'll call you the black duke, since you don't seem to have changed in the least."

"And what's that supposed to mean?" he asked, his eyes narrowing.

"It means that you're still the same heartless brute who sent me away five years ago." She smiled up at him sweetly. "But surely you must be pleased with me now? I have become a perfect Englishwoman. Isn't that what you wished?"

He didn't reply, and Ali saw from the expression on his face that she had finally managed to get a bit of her own back.

"So you have been at Ravenswalk all this time?" he eventually said.

"Yes. All this time, as you put it so well. Your godparents have been very kind to me." She glared up at him. "Without a word of thanks to them from you, of course, or any indication that you cared whether any of us lived or died."

"I wrote," he replied, unmoved. "I suppose my letter didn't reach them."

"And that was it? You washed your hands of me yet again, did you?"

"I didn't wash my hands in the first place. Must you be so absurdly dramatic? I explained it all to you when you left."

"Which is why you took such care to inquire after my welfare?" she asked. "Is this how you plan to continue to treat me now that you truly are a great peer? With the same disregard you give to your family?"

"You little viper!" he exclaimed, missing his step. "My God, England has done your tongue no good at all, has it? You forget what I did for you, all the trouble I went to on your behalf, you ungrateful brat."

"I see," she said, looking up at him. "You toss me away like a bit of old rubbish, and I'm an ungrateful brat. I think the only thing I have to be grateful for is that your godparents were good enough to take me in—and keep me. They taught me how to be a lady. They even presented me at court." She tilted her head to one side. "What do you think of that, Andre? I've met the queen."

He looked down at her, his expression thunderous.

"What do I think? Shall I tell you, Ali? Do you really want to know?"

"Yes, of course," she said, but she was beginning to wonder if her teasing hadn't misfired.

"Very well. I think that you might be dressed like a lady, and you might speak like a lady, you might even behave like a lady, of all idiotic things. But you forget that I know you inside out. You may have fooled everyone else, but you can't fool me, Ali. I know *exactly* what you are."

"What am I, then?" she demanded, but a knot had formed in her throat.

"You're a child playing at dress-up. I suppose I shouldn't be surprised, knowing the penchant you have for pretending to be something you're not."

His words hit Ali like the worst of blows. She thought her heart might shatter into a thousand pieces at their impact. This was not what she had imagined, had waited for all these years.

This was not her Andre, this cruel man who wished only to hurt her. A great flood of sickness and despair washed over her. If feelings could bleed when mortally injured, hers would have bled all over the floor. But instead she held her head high and met his eyes evenly.

"You're wrong," she said coldly. "You don't know me at all, my dear duke." She spoke the last word with quiet contempt. "Not any longer. And I don't know you. The man I knew, the one I cared about, would have smiled at me and told me I'd done well. He would have told me he was proud of me. He would never have tried to make feel inferior, to remind me what I came from."

"That's not what I—"

"It doesn't matter," she said, cutting him off. "It doesn't matter any longer. Funny, isn't it? It used to mean everything to me, what you thought. Well, Andre. Now it's my turn to wash my hands of you."

"Oh? And how do you intend to do that?" he asked, pulling her roughly around in yet another circle, his fingers digging painfully into her back.

"I'm going to marry Matthew Daventry." Ali couldn't believe the words had come out of her mouth, but she took a certain degree of satisfaction in them, even if she didn't mean a single one.

"*You* marry Matthew?" he said with a choked laugh. "By God, Ali, if we weren't in a public place I'd shake you till your brains rattled. What in the name of hell do you think a man like Matthew is going to do with a girl like you?"

"Love me," Ali said fiercely. "Something you know nothing about. And I am not a girl, or a child, I am a full-grown woman who will be twenty-one next month."

"Perhaps your body has matured, Ali, but the rest of you is as childish as ever."

She looked away, feeling as if he'd just slapped her. "And you're as heartless as ever," she whispered. "If you please, I should like to return to my companions. I think it would be best if we never refer to the past again. And I think it's also best if you stay away from me."

"Fine," he said curtly. "That's fine. But it's a damned shame about what's happened to you."

Ali regarded him coldly, although inside she wanted nothing more than to cry. "What else did you expect?" she asked.

"I don't know," he said wearily. "I don't know. Anything but this."

"Civilization has its price, hasn't it?" she retorted. "And you were the one who exacted it on me."

"Well, then damn me for a fool," he said and took her back to her friends.

He left without another word.

Hattie waited until they were preparing for bed before pouncing on Ali. "Oh, Alexis! Tell me all. What happened with the duke? What is he like? What did you talk about?" she demanded the moment the maid had left.

Ali shrugged casually, even though she was falling apart inside. "Nothing, really," she said, giving Hattie the response she'd carefully thought out. "He was curious about Ravenswalk since he's been away for so long, and he wanted to know how it was that I'd become Lord Raven's ward. So I explained Lord Raven's old friendship with my father."

"Oh . . ." Hattie said, climbing into bed and pulling her knees up. "Well, I just wondered when he left so suddenly. I thought he looked annoyed too, and you seemed upset. Did he say something roguish and improper?" she asked hopefully.

"No, not in the least. His manners were impeccable. It was simply that I didn't appreciate being interrogated by a complete stranger, and I told him so." Ali finished braiding her hair and turned to face Hattie. "It was really nothing."

"How fascinating," Hattie said, her eyes dreamy. "Imagine his appearing just like that, and then to have a connection with you . . . Oh, Alexis, you have all the luck." She sneezed.

"Luck?" Ali said, exhausted, emotionally drained, and wishing Hattie would cease her chatter. "I found him perfectly odious, to tell you the truth."

"Odious? But he's so devastatingly handsome! Oh, that dark hair and those light eyes that seem to look straight through one." Hattie sighed ecstatically. "And he's so divinely tall and broad and handsome, even more handsome than Matthew. Did you feel fragile when you danced with him?" she asked.

"No," Ali said, lying. She'd never felt so fragile in her life.

"Alexis? What are you thinking? The oddest expression just came over your face."

Ali sighed. "Nothing. I'm tired."

"Oh. Well, I thought you made a very handsome couple. And I think that the only thing on his mind was luring you into his arms from the moment he saw you."

Ali wanted to laugh, the idea was so ridiculous. If only Hattie knew. *You're a child playing at dress-up.* The words still stung. All that waiting to grow up. All for nothing.

"Alexis?" Hattie persisted, blowing her nose into her handkerchief.

"You are an incurable romantic," Ali said. "Trust me, that was the last thing on his mind."

"No, it's true. I saw the expression in his eyes when Matthew introduced you. He was definitely interested in you."

"Yes, and I told you why," Ali said, longing to stuff a sock into Hattie's mouth.

"I don't think so. He'll be looking for a wife, you know. He was the fifth duke's only grandchild—in fact, the last duke petitioned the Crown to have the succession pass through his daughter because there were no males. That's how important it is for him to produce sons."

"Well, don't look at me," Ali said, crawling into bed and pulling the heap of covers up around her. She'd been inexplicably cold for the last two hours, probably brought on by misery.

"Why not, Alexis? It would be a brilliant match. He's going to be a duke in France too," she said, as if holding out additional bait.

"Then I'm sure he'll have plenty of women falling all over themselves to land him," Ali said, wanting to scream.

"But he chose you. It was a singular honor to dance with you and then leave, you know. And Matthew saw the same thing I did, because he didn't take his eyes off you the entire time you danced. I think he was jealous."

"I doubt it. Matthew dislikes him for some reason or another. But then no one has discussed the duke with me, so I would hardly know. Please, Hattie, let's forget about him and get some sleep." Ali rolled over on her side and squeezed her eyes shut. "Good night."

"Good night," Hattie said, turning the lamp off. Ali heard the mattress creaking, then the sound of Hattie's soft, even snuffles, indicating that she'd fallen immediately asleep.

The same luxury didn't come to Ali. The image of Andre's face refused to leave her. She still felt the imprint of his hand on her waist, her fingers tucked in his, the flesh warm and solid, real. She saw his eyes, his beautiful eyes, filled first with the shock of seeing her, and later with anger and then disillusionment.

What had he expected? A child in *chalvars* with hair still shorn? Or maybe a child who wore pretty dresses but spoke broken English, who gazed at him with unquestioning adoration, who called him master and begged for stories. That Ali was long gone. But who had taken her place?

Perhaps your body has matured, Ali, but the rest of you is as childish as ever.

So he had noticed her breasts, her new curves. And they hadn't meant a thing to him. Nothing. She didn't understand. Wasn't that what being a woman was? Obviously not, if he still considered her a child.

Ali turned on her back and stared at the ceiling, oblivious to the tears that rolled down her cheeks. She thought of the dream she'd held for so long in her heart: Andre would see her and instantly realize that she was the perfect wife for him.

They would go on as they always had, she cooking and cleaning for him, seeing to all his needs, he teaching her and telling her stories and writing his books. They would travel the world together, she and Andre and Joseph-Jean, and it would be just as it had been before, comfortable and happy, but with a few children running about.

But tonight that shining fantasy had been destroyed, smashed into irreparable pieces. Andre was right. It had been the foolish dream of a child, kept alive by an innocent, childish love, by the belief that she could make dreams come true if she wished for them hard enough. But she was no longer innocent. She was no longer a child. And she no longer believed that dreams came true.

She saw life through different eyes, saw Andre through different eyes, saw him not for what she wanted him to be, but for who he really was.

He would never love her. How could he? He was in love with a dead woman, a woman who had taken his heart with her to the grave. And why would Andre want to marry her, of all people? He had baldly reminded her tonight of what she really was, what she had come from. A wife fit for a duke? Only in her childish fantasies.

The hell of it was that Ali still loved him with everything she had in her and always would. That much Allah truly had ordained. But Andre had warned her, long ago, hadn't he?

Don't ever give your heart away and certainly not to me. I have no heart and will only break yours.

Well, he had broken it, and she'd been stupid enough to let him. She had only herself to blame.

In that moment, Ali realized that she had finally grown up. It was cold comfort and came a little too late.

Chapter 11

Andre had a splitting headache, the result of having spent a sleepless night combined with the effect of the heavy and unaccustomed London fog. His mood was foul and his temper short, and it didn't improve when the butler announced that Matthew Daventry was downstairs, asking to see him.

"Show him up," Andre said curtly, internally recoiling from the unwelcome reminder of last night's disaster. "And send for coffee. Strong."

He put aside the flurry of invitations that had arrived in the morning post, now that his presence was general knowledge, telling himself that he was going to need to either hire a secretary or adjourn to Sutherby for the remainder of his life. As much as he loathed Sutherby, it sounded much better than this hell.

He rose from his desk as Matthew came storming through the door, looking like an angry young bull. "Good morning," he said, knowing that his pounding head was not going to improve with this meeting. "Won't you sit down?"

"Let us forgo the pleasantries, Montcrieff. Just what are your intentions here?"

"My intentions? Other than assuming the duties my grandfather left behind, do you mean?"

"You know damned well what I mean. I'm referring to Alexis and the public spectacle you made of her last night." His face reflected barely suppressed rage.

Andre looked the blond giant up and down, thinking that Matthew had inherited his father's quick temper as well as the trademark gray eyes and dark-winged brows of the Daventry family. It did not appear that he had inherited Charlie's sense of humor, however, which was a pity.

"A public spectacle?" he repeated. "And how did I do that? By dancing one waltz with her after a proper introduction had been performed? Are you here to call me out over the matter?"

"Do not trifle with me, Montcrieff. I will not see Alexis's reputation compromised, not after all this time."

"I have no intention of compromising anything," Andre said. "I don't believe I have an established reputation as a rakehell, nor that people regard me as anything more than unpleasant—or at least according to Ali. But you know what her imagination is. Or was." He scratched his cheek. "Did she, ah . . . say something to indicate that I made improper advances toward her?" He could hardly believe that such a thing would even have entered her mind, but this new Ali was probably capable of just about anything.

"Certainly she did not," Matthew replied, "although whatever you did say upset her badly. I could tell, even though she mentioned nothing. But then I know her very well."

"Yes, you probably know this version of Ali far better than I." He waited for the footman to put down the coffee tray and disappear. "I preferred the old one."

Matthew's brow drew down. "You would have. I'm sure you enjoyed having her as your servant at your beck and call, sleeping at your feet, shouting at her, knocking people down in front of her."

Andre had to stifle a smile. So Ali had been telling stories. He wondered just how far she'd gone, if Matthew knew how thoroughly Ali had served him. He doubted it. Matthew's tedious sense of propriety would have been even more outraged than this.

"Yes, I did enjoy it," he said truthfully. "But that was a long time ago, and she and I agreed last night to leave it in the past. I don't want Ali's upbringing or our past relationship exposed any more than you do. Coffee?"

"I think not," Matthew said, his jaw tight.

"See here, Daventry," Andre said reasonably, trying to remember that Matthew was young and still filled with idealistic fervor. "I didn't return to England to sully Ali's name or reputation if that's what you're worried about. I didn't even expect to find her here. I was as surprised last night to see her as she was to see me."

Dear heaven, but that was an understatement, he thought, stirring sugar into his cup. He'd been knocked six ways to Sunday. And if he was honest with himself, he'd been devastated by what he'd found.

"Yes, I realize that," Matthew said. "Nevertheless, you singled her out. You must have realized that would cause a stir? People are already talking."

"Well, they'll stop soon enough, since I don't plan on giving her the time of day from here on out. Now that you know that, why don't you calm down?" He sipped his coffee. "Actually, I'd be more interested in hearing how Ali's managed in London society."

"She has managed perfectly well. There was only a small flutter when word got out about her father, but the story my grandfather concocted about her parents leaving her with relatives in Switzerland took care of that."

"I didn't mean that. Is she well liked?"

"Everyone adores her," Matthew said, looking at him contemptuously. "Alexis is a special girl, one of a kind."

"Odd, it appeared to me as if your family managed to turn her into a carbon copy of everyone else."

Matthew glared at him. "You have no idea how hard Alexis has worked at becoming what you see today. She was like a wild animal when she first arrived, frightened, mistrustful, not even able to speak English. And listen to her now—she speaks it like a duchess."

"Not exactly a duchess, thank God," Andre said,

"although that will probably eventually change too. Pity."

"You fool—don't you realize that she did it all for you?" Matthew cried, then paled as he heard what he had said. "God, I wish you'd stayed away," he said, staring at the floor.

"So do I," Andre said flatly. "And don't think for a minute that Ali did any of it for me. She knows exactly what I think of that kind of behavior."

"What do you mean by that?" Matthew asked indignantly. "She behaves exactly as a lady ought."

"Precisely," Andre said, rubbing his forehead. "So. You fancy youself in love with her. Well, why not? She's pretty enough, I suppose."

"Pretty? Ali is beautiful, you blind idiot. All you can see is the half-tamed, raw-edged girl you sent away. Or maybe that's all you care to see—maybe that's how you can justify your carelessness with her."

Andre chose not to dignify that with a comment. "You're what, twenty now?" he said instead.

"I'll soon be twenty-two," Matthew replied curtly. "Old enough to marry Alexis, which I intend on doing."

"And how will you support her?" Andre asked, suppressing an unexpected surge of anger at the very idea of this boy presuming to marry Ali. "Where will you live? At Ravenswalk?"

Matthew pulled himself up. "I think those are questions my grandfather should be asking me, not you."

"I assumed your grandfather would already know the answers," Andre replied coldly. "Believe it or not, I do have an interest in Ali's future, now that I know she is not in the care of relatives."

"You have no right to anything concerning her," Matthew said furiously. "You forfeited it the day you put her on the boat with that godforsaken Herringer woman who did nothing but call her a savage and a whore—*your* whore, Montcrieff."

Andre clenched his fists at his side, feeling as if a blow had just been delivered to his stomach. "What?" he whispered.

"That's right. Fortunately Ali was too innocent to understand the implication, even when she asked what the word meant."

"I hadn't realized," Andre said, sickened. He thought he'd consigned Ali into the hands of a boring but competent and relatively sympathetic matron, not a vicious, lascivious-minded witch. Poor Ali. It must have been truly dreadful for her.

"I think there's a hell of a lot you haven't realized," Matthew replied, his gaze coldly raking Andre. "My suggestion to you is that you stay out of her life from now on, and my family's as well. All you've ever brought is pain and suffering to the people who have been misguided enough to care about you. Alexis isn't deserving of it, and neither is anyone else."

He turned on his heel and walked out.

Andre watched him go, a mass of conflicting emotions tearing at him, the uppermost of which was rage. How dare the young pup presume to speak to him like that? How dare he talk about Ali as if she were some sort of personal possession?

And then cold reason took hold. Well, she would be Matthew's personal possession, wouldn't she, if she were fool enough to marry him?

"Damn her!" he muttered. "Damn the lot of them."

He strode over to his desk and swept up the handful of invitations, tossing them into the wastepaper basket. London and its attendant miseries needed him about as much as he needed them, and Sutherby had gone neglected long enough. He'd had it with the damned city, with society, and most of all with Ali.

If she wanted to be an empty-headed wife, doing nothing but attending parties and gossiping with her friends, let it be on her head. She could marry Matthew Daventry, and he wouldn't lift one finger to save her from her fate.

Not that he believed for a minute that Nicholas would allow such a thing.

He might not know Matthew Daventry very well, but he knew Ali like the back of his hand, and she no more belonged with Matthew than she did with the man in the moon.

Anyway, she was far too young for marriage.

Ali pushed open the wood door of the enclosed garden that was attached to Raven's Close, the nearby manor house that was part of the Ravenswalk estate. It was a peaceful place, and she sought out the garden whenever she felt troubled. She'd spent a great deal of time here in the two weeks since returning from London.

The relief she'd felt when the season finally ended was enormous. Pretending to be gay and full of life when dying inside was not easy, nor was it easy to disguise her panic that Andre might appear around any corner at any moment.

But at least she was spared that. Rumor had it that Andre had returned to his country seat almost immediately, leaving London rife with speculation about him, most of it ridiculous. She might have been amused, except that any mention of Andre cut straight into her devastated heart.

Ali clipped a spray of roses for her basket, but her mind wasn't on her task; it was on the terrible void that her life had become. All she could see ahead was a long stretch of emptiness and unhappiness without Andre in it.

And on top of all that, there was Matthew's proposal.

She hadn't known what to do when he dropped to one knee in the middle of the Charletons' drawing room, pouring out his heart to her horrified surprise. But he was sincere, and didn't press her for an immediate answer.

But why shouldn't she consider his proposal? Matthew was devoted to her. He was kind. He was all the things Andre wasn't and never would be. Andre had made that more than clear.

She put the basket down and reached into her pocket to read Matthew's letter for the tenth time, carefully unfolding it as she sank down onto the nearby bench.

> ...Alexis, dearest, please do not dismiss my offer out of hand. I realize that I may have been precipitous, proposing marriage so soon after your upsetting encounter with Montcrieff and all the attendant reminders of the past that must have brought.
>
> But now that your eyes have been opened to his character, perhaps you can see that you have no future with him. I can give you a good life, a full life, if you will but let me.
>
> I'll be down at the weekend, darling. I pray you will have an answer for me then ...

Ali rubbed her fingers over her forehead, torn with indecision. She knew he loved her. He knew equally well that she didn't return his love. But he said it didn't matter, that she could learn to love him. Maybe he was right, maybe she could, although she'd never love him as she loved Andre. She knew that with certainty, and it seemed terribly unfair to Matthew.

He had said that it would be more unfair to reject him out of hand. And who else would have her? She couldn't presume on Georgia and Nicholas's kindness forever, and she couldn't marry someone else under a cloud of deception—that would be very wrong. But Matthew knew everything about her and he didn't mind.

Then why didn't it feel right? Why, in her heart of hearts, did every instinct tell her that to throw herself into Matthew's arms would be a horrible mistake? Maybe it was because she couldn't imagine throwing herself into his arms at all.

There was only one man she wanted in that way. For the last interminable month she had dreamed night after night of Andre's mouth, his hands, his body on hers in a way she had never even imagined before. She woke shaking and disoriented, the place between her thighs damp and aching with a heavy longing.

She couldn't think what had happened to her. Oh, she knew all about how babies were made, and that

men and women were not supposed to be left alone
in each other's company, just in case they made one
accidentally. But she'd never before been able to understand why they would want to. Now she understood far too well.

Images of Andre plagued her, memories of the feel
of his muscular body under her fingers, the shape of
his strong back, the planes of his broad chest, the
ridges of his abdomen. She knew how he looked unclothed, every last square, masculine inch of him.

In the past, his body had only been something beautiful to her, something to tend to as part of her service
to him. But now those innocent images had translated
themselves into an entirely different picture, potent
and dangerous, capable of setting her on fire. She
imagined the taste of his skin, the smell and feel of
his bare flesh against hers, his hands touching her most
intimate places.

She couldn't begin to imagine Matthew doing such
things to her—the very thought made her shudder.
And how would she explain it to Matthew when she
woke in the night calling for another man? A man she
could never have.

Ali put her face in her hands and wept, Matthew's
letter falling unnoticed to the ground. She didn't hear
the creak of the garden door softly closing.

"Nicholas, we cannot let Ali go on like this," Georgia said, marching into the library and throwing her
gardening gloves down on the table. "She's lost all her
color, she's losing weight she can't afford to lose, and
just now when I went to work in the garden I found
her crying her eyes out. Again. This is not good for
her."

"What would you like me to do?" Nicholas said,
looking up from his paper. "Go roaring up to Sutherby to knock some sense into Andre's stubborn
head? Or perhaps you'd like me to take him over my
knee? If you want a miracle, apply to Pascal, although
even he hasn't managed to make a dent in his son's
idiocy."

"Nicholas, stop being ridiculous. You're as concerned as I am, so don't try to pretend. I only wish Ali would speak to us about it, but obviously she feels she can't." Georgia gazed out the window, trying to think of a way they could ease Ali's pain. "By the way, I've just had a letter from Matthew in the morning post. He's coming down on Saturday," she said absently.

"I know," Nicholas said, his expression growing serious. "I had a letter from him too. He plans to exact an answer from Ali regarding his proposal."

Georgia's attention snapped back to her husband. "What?" she said in alarm. "You can't be serious?"

"I am. Perfectly." He folded his paper and put it on the table, pulling his spectacles off and rubbing his eyes.

Georgia sat down abruptly. "I hoped that nonsense would all blow over."

"It might well have blown over if Andre hadn't behaved like a complete fool when he returned," Nicholas said with annoyance. "It breaks my heart to see Ali like this, and in this state she might very well do something stupid."

"Then we can't sit by and do nothing. As much as we love them both, an alliance between Ali and Matthew wouldn't be a good idea. Matthew has always been in love with the idea of Ali, not Ali herself. She'd drive him around the bend in no time."

"Yes, I agree," Nicholas said. "Matthew would be far happier with someone a little more conventional. Anyway, Ali is obviously head-over-heels in love with Andre. There's been a big change in her since he came back."

"Yes," Georgia said tartly. "She's been miserable. I can't imagine what Andre said to her, but if the end result was Ali swearing that she never wanted to see him again, it must have been particularly choice." She sighed. "When is that boy going to learn?"

"I have no idea," Nicholas said. "But somehow I'm not surprised that he put his foot in it. His behavior only reinforces what I originally suspected."

"What, that he cares about her? Well, of course he does, or he wouldn't have behaved so badly." Georgia's eyes assumed a faraway look.

"Oh, dear," Nicholas said, "I know that expression. What are you planning?"

"Well ... it's been perfectly clear to me for years that Andre and Ali belong together, and now Andre's home and Ali's of an age where Andre can do something about it. But first we have to open his eyes, not an easy task."

"Oh, God help me," Nicholas groaned. "Not a matchmaking scheme?"

Georgia happily tapped her fingers together. "Yes. As much as I am loath to interfere in other people's lives, age has its privileges. I want you to write a letter."

"Let me guess. You wish me to write to Andre?" Nicholas asked dryly.

"Immediately. The situation has become urgent. Do you think I might have become deathly ill and wish to say farewell?"

"He'd never believe it," Nicholas said, smiling fondly at her. "He knows you have the constitution of an ox."

"Well, even oxen's health occasionally fail," she retorted. "Oh, very well. I'm a terrible actress anyway. He'd know he'd been hoodwinked in a moment. Hmm. Why don't we tell him what Matthew is planning?"

"No good. He already knows. Matthew told him, and according to Matthew, Andre couldn't care less."

"Ha!" Georgia said. "Matthew hasn't known Andre since he was a month old as we have. He doesn't have any idea what a master Andre is at concealing his feelings when he wants to. No, it's imperative to get Ali and Andre together in the same room, so we'll simply have to best him at his own game."

Nicholas regarded her with interest. "How? We inform him that we never wish to see him again?"

"No, because he won't believe that either." Georgia went to Nicholas's desk and pulled out pen and paper, slapping them down on the blotter. "You tell him the exact truth: that Matthew has formally applied to you for Ali's hand in marriage and if Ali should decide to accept Matthew's offer on Saturday, you feel you have no choice but to consent to the marriage."

Nicholas nodded thoughtfully. "Yes ... that might just work. That might just work."

Georgia picked up the pen and held it out. "You can also say that despite being her legal guardian, you are showing him a modicum of courtesy by informing him of the situation, which is more courtesy than he's shown us."

"I hope this isn't a terrible mistake," Nicholas said, crossing the room and taking the pen from Georgia. "You know what happened the last time we interfered in Andre's life."

"Would you rather see Ali marry Matthew?" Georgia asked.

Nicholas sat down and applied himself to writing.

Andre, who had decided upon his arrival a month ago that Sutherby suited his present mood perfectly, stalked across the huge hall to his library to immerse himself in another day's uninterrupted work.

He had managed to arrange his schedule to his complete satisfaction: a morning ride, followed by a solitary breakfast. From nine until noon he worked on his manuscript. At noon he had an hour's interview with his steward, Goodfellow, followed by a light tray of food at his desk.

In the afternoon he read and answered his mail, mostly business, aside from an occasional letter from Jo-Jean. Invitations of any nature all went the same way, into the dustbin. He then went for a long walk, thinking through his work for the following morning. The evening was reserved for reading.

This morning he was grateful for the drafts to which the house was prone. Southern England was in the grip of a heat wave, and although he was accustomed to extreme heat, he found the accompanying humidity excessively unpleasant.

A light tap came at the door, just as he was settling into his notes. "Yes?" he called with annoyance. The servants knew he was not to be disrupted for any reason other than the most extreme.

"Your Grace," Pennyswell said apologetically as he opened the door. "A letter has come. I would have left it for the afternoon, but it is marked urgent."

"Very well," Andre said, thinking it must be revisions from the publisher, who always marked everything urgent. "Put it over there."

"Er, I believe it is of a personal nature, sir, as it is also marked the same."

Andre held out his hand, and Pennyswell proffered forth the silver salver. Andre picked the envelope up, frowning as he saw it was addressed in Nicholas's hand, and tore it open, scanning the contents.

Within one minute he'd arranged for his valet to pack him a case, the carriage to be brought to the door, and a footman to go ahead to hold the train in case he wasn't fast enough to make what Pennyswell informed him was the eleven-twenty, the only direct train on Friday.

He made the train by the skin of his teeth. He spent the next hours stewing furiously, worried he might not arrive at Ravenswalk in time. Oh, he had a fair idea of what Nicholas was up to in dragging him down there—a lecture in family unity was to be expected, but that was only enough to annoy him.

It was the idea that Nicholas would actually be senile enough to give permission for Ali to marry a man entirely unsuited to her that made his blood boil. Ali obviously had no more sense than Matthew did in desiring the match. No, it was Nicholas's idiocy that truly galled, for he'd always thought highly of his godfather, even if he had cut him out of his life.

And where was Georgia in all of this? Didn't she have better sense, either? Dear God, but he would never have sent Ali to them if he'd believed them capable of this kind of stupidity.

On the other hand ... look what they'd gone and turned her into. A prim, simpering miss. He'd never have believed them capable of that, either. Or that Ali was so easily biddable. No wonder Daventry wanted to marry her. He probably thought he could mold her to his exact specifications.

He pulled his valise off the top rack as the train chugged into the station, ignoring the porter and storming down the corridor, pulling the heavy door open for himself. The heat and steam from the engine hit him like a blast in the face as he descended the steps.

He looked around to see if Nicholas had been foolish enough to send his coachman, but he saw no one wearing the Raven livery. That, at least, was auspicious. He might have done the coachman bodily harm from sheer aggravation.

Andre made quick arrangements with the station master to have a hired coach take him to Ravenswalk at double time.

"Miss Lacey?"

Ali looked up as she heard the chambermaid's voice at her bedroom door, open to allow the breeze to flow through from the windows. "Yes, Jane?" she asked lethargically, lowering her book to her lap. "What is it?"

"Mr. Daventry has arrived, miss. He specifically asked me to tell you and no one else."

"But he is a full day early!" Ali said in alarm, utterly unprepared. She thought she had at least until late the next morning to make her final decision. "I— I don't understand."

"He said to tell you that he managed to get an extra day off. He's waiting in the pavilion." Jane spoke in a semiwhisper that indicated she thought she was dealing with high romance.

"Tell him I'll be down shortly," Ali said, cursing Matthew for taking her by surprise. He might be devoted, but he could be irritatingly pushy at times.

She took one cursory look in the mirror, not really caring what she saw, pushed one lock of hair off her damp forehead, and smoothed down her skirt and petticoat, which threatened to stick to her thighs.

"Come along, Sherifay. Let's see what's so urgent," she said, not at all sure she wanted to know.

Matthew was pacing impatiently back and forth in front of the pavilion, and his head snapped up as he heard Ali approach. "Oh—finally," he breathed in relief. "I thought you were never going to come!"

"I came as quickly as I could," she said, trying to force warmth into her voice, but failing. "Why did you break your word? You said in your letter that you wouldn't arrive until tomorrow."

"I couldn't wait a minute longer. I've been in an agony of apprehension," he said, walking rapidly toward her, his hands outstretched. "Have you made a decision?"

Ali had a sudden desire to turn and run, but she stifled it, letting him clasp her hands. "Matthew, this is not a good time. I'm hot, I'm unprepared, and I'm annoyed with you, to be perfectly honest."

"But why? I thought you'd like the surprise," he said with astonishment. "Truly, Alexis—are you not pleased to see me?"

"No," Ali replied, suppressing a very sincere desire to strangle him. "I'm sure you meant it very sweetly, but it's not the sort of surprise I needed. I don't have an answer for you yet, Matthew, and I won't have until tomorrow. I'd like to take the full time you gave me to come to a decision."

"I—I'm so sorry," he said, obviously upset. "I thought that my coming early might make it easier for you."

"Matthew," she said more gently, seeing that she'd hurt him, "I can't make a decision that is going to profoundly affect the rest of my life without giving it the full consideration that it deserves." She pushed the same annoying lock of hair off her sticky forehead. "It's not that I'm not attached to you. It's simply that I'm not sure I'm attached in the way that can make a marriage work."

He kneaded the back of his neck in frustration. "I

don't know what to say to convince you that I love you, that I can make this right."

"I don't know if there's anything," she said, equally frustrated.

"Alexis. Please. Will you let me kiss you at least? I don't want to grab you like a Philistine, given your reservations, but maybe you might see that my feelings are genuine?"

Ali considered this. It wasn't such a bad idea, really. Maybe her addled senses would suddenly burst into flame as they did with imaginary kisses, and she'd finally be relieved of her burden. "All right," she said, lifting her face to his and holding her breath.

Matthew took another step forward and took her face between his hands, and Ali rested her hands on his shoulders, bracing herself.

She closed her eyes as his lips gently touched her own, soft, tender, moving very slightly, like the gentle sweep of a bird's wing. Ali felt as if she were kissing her brother.

He lifted his head again and gazed down at her, his eyes dark. "I love you," he breathed.

Ali couldn't bring herself to breathe the same thing back. All she felt was an overwhelming need to escape.

"I—I'm sorry, Matthew—I need to think."

"All right," he said patiently. "I'll see you at dinner."

Ali didn't respond. The wild part of her took over and she tore off, heading straight to the stables and her horse, Sherifay chasing after her.

She pulled off her encumbering petticoat and stockings, kicked off her shoes, bridled her horse, and leapt onto his bare back. She charged off before the first pursuing stable hand could reach her and headed straight for the high pastures.

The first thing that crossed Andre's mind as he faced his godparents was that they'd aged in his absence. He didn't know why it hadn't occurred to him that they would have; it had been eight years, after all.

They both looked a little more frail to his eye, and a stab of guilt shot through him. Maybe he had been a bit harsh in judging them. At the same time he suddenly realized how much he'd missed them.

"Andre," Georgia said, coming forward, unable to disguise the tears in her eyes. "It is so good to see you."

"And you," he said, kissing both her cheeks. "Hello, Nicholas."

"Sit down," Nicholas said without preamble. "I'm delighted you finally exhibited some good sense in presenting yourself here."

"If your motive is to pull me back into the family circle," he said, taking a chair, "then you're hopelessly deluded. However, Ali is another matter. What can you possibly be thinking, marrying her off to Matthew?" He pushed his fingers through his hair in agitation. "He'll make her miserable and she'll make his life a living hell. Can't you see that? You've had her for five years, for God's sake."

"You're exactly right. We've had her for five years, and I think we know her quite well. We also know Matthew and we happen to agree with you."

"You do?" Andre had been about to take Nicholas's head off but that comment stopped him short. "Then why in hell are you going to give your consent?"

"Ali turned twenty-one years old a week ago. She is old enough to make up her own mind."

"What are you saying?" Andre eyed his godfather with deep suspicion. "Have you dragged me down here on false pretenses?"

"Not at all. It is simply that I feel that Ali is, on the most essential level, connected to you, Andre. You found her, you decided to see to her future, and you sent her here to us."

He clasped his hands behind his back. "And here she still is. I thought that since you once had great influence over her, you might be able to persuade her against the marriage."

"Why? Why would you want me to?" he asked

heatedly. "Is she not good enough for your blasted grandson?"

"Don't be absurd," Georgia said. "We love Ali very much."

"Oh? Then why have you turned her into some kind of an aberration?"

"An aberration?" Georgia asked. "What on earth do you mean?"

"You ought to know what I mean," Andre countered. "That—that girl I saw last month wasn't Ali. I don't know who the devil she was, but she certainly wasn't the same person I sent you from Turkey. She was a travesty."

Georgia looked at Andre keenly, her expression a mixture of exasperation and amusement. "Andre, you know I love you dearly, whether you want to acknowledge it or not. But I've never known anyone so competent at twisting the truth of things around when your emotions become involved."

Andre stared at her. "I beg your pardon?" he said, unable to believe Georgia had gone blithely marching over such treacherous ground. "What in God's name do you mean by that?"

"Never mind," she replied. "You'll work it out eventually, or at least I hope you do. Suffice it to say that in this particular instance, children do not stay children forever."

Andre glared at her. "Do you think I don't realize that?"

"To be honest, I'm not sure that you do," Georgia replied. "But at this moment, that is neither here nor there. The point is that we both believe, as you apparently do, that Ali and Matthew would not make each other happy; they are dear friends, which is very nice, but that does not necessarily make a marriage."

Andre rubbed the bridge of his nose. "Believe me, Ali isn't going to listen to anything I have to say."

"Perhaps not," Nicholas said. "But there's no harm in trying. As I said, you have an unusual connection to her. Maybe you can reach her in a way we can't."

Andre looked hard at Nicholas, then at Georgia.

He saw the sincerity on their faces, saw their genuine concern. It was the last position in the world he wished to be put into, but at the same time he saw their point.

Maybe he could dissuade Ali from this ridiculous marriage, although the thought of having to endure another confrontation with her in her present incarnation was almost more than he could bear.

But the thought of Ali entangled in Matthew's arms was definitely more than he could bear.

Chapter 12

Ali started down the stairs for dinner in a state of anxious anticipation, knowing she'd be faced with Matthew as well as his grandparents, and there would be a horrible, silent, questioning dialogue going on between herself and Matthew during the entire meal. Nicholas and Georgia could hardly fail to pick up on it, and they were bound to wonder.

Her nerves screamed with tension. All she wanted to do was to escape, to run as fast and far as she could so that she didn't have to answer to anything or anyone.

But galloping her horse into a lather hadn't helped with that. It had only cost her an extra hour of walking the poor beast to cool him down, Sherifay panting at her heels, equally exhausted.

"Oh, why can't I pull myself together?" she whispered furiously as she approached the library. She steeled herself to face Matthew after her humiliating reaction to his kiss. Ali colored, just thinking about it. She felt like a fool, a silly, naive fool who couldn't even cope with a simple kiss from the man she was considering marrying.

But she couldn't marry him. How could she, after that? Poor Matthew. Hattie was right, after all. She was going to break his heart—she should have turned him down the moment he first proposed.

She took a deep breath, then opened the library door. And stopped cold. For a moment she thought she was dreaming again or that the heat had affected her senses.

Andre stood directly in front of the cold fireplace, a glass of sherry in his hand.

She blinked. He was still there, regarding her with a steady gaze devoid of any expression at all.

Ali's world spun for an infinitesimal moment, fractured images clashing together. Andre sitting in a tent, trying to explain a complicated piece of history to her, Andre standing across a ballroom gazing at her stunned, Andre here, now, one shoulder propped against a mantelpiece with a glass in his hand as if he'd always stood like this, always looked at her in this indifferent manner.

Had she been holding a glass herself, it would have splintered on the floor.

"Ali?"

She spun around. Georgia came toward her, one hand extended, and she laid it on Ali's shoulder. "Are you not going to greet Andre?"

"I—yes, of course," she said, her throat ridiculously tight. "I was merely taken by surprise. Good evening, Your Grace."

"Andre will do," he replied, straightening to his full height. "How are you, Ali?"

"I—I am well," she replied, grateful for Georgia's steadying hand. "And you?"

"I am also well."

She didn't believe it for a minute. He appeared pale and strained. Oh, God, she wasn't sure she could bear this. But she had no choice. For whatever perverse reasons he had chosen to come, she would not gratify him by falling apart. She would not.

"How are you enjoying life in England?" she asked politely, desperately trying to collect herself.

"Exactly as you might expect," he replied. "Or have you really forgotten so much?"

Ali stared at the ground. She had forgotten nothing. That was the trouble. The very sight of him cast her into full memory. All kinds of memory. She felt her face growing hot.

"Has the cat got your tongue, Ali?" he said. "I don't believe I remember your ever being at a loss for words. But then so much has changed that I no longer know what to expect."

Her head shot up. "Are you trying to provoke me? If so, you are doing a good job."

"Why should I wish to provoke you?" he replied evenly. "I've come to see Nicholas and Georgia. Since you are also here, don't you think we might be pleasant?"

Ali nodded, looking away. "Of course." Oh, how she wished he'd disappear, vanish into thin air. This was a nightmare come true.

And then Matthew appeared in the doorway. Ali, her stomach sinking, took in the grim expression on Matthew's face as he registered Andre's presence. Anger flashed in Andre's eyes, quickly concealed.

If she thought she'd been caught in a nightmare a minute ago, now she knew she had just been dropped into the jaws of hell.

Andre summoned every reserve of control to behave politely throughout the drinks before dinner. He managed to remain civil throughout all three courses of the meal, answering questions about his work and his travels, although his attention wasn't fully on the job. He knew that Ali was listening closely, although she feigned disinterest, the brat, behaving as if she had no idea of what he was talking about.

Her gaze remained demurely fixed on her plate and she pushed her food around exactly like every other silly miss he'd ever come across, as if she were too delicate to eat. That was a joke in itself.

She also behaved as if she had no idea that Matthew was staring her down, or that there were subtle but intense undercurrents running between himself and her, charged with the force of a hundred unspoken things. And she certainly did not behave like a woman in love with the man sitting next to her.

Ali. What had happened to her? Where had his sweet, funny child gone? What had happened to all that innocence, her lack of artifice? It had vanished beneath a swirl of skirts, an arrangement of lush dark hair.

His gaze traced the lines of her cheekbones, the square angle of her jaw, and the long sweep of her neck. Now that he had a chance to observe her at leisure without the gaze of most of the polite world upon them, he could also assess the other changes, the curves and swells that he'd never thought to see.

His fork slowed on the way to his mouth. She was still gamine in her own way, but he wondered how he could ever have so easily thought her to be a boy, for there was nothing boyish about her. She was ... feminine. Very feminine, her ripe mouth begging to be kissed.

Andre fumbled and dropped his fork. "I beg your pardon," he said, appalled with himself. What was he thinking, for God's sake?

"No, there's no need to fetch another," he said to the footman who scurried to retrieve the fallen object and replace it. "I've had enough. Forgive me, Georgia. The meal was delicious, but I think the heat has affected my appetite."

"Yes," Nicholas said gravely. "I believe we are all feeling the heat this evening. Perhaps it would be best to retire early."

"What a good idea," Georgia said. "Both Matthew and Andre must be tired from their journeys as well." She rose, giving the signal that the meal was over. "But, Matthew, dearest, would you first come upstairs with me? I have a letter to write that must go in the morning post, but my eyes are tired. I hoped you might let me dictate it to you."

Andre silently applauded Georgia as Matthew opened his mouth to object, then closed it again.

"Very well, Grandmama," Matthew said reluctantly as Georgia tucked her hand in the crook of his elbow. "Good night," he said. "I'll speak with you in the morning, Alexis."

Ali glanced up at him and nodded, her color heightening.

Andre wanted to be sick. Since when did Ali blush? Was it in memory of some stolen kiss, or worse?

Ali was on her way out the door, and he quickly stepped up behind her, placing a hand on her arm. She turned around, alarmed, her color fading. "What—what do you want?" she asked, her voice shaking.

"A word with you," he said. "In the library."

"But I was going to bed," she said. "I have a headache."

"The hell you have," he said, steering her out of the dining room and taking her down the hall. He shut the door firmly behind them. "Now suppose you tell me," he said, biting out each word, "what you damned well think you're doing?"

"Don't blaspheme," Ali automatically replied, but her hands tightened into fists at her sides.

Andre's heart unexpectedly tightened as he heard the familiar words, last spoken in what seemed a lifetime ago, but he pushed the old memory away. "Don't blaspheme?" he said. "Tell me, what is worse, my blaspheming or your marrying a man whom you obviously don't love? Is this your idea of becoming an Englishwoman, Ali?"

"Is that why you're really here?" she asked, frowning. "Because of Matthew?"

"Yes. That's exactly why I'm here, to stop you from this idiocy. Nicholas had the forethought to write me and inform me of Matthew's proposal."

Ali turned away from him. "He had no right," she said, her voice thick. "It is between Matthew and myself, no one else."

"He had every right," Andre countered. "Every right, when both he and Georgia saw you about to make the mistake of a lifetime."

Ali whirled around to face him. "And you? What right do you think you have to come here and tell me what to do?" she cried, her eyes bright with unshed tears. "What has any of it to do with you any longer? What do you care?"

"Damn you!" he said, his hands itching to wring

her neck. "Do you really think I have no interest in what happens to you? Do you think that I picked your blasted scrawny, starved body up off a mountaintop and nursed you back to life to see you end up like this?"

"Like this?" Ali asked coldly. "Is that why you object so strongly to what you see, Andre? Because I am no longer the scrawny child you rescued? Because I have no more need of you?"

"What I object to is that you have become the one thing I cannot bear," he said, truly wanting to throttle her.

"Oh, and what is that? What are you going to accuse me of now?" Ali said, her eyes now not only bright with tears but also flashing with rage. "Perhaps you think I have become a cold fish?"

"You'd have to be that to do what you're planning. But you've become something far worse, by God. You've become a hypocrite, Ali. You're going to marry a man you don't love just for the position he will give you. Can you deny that's true?"

Ali stared at him a long moment, two spots of red flaming on her cheeks. And then she turned and ran across the room, wrenching open the French doors that led to the outside and disappearing into the night.

Andre swore under his breath until he'd exhausted nearly every English oath he could think of and a few French ones as well. What was it about Ali that crawled under his skin, made him lose all semblance of control? She was a child, a silly little empty-headed fool who hadn't one iota of common sense and never had.

He counted to twenty, trying to get a grip on his temper, and then he went after her.

Ali headed straight for the lake, so angry and upset that she could barely think straight. All she wanted was a swim to cool down her body and calm her raging emotions, although she'd have been just as happy to drown herself.

She stopped only to pull off her shoes and throw

them over her shoulder. A few yards later came her dress, and then her stockings and petticoat and drawers. She hated her clothes. They made Andre look at her with disdain, as if she were beneath his contempt. And what had she done to anger him so? Nothing, except to consider a proposal of marriage. People did that every day of the week.

A hypocrite? *He* called her a hypocrite? Ohhh! How she despised him. It was an impossible paradox, loving and hating the same man all at one time, but she seemed to have mastered the art. How dare he accuse her of wanting to marry Matthew for position, the idiot? Andre had no idea—none—of the agonies she'd suffered on his behalf.

She finally reached the water. It took her only a moment to pull the pins out of her hair and let it tumble free. She was about to take off her shift when she heard something behind her. She spun around with a little squeak of fright.

"Did you lose something?" Andre asked, holding up her dress in one hand and her petticoat and drawers in the other. "You don't cover your tracks very well."

He looked at her with an expression she'd never seen before, his eyes reflecting the silver of the moon, but the heat of the sun blazed from them.

"How long have you been standing there?" she asked in alarm.

"Long enough to see that your hair has grown a considerable amount. I never thought to see it touch your hips," he said.

"Go to hell," she said, appalled with herself as she heard the words come out.

"Oh. So Allah no longer holds such a great sway over you? I suppose I shouldn't be surprised about that, either. There seems to have been much that's been lost in the translation between Turkey and England."

Ali glared at him. "You are what has been lost in the translation, Andre. Only you. If I choose to marry Matthew, I will, and nothing you can say or do will make any difference to me. And that does not make me a hypocrite or a cold fish."

"No? Tell me, Ali. Do you think he'll warm your bed? Do you think he'll make you cry out in the night?" Andre said, taking a step toward her.

Ali took a step backward, alarmed by the sudden change of expression on Andre's face. "Wh-what?" she said, her heart beginning to race. It was only then that she realized that she stood nearly naked, the moonlight probably making her shift as good as transparent.

He took one last step and grasped her by the shoulders. "Tell me. When he kisses you, does he make your blood run hot?"

Ali swallowed. Matthew's kiss had made her blood run cold, but just the way Andre looked at her made her feel as if she'd stepped into a furnace.

"Is that how you want to spend the rest of your life, Ali? With someone who hasn't the first idea of what you need or how to give it to you?"

"And you think you know anything about it?" she said, her heart in her throat.

In answer his mouth came down hard on hers, and it was not the tender, chaste kiss that Matthew had given her, but something else entirely, his mouth opening on hers, his breath hot, mingling with hers, his tongue making her senses swim and her knees threaten to buckle.

She held on to him for dear life as he played out the kiss, bruising her mouth, crushing her body against his, the hard length of his erect manhood pressing into her belly.

That brought her to her senses and a sudden rush of fury coursed through her that he would manipulate her so callously, so heartlessly, just to prove a point about Matthew, with no care for her feelings. With all of her strength she tore herself away.

"And you called *me* a hypocrite?" she sobbed, and shoved at him with both hands.

Andre, unprepared, overbalanced. He toppled backward, but not without grabbing her arm as he went.

Ali gasped as he dragged her into the lake with him, the cold dark water submerging her for a moment. And then Andre's arms came around her and lifted her up above it as he found a foothold on the bottom. He pulled her against him, his breath coming hard.

"Damned vixen," he said, rubbing the water from his face with one hand. "What the hell did you go and do that for?"

"Don't be stupid," she said, trying to ignore the heat that radiated from his body to her own, through the cold wet linen of his shirt, through the cold wet cotton of her shift, all the way to her skin. The sensitive erect nubs of her nipples pressed against his hard chest, and she knew he must feel them as surely as she felt the rapid pounding of his heart.

"Ali," he whispered hoarsely. "You can't marry—"

"Don't you dare mention Matthew's name," she hissed furiously, shoving at him again and scrambling up the bank.

It took him four easy strides to reach her. "Oh, no. No," he said, his breath coming fiercely as he caught at her arm and pulled her around to face him. "You're not running away. Not again. Not now. We're going to have this out."

"What?" she said on a sob. "What more is there to say? You think I'm a scheming child who wants nothing more than the empty promise of a title." She pushed the dripping strands of her hair out of her face. "Well, you're wrong, Andre, on both those counts. I'm not a scheming child, and a title means nothing to me. Nothing."

"And you expect me to believe that after the way you've been behaving?" he asked, grasping her arms tightly.

"Yes," she said, tears starting to her eyes.

"For the love of God, how can I? What else have you given me to go on?"

"How can you so easily forget what you and I always were together?" she asked brokenly.

He closed his eyes for a moment. "That's the problem. I haven't forgotten. Not one blasted minute. And

I never thought it possible for anyone to change so much."

"But I haven't changed," Ali said desperately, her heart feeling as if he had just bruised it. "You only want to think I have, and God help me, I don't know why. Do you object to the fact that Matthew wants me when you don't? Or that I learned to speak English? Or even that I finally grew breasts?"

"Don't be a bloody idiot," he said, giving her a hard shake. "Can't you see what's happened to you? Or have five years in England really done so much damage?"

Ali shook her head. She pulled free and turned her back, not wanting him to see the tears that threatened to spill over. "I don't know any longer what you want, what you expect me to be," she said in a muffled voice, wiping her eyes with the back of her hand.

"Will you please stop turning away?" he said, twisting her to face him. "I don't intend to have a conversation with your back. Actually, it's very simple. I only want you to be yourself, not a duplicate of everyone else."

"But I am not like everyone else!" she cried. "Just because I wear European clothes and know how to waltz and can eat with a knife and fork . . ."

And in that moment a conversation she'd had with Andre's father years before in this very spot floated into her mind.

Are you any different if I call you Alexis instead of Ali? I don't mean on the outside, but on the inside where it counts?

And later that same night, also here, she had finally come to peace with herself and the destiny that God had chosen for her.

It all became crystal clear. She hadn't been wrong. Her future with Andre hadn't all been a childish dream. But it had been a dream that couldn't be realized until she'd truly become a woman and understood what that meant. She knew now what it was to hurt as a woman, and she knew now that she could love as a woman, as Andre needed to be loved if he was ever to heal.

She understood that God was giving her this one chance to realize their destiny for both of them. She'd been wrong about Andre not caring. He cared very much. All it took was looking into his stormy face to see that.

Judging by his behavior tonight he realized perfectly well that she was no child. And that was good. Because she knew exactly what she had to do, and she was going to do it with every last shred of love she had. She didn't give two figs whether it suited propriety or not.

She summoned up her courage, then reached down and grabbed the hem of her wet shift, pulling it over her head. She tossed it on the ground and stood before Andre as she had once stood before Allah.

"Ali," Andre said, staring at her in disbelief. "What in the name of God do you think you're doing?"

"I am showing you what I am," she said, her voice shaking. "And what I am has nothing to do with the clothes I wear on my back, or the language I speak, or even the people who gave me life. If you cannot understand that, Andre, then you will never understand me." She bowed her head. "And I will have loved wrongly."

Andre passed a hand over his face as a sharp pain stabbed through him. He wanted to tell her that she didn't know what love was. He wanted to tell her to put her clothes back on, that he was on the verge of doing something outrageous. But the words wouldn't come.

She stepped up to him and took his face between her small hands, her touch burning into him, her wide dark eyes looking into his, not with anger or artifice but with honesty. Her touch nearly undid him, but her eyes—oh, her eyes—they inflicted far worse damage. "Ali," he said, his voice choked. "Ali . . ."

"Yes," she said. "It is me, Ali. I didn't go away, or change into someone else. I only became a woman. Was that really such a crime?"

Andre groaned and lowered her hands from his face. "Please, don't do this to me. I'm only a man, for God's sake."

"I know," she said softly. "And that is how I want you."

He couldn't help himself. He crushed her to him, taking her mouth again, this time not in anger but in need. He played with her lips, brushing her own back and forth against them, stroking them with his tongue, opening her mouth to his and tasting her sweetness.

This time he took care with her, slowly building her response from a smolder into the full-furied blaze that he intuitively knew she was capable of, stoking it with his hands, his tongue, until Ali moaned low in her throat, the sound of her pleasure alone making his heart pound so hard that it hurt nearly as much as his groin.

Andre lifted her in one easy movement and carried her away from the bank, placing her on the mound of clothes he'd dropped. He stripped off his boots and his wet shirt, wondering how in hell he was going to manage to stay in control. He abandoned the question almost immediately as he saw how Ali watched him, her face flushed, her breasts rising and falling with the rapid rhythm of her heartbeat. She was so beautiful, so slight, so delicate . . . so desirable.

He lowered himself over her, his mouth claiming hers again. "Ali," he whispered, already lost, his hands sliding up her soft thighs, over her slim hips, skimming over her smooth abdomen, his palms cupping her small ripe breasts, stroking and kneading, until her back arched under him and she whimpered. He dropped his head and he took one delicate pink nipple in his mouth, suckling it.

Ali cried out in a rush of pleasure, her hips pushing up against his erect penis. He shuddered at the contact, and her hand slipped down between their bodies to touch him through the material of his trousers. A fresh surge of desire coursed through him and he couldn't help pushing up against her palm. It became unbearable as Ali traced the outline of his erection with her fingers.

"Wait," he whispered, taking her hand away and rolling to one side. He stripped his trousers off and came back to her, but this time his hand reached low and slipped between the soft curls at the juncture of her thighs.

Ali moaned as he found her cleft and slid his fingers between the soft folds. God, but she was ready, slick and hot. Sweet, so sweet. His fingers stroked skillfully between her swollen female flesh, drawing a frenzied response from her, her breath hot on his cheeks, her whimpers soft in his ear. He kissed her mouth, her cheeks, her neck, lifting her head to trace the delicate outline of her ear.

He honed in on the little nub of exquisitely sensitive tissue at the apex of her cleft and circled it with one finger. Ali gasped, her fingers clutching in his hair, and she lifted her pelvis, her thighs opening to him.

"Good," he murmured, stretching her, and he pushed one finger inside her. "That's so good. So wet, so tight." He touched her at first shallowly, rhythmically sliding his finger in and out, and then he pushed deeper, gently rocking.

"Ohhhh!" she cried, lifting up against his hand, her entire body straining toward climax. He cupped her in his hand, his thumb lightly touching her erect nub as he pushed his finger into her.

Ali's eyes squeezed shut and her head fell back, her back arching as she cried out, sharp little noises, her tight muscles throbbing convulsively. Andre thought he might just explode himself and he gritted his teeth, trying to keep that from happening.

But the minute he pulled his hand away, Ali's slim fingers wrapped around his wrist, staying him. "No— no!" she whispered. "Don't go. Oh, please?"

It broke the last slender hold he had on control. "Only for a second," he managed to say, his head reeling with her impassioned response, all rationality fleeing in the face of his need and her pleas.

He quickly repositioned himself over her, guiding

himself to her entrance, his tip spreading her wide with a steady pressure as he eased himself into her tight passage, waiting for a moment for her body to adjust to him. God, she felt unbearably good. He couldn't ever remember any woman feeling quite this right. It was as if she'd been made for him.

He thrust his hips forward, sheathing himself in her. Ali sucked in a sudden breath, clutching on to his shoulders, then released it in a long moan. "Andre," she breathed. "Andre."

He rested his forehead against hers for a moment, trying to calm himself. Then he began to move in her, at first slowly, long smooth strokes, pulling out of her nearly completely, easing back, taking his time, intent on pleasuring her. His hands smoothed back and forth over her hips, and he lifted up her knees, moving her closer to him as he gradually increased his rhythm, thrusting hard and fast. Ali met him stroke for stroke, her high little sobs echoing into the night.

"Ali. Ah, God," he whispered, hardly able to catch his breath. It had been a long time since he'd had a woman, but this was unlike anything he'd ever experienced. Ali had the ability to turn him inside out. The touch of her hands moving on his back, his shoulders, his buttocks, the soft heat of her mouth sweeping across his skin, inflamed him to even greater heights as his body moved in hers.

He wanted to bring her to another climax, but he couldn't wait another moment. He rose up and pushed into her, hard, dimly hearing himself cry out as he exploded into her in gut-wrenching spasms.

And then, finally spent, he collapsed, his cheek pressed against her neck as his rough breathing gradually returned to normal. But as it did, so reason also returned, as chilling as a bucket of ice water thrown over him.

"Oh, dear God," he said, lifting his head, horrified at the implications of the act they'd just indulged in. "What have I done?"

She stroked his face. "You don't suppose you've made me a baby, do you?" she asked.

Andre groaned, his heart sinking about as far as it could go. A baby? He might well have. He squeezed his eyes shut. Nothing, nothing excused the mess he'd just made of things. "Ali, I'm sorry, I don't know what happened—"

"Then you are very silly," she said, lightly kissing his mouth. "Even I know what happened, and I'm only an ignorant female. Shall I explain it to you?"

He frowned, wondering how she could possibly be so blithely ignorant to the repercussions of their love-making. He was obviously going to have to explain some things to her. He opened his mouth, then realized he was still buried in her, extremely inappropriate under the circumstances. "You really haven't changed, have you?" he said, slipping out of her.

"What do you think I've been trying to tell you? Oh! What an odd sensation. I think I liked it much better the other way around." She smiled up at him.

Andre rubbed his forehead, wondering how he'd managed to be so monumentally stupid. And then he saw the blood smearing her thighs and it only drove the situation home with more finality. "Do you have any sense of what we've just done?" he asked.

"Yes, of course I know what we've done," she said. "We made love, and I am no longer a virgin." Ali's smile widened. "It was very wonderful, Andre. I don't think you can call me a cold fish ever again."

"Ali. Oh, Christ." He sat up, running his hands through his hair. "This is no joke. You can't marry Matthew, I'm afraid, not after this."

"I can't?" she said, looking not the least concerned.

"No. You can't. I—um . . . I'm afraid you're going to have to marry me."

Ali's eyes filled with a brilliance he'd never seen before, so radiant that it almost blinded him.

"I would be honored to marry you," she said simply. "And it took you long enough to ask."

Chapter 13

Andre splashed cold water on his face, not looking forward in the least to going downstairs and facing Nicholas. How was he going to explain his sudden engagement to Ali? Say that he'd offered himself up in place of Matthew?

He couldn't believe that his entire life had been turned upside down by one impulsive sexual act. He wasn't even prone to that kind of behavior, sexual relief being something he regarded as one of the occasional necessities of life. Furthermore, he'd always been so cautious when he did indulge, taking care to avoid involvement, being equally careful to avoid any chance of leaving a child in his wake. And he avoided virgins like the plague.

Yet in one fell swoop, Ali had managed to undo the habits of his entire adult life. No, he amended. She had managed to undo his entire life, period.

He dried himself off with a towel and shrugged into a clean shirt, then gave his hair a quick brush. Better to get it over with now, before breakfast, he decided, since he didn't have much of an appetite anyway. And he really didn't think he could face Matthew over the table, not when he'd just compromised the woman Matthew had planned to marry.

"Idiot," Andre muttered, pulling on his boots. "Fool." And yet ... he didn't know what he was so upset about. He needed a wife. He hadn't looked forward to finding one. Ali was conveniently there, and they'd always gotten along. Well ... almost always. Last night was a shining example of Ali's uncanny ability to get under his skin.

But that wasn't all bad either, he thought with a faint smile as he pulled on his jacket. In a way it was an unexpected bonus. His impassioned response to her had certainly come as a surprise, as had the ease with which he'd held her afterward, quietly questioning her about what had happened in the years since he'd sent her away, listening with pleasure to her relaxed, amusing replies. Yes. Ali was comfortable, he decided, rather like the fit of an old shoe. So why not?

Still, there was always the possibility that Nicholas might not approve of this match, either, not that there was much Nicholas could do. If Andre had to confess, he would, and he could only hope that Nicholas wouldn't put a gun to his head.

He was offering Ali a duchy, after all. Andre shook his head with amusement as that facet of the situation occurred to him for the first time. Ali, a duchess. Now there was an extraordinary concept.

Andre gave a snort of laughter, and headed down to the library.

"Ah, good morning, Andre," Nicholas said, putting down his pen as Andre came into the room. "Please sit down. I assume you've come to report on your conversation with Ali last night? Did you have any success?"

"In a manner of speaking," Andre said, taking the chair opposite the desk.

"Oh? Well, did you dissuade her from marrying Matthew?"

"I did," Andre replied.

"Good. Excellent. I'm delighted to hear it, although Matthew's bound to be unhappy about it. Never mind, it's for the best. Georgia will be so pleased."

"I'll be pleased about what?" Georgia said, coming into the room. "Good morning, Andre." She examined his face a little too carefully for his liking. "You're looking tired. Did you not sleep well?"

He stood out of courtesy. "Actually, I slept like a log," he said. It was true. He'd slept better than he had in a month. His only problem was that he hadn't gone to bed until four hours before.

"I'm so pleased. The heat doesn't make it easy," Georgia said. "I myself had a terrible time sleeping last night, but I suppose it's old age. Please, sit. Coffee?"

"Thank you," Andre said, not entirely comfortable. There was an undercurrent to Georgia's words that made him uneasy. He took his chair again, but he watched Georgia carefully.

She stirred the sugar into his cup as he liked it, and handed it to him as casually as if it hadn't been eight years since the last time she'd done it.

"Thank you," he said, regarding her with the faintest degree of suspicion. He *knew* Ali was sound asleep. He'd checked with the footman. And he knew Ali had gone straight to bed, since he'd seen her to her door. He dismissed his concern. Ali couldn't have told Georgia anything. He was just on edge, he decided.

"So," Georgia said, pouring her own cup. "What is it that I am to be pleased about?" she repeated.

"Fortunately," Nicholas said in a satisfied tone, "Ali has decided against marrying Matthew. Andre successfully convinced her that it wouldn't be a good idea."

"Oh?" Georgia asked with an arched eyebrow. "And how did you manage that?"

"I ... well," he said, deciding to face the matter straight on, bracing himself for the explosion. "The truth is that I persuaded her to marry me instead."

Nicholas's mouth dropped open. Georgia simply nodded. "Wise, I think," she said calmly.

Andre couldn't believe his ears. He couldn't believe that it was that easy, but he was damned if he was going to tip his hand and let them see his astonishment.

"Yes," he said, equally calmly. "I think it's a good solution. As you pointed out to me yesterday, Ali really is my responsibility, and I've neglected it far too long, leaving her to you. It is time that I take her off your hands."

"Mmm," Georgia said. "It does make sense that you should do that. So. You wish to marry Ali."

"I do," he said, to his surprise meaning it.

"Soon?" she asked.

"Soon enough," he said. "I see no reason for a lengthy engagement. Can it be arranged within, say, a month?"

"A month?" Nicholas said, frowning. "Isn't that a little hasty?"

"Oh, no," Georgia said quickly. "Why wait? I can make all the arrangements easily enough. All you have to do, Nicholas, is write away for a civil license. Both Ali and Andre are Catholic, so that's simple enough. You do plan on being married within the church, Andre?"

"I—well, yes, I suppose," he said, not having considered this aspect. "I suppose it's a hypocritical on my part, but I'd like to make the marriage appear as correct as possible."

"Why wouldn't it appear to be correct?" Nicholas asked, puzzled.

A faint sweat broke out on Andre's brow. "Well, people assume that we only met that one time at the Umbersville ball," he said. "They might wonder why we—why I . . . The marriage might appear precipitous, and naturally I don't wish for the matter of Ali's past to come out," he said, trying very hard to keep a composed demeanor. "I don't want to subject her to a scandal," he finished, feeling ridiculous.

"But there's no reason why your work shouldn't create a middle ground," Nicholas said reasonably. "Ali is Frederick Lacey's daugther, after all, and anyone who would be interested in that sort of thing would know how much you admired Lacey."

"Yes," Andre said thoughtfully. "That's true."

"And on top of that," Nicholas continued, "I am your godfather and Ali is my ward. Neither of those facts is secret. Why should you not have met again here and made a match of it?"

"Why not indeed?" Georgia said, looking at him over the rim of her cup. "But tell me, Andre. Despite all of this talk about responsibility, do you, in fact, love Ali?"

Andre froze. Love? That was a word that didn't even enter into the equation. It couldn't. It never would again, and Georgia ought to damn well know better than to ask.

"Love her?" he said, meeting Georgia's gaze squarely. "No. The truth of the matter is that I need to secure the succession. Ali and I ought to suit well enough, and I am fond of her. Or at least I was, and I'm sure I will be again." God, he was making a hash of the thing.

"At least you're honest," Nicholas said. "Well. I hope she grows on you."

Andre didn't know quite what to say to that, so he said nothing.

"Georgia and I have enjoyed a marriage filled with many years of love and happiness," Nicholas continued, "even though we initially married for convenience rather than love. I have every reason to hope that you will find your way to the same happiness."

"I assume that means you give us your blessing?" Andre asked, not wanting to delve any further into the subject. The way things were going, Genevieve's name was going to pop up at any moment, and he wasn't sure he could handle that. He knew that the only way he was going to get through the situation at all was to be as matter-of-fact as possible, to treat it as a business arrangement, which was really what it was.

"Yes, you have our blessing," Nicholas said, rising. "I have to admit, I'll miss Ali, though. She's given us years of pleasure, but I suppose we couldn't expect to keep her forever."

Georgia came over and kissed his cheek. "Make her happy," she said. "It's all I ask."

"I will do my best," he said. His fingers tightened around the handle of his cup. "I, ah . . . I'd like to take this opportunity to thank you both for all you've done for Ali. I—I was mistaken in what I said yesterday about your turning her into a travesty. You've done a fine job."

"Thank you," Nicholas said gravely, but his eyes held amusement. "I am pleased that you approve of our efforts."

Oh, hell, as long as he was eating humble pie, Andre decided, he might as well go all the way. "I realize that you went far beyond the call of duty in looking after Ali for me, especially given the disagreement we had the last time we met."

Nicholas idly picked the pen off his desk and toyed with it. "Oh, do you mean the time you damned us all to hell for caring enough to try to knock some sense into your head?"

Andre colored. "Perhaps I spoke too strongly," he said in what he considered to be an enormous concession. "My argument is not with you. But please, let us leave it there, for I have no desire to argue with you again."

Nicholas nodded. "Very well. We'll consider it forgotten. I assume this means we won't be seeing your parents at your wedding?"

Andre's eyes glinted steel. "No, you will not. And the subject is closed."

"Naturally," Georgia said. "Well. I suppose I had better find Ali and start making arrangements. It will be nice to see her looking happy for a change."

She placed her coffee cup on the tray near the window and took a moment to look out. "Do you know," she said, her tone reflective, "I've always loved this view above all the others at Ravenswalk. There's something about the stretch of lawn, the glimmer of the lake, that draws one's gaze so compellingly, especially in the moonlight."

Andre nearly dropped his cup.

Georgia turned and smiled at him. "Don't you agree? But I suppose this is no time to be discussing the view. You and Nicholas probably want to go over the marriage settlements and so forth. I'll see you both at lunchtime."

Andre watched her go, feeling like an utter idiot.

* * *

Something loud penetrated the haze of Ali's dream, and she rolled over and stuffed her pillow over her head, unwilling to be snatched away from Andre's embrace. But it came again, persistent, and she realized that someone was knocking at her door. Her eyes flew open as she registered the position of the sun, already high in the sky.

"Oh!" she cried, horrified that she'd slept so late. She was an early riser by habit, and they were bound to think something was wrong. "Come in," she called, quickly pulling her robe on.

"Good morning, darling," Georgia said, entering with a tray. "I told the servants not to disturb you this morning, since you went to bed at such a late hour. I thought you might like some tea and toast." She rested the tray on Ali's lap.

"Thank you," Ali said, wondering curiously how Georgia knew what time she'd gone to bed.

"So. Andre tells us that you have very generously agreed to marry him," Georgia said, settling herself into the armchair near Ali's bed.

Ali looked at her in alarm. "He did?" she said. "But I—that is ..." She gulped. "Oh. Are you angry?"

Georgia laughed. "Not in the least. I think it's wonderful. It's what you've always wanted, isn't it?"

Ali's face lit up like sunshine. "Yes. Oh, yes," she said, hugging the covers to her chest. "I can hardly believe it's true." But then she remembered Matthew, and her heart fell. "Does he know yet? Matthew, I mean?"

"No, darling. Not yet. That's for you to tell him. But that's not what I want to discuss with you."

Ali's gaze examined Georgia's well-loved face, every line, every expression known to her. She knew that Georgia had something important on her mind, and she prepared herself to listen, for Georgia had never once given her bad advice.

"Ali ..." she said, "Nicholas and I have said nothing about the unhappiness and confusion you've felt this last month. We wanted you to feel free to make your own choice." Georgia measured her words carefully. "I believe that in choosing Andre, you've chosen wisely. But you haven't chosen easily. Andre is a wonderful man, but he will be a challenge."

Ali chewed on her lip. "I know," she said. "And I also know that he doesn't love me, if that's what you're worried about."

Georgia's eyebrows rose. "Oh? Did he tell you so?"

"No, not in so many words," Ali said. "But he didn't have to. He still loves Genevieve and he doesn't think he has room in his heart for anyone else."

Georgia was silent for a long moment. Then she released a heavy sigh. "I hadn't realized you knew about Genevieve."

Ali nodded solemnly. "Yes. I have known about her from almost the beginning, although Andre never speaks of her, of course. She is his great tragedy."

Georgia rubbed the side of her mouth. "I suppose you could say that."

"Mmm," Ali said, munching on a piece of toast. "You see," she said through her mouthful, "I had a choice last night. I could either let Andre spend the rest of his life mourning his fairy-child, or I could give myself to him as Allah meant me to do. I thought it was far better to listen to Allah than to Andre."

"I see," Georgia said, looking away for a moment, the corners of her mouth trembling. "Well," she said after a minute, "you've always had an interesting relationship with both God and Andre, and given the frame of mind Andre was in last night, I suspect you listened to the right party."

Ali grinned. "Andre was very upset with me. I pushed him into the lake."

"Did you?" Georgia said absently. "I'm sure he deserved it. Listen, my darling. I know that you love Andre very much and always have. I only want to be sure that you understand what you're taking on."

"Do you mean that I will be a duchess?" Ali asked. "I don't see what difference that makes."

"No, that's not what I meant. I'm sure you'll make

a fine duchess, but I was actually speaking of Andre. You're going to have to be very patient with him."

"Yes, I know," Ali said. "What has happened to him is like what happens to oysters."

"To *oysters*?" Georgia asked, nonplussed.

"Yes." Ali pushed the tray aside and slid out of bed, going to kneel at Georgia's feet and taking Georgia's hands between hers. She looked earnestly up into her face. "Every now and then a grain of sand slips inside the shell that the oyster can't rid itself of," she said.

"Ahh," Georgia said. "I think I see."

"Do you?" It was terribly important to Ali that Georgia understood what she was trying to say. "All I want is for Andre to be happy again. Maybe my love can be like the soothing coating that wraps around the oyster's grain of sand. Maybe it can heal him and protect him, and together we will make something as fine and durable and lustrous as a pearl." She squeezed Georgia's hands tightly. "This is why it doesn't matter so much that Andre doesn't yet love me. It's enough that he cares. A pearl must begin somewhere."

Georgia smiled at Ali with great fondness. "Andre has no idea how lucky he is to have found you," she said, then hesitated. "It is not my place to speak of the past," she continued carefully. "That is Andre's story to tell you when he's ready. But I will say this much: I don't think he could have found anyone better suited to be his wife than you."

Except his fairy-child, Ali thought, her chest squeezing painfully. But she chose to keep her peace, for that was her greatest regret, that even if Andre did learn to love her, he would never be able to love her as he'd loved Genevieve.

"Thank you," Ali said, her throat tight. "You could not have given me a kinder blessing. And I promise that I will look after Andre as best as I know how, now that it's my turn."

"Be happy, Ali. And know that Nicholas and I love you always." She cleared her throat and reached for a handkerchief, wiping her nose. "Now," she said, returning to her usual practical self, "I believe Matthew has been beating a path around the pavilion again. Best if you put him out of his misery before lunch."

Ali swallowed hard, the grim reality of that situation returning. "Yes. Yes, I will," she said.

Georgia turned on her way out. "It will be all right, Ali. You and Matthew were always great friends. I'm sure that's how it will work out in the end."

"Oh, I hope so," she whispered. "I really hope so."

There was nothing worse than breaking someone's heart.

She found Matthew inside the pavilion, his hands folded against his knees, his head bowed. He looked up as she approached, but his eyes held foreboding.

"Alexis," he said, standing. "You came."

"Yes, of course I came," she said, her heart feeling like a shrunken thing in her chest. Treacherous. Mean. She was a hideous monster, treating him like this when he'd been so kind to her, so sweet and loving and unfailingly generous. To know she was about to hurt him so terribly was unforgivable ...

But Matthew, with his infinite grace and innate sweetness, saved her the moment. "It's over, isn't it?" he said, walking toward her. "Don't say anything, Alexis. I can see it on your face. I felt it yesterday afternoon, and I saw it last night."

"Matthew," she said, barely able to get the words out. "You've been such a dear friend to me. You've always been there, always so true. I—I'm sorry ..." She took a deep, shuddering breath. "I'm not the one for you. I will always love you, Matthew, but not as you need to be loved. Not as a wife should love her husband."

He only shook his head. "It's Montcrieff, isn't it? He's done something, said something to dissuade you from our marriage."

Ali met his eyes evenly. "You know how I've always felt about him. Had you and I married, Andre would have been between us forever. I tried to tell you that."

"And I still don't believe it," Matthew said. "We

had a good chance at happiness before he came back. Alexis, love, don't be a fool. You can't really think Montcrieff will offer for you?"

He stood with both hands shoved low on his hips, so masculine, so beautiful in his own way. Ali saw for the very first time how splendid he was, what all the other women had been fluttering about. Perhaps it was because her own senses had finally been awakened that she could see it. But she could only admire him as she might admire a brother. To her own mind, nothing would ever compare to Andre. And oh, how to make Matthew understand?

"Matthew," she said tentatively, feeling her way along as carefully as she might negotiate the edge of a precipice, "as much as I care for you and always will, it would have been a terrible mistake if we'd gone beyond that."

He looked away. "You only say this because that— that damned excuse for a man has swayed you, reminded you of your life before this, before us."

Ali reached up with one hand and touched his shoulder. "No. He didn't sway me. All he did was come home, as I always prayed he would," she said, willing him to hear her, to know that what she was saying was true. "As much as you and I are friends, you only know me for what I have become here. Andre knows my origins, and he doesn't just accept them, he understands them in a way that no one else does."

"Understands them?" Matthew said, the bitterness in his voice causing Ali to cringe. "Do you really think he understands you? My God, he sent you to this country to rot for all he cared. And now he comes back and you fall at his blasted feet like a dog begging to be kicked yet again."

"That's not true," Ali said, piqued by Matthew's unfair assessment. "Far from kicking me, he asked me to marry him. And I accepted."

"You—you what?" Matthew stared at her, his face paling. "No. No, you couldn't have."

"I did," she said more calmly, already regretting her

outburst. "I'm sorry that you're hurt, I truly am. But oh, please, please believe that this is for the best." She held her hands out to him.

Matthew stepped away. "Never. Never. I can see that your mind is made up, but by God, I think you're making the worst mistake of your life."

"No," Ali whispered as he turned on his heel and walked swiftly away. "I've just saved us both from the worst mistake of both our lives. And one day you'll know it, Matthew. One day, pray God, you'll know it."

She took a deep breath, then started toward the house, her face turned toward the future.

Andre's face unfortunately was turned toward a stall box, his attention on the horse inside it when Matthew came storming into the stables.

"Montcrieff?"

The slightest prickling on his spine warned Andre, but not quite in time. As he turned, Matthew's fist flew toward him. He could have deflected the blow easily enough, but instead of ducking or knocking Matthew over with his own fist, he moved into it.

The swing caught him on the underside of his jaw and sent him reeling back against the wall, his head rebounding against the wood. He sank down, his hand cupping his bruised face. There wasn't much he could do about the stars dancing in his eyes.

"Nicely delivered," he managed to say, massaging his jaw, wondering whether it was broken.

"What the *hell* did you do that for?" Matthew asked, shaking his hand and regarding Andre as if he'd just met a madman.

"Call it sheer stupidity," Andre said, struggling to his feet. "Or call it an apology. I don't much care. Christ, you've got one hell of an uppercut." He abruptly sat down again and lowered his head onto his knees. The blood in his mouth was nothing compared to the dizziness in his head.

"Damn you to hell," Matthew shouted.

"Probably already done," Andre replied from the

shelter of his knees. "Now be a good sport and go away."

Matthew frowned. "I—you're not badly hurt, are you?"

Andre managed to look up, a gleam of irony in his eyes. "Nothing I won't survive. Sorry about all this, coz. But then it's nothing you won't survive, either."

Matthew looked as if he might well come at him again, and Andre held up a forestalling arm. "Go on, get out of here before you kill me properly," he said. "I'm not worth a murder charge. Ask anyone but Ali, and she'll probably change her mind within a year or two."

"You had better do right by her," Matthew said, regarding Andre with a peculiar mixture of resentment and admiration. "If nothing else, at least you know how to take a blow like a man."

Andre had to fight a desire to burst into nonsensical laughter. "Thank you," he managed to say with a straight face, saved primarily because his face couldn't move at all. "And I will do my best to do right by Ali. That I swear."

Matthew looked down at him one last time, then turned on his heel and left.

Andre just managed to hang on until Matthew was out of sight before passing out. The very last dim thought that occurred to him as the world spun away was that life with Ali would never be dull.

Chapter 14

Ali looked around the drawing room, which had been commandeered for wedding preparations. Boxes upon boxes of wedding presents were strewn about, each one labeled and readied to be shipped to Sutherby. She imagined Andre had an equal number of boxes strewn about, and probably the same huge pile of correspondence on his desk, mostly letters of congratulations from well-wishers, or those jockeying for an invitation.

Ali was still astonished by the fuss that had ensued once the engagement announcement was placed in the papers, and she was thrilled that today was the last of the preparations. By tomorrow evening, she and Andre would be on their wedding trip with not a single detail to attend to and nothing to think about but each other.

She couldn't wait. She'd missed him terribly over the last month, although she doubted he'd missed her in the least. He'd probably spent the entire month wondering how he'd managed to get himself into such a fix. Ali grinned. Poor, poor Andre.

He'd been so subdued when he'd said good-bye to her, Nicholas and Georgia watching him like a hawk as he kissed her cheek. He told her only that Nicholas would explain the settlement to her, then swiftly left.

No, Andre hadn't been himself at all. He'd behaved more like someone stunned from a bad blow, which she supposed he was.

But at least his two letters since had been friendly and relaxed, and she hoped that meant that he'd adjusted to the situation. Andre had always been nothing if not practical, and since he knew there was no going back, she imagined he'd decided to put the best possible face on their marriage, even if he wasn't awash in love for her.

Ali looked around the room again, wondering if there was anything she'd forgotten in the endless list of things that had to be done. Thank God efficient Hattie had come down to help out, or they all would have been exhausted.

"Well, I think that's it," Hattie said, coming into the room with her checklist. "Your trunks are packed, and all that's left to do is change into traveling clothes."

"I can't believe it's finally over," Ali said. "Hattie, thank you for all you've done."

"Don't be silly," Hattie said. "I wouldn't have missed this for the world. Just think, tomorrow morning and you'll be a duchess."

Ali shook her head. "Sometimes it all seems like a dream. Imagine. Me, a duchess."

"I don't know how you did it, but it's the coup of the decade," Hattie said. "I still don't think you realize how coveted the invitations are."

"I don't know why," Ali said. "People get married all the time."

"Not to dukes, they don't. Lucky, lucky you for having been born a Catholic," Hattie said wistfully. "I think everyone had forgotten Montcrieff's religious affiliation, that he would have to think of the church when he picked a wife."

It was all Ali could do not to laugh. Andre was on precisely the same speaking terms with God as he was with his parents. And that was the one thing that dimmed her joy at her forthcoming wedding, that they would not be there to see their son be married.

It seemed terribly unfair of Andre to behave this way toward them—and so baffling, all this mystery about the past that no one would speak of. She frowned and stared down at the ground, wondering if there was any way that she could find to mend the rift between them. But how, without incurring Andre's wrath?

"Alexis? What's the matter?" Hattie asked. "I didn't mean to imply that Montcrieff only chose you because of your religious faith. I'm sure he finds you very attractive too, and clever and fun. But since he hardly knows you, it only makes sense that it would be a factor."

Ali glanced up. "What?" she said, distracted.

"Oh, dear, are you having an attack of nerves? Brides do, you know, and it's little wonder." Hattie blushed. "Are you, um ... worried about tomorrow night?"

"Tomorrow night?" Ali said, trying to work out what Hattie was talking about. "Oh," she said as the light dawned. "No, not at all."

"Alexis," Hattie said, blushing even more fiercely, "it's very indelicate of me to speak of such things, but do you actually know what happens on your wedding night? You do realize that you must submit to Montcrieff in every respect?"

"Mmm," Ali said happily. "Isn't it wonderful?"

"Wonderful?" Hattie said, horrified. "I think it sounds appalling!"

"Oh, I don't think it can be appalling," Ali said lightly, wishing she could tell Hattie that she knew just how wonderful it was. "Look at Caroline," she said instead. "Do you think she'd blush and squirm the way she does whenever she looks at Langley? I think that whatever he does to her in bed must be heavenly."

Hattie's mouth fell open. "Alexis, you are wicked," she said, looking delighted.

"Why is that wicked? It seems a perfectly natural thing to do, and it's not as if Andre is old and shriveled and has stinking breath."

"But he's practically a stranger," Hattie exclaimed. "Do you really not mind the idea of a stranger touching you like that?"

"I like the way he touches me," Ali said.

"You—you do? I mean, he has?" Curiosity crept

into her voice. "Did he, um . . . did he touch you when he proposed?"

"Do you mean did he press his mouth to mine?" Ali asked innocently.

"Yes—or did he just bow over your hand and murmur all the right things? He seems so cool and collected that I would imagine that would be more his style."

Ali burst into laughter, thinking of exactly how Andre had proposed, stark naked in the moonlight, looking anything but cool and collected. "No, he didn't bow over my hand. And he didn't coolly press his lips anywhere."

"Oh," Hattie said with strong disappointment. "What a pity."

"I don't know," Ali said, considering. "I rather liked being pulled into his arms and kissed as if nothing else in the world existed."

Hattie's eyes widened. "Really?" she whispered. "Oh, Alexis *really*? He did that?"

"Really," Ali said. "He does it very nicely too," she added with enormous understatement. "I know he'll do everything else the same way. Actually, I'm looking forward to it."

Hattie's hand slipped to her mouth and a giggle escaped. "Only you would say such things, Alexis."

"Well, it's true. I never would have agreed to marry Andre if I didn't think we'd be happy together. You must know that my acceptance had nothing to do with his position—I couldn't bear it if that's what you're thinking when I take my vows tomorrow."

Hattie chewed on the tip of her finger, a habit she had when she was about to say something she thought she shouldn't. "Since you brought it up," she said, her tone contrite, "I honestly don't know what to think. I don't mean to imply that you shouldn't marry Montcrieff, but you always said that the reason you never took your suitors seriously was because you were waiting for someone very special." She looked away. "I thought you believed in true love."

Ali, her heart sinking, realized that Hattie had been

keeping her peace all this time, putting a good face on celebrating her friend's good fortune and worrying about her happiness underneath it all. It spoke well to Hattie's devotion that she was taking this last moment to try to dig out the truth. She owed it to Hattie to give her as much of the truth as she could.

"Hattie, do you remember asking me why I was upset after the Umbersville ball?" she said, choosing her words carefully.

"Yes," Hattie said solemnly, her ginger curls bobbing with the earnestness of her reply.

"I couldn't tell you the truth then, but I can now. I *was* upset, very upset. You see, the moment I saw Andre across the room, I knew that he was the special person I'd been waiting for all these years." Ali quite liked the ring of that, and it was the truth, after all.

Hattie's eyes widened. "You did? Oh ... I remember now! You suddenly turned pale. And—and then you looked so odd when he came up to be introduced. Did you really and truly know in your heart of hearts that he was the one?"

"I really and truly knew in my heart of hearts. But then when we danced I inadvertently did something to anger him, something foolish and childish," Ali said, also truthfully. "I thought I had ruined everything. And then he came to Ravenswalk, and I was so grateful to be given another chance."

"Do you mean he didn't come down to propose?" Hattie said, astonished.

Ali shook her head. "He came down for something else altogether. But when we spent some time together, he realized that he had a strong attraction to me, as I had to him. And so he asked Nicholas for my hand." Ali felt very satisfied with her new version of events, which was more a story of careful elimination than falsehood, but carried a nice emotional punch.

"Oh," Hattie said breathlessly, "oh, Ali, how absolutely divine! So it really is a romance? But why haven't you said anything before this? You made it all sound so businesslike."

"I—I wasn't sure you'd believe me. It seems so improbable, I know, and it's probably better if the rest of the world does consider it a business arrangement. But you see," she said, crossing the room and giving Hattie a quick hug, "tomorrow, when I swear to love and honor and obey him, I will mean it with all my heart, each and every vow."

Hattie looked as if she might swoon. "I wish my true love would come along for me," she said faintly. "It is all I want in life."

"Shall I tell you something?" Ali said, hoping she wasn't speaking prematurely. "The way Matthew has been spending so much time with you of late makes me think love might be right around the corner."

Hattie colored to the roots of her ginger hair. "Don't be absurd," she said. "He only sees me as a friend who is of comfort to him while he recovers from his heartbreak. You're the one he loves, even if he does hardly speak to you."

"If that's what you think, then you're blind, Hattie Charleton, for Matthew never loved me. I swear to you, he has yet to know what real love is, the kind that sustains a marriage. I think that if he's lucky, he'll find it in you."

Hattie looked down at the ground, twisting her ever-present handkerchief between her hands. "I am plain," she said, her voice low.

"You are no more plain than I am," Ali said impatiently. "You are no beauty like Caroline, it is true, but neither am I. And as much as I love Caroline, I will tell you that you have more personality and certainly more intelligence in your little finger than Caroline possesses in her entire body. So there."

Hattie peeped up at her with a shy smile. "Do you really mean it?" she asked.

"Don't be silly. Of course I do. Have you ever known me to say anything I don't mean?"

"No ... I suppose not. Oh, Alexis, do you really think there's a chance? I care for Matthew so." She blushed again.

Ali's heart went out to her in sympathy. "I know

you do. And if I didn't think there was a good chance, I wouldn't have said anything. You're exactly what Matthew needs; you're strong and solid and dependable, and you have a heart of gold."

"And ginger hair and freckles to match," she said despondently. "And I sneeze constantly."

"I don't know what is wrong with ginger hair and freckles, and furthermore, when I consult with Andre I'm sure he can tell me what to do for your sensitivities."

Hattie looked perplexed. "What in heaven's name makes you think he'd know anything about those?"

"Well . . ." Ali said, realizing that she'd said more than she ought to have, "being a scholar he must know about everything, so he's bound to know something or someone who can help."

Hattie, bewildered, nodded. "It would be nice if he did. No one, including all the physicians Papa has consulted, has come up with anything helpful. I'm so tired of sneezing and sniffling and itching all the time."

"We shall see," Ali said. "But I think it's probably nearly time to leave. We should change our clothes, and I must find Sherifay. I hope she won't be too lonely while I'm gone, but Nicholas promised to keep her happy until we've returned from our wedding trip and she can be brought to Sutherby."

Hattie, who sneezed at the very idea of Sherifay, vigorously rubbed her nose, then returned to her efficient self and immediately set about making the final arrangements, leaving Ali to take an hour to herself.

She spent it saying good-bye.

To Ali's great surprise, Andre was waiting at the station as the train pulled in, his hat in his hands, the wind ruffling his dark hair. Just the sight of him gave her a rush of joy, and she could barely wait for the train to come to a halt. Although she allowed the porter to help her down the steps, she abandoned all restraint the moment her feet touched the ground.

"Andre!" She flew across the platform, oblivious to

the amused glances of the onlookers, and flung herself into his arms.

"Ali," he said, his hands going around her back, steadying them both. "Well, hello."

She raised her face and gazed up at him. "Oh, it's so good to see you. I missed you."

"It's good to see you too," he said, the warmth in his eyes telling her that he meant it.

"Do you mean you haven't come to cry off?" She tucked her fingers in the lapels of his jacket. "I can't think why else you came to meet the train unless it was to put me back on it."

Andre smiled down at her. "Actually, I came to escort you personally to your new home. I thought you might need some moral support—I didn't want the shock of Sutherby to send you running in the opposite direction."

"Would you have wept bitter tears if it had?" she asked, cocking her head.

"I don't generally weep, but I would have been sorely disappointed," he said, setting her away from him. "And as much as I loathe decorum, I think we had better observe it for at least the next twenty hours or so. We didn't spend the full month apart to go and slip up now. Do try to behave like a timid bride, will you, at least once we get to Sutherby?"

Ali grinned. "All right. I can wait another twenty hours to show you how I really feel."

"If that greeting just now was anything to go by, I have a fair idea of what's ahead," he said with a light laugh. "But that's what I mean. Don't forget that we're barely supposed to know each other." He lifted her gloved hand to his lips and placed a kiss on its back. "Just this much and not a millimeter more."

He glanced at her over her fingers, the heated expression in his eyes implying that he hadn't forgotten a millimeter of what he did know, and Ali drew in a sharp breath.

Andre flashed her a wicked smile. "Exactly. Now let me greet everyone and see them to the carriages. You and I are going alone in mine. We need some time to talk before we enter the madhouse. And I warn you, I don't exaggerate."

"Oh," she said breezily, "I'm not worried."

He raised an eybrow. "Then you're a braver soul than I. Sutherby feels like an occupied country."

He strode off across the platform, leaving Ali with a heavy longing that throbbed deep in her abdomen and echoed in her heart.

Ali stared as the carriage rattled through the gates of Sutherby. The Elizabethan house was enormous, a vast, imposing square of stone capped by balustrades, domed turrets, and chimneys. It was easily twice the size of Ravenswalk, which was nothing modest, and the lawn that stretched around it could have accommodated an entire cavalry regiment. The reality of the situation suddenly hit her with enough force to jolt her entire being.

"Andre . . ." she breathed. "It's—it's huge." She ran her tongue over her bottom lip, overwhelmed with unexpected panic.

"Fit for a great pasha?" he asked with amusement from his seat across from her.

"Fit for a very great pasha," she said shakily, pressing her hands against her cheeks. "But how am I to run a house this size?"

"The same way you ran our camp. Like a tyrant. The only difference is that you will be my wife. Which reminds me." He reached into his pocket and pulled out a little box. "Here is your engagement ring."

Ali gasped as he opened the box. Inside was the most enormous emerald she'd ever seen, square cut, flashing with green fire. "Andre," she choked. "It's almost as big as your house."

"Fit for my duchess," he said, slipping it onto her finger. "What's the matter, Ali? I thought you liked jewels and castles and all that sort of thing, and now you shall have them."

His words, so casually spoken, startled her. She tore her gaze away from the ring and gave him a searching look. "You don't think that's why I'm marrying you, do you? So that I can be a duchess and be given jewels and live in a big house?"

The smile faded from his face. "No," he said softly. "I don't."

Ali nodded, but the question that had been paramount on her mind for all of the last month still burned at her. She knew this would be her last opportunity to ask it before they were married, but it took all of her courage to bring it to her tongue.

"Andre," she said hesitantly, but forging ahead anyway, determined to have honesty between them. "We have talked of the dinner tonight, and who will be there, and the seating arrangements. We have talked of the details of the wedding tomorrow, and the breakfast to follow, and we have even talked of Mrs. Grimes the dragon housekeeper and Pennyswell the butler, and how they will all be lined up to greet me." She paused.

"But we have not talked of the arrangement between the two of us, is that it?" he said, as if he'd read her mind.

Ali stared down at her hands, the ring flashing in the sunlight. "I—I only wish to know how you'd like for us to go on."

"Ali," he said, his voice gentle. "I know that you think you love me, and I'm honored that you do, although I believe you to be completely misguided."

Ali's head snapped up and she glared at him. "I am not misguided in the least," she said. "I do love you."

"All right," he said, holding his hands up to forestall her. "I think you must, or you'd never be so foolish as to marry me. But I have to be honest with you." He leaned forward and took both her hands in his. "I told you long ago that I had no heart, or at least not one worth anything. It would be wrong of me to pretend to love you, or at least to love you as you might wish, and for that I'm deeply sorry. But we are friends, are we not?"

Her eyes crept up to meet his steady gaze. "Yes," she murmured, willing away tears, for his words, as much as she'd expected them, still tore at her soul. "We have always been friends, I think. Good friends."

"Yes. And I hope we always will be. We know each other fairly well, although five years is a long time to be apart, and we have things to learn about each other—mostly on my part, I think. It hasn't been easy adjusting to all the changes in you."

"But you don't mind those changes anymore, do you? At least you didn't seem to mind the last time we were together."

"Ali, ever blunt," he said with amusement. "No, I don't mind, not in the least. I don't regret what happened between us." He stroked her fingers, his touch firm but sensual at the same time. "I hope you don't regret it either."

Ali's blush covered her from head to toe. "No," she murmured. "Not one minute of it. It was right, Andre. But I have worried that you felt forced to marry me because of that." She pulled her hands from his and clenched them together. "We didn't make a baby after all."

He chucked her under the chin. "I don't feel forced to marry you, and furthermore, I assumed you would have told me if you were pregnant."

"You don't mind that I'm not?" she asked.

"Good God, no. It's a relief. We have enough to deal with as it is without people wondering about a baby arriving in eight months."

"I suppose so," she said. "But I do want to make you a son as soon as I can."

"There will be plenty of time for that after our wedding, although I promise you that when I make love to you, the last thing on my mind is going to be babies."

Ali's mouth curved up in a provocative smile at the thought of being back in Andre's arms and she gazed at him, thinking of the exquisite pleasure they were going to share.

A strangled sound emerged from his throat. "For God's sake," he said hoarsely, "don't look at me like that—or at least not until I have you where I can do something about it."

He glanced out the window. "We're arriving, so let me just say this much, since I probably won't get another chance. I'm very fond of you, Ali, and I intend to make you a good husband and a faithful one. Even if I can't love you, I swear I will do nothing to dishonor you."

Ali didn't answer. She couldn't, for fear of bursting into wild laughter. Andre looked so earnest, as were his words, but the stiff bulge that pushed against the front of his trousers put the whole situation into perspective.

Andre thought he was going to jump out of his skin at dinner. Guests had been arriving at Sutherby for days, and he'd been marginally able to cope with that, but now that Ali was here, the situation had become unendurable.

If Joseph-Jean had showed up he might have found it easier, but there hadn't been a single word from him, and that cut badly. Jo-Jean obviously didn't approve of the latest development concerning Ali, and Andre couldn't really blame him.

He stared into his pudding, thinking that if he could have his druthers, he'd clear everyone out of the house, with the exception of Ali, of course. Ali he would march straight up the stairs to the bedroom. No—wrong thought, he realized as his groin tightened yet again. God, how he wanted her. He couldn't believe how badly.

He'd gone to the station, thinking to reassure her, to make her feel welcome, for he'd been fairly sure that she'd be overwhelmed. But instead, she had bowled him over with her sweet and uncontrived greeting, so reminiscent of the old Ali. What was new was his immediate and intensely physical reaction to her, and he didn't seem to have much control over it.

He lifted his head and gazed at Ali yet again down the interminable length of table. He'd been impressed with the way she'd greeted the staff who had assembled outside the house to meet her, charming even Mrs. Grimes. Pennyswell had looked as if he wanted to fall at her feet in adoration. And tonight she was handling herself as if she were in her element.

Well, almost. It was more as if Ali had changed the element to suit herself, since at Ali's end of the long table everyone was in fits of laughter.

Watching her, Andre had a strong flashback of Xanthos, Ali sitting by a campfire, telling ridiculous stories, reducing the Yourooks to the same helpless state of mirth. Lord, it would have been dismal tonight without her. The last few days had been hell. And yet Ali was like a beam of sunshine, cutting through the gloom, bringing her own particular brand of originality to the usual dull mix.

"A little more attention to the blancmange and a little less to your bride-to-be might be in order. You look like a stallion sniffing out a mare in heat."

Andre's gaze snapped over Georgia who sat at his right, settling directly on Nicholas. "I beg your pardon?"

"Just a suggestion." Nicholas only smiled and returned his attention to his pudding, leaving Andre with no reply, but hoping to God that his feelings weren't as obvious to anyone else. Here he'd been thinking that he'd kept himself carefully under wraps. It horrified him that anyone else might have divined his thoughts, especially Matthew, who had been watching his every move all night. The last thing he needed was another blow to his jaw.

He did exactly as Nicholas suggested and returned to staring at his pudding. Fifteen hours and counting.

"For the love of God, what happened to you? I thought you meant to abandon me to my fate," Andre said, ushering Joseph-Jean into the library. It was late, but he didn't care, and he hoped Jo-Jean didn't either.

"I only received your letter three days ago. I was in Paris."

He waited until Jo-Jean had been given a cigar and a glass of cognac before he settled back in his chair, trying to calm his frazzled nerves. He thanked God for the inviolate peace of the library.

"Thank you for coming," he said, the moment the servants had melted away. "I realize it was a great deal to ask."

"Not at all," Joseph-Jean said. "I've been curious on a number of counts. So," he said, gazing around. "This is Sutherby."

"Yes. A bloody hellhole, despite outward appearances," Andre replied, then shrugged. "Never mind. It's not worth complaining about. The assembled guests seem duly impressed."

"Where's Ali?" Joseph-Jean asked. "I was hoping to see her before the wedding tomorrow."

"No chance of that, I'm afraid," Andre said. "She's gone to bed. Georgia ushered her off a good hour ago. Something about brides needing their sleep. So tell me—what were you doing in Paris?"

Joseph-Jean gazed down into his glass. "I was there on Saint-Simon business. I've taken a job in the winery, feeling that since your father provided my entire education, I might do something to pay him back." He looked up. "The duke is well, in case you were wondering."

Andre blinked in surprise at both Jo-Jean's cool tone and also the casual way he had just tossed the forbidden subject of Andre's father into the conversation. "Actually, I wasn't wondering," he said curtly.

"Oh. Too bad. He asked about you, naturally. I said that I assumed you were well, but perhaps suffering from a spot of brain fever."

Andre's fingers tightened on the glass. "Brain fever?" he asked, seeing that they were going to come right down to it.

"Yes. Brain fever. Amazingly enough, your father was sympathetic. He seemed to think you'd recover. Eventually."

Andre steeled himself against the surge of anger any mention of his father brought. "My father's opinion is of no concern to me," he said tightly. "And I'd thank you to leave the subject alone. What is this about, Jo-Jean? You came in here like a blast of cold air and the climate is not growing any warmer."

"Forgive me, but as Ali once said, you can be remarkably stupid for such a smart man," Joseph-Jean said.

Andre put his glass down and stood, walking over to the bookshelves. He carefully ran his finger along the leather spines, his head bowed for a moment. "Do you know," he said very softly, "when I spent my years at Oxford, and you were at the Beaux-Arts in Paris, I never once felt a distance between us. You were the only person I didn't feel distanced from in the years after—in the years we spent in Asia Minor. And yet tonight, of all nights, I feel that distance acutely." He turned and met Joseph-Jean's eyes. "Why is this?"

"Do you honestly not know?" Joseph-Jean said. "Ah, well. As I said, sometimes you can be incredibly stupid, but we'll leave it there. Maybe I should at least tell you that your parents approve of your marriage, since you couldn't possibly know that for yourself."

Andre rubbed his forehead, then sighed. "You know I could care less what my parents think. I have to assume that it is you who disapproves of the marriage, which is why you're behaving in this absurd fashion."

"What makes you think I disapprove?" Joseph-Jean asked, swirling his cognac around in his glass.

Because you think I'm betraying Genevieve's memory. Because my damned parents didn't approve of that marriage, but they approve of this one, and it annoys you. Of course they would approve. Ali might have been raised by Yourooks, but she still has acceptable bloodlines.

But although it cost him, he held his peace. "Because while everyone else thinks the marriage and Ali are both perfectly proper, you know the truth," Andre said instead.

Joseph-Jean puffed thoughtfully for a moment, his legs stretched out before him, his jacket open, his neckcloth loosened. "Yes. I do know the truth. And you know how much I have always cared for Ali."

"Ali as a child, yes. Ali as a wild Turk, yes. But Ali

as my wife? Somehow I don't see you accepting that so easily, for a number of reasons." He watched Jo-Jean carefully for his reaction, the subject of Genevieve hanging between them.

To his great surprise Joseph-Jean grinned lazily. "Mmmm. I have to confess, I haven't seen Ali in a number of years, so it's not easy to visualize her as she must be now. But I'm sure you have your reasons for wanting to marry her."

"Trust me," Andre said dryly. "Once you see her, you'll understand better. Ali comes with all the trimmings."

"Ah. Well, that's good," Joseph-Jean said, raising his glass in a toast, further baffling Andre. "I thought she must have some trimmings by now. But I must confess, I've been wondering how this all came about. You were extremely vague in your letter." He sipped his cognac and savored the taste. "Did you feel the need to lay claim to her, or perhaps to rescue her from her present situation?"

Andre scrubbed his hands through his hair, entirely unclear on the situation himself, as much as he'd tried to puzzle it out over the last month. Taking Ali's virginity was one very good reason. Needing a wife was another. It was the vast gray area in between that confused him.

"To tell you the truth," he said, "marriage was the furthest thing from my mind when I met her again. And my God, that came as a shock, Jo-Jean."

"Oh?" Joseph-Jean asked mildly.

"Well, yes. She's ... changed. Grown up, you know. In a manner of speaking. Don't mistake me—I'm not in love with her. But she has become very attractive. Beautiful, actually," he added.

Joseph-Jean took a moment to absorb this piece of information. "I see," he said after a moment. "And it was at this point that you decided that Ali would make a convenient wife."

"No," he said in frustration, pulling open his neckcloth and taking a large swallow of the fiery cognac. "I was left with no choice." Andre felt the back of his neck growing hot, but he desperately needed Joseph-Jean to understand that he hadn't betrayed his vow to Genevieve, that his attraction to Ali was primarily physical.

"No choice?" Joseph-Jean asked, his gaze sharp on Andre's face. "What do you mean? Nothing came out, did it?"

Andre couldn't help grinning. "Well . . . in a manner of speaking it did." He rubbed the corner of his mouth. "If you really must know, the truth of the matter is that Ali compromised me."

Joseph-Jean stared at him for a long moment, then lowered his face into his hands with a smothered laugh. Within another minute his shoulders were shaking so hard that he nearly tumbled off his chair. He finally managed to collect himself long enough to look up. "She did? Truly? Oh, merciful Lord above. Ali. Only Ali. Ha!" He fell back into hysterics.

Andre walked over to the window, trying very hard to maintain some sense of decorum in the face of his own stupidity. He felt like a complete idiot. But when he glanced over his shoulder, it was only to see Joseph-Jean wheezing wildly, tears pouring down his cheeks.

It was too much for Andre. The absurdity hit all at once, and he sank onto the floor, tears of laughter streaming down his own face. "I—I swear to God, that's how it happened," he choked. "She took all her clothes off to prove a point, and I—I was unable to help myself."

Jo-Jean doubled over. "Ah, no. Stop. Please stop."

"Well," Andre said, wiping his eyes, "maybe I could have if she'd asked me to, but she did just the opposite."

"Oh my God." Joseph-Jean groaned, grabbing his sides. "My ribs. Ah Lord, my ribs."

Andre wiped his eyes again. "So here we are, and God help me, I really can't find a thing to complain about. It's a good thing we're getting married tomorrow, for I swear, it's everything I can do to keep my hands off her."

"Ali. You can't keep your hands off Ali," Joseph-Jean said, slowly straightening, his hands clutching his tender stomach. "This um—oh, how to be tasteful? In Turkey you didn't have this alarming physical attraction, did you? I mean, all those months sharing a tent?"

"Jo-Jean!" Andre said, grinning hugely. "Certainly not. Don't you think I would have discovered the truth of the matter long before I did, if that had been the case?"

"I only thought I'd ask," Jo-Jean said, his grin matching Andre's. "You must understand, this is hard to imagine."

"Yes," Andre agreed. "I know it's hard to imagine, but I swear to you, the girl sets my blood on fire. Who ever would have thought it? Scrawny little Ali . . ."

Before they knew it, they were back in the long summer of 1864, the year that Ali had first come into their lives.

The soft, pale light of early morning streamed through the window, and Ali came instantly awake, knowing in every fiber of her being that this was the day she had been waiting for since God had left her on a mountaintop for Andre to find her.

She slid out of bed and pulled on a simple dress, tied her hair back with a ribbon, then crept out of her room, down one branch of the double staircase, and padded across the vast marble hallway, a mission on her mind.

Only a housemaid was about, busily cleaning the floor. She saw Ali and started, then clambered to her feet. Ali smiled and put her finger to her lips, and in another minute she had safely made it through the front door undetected by anyone else. She ran lightly down the steps and followed the path across the lawn to the fifteenth-century chapel with its high leaded windows, where she was to be married in only a few hours.

The door creaked slightly as she pulled it open and it took her eyes a moment to adjust to the dim light.

The chapel had already been prepared for the wedding. Flowers decked the altar, and the ends of each pew had also been decorated with more of the same. She went directly up to the altar rail and knelt.

"I wanted to say thank you, God," she whispered. "Thank you for giving me to Andre. I will love him with all my heart and soul, always, and I will be a good wife, and do everything in my power to make him happy." She gazed up at the Cross. "But if it's not too much to ask, do You think You might help Andre to love me just a little? It would be so nice if he could. And perhaps You could help him find his way back to loving his parents too?"

She said a quick Hail Mary for luck and rose, turning to leave, but stopped in surprise as a man moved out of the shadows by the door.

"Having one of your endless conversations with Allah?" he asked, walking toward her.

Her eyes widened in disbelief. "Jo-Jean!" she cried. "Oh, Jo-Jean, I can't believe it! When did you arrive?"

She ran toward him, and he caught her up in a hug, then stepped away, holding her by the shoulders and looking her up and down with a smile. "I got in late last night. So. Everything I've heard is true. You've grown into a beauty, Ali."

"I have?" she said, her face lighting up with pleasure. "Do you *really* think so, or are you just being kind?"

His blue eyes sparked with amusement. "I really think so. Andre's parents told me as much, and Andre himself said the same last night."

Ali looked at him suspiciously. "He did?"

"He did indeed. I think you're going to make him very happy, Ali. I couldn't be more pleased."

"Oh," Ali said, flushing with pleasure. "Oh, Jo-Jean, that's the nicest wedding present you could have given me."

"I don't know about that. Actually, I followed you down here because I have something else for you, and I needed to give it to you privately. Come over here."

He led her to a pew and sat down next to her, looking around the chapel for a moment. "Did you know that Andre's parents were married here?"

"They were?" she said with surprise. "I thought they'd been married at Saint-Simon."

"No, here in this very chapel. The duchess asked me to tell you that, and to give you her love. And the duke asked me to give you this." He reached into his pocket and pulled out an envelope. "They came to Paris to deliver this and two other things so that I might bring them to you to have on your wedding day."

She took the envelope and opened it, unfolding a letter written in Pascal's lovely flowing script.

My dearest Ali,

Lily and I wish with all our hearts that we could be with you both today, but know that we will be with you in spirit. We are so very happy that you are to become Andre's wife and our daughter.

Look after him, dearest one. Do not worry for us. As you once said, God will return him to his proper place when the time is right. Love him well, for he needs that above all else.

We send our love and our blessing to you both. Joseph-Jean has a wedding present for you from Lily, which I hope you will wear in health and happiness. I also have a smaller present for you. I think you will understand.

He had signed it simply "Pascal."

"He is a very good man," Ali said, wiping her eyes with the back of her hand.

"Yes," Joseph-Jean said. "He is. It's a shame Andre doesn't see it that way. I can't tell you how angry it makes me that he continues to turn his back—ah, well," he said, cutting himself off abruptly. "It's his wedding day, and yours, and we should concentrate on happiness." He sighed, then reached inside his breast pocket. "These are from the duchess. She hopes that you will wear them today." He handed Ali a cloth pouch.

Ali opened the strings and tipped the pouch upside down. Out tumbled a triple strand of perfectly matched, milky-white pearls. She caught her breath in wonder. "Oh ... oh, Jo-Jean, look at them. They're beautiful!"

"They are indeed. You will do them honor, Ali."

She smiled at him. "Thank you."

"I mean it most sincerely." Finally he handed her a little packet wrapped in ribbon. "From the duke."

She undid the ribbon and folded the paper back. "Oh—oh, Jo-Jean," she said, covering her face with her hands for a moment as hot tears started to her eyes. She thought her heart might break with love. "He—he remembered," she said, her voice choked.

For lying nestled in the paper was a gold chain, and suspended from the chain was a golden angel that held a tiny diamond lily in its hands, the symbol of the Archangel Gabriel.

"He had it made for you."

"Did he?" Ali said, blinking back her tears. "Oh, Jo-Jean, you have no idea ..."

"How appropriate that he chose to give you an angel," Joseph-Jean murmured.

Ali looked at him with surprise. "But how could you know about that day?"

"What day? I only meant that the duke has an interesting, um ... attachment to angels. What are you talking about?"

"The day I first met Pascal. We had a long talk, and he taught me something very important about God and acceptance and myself. It meant a great deal to me." She held the chain out. "Please. Would you put it on me? I would like to wear it close to my heart." She turned her back to him, and he fastened the clasp around her neck.

"Thank you," she said, looking down at the little Gabriel. "I know what you mean about Pascal liking angels. He says his favorite is Rafael, but I suppose that's because Rafael is the archangel of healing, and Pascal is a physician. But you must know that."

Joseph-Jean gave her a long look. "Yes," he said.

"I do know that. He not only delivered me, he also saved my life."

Ali's hand flew to her mouth. "He did? Oh, Jo-Jean, how wonderful! He never said, even though he's often spoken of how fond he is of you."

"He wouldn't say," Jo-Jean replied. "He's never even spoken of it to me. But it is the truth. And now I think you had better get back to the house before you're discovered missing and everyone starts to think you've bolted."

Ali slipped her arms around Joseph-Jean's back and gave him a hug, then tenderly kissed his cheek. "I am so glad you could be here today. It's wonderful to see you again."

He smiled. "This I wouldn't have missed for the world. I'll see you here a little later, Ali. You will make a lovely bride. And I look forward to being formally introduced to you after the wedding. It will be a trial, trying to keep a straight face."

"I know. I'm already having great difficulty pretending to know Andre only slightly. I nearly died at dinner last night. I couldn't look at him without wanting to burst into laughter, so I tried not to look at him at all." She shook her head. "but you should have seen him. Do you know that strained expression he has, the one that makes him look constipated?"

"Of course," Joseph-Jean said, choking back a laugh.

"He barely spoke to anyone. It's no wonder they used to call him the black marquess if that's how he conducted himself," she said, rolling her eyes. "Anyway, Georgia said it all worked out, because he behaved exactly as a nervous bridegroom ought, and I behaved like a shy bride, and no one is the wiser."

Joseph-Jean took her hand between both of his. "It's amazing, you know. You haven't changed an iota, not really. Here we are, sitting in a chapel in England, you now a beautiful young woman about to marry my dearest friend, yet I feel as if it's exactly like old times."

Ali smiled softly. "Just another adventure, Jo-Jean.

But this one will carry me through my entire life." A spark of mischief leapt into her eyes. "At least now I can go back to giving Andre baths without anyone to object. Who is going to argue with a duchess?"

"You really haven't changed, have you?" Joseph-Jean said. "God help England."

She scooped up her pearls and her letter and jumped to her feet with a grin. "My first command as a duchess is going to be that from now on, everyone must ride camels in Hyde Park."

"Maybe you should first consult with the queen," Joseph-Jean said dryly.

"Oh," Ali said with a toss of her head, "she's in perfect agreement." She dashed out the door.

Ali made it back to her room with no one the wiser. She washed, she ate, she dressed, her thoughts centered on nothing but Andre and the life that she would lead with him from this day forth. Hattie's stream of chatter punctuated by sniffs and sneezes went unheeded.

She did register Georgia's warm hug and whispered words of love and encouragement as Georgia left for the chapel. Hattie pressed something into her hand, which she only later realized was Hattie's lucky silver six-penny piece. That alone nearly brought her to tears. She tucked it inside her bouquet of roses, knowing just what she wanted to do with it. Lily's strands of pearls hung about her neck, and Pascal's angel rested safely inside her dress.

Nicholas's warm hand held hers in reassurance as they walked down the flower-strewn path to the chapel. All she could think of was that inside—oh, inside waiting for her was Andre.

As she adjusted the wide satin skirt of her wedding dress, let Hattie pull the long lace veil just so, she thought only of how she had loved Andre for so long, and now Allah was finally, but *finally* giving her to him properly. Goodness, she'd been patient.

And now it was time. The door opened and Ali walked into the chapel on Nicholas's arm. Andre stood at the altar, tall and straight, looking directly at her, his eyes not guarded but instead clear and filled with welcome.

Ali didn't realize it, but she wore a smile of such pure happiness and simple love as she walked into the chapel that it shocked half of polite society when the story circulated for months after. The other part of the shocking story was that the black duke's face reflected an extraordinary amount of pleasure and affection as they exchanged their vows.

But most shocking of all, everyone agreed in hushed tones, was the kiss they exchanged at the end of the ceremony. It could only be called unusually heated, despite the overt restraint.

And horror of horrors, the best man laughed.

Chapter 15

Ali slipped out into the garden, desperate for a moment of peace. Even though the breakfast was over, the party was not, and she and Andre still hadn't had a minute to themselves. She looked down at the plain slim band on her finger, thinking it the most beautiful thing she'd ever seen, a symbol not only of marriage, but of the full circle she and Andre had made back to each other.

She rubbed her forefinger lovingly over the rich gold, remembering the moment that Andre had slid the ring onto her finger, his touch firm but gentle, his voice so deep, so beautiful. *With this ring, I thee wed ...* They were words she would treasure forever—she particularly liked the part about his body worshiping hers. Ali smiled, thinking of the kiss he'd bestowed on her. There'd been nothing noncommittal about that.

"Alexis ... may I have a quick word with you?"

Ali spun around to find Matthew standing behind her, and her heart sank. "Yes, of course," she said. "But I—I hope you can find it in your heart to wish me happiness, Matthew, because I don't think I could bear it if you can't."

"That is what I wanted to say. I ... Alexis, I've been a fool. It took watching you at the altar today to realize that you were right about us. It wouldn't have worked." He rubbed his neck. "I was holding on to a childhood fantasy, and I believed you were doing the same with Montcrieff. But I see that what you have with him is real."

"Oh, Matthew, thank you for understanding," she

said with a sigh of relief. "That means a great deal to me."

"There is something about the two of you together that ... well, you just seem to belong to each other. I—that's all. Excuse me, I must get back. I promised to bring Hattie a glass of champagne."

"Of course." Ali stood on her tiptoes and kissed his cheek. "Friends?"

"Friends," he agreed.

Ali grinned. "Good. Then take some friendly advice. Don't ignore what's right under your nose."

Matthew nodded, but looked puzzled nonetheless, and Ali shoved his chest. "Go on. Go fetch Hattie some champagne."

He took a step backward to regain his balance, and nearly bumped into Andre, who came into the garden just at that moment.

"You're not harassing my wife, I hope?" Andre said calmly enough, but Ali thought he looked surprisingly dangerous.

Matthew put out his hand. "Just the opposite. My apologies, Montcrieff."

Andre, surprised, shook his hand. "I accept them. You're safer when you're feeling tame. And please, will you call me Andre? We are family, after all."

Matthew smiled faintly. "I suppose we are. Well. Best of luck to you both." He headed back to the house.

Andre turned to Ali. "Thank God for a moment alone. And thank God I can now do this with impunity." He pulled her into his arms and lowered his head, taking Ali's mouth in a fevered kiss.

She slipped her arms around his neck, her blood racing in her veins as his tongue found hers and his kiss deepened until she shook with desire.

"Oh, no, they're at it again. That performance in the church wasn't enough?"

Ali sprang away from Andre, belatedly realizing that the words had been spoken in Turkish and that Joseph-Jean was grinning at her. "You beast," she said.

"Bugger off," Andre said more succinctly, pulling her back into his arms.

"Actually, Georgia sent me to find you. She says it's time for Ali to change into traveling clothes. But I imagine she really sent me to avoid having you discovered in flagrante delicto by one of your less enlightened guests."

"We can leave?" Ali said, catching on the words she'd been waiting to hear. "Oh, how wonderful."

Andre chuckled. "Patience never was your strong suit. But at the moment it's not mine, either. Go on then, Ali. Change your clothes and say your good-byes, and we'll be on our way."

"I promise, I won't be long." She gave him one last brilliant smile and hurried away.

"So," Andre said as soon as she'd gone, "what do you think? Isn't it amazing? Would you know that was the same girl we sent off from Izmir?"

Joseph-Jean was silent.

"Jo-Jean? Surely you must be surprised?"

Joseph-Jean looked at Andre long and hard. "I would know Ali anywhere. And you, my friend, are an even bigger fool than I thought." He walked off without another word.

"Alexis," Hattie whispered, kissing her good-bye. "I shall miss you."

"Don't worry, Hattie. I'll be back. You can be sure of it. It's only a month after all." She pushed her bouquet into Hattie's hands, the silver sixpence still tucked inside. "For you," she said. "May it bring you all the luck and happiness you deserve."

She said a tearful farewell to Nicholas and Georgia, then turned to Joseph-Jean, who stood next to Andre. As frustrating as it was, all she could do was to let him bow over her hand in front of all the guests and staff who watched them. "Thank you," she said. "You were most kind to come."

"It had nothing to do with kindness, Duchess, and everything to do with friendship. Please. Look after him for me?" he asked in an echo of years before when the situation had been reversed.

"You know I will," she said, completing the phrase. "Good-bye." The love in her eyes spoke the rest.

Joseph-Jean walked with them to the carriage. "And you look after her," he murmured, taking advantage of the proximity of Andre's ear. "Or I swear I'll kill you."

Andre clapped Joseph-Jean on the back, not gently. "I wish to hell you'd make up your mind about this," he said. "But regardless, I'll be in touch."

And then, the farewells finished, Ali climbed inside the waiting carriage, Andre joining her. The door shut behind them and the carriage rolled off, cheers following after them.

Andre pulled his gaze from the window as soon as the last person was out of sight. He looked at Ali. "Well, wife. What now?"

Ali was unclear on the matter. "I was about to ask you. Where are we going? Georgia said only that we weren't leaving England."

"We're taking the four o'clock express to the coast, and then I'm taking you to your wedding present."

"My wedding present?" Ali said, clapping her hands together in delight. "Oh, Andre—you bought me a present? What is it?"

"You'll see soon enough." He settled back against the plush squabs and folded his arms across his chest. "We ought to be sitting down to dinner in about four hours. Can you last until then? I seem to remember your prodigious appetite, and you didn't eat much at noon."

"I was too hapy to eat," she said. "And now I'm too excited even to think about food." She sighed. "I like being a bride, but I think I like being a married lady much better." She smoothed down the silk skirt of her new dress. "Do you think I look like a married lady?" she asked him mischievously.

"Hmm. I'd have a peek, but it will have to wait till later," he said with a little smile. "As much as the waiting might be torture, I'm damned if I take you this time in anything less than a bed."

Ali chortled. "You'd have a hard time in the confines of a carriage, especially with all the underclothes I'm wearing."

He cocked an eyebrow. "I think you underestimate my ingenuity. But that's enough talk about that, or I'll break my word here and now. Actually, in preparation for your role as mistress of Sutherby, I've been meaning to tell you everything I know about crop rotation ..."

The brougham that met them at the other end of their journey was a far cry from the one that had taken them from Sutherby. It had no ducal coat of arms on the side, and although it was in good repair, it was not elegant. Nor was the driver who hopped down off the box and tipped his hat. He was dressed not in livery but in farm clothes, and his weathered face and hands had seen their share of the outdoors.

"Good evening, sir," he said in a thick country accent, tipping his hat. "Welcome, madam. I'm Lummus. Hop on in, and I'll have you sitting at your dinner in no time flat. The missus is making you a nice roast for your wedding supper, and may I wish you very happy?"

He loaded the baggage, and he was as good as his word. Within half an hour of rolling down country roads, they turned into a long lane and a few minutes later the carriage pulled up in front of a limestone farmhouse, surrounded by outbuildings and fields. Ali looked at Andre in question. "Is it an inn?" she asked.

"No, and it's not a tent, either, but it's the best I could do. This is Milford Farm, where we're going to spend the next month."

Ali gazed at the farmhouse, taking in the lead-paned windows, the pitched roof, the sheep grazing in the pastures beyond. "Oh, Andre, it's so sweet. Whom does it belong to?"

"You," he said, opening the door. "This is your

wedding present. You own it free and clear, all six hundred acres."

Ali's jaw dropped. "It's mine?" she whispered.

"Yes. I wanted you to have a place to come to when you don't feel like being a duchess, where you can be plain Mrs. Saint-Simon and live a simple life with your animals." He held out his hand. "Lummus farms the land with his wife, who will housekeep for us while we're here. They live in a cottage on the other end of the lane."

"Andre, I don't know what to say ..." Ali could barely get the words out, she was so overwhelmed by his kindness and touched by the thoughtfulness of such a gift, not to mention the time he must have spent finding it.

But at the same time she couldn't help but wonder if he thought her too uncouth, too childish to withstand the responsibilities of being a duchess, that she needed a convenient escape. She wondered too if this was the reason he'd decided to bury her in the country instead of taking her to the Continent. Both thoughts worried at her, but she chose to remain silent. She was the last person to complain about being buried in the country.

"You really are without something to say?" he said, helping her down. "I don't believe it. Now come inside and inspect your humble abode." He tucked her hand into the crook of his elbow and led her through the door, ducking his head to avoid hitting it on the frame.

"Welcome, Mrs. Saint-Simon," said a middle-aged woman, hurrying out of the kitchen into the little entrance area, wiping her reddened hands on a towel. "Martha Lummus, and it's a pleasure to meet you at last, to be sure. Everything is in order, just as your husband requested, and I'll bring up some hot water to your bedroom in just a tick when Arnold is finished carrying the bags up."

"Thank you," Ali said, smiling at this small, kind woman with a face as weathered as her husband's. "It's very nice to meet you too."

"Well, isn't that kind of you. Oh, and there's a surprise waiting for you outside the back door, just through the hall there. Came this morning off the train. Never seen anything so bossy and scrappy."

Andre chuckled and strode through the hallway, opening the door. A small white and black polka-dotted streak came bolting through and went into a dance of ecstasy upon seeing Ali, turning frantic circles at her feet.

"Sherifay!" Ali cried in disbelief, scooping her up into her arms. "How did—oh, *Andre.* Andre, thank you!" She submitted to a thorough face-licking, then put Sherifay down. "But how did you even know about her? She was shut away for her heat in the kennel the last time you were at Ravenswalk."

"Nicholas told me, of course. He seemed to think that having her here would make you happy. But come." He took her hand and opened another door, drawing her inside.

Ali blinked. It was a large and cozy sitting room, but what astonished her was the manner in which it was decorated. Ornate Turkish carpets covered with stone floor, and richly decorated pillows in familiar patterns adorned the sofa and chairs, more scattered about the floor. A brass coffee table, worked in an elaborate design, stood in front of the sofa, and even the prints on the wall were of Turkish scenes. She recognized a few watercolors that could only have been painted by Joseph-Jean.

Andre's writing table sat against one wall.

Ali could only shake her head, her eyes welling with tears.

"Mr. and Mrs. Lummus didn't know what to think until I explained that I was an eccentric historian." He pointed at the bookshelf, which was filled with tomes on that part of the world. "I said nothing about you, naturally. But I do want you to feel you have a safe and comfortable haven, Ali, despite what I'm dragging you into elsewhere."

Ali, deeply shaken, moved into his arms and buried her head against his hard shoulder. She couldn't help it—her tears came unbidden, and she began to cry soundlessly, overwhelmed with love for him.

"What is it?" he murmured against her hair. "Do you not like it? I thought it would bring you happy memories, not sad ones—oh, come, sweetheart, don't cry. If you really don't like it, I'll pack it all away and you can have an ordinary old farmhouse. Whatever you wish."

Ali shuddered and pulled herself together. She rubbed her face against his coat, then looked up at him. "Don't be silly. I love it. How did you do it?"

"I had a number of things shipped before I left," he said, appearing relieved that she'd returned to her senses. "When I realized we were to be married, I knew exactly what to do with them," he said, wiping away her tears with his thumbs. "Wait until you see the bedroom."

"You haven't re-created a harem, by any chance?" she asked with a wobbly smile.

"Now what would I know about the inside of a harem?" he replied, his fingers moving down to stroke her neck.

"Probably far too much," she said tartly. "Oh, Andre, I honestly don't know how to thank you for all this. It's—it's like being home again."

"Well, thank God," he said with real relief, "since that was the idea. I meant this to be your own You-rook encampment in the heart of England. The only thing I can't do anything about is the weather, but the fireplace draws nicely."

Ali reached up with both hands and drew his head down toward hers, kissing him softly. "You couldn't have given me anything more perfect."

"Well . . ." he said, nipping her bottom lip with his teeth, "the night has only just begun."

Ali caught her breath at the note of husky promise in his voice. She suddenly couldn't wait for dinner to be over.

"Let me take you outside for a walk and show you some of the outbuildings," he said, reluctantly releasing her. "That should give Mrs. Lummus plenty of time to unpack your clothes, heat water, and finish preparing the dinner. And you need to dry your eyes before she sees you and thinks I've already begun to beat you."

Ali had to laugh when he did finally take her upstairs. The main bedroom was exotic indeed for a simple English farmhouse. Although he hadn't gone so far as to put the mattress on the floor, he'd had the bed draped with a silk kilim woven in rich burnt umber and reds and blues. It was the only strong note of color in the room. A large wooden chest with hammered brass filigree sat at the foot of the large bed, a pile of typical Yourook furs on top of it, and delicate white gauze fabric adorned the windows, not obscuring the views in the least or even occluding the light, but adding a note of Eastern grace.

But best of all, a lovely brass hip bath stood in one corner, and on a table next to it sat a large mahogany box filled with all sorts of precious oils.

Ali, left alone to wash and change, lovingly fingered the dark glass vials filled with her favorite scents. Jasmine, rose from Damascus, orange blossom, frankincense, sandalwood, cinnamon, nutmeg, there were more than she could count.

She knew that Andre had probably brought most of them back for medicinal purposes, for she'd learned much from him in Turkey about their healing properties and taught him remedies too, things that she'd learned from her people.

But she'd also learned from her people that some of the oils served dual purposes and were used to stimulate and heighten desire. She didn't think either of them needed any extra stimulating tonight, but it couldn't hurt to dab a little precious jasmine behind her ears and on her wrists.

Ali washed and changed from her traveling dress. It amused her to find that hanging in the armoire were not the fashionable and expensive clothes that had been made for her trousseau, but the older and more comfortable dresses that she'd worn at Ravenswalk.

Georgia and Nicholas must have had a fine time conspiring to keep this secret from her. Ali smiled at the thought.

She slipped on a simple green dress, not bothering with the petticoat that went under it. She didn't bother to put her hair up either, pulling it back in her favorite style, with just a ribbon to hold it. Andre wouldn't mind, and she doubted Mrs. Lummus would care.

Andre had changed too, and as she paused on the threshold of the sitting room, she was delighted to see that he was dressed as simply as she was, his linen shirt open at the neck, no jacket, no waistcoat, wearing a casual pair of trousers. He sat reading on the sofa, his feet propped up on the table, his attention fully on his book, so like the old days.

The sight was enough to make her heart hammer painfully, not so much with desire, although that was there too, but with the understanding that had dawned when she had first walked in and seen what he'd done.

This house was his silent acknowledgment to her. He had not bought it because he thought the pressure of being a duchess would be too much. He needed the escape from the pressures of the duchy as much as she. Just looking at him now told her that.

No, he had bought it and decorated it in this fashion as a statement of what they were together—easy, comfortable, two people with a shared past and a shared affinity for a special part of the world.

He had done it to tell her that he knew at heart she was the same Ali and brought her here to make that rediscovery for them both, to blend their two worlds together. And he had somehow managed to evade the laws of marital property and put the farm in her name to tell her that he honored her as a woman in her own right.

If that wasn't love, she had to wonder what he thought love was.

Andre listened to Ali's cheerful chatter during dinner with only half an ear. His attention was caught instead by her sparkling eyes, looking even brighter by candlelight, caught by the sweet curve of her mouth, by the sensuous tumble of hair down her back, the loose strands carelessly caressing her slender neck exactly where he wished his fingers could be.

It served to remind him of what lay ahead, and he found that he didn't want to wait another moment. But he didn't want to rush Ali, either. He owed her the fullest night he could give her, since there was so much else he couldn't.

"Andre?" she asked, putting down her fork and knife. "May I stop talking now, please?"

"I beg your pardon?" he said, jolted out of his wayward thoughts.

"I said I'd like to stop talking. It's not easy trying to make conversation for two, especially when one's heart isn't in it. Mrs. Lummus has gone home, we did justice enough to her meal, and I think we can safely go up to bed. Although I think I need to teach her about spices, don't you?"

It was such a typical Ali statement that he wanted to laugh. "Yes, I agree on all counts," he said as seriously as he could manage. "Why don't you go on up? I'll join you shortly."

Ali took a last sip of wine, then put her glass down and wiped her mouth with her napkin. "You had better," she said, standing. "Or I shall come down and drag you to bed myself."

"I'm not in need of persuasion," he replied, slipping his arm around her slim waist as she passed and stroking her hip. "I only thought to give you a few minutes to prepare yourself."

"I have been prepared for years," she said with a mischievous smile. "It is you who is always being taken by surprise." She danced away from him and disappeared down the hall.

"Brat," he murmured under his breath. But she was right. One way or another, Ali always did manage to catch him off guard.

Ali brushed out her hair in long careful strokes, grateful there was no lady's maid tonight to distract her. She undressed and washed, then put on the simple white nightdress she had chosen for this night. And then she climbed beneath the covers, suddenly nervous.

Her last experience with Andre had been unmeditated, an act of spontaneous love on her part, even though she had been fully aware of the consequences when she'd given herself to him. This night was entirely different, the first in their married life, and she couldn't help but wonder what was going through his mind.

She stroked the kilim, a strong sensual memory running through her fingertips, bringing back sharp images of her childhood. And later, in her time with Andre, she had spent many hours sitting on rugs just like this, in his tent, or with the Yourooks, or watching closely as he negotiated with Gemil or others in the marketplace. Her life in Turkey felt like only a breath away. But her life in England felt just as immediate to her.

Andre was the only bridge between the two.

And now she sat here, waiting for him to come to her bed and take her as his wife. Was he thinking of her? Or was he thinking of Genevieve, who should have lain in his marriage bed with him, instead of a little Turkish stray?

Ali folded her hands together and prayed as hard as she ever had that she would be equal to him on this night, that she might make him forget. Tonight she wanted to wrap the first layer of her love around him, to form the first coating of her pearl. Nothing else could be more important than that.

A light tap came at the door, and she looked up with renewed determination. "Come in," she said, trying to control the ridiculous trembling of her fingers.

Ali forgot her nervousness in sheer surprise as Andre appeared. He wore only the classic Turkish piece of linen wrapped around his waist, the simple blue stripe across the bottom the pattern of the Yourooks of Xanthos. She'd seen him like this so many times in the past, and to see him now dressed in this manner dissolved the very last of the gap between the worlds.

"The last time I saw you wearing that, you were waiting for your bath," she said softly, gazing at him with an inviting smile.

He crossed the room in a heartbeat. "A bath is the last thing on my mind," he said, moving onto the bed and taking her in his arms. "I think you know exactly what I want." His hands smoothed and stroked her hair, her neck, drew her closer to him, his breath fast and light on her cheek, but hot, so hot.

"I—I do," she gasped as he turned her, folded her against him, and carried her down onto the bed.

"Ali, sweet," he murmured, his hands restlessly stroking over her, his mouth doing outrageous things to her ear and then descending to take her mouth with no thought to her senses. He thought nothing either of cupping her breast, stroking the nipple with his thumb until it sprang up hard under his fingers.

"God, how I've wanted you," he said hoarsely, sweeping his mouth down her neck and opening the ribbon of her nightdress. He pushed the material aside, exposing her breast. His tongue traced one delicate blue vein, then circled the underside and moved up to capture her throbbing nipple, pulling it into his mouth and lightly rolling it between his teeth.

Ali's fingers slipped into his hair, and she pressed up against his touch, reveling in every sensation. "Andre—Andre, oh . . ." she moaned, twisting against him. Every little tug of his mouth sent fire racing through her belly. She thought she might die from pleasure, and just as the thought occurred, he moved his head and adored her other breast, creating another scene of unholy chaos.

He lifted his head and gazed down at her. "I want this to be right for you," he said raggedly, his eyes blazing pure silver fire, his hands stroking the hair back from her fevered brow. "Let me know what you like, what you want."

"All I have ever wanted is you," she whispered. She lifted the hand that bore his ring and touched it to his face, tracing the line of cheekbone, her shaking fingers drifting to his mouth. "Teach me now, Andre, as you have taught me so much else?"

His hand closed around hers and he bowed his head, his cheek resting against her hair. "Ali. What do you do to me?"

She moved her head so that her mouth pressed against his neck. "Nothing but love you," she murmured against his heated skin. And then she opened her mouth and stroked him with her tongue, reveling in his taste and smell, pulling the lobe of his ear between her lips and suckling it, much as he had done to her nipple.

Andre shuddered and moved over her, this time taking her mouth in a furious kiss that held nothing back and sent Ali into a state of wild abandon as his hands stroked over her, kneading her breasts, slipping behind her hips, lifting her toward him. She writhed against him, his erect penis rubbing against her belly in a manner that made her want to scream with desperate longing.

Just being in his arms was enough to set her on fire, but the knowledge that she had the ability to arouse him to such a degree only added to her fevered desire. Her fingers raked down his back in frenzied need and her hips pressed against his, rubbing against his hard length. "Oh, Andre, please," she begged. "Please now?"

He pushed her shoulders back against the bed. "Wait," he gasped. "Wait, for God's sake, or I'm going to lose myself here and now."

Ali, her chest heaving desperately, squeezed her eyes shut and nodded, but that did little to quench the flames that threatened to consume her.

He waited a moment, panting heavily, then swallowed hard and threw his head back, staring up at the ceiling. "I can see," he said, his breathing labored, "that this is not going to be as easy as I thought."

Ali ran her tongue over her parched lips. "Did I do something wrong?" she asked, breathing as hard as he.

"Ah . . . no. Just the opposite." He rolled over onto

his back, his erection holding the cloth of his wrap up like a tent pole. "God, Ali. Dear God. All right. Better now." He looked at her sideways. "I refuse to take you like an untried schoolboy, which is exactly how I'm feeling. But I swear, you don't make it easy."

Ali wasn't exactly sure what to make of that, but she looked at him and then at his rampant erection and decided that the problem wasn't serious. "Maybe we should take our clothes off?" she suggested, thinking that might help.

Andre groaned, then gave a choke of laughter. "Ah ... ah. Yes. Why don't we do that?" He rolled onto his side and skimmed his hands up Ali's hips, taking her nightdress with him. In one deft move he lifted it over her head and tossed it onto the floor.

Ali, equally obligingly, untucked the fold of material at his waist and loosened the cloth with practice fingers. Only this time what she found was an entirely different sight to what had appeared in the past.

Andre was magnificent in his arousal. His shaft jutted out from his belly hard as steel, arcing up toward her in obvious need.

Ali caught her breath. "You are beautiful like this," she said in awe, reaching her hand out.

To her surprise Andre caught her wrist, holding it tightly away form him. "No," he said. "Oh, no you don't."

"It is not permitted?" she asked, bewildered.

"It is permitted," he answered, sweat beading his forehead. "It is very much permitted. Just not now."

"But why?" she asked. "If it is all right for you to put this wonderful part of you inside me, then why may I not touch you on the outside?"

Andre grinned. "Let me show you? It's easier than explaining." He moved her onto her back, and began to stroke her legs, from the bottom of her feet all the way up to the juncture of her thighs, long, languorous strokes that soon had Ali shaking uncontrollably.

"Now," he said huskily, gently spreading her thighs and moving his hand into her soft curls, damp with desire. His fingers began to move on her flesh, sliding between the lips, teasing, stroking, causing her to sob with renewed need, her hips moving convulsively.

"Oh," she moaned. "Oh, please, Andre, I can't bear it."

"Good, because that's how I was feeling a few minutes ago," he said raggedly. "Had you laid one slender finger on me then, it would have all been over."

"It feels this wonderful to you too?" she asked, wondering how that could be when they were made so differently.

"Oh, yes," he said, exploring her more deeply with his finger. "Oh, yes."

He pushed them into her and the next thing Ali knew, all sensation gathered together in one unbearable knot of pleasure and burst apart.

"Andre!" she cried, spasms of release overwhelming her. "Oh, Andre," she whimpered as they finally began to subside and he took his hand away.

He kissed her, his breath coming hard and fast. "That, my sweet, was very nice, and you may do that as many times as you wish while we make love."

"I may?" she said, dazed and limp and wondering how her body could possibly survive it more than once.

"Mm hmm," he said, circling her ear with his tongue. "I, however, have to be more careful."

"You do?" she murmured, shivering with pleasure as he moved his mouth down to her throat, lightly nipping.

"Mmm," he said, his breath hot against her sensitive skin. "Once I reach that point, there's no return, and then I can't continue to pleasure you—at least not like this."

He rose over her and moved her legs apart with his thigh, entering her in a smooth thrust. He stayed still inside her for a long moment, his face buried against her neck, and Ali relished his fullness, pushing her hips up, testing, slowly stretching around him until she had taken his full length into her.

Andre groaned again. "You," he said, lifting his

head and shifting his weight so that it rested fully on his forearms, "are unbelievable."

"I am?" she said, smiling up at him happily, her face flushed with a renewed rush of desire.

"You ... were ... born for this," he said, beginning to move in her, and Ali opened her legs wider to accommodate him. She quickly discovered that if she wrapped her legs around his back he could move even more deeply.

"Ali—sweet, sweet girl," he whispered, increasing the rhythm of his thrusts until he had her pinned on the bed unable to do anything but moan as he pounded into her, deeper and deeper, harder and harder, pushing her closer to that precipice of oblivion.

He held her arms over her head, his fingers entwined in hers, his face taut, his eyes fixed on hers, and Ali felt as if his gaze burned into her very soul.

"My God," he groaned, his face suddenly contorting as if in pain and he thrust deeply with a hoarse cry.

That final thrust threw Ali straight off the edge she'd been hovering on and she convulsed around him at the same time that he pulsed into her, fiercely milking the seed he poured into her, her cry like the long wail of a she-wolf in the night.

Andre's entire body shook as another groan was torn from his throat and his fingers tightened painfully around hers. And then they gradually released, and he fell against her, his heart pounding slowly.

She wrapped her arms around his slick back, one hand stroking the damp hair at the nape of his neck, the other running lightly over the hollow of his spine down to the hard curve of his buttocks and up again.

He was quiet for many minutes, and she wondered if he'd fallen asleep. But then he stirred in her arms. "Ali?" he murmured.

"What?" she said softly.

"I'm very glad I married you."

Chapter 16

Andre woke early the next morning to the extraordinary sensation of his toes being expertly licked. For a foggy moment he thought it was Ali, but that was impossible since he had her securely in his arms and any licking that she felt compelled to do would have occurred in the region of his neck.

Granted, it had been a long night and he hadn't had much sleep, but he wasn't that muddled. He gently disentangled Ali and sat up, lifting the covers.

Sherifay's little face looked up at him, not a trace of guilt on it. She gave his big toe one last thorough lap, then inched her way up his side and poked her head out, looking very pleased with herself.

"If you think you're sharing the marital bed, my friend, you have another think coming. I have plans for this morning." He located his wrap, then hoisted Sherifay under one arm and marched her straight back through the open bedroom door and down the stairs, firmly putting her out the back door.

He made a fire, put two large pots of water on to heat, and went out to the well. He'd instructed Mrs. Lummus to stay well away from the house until dinnertime, so he knew he could strip and wash without the risk of sending her into strong hysterics.

When he returned to the bedroom, Ali was still asleep, curled up on her side in the manner in which she had always slept, her fist tucked under her chin. The only difference now was the hair that tangled around her arm—and the rise and fall of her breasts beneath the sheet.

Propping himself on the end of the bed, he watched

her, the morning light playing softly over her features. Ali slept with the same enthusiasm that she brought to everything else. A slight smile curved up the corners of her ripe mouth, and her sooty lashes swept the curve of her finely drawn cheekbones.

It was the oddest thought that he'd spent a good portion of the night making love to the same person who had once served him intimately in other ways. And yet Ali wasn't the same person.

Oh, she was still the same fiery, determined, quixotic soul she'd always been, but this Ali ... this Ali was no child. No child at all.

He ran his eyes over her face, thinking of the fierce joy that Ali had brought to their lovemaking, her complete lack of inhibition, her generosity. Her love.

Andre squeezed his eyes shut as guilt stabbed sharply through him. Ali deserved so much better, so much more than a man whose heart would always belong to someone else.

Still. It was done and, selfishly, he could not be sorry. He could only hope that she would not eventually grow to regret their marriage. He also hoped that she didn't ever learn about Genevieve, for the last thing Ali needed was to feel diminished in any way. But he intended to do everything in his power to see that didn't happen.

The sound of water splashing penetrated Ali's consciousness, and she opened her eyes to see Andre pouring a bucket of steaming water into the tub. She shivered at the sight of his broad, bare back, the play of muscles as he lifted another bucket and tipped it in. He truly was the most handsome man she'd ever seen, and it didn't make any difference whether he was in formal clothes or none at all; just the sight of him made her heart turn over.

She assumed the bath was for him until the scent of roses drifted across the room. Since Andre had never been inclined to smell of anything but himself, she realized he'd prepared it for her, and Ali's throat tightened with love.

Everything he'd done from the moment she'd arrived at Sutherby had been so generous, down to the way he had loved her the night before, making sure she took as much pleasure in the act as he. Well, *that* hadn't been any problem.

She sighed and sat up, stretching in contentment, and he turned.

"Good morning," he said, looking deliciously like her Andre of old, a hint of beard on his cheeks, his hair tousled.

Ali smiled at him. "Hello," she said, feeling a little shy considering some of the things they'd done to each other in the dark. But Andre didn't look the least perturbed. If anything, he appeared more relaxed than she had ever seen him.

"Your bath is ready, madam," he said, crossing the room and lightly kissing her. "I'll leave you to it, shall I? I'm going down to make some tea and feed Sherifay. Your dog, by the way, is very forward. I found her taking her pleasure with my toes earlier."

Ali's smile widened. "Oh, dear. I suppose she knocked the door open. She's very fond of feet, I'm afraid."

Andre raised his eyebrow. "They have a name for that, you know," he said with a wicked grin. "But I'll explain later. Have a nice long soak. You could probably use it after last night." He lifted her hand to his mouth and kissed her fingers. "By the way, thank you," he murmured, glancing down at her.

"For what?" she asked.

"For being you. For taking me on. For not asking for more than I can give."

"Andre," she said very quietly, "I meant what I said that horrible day in Izmir. I belong to you. That will never change. The only difference is that now I belong to you in body as well as in soul."

A flash of pain came and went in his eyes. He didn't answer her, just kissed her hand again and swiftly left.

Ali tucked her knees up and rested her chin on them, considering. She thought she'd done a good job with the first layer. But it was going to take a lot more wrapping herself around him before Genevieve was no longer an unspoken ghost hanging between them.

The bath was wonderful. She didn't realize that she was sore until she climbed out of bed, but the bath took care of that. The hot water eased the ache from her muscles, the rose oil soothed her senses. She closed her eyes and rested her head against the back of the tub, humming softly to herself, counting her many blessings.

She had a house of her very own, a husband who clearly cared for her, and a loving family. She had good friends, a wonderful little dog, and maybe even a child starting inside her.

Ali placed her hands on her belly, imagining a tiny seed growing inside. Goodness, with the amount Andre had put in her last night, she ought to have an entire army of babies in there.

She smiled blissfully.

A warm cloth slipped over her breasts and her eyes shot open in surprise. "Andre . . . what are you doing?"

"Bathing you," he said, kneeling next to the tub and squeezing the washcloth out, dribbling silky water down her neck. "I think it's time we establish some dominance in this relationship. I therefore am asserting my rights, or I'll never have the upper hand. I learned my lesson in Turkey."

Ali thought this over. "Do husbands generally bathe their wives?"

"Not generally, no, or at least I don't believe so. But that is neither here nor there. I don't know that we've ever done things the way other people do, and I don't intend to start now." He picked up her arm and stroked the cloth down it.

"Oh, good," Ali said with a contented sigh, enjoying the sensuous feel of the cloth sliding over her skin, of Andre's hand supporting her arm. "But don't think that means that I don't get to bathe you too."

"Another time. I've already doused myself in cold water."

"You hate cold water," she said as he stroked her other arm.

"You're right. But it has its purposes. It gained you an extra hour's sleep."

Ali opened one eye. Andre wore a broad smile that she was pleased to see, since it meant he'd put aside whatever had upset him. "You are insatiable," she said.

"It's looking that way," he replied, slipping the cloth between her legs and moving it in a sensuous circle. She was sorry when he removed it. "You know, for a little Turkish lad, you're surprisingly appealing," he said.

Ali opened both eyes. "Are you finally admitting that you're impressed with my magnificent breasts?" she said.

"Impressed is not the word I'd use," he replied, lifting her leg and washing that. "I'd say I was more, ah . . . enthralled. Yes. Enthralled."

He completed his tour of her body, then held out a large white towel. "Up you go."

Ali let him wind her in it, and then he lifted her in his arms and carried her back over to the bed.

He'd spread another towel out on that, and he gently lowered her onto it, then rubbed her dry. "Roll over onto your front," he commanded, taking the first towel away. "I'm going to give you a massage. This is part two of establishing dominance."

Ali happily complied, thinking that marriage had its advantages. He produced a bottle of oil and moved her hair off her back and over her shoulder. And then his hand froze.

"Ali," he whispered. "Dear God."

"What?" she asked, wondering why he'd stopped.

"These—these scars. What happened to you?"

Ali, who had forgotten all about them, looked up over her shoulder at his appalled face, feeling equally appalled. "They're nothing," she said, dismissing them. "They're old."

"I can see that. But what I'm asking is how you got them."

Ali didn't want to discuss it in the least. "I fell off a horse," she said in a blatant lie.

"I don't think so," he said, frowning. "You don't get a crisscrossed webbing like that from falling off a horse. Who whipped you, Ali?"

"It doesn't matter," she said, furious with herself. She should have remembered about the stupid scars, been prepared for his quesions, for Andre always noticed everything. Something like that wasn't likely to escape his attention.

"It damned well does matter." He took her chin and pulled her face up to meet his furious gaze. "Was it Hadgi?"

"If you insist on knowing, yes, it was Hadgi," she said tightly. "Now, please, can we talk about something else?"

"No," Andre said, his voice rough. "Why? For God's sake, why would he do something so brutal to a young girl?"

Ali pulled away from him and wrapped the towel around herself. "He was angry with me," she said, slipping off the bed and crossing to the window as if she could walk away from the questions and the unwelcome memories they provoked.

But Andre came up directly behind her and took her by the shoulders, his hands gentle. "Ali. I'm not going to let it go. Please, tell me what happened."

"You know my country. You know that punishment is often harsh." She stared down at the floor, a hard knot forming in her throat. She hadn't cried then, and she was not going to cry now. She was not. Not over Hadgi. Not ever.

"Yes, of course I know that," he said. "But what did you do to provoke this kind of treatment? Did you steal something from him?"

Ali's thin thread of control snapped. She spun around, her fists clenched by her sides, fury taking hold of her that he would even think such a thing. "*Steal* something? He was trying to steal from me!"

"What—what do you mean, he was trying to steal from you?" Andre said, his voice very low.

"Andre—please. Can't you see I don't want to speak of it? If I tell you the truth, you'll only be angry and upset, and it's long in the past. What difference can it make now?" She rubbed a shaking hand over her forehead.

"I'm already angry and upset," he said. "And I'm getting more so by the minute. You know I'll get it out of you one way or another, so you might as well tell me now. The truth, Ali."

Ali closed her eyes for a moment, wishing God had made Andre a little less persistent. The truth. Very well. If he wanted the truth so badly, he could have it, but he wasn't going to like it.

She looked him directly in the eye. "He tried to rape me."

"*Rape* you?" Andre whispered, his skin paling. "But you were no more than a child ..."

"Oh, he wasn't going to take my virginity—that was too valuable," Ali said tightly. "I was worth far more to the Turkomen if I was a virgin, and he knew it. He went so far as to tell me that before he ..." She swallowed hard. "He said he was going to teach me humility before he sold me."

"Ali. Oh, God, Ali," he said brokenly.

She shrugged. "He didn't succeed. I had a knife under my pillow, and I came close enough to maiming him with it. The whipping was what I received in retaliation."

Ali clenched her hands into fists, her knuckles turning white as the scene came back far too clearly— Hadgi's attack in the night, the struggle and his enraged face as she fended him off, slashing his thigh. And after, when he'd tied her to the pole, her hands over her head, and torn her overtunic to her waist, stripping the skin from her back with a knotted whip as the villagers watched her humiliation ...

She shuddered in memory. Well, at least Allah had made her faint after a time.

"Dear God in heaven," Andre murmured, his face white and strained.

"Ten lashes was a small price to pay," she said. "But I thought it wise to run away as soon as I was able. And also wise to dress as a boy so that I wouldn't be in the same danger again."

He pulled her fiercely into his arms, burying his face in her hair. "If I'd only known," he whispered. "I swear I would have killed him that day."

His words had the effect of bringing Ali back to the present, and she pulled slightly away from him, her face as pale as his.

"No," she said. "You wouldn't have—you don't have it in you. It's one of the reasons I love you so much, and why I loved you from the first. Because you are gentle." A little smile crept onto her face. "But still, I was very pleased when you knocked him down."

Andre stroked his hands over her back as if he could smooth the hurt away. "I'm sorry, sweetheart. I'm so, so sorry. Not for knocking him down—I'm glad for that. God I'm glad for it. But I am deeply sorry for all the suffering he put you through."

Her gaze searched his face. "I don't mind so much about the suffering," she said. "After all, it brought me to you. I don't even mind about the scars. But do you, Andre? Do you find them ugly?"

His only answer was to pick her up. He carried her back to the bed and laid her down on her side. And then he came down next to her and lowered his head.

One by one he tenderly traced each pale, raised stripe with his mouth.

"I find them beautiful," he said, lifting his head. "Each one is a mark of your courage, sweet Ali. And no one . . . *no one* will ever harm you again," he added savagely. "If anyone should try, he will have me to answer to. This I swear to you."

Ali rolled over in his arms to face him. "Then I am very lucky to have you as a friend," she said, winding her fingers through his hair, knowing that he spoke the truth. "And as a husband," she added, softly brushing her lips across his.

Andre responded with a groan. He opened his mouth against hers and kissed her hard, plundering her with his tongue until Ali forgot everything but the pounding of her heart and the feel of his body on hers.

He made love to her that morning with a ferocious tenderness that left Ali thinking maybe he was wrapping a protective layer of his own around her too.

Ali lounged on a pile of cushions, her book lying forgotten on her lap, mulling over the last three weeks. It had been a good time, a peaceful time. They spent hours making love, more hours discussing history, politics, all sorts of fascinating subjects.

Ali had always been infinitely grateful for the education Nicholas had given her, but now that she could use it to converse with Andre, it became even more precious to her. He had an acute brain and enjoyed teaching her, so she learned new things every day.

At the moment his extraordinary powers of concentration were focused on his book, his feet propped up in his favorite position. He'd been reading the *Odyssey* in the original Greek for the last week, a wonderful story.

Ali knew. She'd read it, also in the Greek. But she hadn't told him that, since she much preferred his recounting the chapters in his own words. She begged him to do just that every night over dinner, since she found Andre's humorous interpretation as interesting as Homer's original intent.

Anyway, there were things that he didn't yet know about her, which might be better for him to discover in small increments. Such as her ability to speak Italian and Arabic now—and also to read Greek and Latin. She didn't want to shock him, since he'd been upset enough about her managing the waltz. Ali grinned to herself.

But then he'd come a long way since then. Every day he seemed a little more carefree, as if the deep unhappiness he'd carried around for years was finally releasing its wintry grip on him. A man she'd never seen before but had always known was in there was slowly emerging, and Ali delighted in watching it happen.

She suspected his progress was a result of so much lovemaking. It wasn't easy keeping one's emotions tucked away when nothing else was. He smiled often, and laughed out loud all the time. He didn't measure his words as carefully. He didn't retreat nearly as often, either, and although there was a part of him that he still held far away from her, she didn't mind. She couldn't expect everything all at once.

Her eyes lovingly traced the high arch of his nose, the sharp definition of his cheek, the beautiful sculpted shape of his mouth, wondering if he was aware of the changes in himself. Probably not, but then that was typical of Andre. As acute as his brain might be, he was remarkably good at concealing his feelings from himself. But he couldn't conceal them from her.

Andre's heart was beginning to open. Now it was just a matter of time.

Ali sighed happily, and Andre glanced up.

"What are you looking so pleased about?" he asked.

"Dinner," she lied. "I taught Mrs. Lummus how to make *imam bayildi*. She didn't mind the idea of stuffing an aubergine, but I think she had a hard time accepting all the garlic. But it ought to be delicious."

"Mrs. Lummus," he replied, "is becoming a paragon of Turkish cuisine, even if she does think us both mad as hatters." He smiled. "But then she's a good country woman. I can't wait until you get your hands on the Sutherby chef, who's French. We're bound to have hysterics in the kitchen."

"No, no," Ali replied. "The secret of managing chefs is to flatter them wildly while slowly bending them to your will."

"And where did you learn that?" he asked, finding his bookmark and marking his page.

"From Jo-Jean," she said. "He made such a fuss about my seafood stew that I felt obliged to make it at least twice a week. Personally, I think he made a fuss because it saved him the trouble of having to hunt, but it worked."

Andre reached his arm out, wrapping his fingers

around Ali's ankle. "If you're so susceptible to flattery, then I have a few sweet nothings to whisper in your ear." He pulled her toward him, stretched his body over hers.

"Mrs. Lummus?" she murmured as he began to nuzzle her neck.

"Not expected for at least half an hour. I'll be quick."

Ali began to unbutton his shirt.

"You fiend," Ali cried the following afternoon, kicking her horse into a gallop behind Andre as he took off in front of her.

"Then catch me up." Andre headed straight for the beach, knowing that although Ali might be a fast and brilliant rider, he had the advantage of superior strength and a larger horse capable of carrying his weight. Ali hated it when he beat her, which he did regularly. In races.

The rest of the time she managed to bring him to his knees. He could only be grateful that the initial spontaneous combustion Ali had inspired in his loins had settled down to a more manageable, if perpetual, simmer, or he wasn't sure how he would have survived the rest of his life.

He maneuvered his horse down the sandy slope, carefully watching the slippery footing until he had gained firm ground. He was busy reflecting on the pleasures of Ali's bed when a whoop came from above him, and he looked up only to see Ali making a mad—no, a completely insane—leap with her horse from the embankment.

"Ali, for God's sake!" he cried, pulling his horse to a halt, his heart stopping in terror as she flew through the air on a certain course of death, hunched over her horse's neck.

In that second he thought he might die himself.

But incredibly enough, she and her mare landed safely a few yards in front of him.

Ali laughed, her hair whipping in the wind. "Beat you," she called.

Andre dismounted, a wild anger taking hold of him. He stormed over the sand and grabbed her by both arms, dragging her off the horse to face him.

"Don't you ever, *ever* pull a stunt like that again," he shouted, his fingers biting into her shoulders. "Ever!"

"Why?" she asked nonchalantly enough, but she looked startled by his anger. "It's not as if I haven't jumped a horse hundreds of times before."

"Because," he said, furious with himself for feeling so shaken, "one of these days you'll break your neck. Is that reason enough?"

Ali glared at him. "And if I do? It's my neck, isn't it?"

"What kind of question is that?" he said, the blood pounding in his ears, his groin suddenly inflamed by the rebellion in her eyes. "You gave me your damned neck along with the rest of you the day you married me, and by God, I'll keep what's mine."

He pulled her to him, savaging her mouth, his hands moving to her skirt, lifting it over her hips, crushing her against his aching erection. Ali savaged him right back in instant, furious response.

"And I'll have what's mine," he muttered roughly, picking her up and quickly carrying her to the shelter of an overhanging berm. "Now, Ali, because it pleases me. Do you hear me?"

In answer her fingers went to the front of his trousers, undoing them, releasing him. She took him in her hand, stroking him hard and fast.

Inflamed, driven beyond control, he pushed her against the wall of sand, moving her underclothes to one side and spreading her legs, his mouth possessing hers at the same time he entered her, standing.

He took her swiftly, furiously, as if he were unleashing the desperate fear he'd felt at the thought of losing her, claiming her primitively, his emotions scraped raw.

Ali accepted him equally primitively, crying out, clawing at his back, her head tossing frantically in the sand as he pummeled her, faster and harder and deeper than he ever had before, needing to possess her completely, to own her, to leave his mark on her.

He lifted her higher up on his hips and banged her back into the hard sand. "By God, you won't do that again, will you?" he said savagely, giving her no respite. He drove into her again, determined to force her promise. "Will you?" he demanded, with another pounding drive. "Swear it."

"I do," she cried. "I swear it—oh, Andre ..." She rose up to him and met him thrust for thrust, her body shaking under his, straining toward him as he hammered into her, gone far beyond reason, only knowing that he wanted to drink in her life, to blindly wipe out the terrifying specter of death that he'd envisioned in that one split second.

She moaned, grabbing his hair and pulling his head down, frantically taking his mouth, and he bit her lip, drawing blood. Ali cried out, raking his back with his nails, her hips thrashing against his in a need to draw him even closer.

He grabbed her buttocks and pounded her back against the sand once again, his fingers digging into her flesh, his breath fast and hot on her cheek. "Tell me, Ali. Tell me."

He didn't even know what the question was, only that he needed her answer.

"Oh, Andre!" she sobbed. And she screamed then, a cry of sensation that had become too much to bear. It carried into the howl of the wind and the crash of the surf, blending into the elements as if it had been born from them.

His own desperate cry echoed hers, his ejaculation searing them both as he branded her with the same fury with which he'd taken her.

And then as sanity slowly returned, Andre sank down onto his knees, bringing Ali with him, his head bowed, his eyes closed, torn apart by what he'd just done—torn by how much he needed her, torn by the violence with which he had expressed that need.

Had he but realized it, he had just assumed the posture of prayer.

*   *   *

"Andre—Andre, please tell me what's wrong?" Ali asked, tugging on his arm to get his attention. From the moment he had abruptly pulled away from her on the beach, he'd been behaving in this cold, distant fashion.

"Nothing's wrong," he said, detaching himself from her and resuming his packing.

"Then why do we have to leave?" she said. "I thought we weren't going back to Sutherby for three more days."

"We weren't," he said. "But I have work to do. We can't live in an idyll forever."

"I don't see why not," Ali said, picking Sherifay up and cuddling her, desperately needing comfort.

"Because I have a book to write, and an idea is nagging at the back of my mind. I don't want to let it slip away."

"Oh," Ali said, trying to stifle her disappointment. She knew what Andre was like when he started thinking about books. "Why didn't you just say so?"

He glanced at her over his shoulder. "Because the idea only occurred to me this afternoon. Now get on with your own packing, Ali. I'd like to catch the six o'clock train."

She turned back to the armoire, her feelings terribly hurt. He was impossible to understand sometimes. How, after their incredible experience on the beach, could he have immediately started thinking about a book?

Maybe, she thought sadly, only she had thought it incredible.

She was beginning to discover how difficult it was to love so deeply and not be loved in return.

Chapter 17

A li came awake, alone once again save for Sherifay, who was snuggled at her feet. She sat up in
her vast bed, as vast as the distance that Andre had
created between them.

Oh, he still came to her bed, but his lovemaking
was restrained in comparison to what it had been, and
although he stayed long enough for her to fall asleep,
he was always gone before she woke. Maybe it was
the chilly atmosphere of Sutherby that affected him—
it didn't do a thing for her either. It just wasn't the
sort of place to make sons, not that she'd been successful in that either, to her great disappointment.

She looked up at the magnificent canopy, as magnificent as everything else at Sutherby. She looked at
the silk hangings, the gilded chairs, the Mortlake tap-
estries worked with the Acts of the Apostles.

Sutherby had one hundred seventy-five rooms and
almost every single one had a religious theme. As
much as she loved God, it depressed her, for there
wasn't any joy in the house, and she had to find a way
to change that. Sutherby, like any house, should be a
reflection of the people who lived in it, not a mausoleum to the past. How could they possibly be happy
in a mausoleum?

But before she could do anything about Sutherby,
she had to do something about Andre.

"Please, God," she whispered, "I need Your help.
Andre's behaving very strangely, and I cannot think
why. I know it's not his book—it's more as if he's
closed himself off."

She sat quietly, waiting for an answer, should God

feel like giving her one. It might take some time, she knew. This wasn't the first time she'd asked. Andre was so complicated that his inner workings resembled a maze. She'd never known anyone as talented at concealing his emotions. Take his incredible love for Genevieve—and yet never once had he spoken of her. And take his temper—it was something to behold, yet he rarely showed it. Usually he kept a tight clamp on it and carried it around inside himself instead. Yet she had an uncanny ability to make him lose it.

And then like a light exploding in her head, the answer came to her clear as day. Andre really was still angry with her, but pretending not to be. Typical. He could carry a grudge to his grave. "Well, I suppose the only way ever to change things is to meet the problem head-on, isn't it? You taught me that long ago."

She smiled happily, feeling much better. "Thank you, God. You've been very helpful."

She hopped out of bed and dressed, wondering if Andre's fairy-child had ever annoyed him. Somehow she doubted it.

Oh, it was unfair that she wasn't fair and fragile.

"Andre," she said, bearding him in the huge study where he sat with a mound of foolscap at his elbow, "I must speak with you."

He raised his head, his expression distracted. "Certainly. What is it?"

"It's very serious," she said, sitting down opposite and summoning her courage. "I have an apology to make to you."

"An apology?" he replied, frowning. "An apology for what? Have you broken something? Don't worry, just tell one of the footmen. It's all yours to break, anyway."

"Andre. Will you please pay attention? I haven't broken anything, although I ought to, and directly over your head."

Andre scratched his temple with his pen. "Are you about to subject me to a fit of temper? Because I warn you, Ali, I'm in no mood. I have to finish checking this chapter, and it is *not* going smoothly."

"Never mind the chapter," she said. "This is much more important. You are angry with me," she said bluntly.

"I am?" he said, raising an eyebrow. "Do I know what I am angry about?"

"Of course you do. You're still furious with me about jumping my horse when I might have been carrying your child."

"What?" Andre groaned, then threw his pen on top of his papers, abandoning his work. "What in God's name gives you that idea? And why is this coming out of the clear blue sky?"

"It isn't coming out of the clear blue sky. You've behaved very strangely this whole last month, and the only reason I can think of is that you're angry with me, and you've been waiting for a formal apology."

"Ali," he cried, then stopped and brushed his hands through his hair. "I promise you, I am not angry with you," he said. "You swore you wouldn't do anything foolish like that again and I trust you to keep your word."

"Naturally I will keep my word. But that's not the point." She placed both hands on the cool wood of his desk. "I made you lose your temper, and you hate to lose your temper."

"It's not something I particularly enjoy, no," he said, fiddling with his papers.

"And I don't want you to cut me off as you did your parents when they angered you, or your godparents, even though you've finally forgiven Nicholas and Georgia," she said in a rush. "I couldn't bear it, Andre, really I couldn't. So will you please forgive me so that we can get on with our lives?"

He rubbed a finger over his temple, then folded his hands together. "Ali," he said after a moment, "I don't know where all this has come from, but believe me, you are barking up the wrong tree." He drew in a deep breath. "I am not angry with you, and you've done nothing wrong. It didn't even occur to me at the time that you might be pregnant. If you remember, I was more concerned about your life."

"Oh," Ali said. "Well, that's a relief. Then why have you been so distant?"

"If you feel that I've been ignoring you, I'm sorry, but I've been awash in work, and I can't give you my undivided attention as I did at Milford."

"Arghhh!" she cried in frustration, banging her fists on his desk. "You are impossible. Just as I thought you were becoming human, you go and bottle yourself up again." She clenched her hands in her lap. "If you're not angry with me, then what is your problem?"

"I wasn't aware that I had a problem," he said coolly. "I was also unaware that I was lacking in humanity in your opinion."

Ali stood. "That's it," she said. She marched over to the massive double doors of the study and stuck her head out. "Pennyswell," she called to the butler, who was just approaching the study with a tray of coffee. "My husband and I are not to be disturbed under any circumstances. He can have his coffee later."

"Certainly, Your Grace," Pennyswell said, turning obediently on his heel and retreating with no change of expression.

"Pennyswell," Andre called. "Come directly back here."

Pennyswell vanished, and Ali smiled victoriously and pulled the doors shut. She turned the key in the lock and dropped it in her pocket, crossing the room and facing him. "You and I are going to have this out here and now, because I refuse to endure another minute of your nonsense."

Andre's eyes glittered dangerously. "Do not think to provoke me, Ali."

"What will you do?" she said, throwing down the gauntlet. "Take me over your knee? I think not. You don't believe in violence."

To Ali's surprise, a faint blush stained his cheeks.

"No," he said. "I don't." He looked down at his hands.

"Well, then. You could threaten to remove me from my friends, but they are all in London for the little season."

"Are you saying that is where you wish to be? Attending parties with your friends?"

The paperweight on his desk suddenly took on a whole new appeal. "No. I want to be here with you. But *with* you, Andre. Not as a shadow in your life. Not someone to whom you're unfailingly polite, and whose bed you visit only as a duty."

"As a duty?" he said, looking astonished. "*That's* what you think I've been doing?"

Ali folded her arms across her chest. "Yes. I do. I'm not stupid, Andre. I know what it is like when you choose to make love to me instead of politely servicing me like a mare. And so do you."

His cheeks flamed, and for a moment she saw a flash of the old Andre in his eyes before he put his head in his hands. "You are very wrong," he said tightly.

"Am I? I don't think so. And I don't think this has anything to do with our wedding trip being over, unless Sutherby has addled your brains so badly that you can't think straight. Or you are constantly reminded of things you'd rather not be reminded of."

He looked up at her then, his eyes sharp on her face. "What do you mean by that?"

"I am referring to your grandfather, the horrible old man," she said, looking around the room. "I can't think you ever found much happiness here."

He relaxed slightly. "No. No, I didn't."

"Well, then. It's time for that to change. We need to fill the house with people, with friends and family, and I think Christmas is the perfect time to do it. I'm going to ask Nicholas and Georgia, and Hattie of course, and Matthew, and anyone else in the family who wants to come."

Andre rubbed his neck. "Don't you think that's a

little much? We're only just married. You haven't had a chance to learn the running of the house."

Ali snorted. "While you've been buried in here, I've been busy. I know the house backward and forward, I know every member of the staff by name, indoor and out, and I know that the one thing this place needs is some happiness brought to it. A little less stuffiness and a lot more fun would be in order."

Andre nodded, but he still looked disconcerted. "Do as you like then. As I said before, it's your house too."

"It is my house, isn't it?" Ali said, grinning. "And I will do as I like. Since you've given me your permission, I know just where to start."

"Oh? Where is that?" Andre asked, but he watched her carefully, as well he should have, for Ali began to undo the buttons of her dress.

"Here," she said, pulling it off and stepping out of her crinoline.

Andre groaned. "For God's sake, not again. Please, Ali, get a grip on yourself."

"That's exactly what I've done," she said, coming around the desk. "Sutherby needs a good turning-around, and if it takes carnally christening all one hundred seventy-five rooms to exorcise the past, we're going to do it properly."

She pulled his shirt out of his trousers and ran her hands up over his broad chest, her fingers playing with his nipples, which instantly became taut beneath her touch. His muscles flinched involuntarily as she caressed them, and Ali, well pleased, lowered her mouth to his and kissed him heatedly, her teeth nipping his full lower lip as she straddled his lap.

"Ali, please—please don't do this," he said desperately, his hands trying to restrain her hips.

"Why not?" she asked, rocking on his stiffening penis, relishing the feel of his length rubbing between her legs.

He buried his forehead against her breasts, breathing hard, his heart pounding as if he'd been running too fast, his skin suddenly on fire under her touch. It was the most uninhibited reaction that she'd had from him in the entire month they'd been at Sutherby.

"Why not?" she asked again, murmuring the question into his soft hair.

"Because I don't want to hurt you," he said brokenly. "Dear God, I don't want to hurt you again."

"Hurt me? But why would you—" Ali froze as understanding finally dawned. "That's it? That day on the beach is what all of this distance has been about? Oh, Andre," she said, starting to laugh and cry all at the same time in relief, in infinite love, stroking his hair, his cheek. "You didn't hurt me—you would never *hurt* me. How do you manage to turn the most obvious things inside out?"

He closed his eyes. "I hurt you, Ali," he said. "My God, I as good as raped you. There is no forgiveness for that."

Ali gazed at him in wonder. "You truly believe that?"

"I—I wanted to force you to submit to my will. And God help me, I did." He shuddered.

She cupped his face in her hands, her eyes burning into his, desperately wanting him to understand. "You didn't force me to do anything I didn't want to do," she said. "Andre—you didn't force me and you didn't hurt me."

"That's not how it sounded to me," he said, looking away.

"Do you honestly think I would have cried out for anyone else in such a way? I never even screamed when Hadgi flayed the flesh off my back, Andre, and I've *never* felt such pain as that." She smiled. "Pleasure is an entirely different matter."

He shook his head soundlessly.

Ali gently stroked his face. "If you had done anything to cause me real physical pain, I would have let you know in a way that was unmistakable, believe me. I would never have let you continue. What you gave to me that day is something I will never forget."

Andre met her eyes and the uncertainty, the guilt

he was feeling, were laid bare. "Do you honestly mean it?"

"Of course I do." Ali lowered her mouth and kissed him. "You're a wonderful lover. I would far rather have that part of you, the part that really means it instead of the part that holds back." She smoothed her hands down his muscled rib cage. "I like you much better when you're my Andre, not the Andre you become when you're trying to behave like a proper Englishman."

"The last thing I am is a proper Englishman," he said, a flash of humor in his eyes. "Just as the last thing you are is a proper Englishwoman," he finished.

"Then stop treating me like one," Ali said, cupping the outline of his erection and lightly squeezing.

It finished him off, as she knew it would. Within a moment he had her on the floor, his hands inside her chemise, her petticoat worked up around her waist.

"Ali, God . . ." he whispered, his mouth taking her breasts in a frantic suckling, squeezing them until she winced, his hands kneading her buttocks, his fingers wasting no time slipping into her folds, touching her with the old frenzy, causing Ali to buck underneath him in delirious pleasure.

"Better," she managed to say. "Oh, much better. And under the starchy old duke's desk is best yet."

Andre choked with laughter, then pulled her drawers off in one swift movement and flung them behind him. "Then let him watch this," he said, positioning himself to enter her. "Because I'm going to exorcise his ghost once and for all."

He christened Ali, the rug, the room, and Sutherby in one almighty storm of lovemaking that he never expected to occur under that particular roof. It was as much an act of vindication as anything else. Ali, bless her, made it easy.

Andre shivered as he watched Ali fly around the frozen lake on her ice skates, laughing with sheer enjoyment, two of Ghislane's grandchildren holding her gloved hands and squealing with pleasure, Sherifay leaping about on the bank, barking insanely.

He laughed himself as all three took a tumble and Matthew and Hattie, who had been holding hands and watching nothing but each other tumbled over on top of them. Cold, he decided to let them sort themselves out and started back to the house where Nicholas and Georgia and Charlie and his wife had sensibly retired to the warmth of the fireplace.

Christmas Day. It was the first he'd celebrated in nine years. Well, he amended as he approached the house, he wasn't exactly celebrating it as such, but he had to admit that much to his surprise, he was enjoying himself.

It wasn't easy having the ghost of Christmas at Saint-Simon hanging over him, but since Ali busily filled every moment with one activity or another, there wasn't much time to think about it. And that was fortunate, since in moments when he wasn't paying strict attention, memory came flooding back. It hurt. God how it hurt. Yet Ali unconsciously assuaged the pain that he kept closely guarded, just by being her sweet, funny self. She made it damnably hard for him to keep himself guarded, period. But he managed. Not entirely successfully, but he managed.

Ali also had turned Sutherby into a place of laughter, a feat he would have thought impossible only a month ago, and yet it was now filled with not only laughter but with nearly the entire Daventry family, who had arrived the week before to spend the Christmas holidays. Oddly, although he had only agreed to the house party to make Ali happy, he didn't really mind that either. He loved to see Ali happy, loved to see the happiness she created in others.

"A chilly afternoon, Your Grace," Pennyswell said, taking his overcoat in the hall, which sported a large Christmas tree complete with all the decorations. Ali and the others had spent all of the last week strewing holly and evergreens and mistletoe in every conceivable location.

"It is indeed, Pennyswell. I hope the fire is roaring.

The duchess refuses to come in until the last possible moment, but I'm not so brave a soul."

"Your wife does not feel the cold as you do, Your Grace. Hot punch is coming out of the kitchen right now."

Andre smiled. "Thank God for small mercies. I'm about frozen through."

He walked down the hall to the sitting room, relieved that the chilly reception he'd first been given by various members of the family had thawed, largely again thanks to Ali's warmth and the family's desire to see her first Christmas as his wife be a happy one.

He was absolutely certain that was the only reason they'd decided to come. Mercifully though, no one had brought the past up, and for that he could only be grateful. But then, they were all bending over backward to be careful anyway, so that no slip was made in front of Hattie or the staff regarding his and Ali's shared time in Turkey.

"You too?" Charlie asked as Andre marched over to the fireplace and practically climbed inside. "India has thinned my blood. I suppose Asia Minor has done the same to you."

Andre held his hands out, rubbing them together to encourage the circulation. "I don't know about that," he said. "I managed to spend time in some incredibly cold locations. But yes, I suppose my blood must have thinned in the eight years away."

Charlie looked at him sideways. "You were never homesick in all that time?"

Andre went very still. "No. I was never homesick," he said, knowing his luck had just run out. Charlie was gifted at prying things out of people and doing it with extraordinary insouciance.

"Liar," Charlie said succinctly. "I may only be your nominal uncle, but I know you better than that, my boy. Saint-Simon is a part of you every bit as much as it's a part of your father."

Andre turned to face him, doing his level best to remain civil. "Charlie, as pleasant as it is to see you,

I am going to find your company extremely unwelcome if you pursue this particular subject."

"You know, the first time I met your mother, she had the same prickly skin." He scratched his head. "Of course, growing up here at Sutherby with no one but her half brother and misguided father and that blasted priest didn't help, but it was a good thing that your father managed to bring her out of it. Too bad he wasn't as successful with you." He gave Andre the characteristic grin he was rarely without. "It's a good thing you have Ali to do it for you."

Andre fixed Charlie with a chilly eye. "Back off, Charlie."

"Me?" Charlie said innocently, raising his winged eyebrows. "I was just giving you my blessing. After all, you did steal Ali right from under my son's nose, poor boy."

"Poor boy?" Andre said, having to admire Charlie for his ability to wiggle out of a tight corner. "Trust me, Matthew can look after himself. And given what he's been doing under the mistletoe and God knows where else every chance he has, I expect an announcement soon."

"Mmm. Hattie's a fine girl, and I think they'll be happy. I don't believe that stuff you gave her for her sneezes is responsible for the stars in her eyes, but it might be responsible for the stars in Matthew's. She looks an entirely different girl."

"I think she feels like an entirely different girl. It must have been awful, suffering like that all her life. Bloody unnecessary too."

"What did you give her, anyway? Eye of newt mixed with a little camel dung? She says it tastes foul but works as nothing else has."

"Ma Huang," Andre said. "Or if you prefer the genus, *Ephedra*. It comes from South China, which is probably why none of her physicians knew of it. It's a highly effective medication."

"Must have learned about that from your father, eh? He was always coming back from Asia with all sorts of strange and interesting things. But then Pascal is a strange and interesting person."

Andre's fist worked at his side. "Charlie. I realize you think you are being helpful by chasing this topic, and maybe you think Christmas has made me feel sentimental. But I assure you it hasn't."

"Pity," Charlie said. "I must say, I thought you were looking particularly annoyed in church this morning. Or was that because Ali kept nudging you in the side?"

"Ali," Andre said with exasperation, "thinks God is her best friend. She becomes offended when not everyone likes Him as much as she does. Or in my case, has no use for Him at all."

"Ah. Yes, I can see why she was poking you, since Ali does seem to relish Christmas. I have fond memories of one I spent with her—oh, what was it—about four years ago, when we last came over to see the family? Ali has the most interesting version of the birth of Christ I've ever heard." He chuckled. "You ought to have her tell it to you."

Andre had to laugh. "Believe me, I've been subjected to Ali's stories. They are original, to say the least."

"Yes ... I particularly enjoyed hearing about the two of you, and Joseph-Jean, of course, romping about on camels and so on." He clapped Andre on the back. "You made a good marriage, Andre, and I wish you great happiness. It's long past time for that, although thinking about it, you're about the same age as your father was when your mother fell at his feet. Late bloomers, you Saint-Simons."

Andre was stunned by that piece of effrontery. Charlie knew perfectly damn well that he had fallen in love with Genevieve at the tender age of fourteen and had never looked at anyone else before or since. "I don't think you can say that," he snapped.

"Can't I?" Charlie said, not the least perturbed. "Oh, well. Too late. I'm forever putting my foot in my mouth, aren't I?" He grinned. "Never mind, Andre. It's part of my job."

Charlie wandered over to his wife, leaving Andre by the fire, trying to work out what Charlie had really been getting at.

"It was a lovely day, wasn't it?" Ali said as they prepared for bed. "Did you see the children's glowing faces when the dining-room door was opened?"

"Yes. And did you see Hattie's face when Matthew found the lucky silver sixpence in his Christmas pudding?"

Ali nodded. "I thought she was going to burst into tears of happiness. Now they both have one, which bodes well. She told me just this afternoon that Matthew hinted he was going to apply to her father for her hand."

"Well, thank God for that. At least he's not staring you down like a lovesick calf anymore."

"Jealous?" Ali asked with a sparkle in her eyes.

Andre came over to her and delivered a kiss on the top of her head. "Insanely," he said. "Thank you, by the way, for my new dressing gown."

"Did you like the camel I embroidered?" she asked, looking at him.

"Very much so, and the tents in the background as well. I can't help but wonder what Hambley will make of it."

"Hambley already thinks you eccentric, so I doubt he'll think much of anything. And thank you again for my bracelet. The emeralds are very beautiful, although I'm sure you spent far too much money."

"I'm delighted you like it, and let me worry about how much money I spend."

"Well, I hope you bargained with the jeweler," she said and picked up her hairbrush again.

Andre took it out of her hand and began to brush her hair in long smooth strokes.

"Mmmm" Ali said, tilting her head back. "I particularly liked the carolers coming into the front hall, and Pennyswell's proud face when he handed around punch to them. It was the first time ever at Sutherby, he said."

"Oh?" Andre asked absently, more interested in Ali's long shining hair.

"Yes," she said, twisting on the chair to look at him. "There was no Christmas tree, either, no decorations, no Yule log, not even a Christmas feast." She screwed up her face. "Your grandfather spent the whole day in prayer in the chapel. Pennyswell said that if the old man had seen the chapel last night with all the candles and the crêche, and the beautiful evergreeen boughs, he would have had apoplexy on the spot."

"Too bad you didn't come along to decorate sooner," Andre said dryly. "He might have gone years ago and spared everyone."

"But then you would have had to come home to be the duke, and we would never have met."

Andre tried to make sense of that, then gave up. "I suppose he objected to all the decorations because of their pagan connotations." He put the brush down and started to undress.

"What pagan connotations?" Ali asked, crawling into bed.

"Well, first of all, the Yule log, the greenery including the fir tree, the exchanging of gifts and so on, all come from much earlier traditions of celebration associated with the winter solstice." He glanced at her over his shoulder. "The Celts, Teutonic tribes, all sorts of pagan religions celebrated the same way," he said, pulling off his shirt. "I believe the Egyptians as well as the Chinese and the Hebrews used evergreens as a symbol of eternal life, which makes perfect sense, of course."

"Andre," Ali said, wrapping her arms around her knees, "sometimes you are much too analytical. Why can't you simply enjoy Christmas without picking it to death?"

"Aren't you interested? Candles in the tree, for example, are a symbol of Christ, as well as a damned good way to burn the house down." He yanked off his shoes and removed his trousers.

Ali glowered at him. "You were the one who had

all those ugly buckets of water put in the hall? Pennyswell wouldn't say."

"Ever loyal Pennyswell, although to whom I'm not sure. But I didn't want to spend the evening fighting a fire."

"Andre, it's Christmas—the day of the birth of Christ. Can't you allow yourself a little whimsy?"

"Why?" he asked, sliding into bed next to her. "You provide more than enough whimsy for both of us. I'm an historian, sweetheart. It's a natural function of my mind to be analytical."

"Pooh," she said. "That's just an excuse you use. Even you can't be immune to the story of Christ's birth."

"Oh?" he asked, propping his head on his hand and gazing at her with fascination. "And I suppose you're now going to subject me to it?"

"Yes. And you're going to listen to every last word." She dimmed the gas lamp, then crossed her legs and placed her hands in her lap, preparing to begin.

Andre saw he was in for a long one this time, and although the very last thing he wanted to hear about was the birth of Christ, Charlie had piqued his curiosity. "All right," he said. "I'll do my best. Just don't expect to make a believer out of me."

"Quiet," Ali commanded. "Once, a long time ago in Nazareth, which is a city in Galilee—"

"I've been," he said. "Filthy place."

"Oh. Well, I'm sure it was different back then. Anyway, there was a woman named Mary. She was very kind and good, and she loved a man called Joseph with all her heart." Ali smiled softly. "Just as I love you."

"Ali—" he said on a warning note. "You know I—"

"Shh," she replied, putting a finger over his mouth. "Of course Mary was much, much purer than I, for the angel Gabriel came to her in her house and put a baby inside her without the usual method." She sighed. "I wonder if it felt as nice. Anyway, Mary was amazed, of course."

"I'm sure Joseph was as well," Andre said wryly.

"Andre. Joseph understaood perfectly. How could he not?" Ali's brow furrowed. "I'm not sure everyone else took it as well, but then, you can't ask for everything."

"No, I suppose you can't," Andre said, suppressing a smile.

"It's a pity," Ali said, "but there you are. Mary's belly grew large with her baby, so they did just what we would have done in Turkey. They married her off to Joseph, since despite both their protests, the family assumed they'd slept together."

"Ah," Andre said. "Practical."

"Of course. People are not so histrionic in that part of the world as they are in this part. Well. Off Mary and the unborn baby went on a donkey—Joseph walking beside—to Bethlehem, since a perfectly horrible man called Caesar Augustus was taxing everyone." Ali tapped his arm. "Not unlike your friend Brutus."

"I never said I approved of Brutus. That was your piece of fiction." Andre stroked her knee, but Ali pushed his hand away.

"Not now. I'm concentrating," she said. "Poor Mary and Joseph ended up miles and miles away in Bethlehem, all because it was the place that Joseph's people, the people of David, had come from. They were hot, tired, and thirsty, and not a single beastly innkeeper would give them a room, even though dear Mary was about to have her sweet little baby. So what do you think happened?"

"I have absolutely no idea. What happened?"

"Mary ended up in one of the kinder innkeeper's stables where the animals were far more hospitable than the people of Bethlehem, that's what happened. Imagine. A woman trying to have a baby, and no one would let her into his house."

"Well ... you have to understand, with everyone running around being displaced because of the taxes, the innkeepers were stretched to the limit, Ali. First come, first served and all that." Andre rolled over onto his back and stretched his arms behind his head.

"Suppose they had great pashas filling the rooms? You don't think they'd toss one of them out to suit a mere woman in labor?" He grinned at her.

Ali threw a pillow at him in response. "I'm sure God wanted His little son to be born in a stable with the animals all around or He would have arranged a room. He even put a great star in the sky so that people could find the infant. Who would think to go looking in a stable for the son of God?"

"I assume you're referring to the three kings bearing all those precious gifts of oils and incense?" Andre asked, his expression one of supreme innocence.

"Yes," Ali said, "but also to the shepherds in the field, who were just as important. And all the angels too, although I suppose they would know where the baby was anyway."

"Hmm. I suppose they must have, given all that singing they were supposed to be doing."

"I think it must have been very beautiful. Just like home, with the bright stars clustered in the night sky, and camels and sheep and cows in the fields, and not a single glimmer of snow, except maybe on the mountaintops." She smiled dreamily. "And maybe a nice soft breeze blowing, bearing the scent of orange blossom . . ."

Andre's patience ran out. The sight of Ali sitting half-naked on the bed, her hair falling down her back, was too much for him. He hoisted himself into a sitting position and reached for her, pulling her down on top of him, spreading her hair over his arms. Oh, yes, Ali was a far better source of heat than anything else that existed at Sutherby.

"My turn," he said, cupping the back of her head and pulling it down toward his. "Once, in a bedroom in a large and drafty house in a cold, damp country called England, which had never known the scent of orange blossoms, there was a man who very badly wanted his chatterbox wife. So to silence her, he kissed her like this."

Andre traced the outline of her lips with his tongue, then covered her mouth with his own, tasting the sweet moist depths. Ali's arms came around his back, her small hands stroking over his skin as she returned the kiss.

"He wasn't sure he had her complete attention," Andre continued, raising his head. "So he decided to be a little more blatant about the matter." He moved his head down to Ali's soft round breast, the nipple already hard, and he tongued it through the fine material of her nightdress.

Ali squirmed on him, her head arching back, her hands pushing hard through his hair. He took her nipple between his teeth and lightly bit down, and she gave a little cry of pleasure, which only encouraged him to do the same to the other breast.

Ali lifted her head and did exactly the same thing to his bare nipple, and he groaned.

"And then the wife," she said softly, putting her hands on his chest, "decided to give her husband one last taste of Christmas. But you have to stay absolutely still."

"Oh, sweet Christ," Andre groaned, with a fair idea of what was coming.

"And no blaspheming, either," Ali said, holding his arms down. She bent her head and suckled hard on his nipple, which nearly caused him to lose his mind. It was everything he could do to not move as Ali brushed her mouth back and forth over his chest, then moved lower over his abdomen, pushing the covers down as she went.

He didn't feel the cold—his skin was on fire. He closed his eyes and grimaced in a monumental effort at control as Ali's mouth found his erection. She kissed him softly, running her tongue up and down his length, her hand cupping him below as she opened her mouth and took him into its soft recesses, suckling him much as she had done his nipples, with a gentle pressure that gradually increased and threatened to send him through the ceiling.

"Mercy," he moaned, his entire body trembling with the effort of keeping still. Ali's soft hair swept rhythmically over his skin, only making the situation worse.

"No mercy," Ali said, lifting her head and moving up over him. She kissed him then, her tongue stabbing in and out of his mouth, and a renewed sweat broke out on his brow as she took him in her hand and guided him between her thighs, sheathing him in her, her breasts brushing against his flaming chest as she took his full length all at once.

"Ahhh—God," he groaned as she straightened and began to move on him in long, sweeping plunges.

"Don't move," she whispered again, beginning to ride him as expertly as she rode her horses, sinking down on him again and again.

Andre closed his eyes, all sensation centered in his groin, the only part of his body that had contact with Ali, and it became the center of his universe, Ali's hot wet silky flesh sliding frenetically up and down on his. He dimly heard her cries as the world began to spiral out of his control.

Control ... somewhere in the recesses of what was left of his mind he realized that Ali was doing to him what he had done to her two months before. She was not giving him a choice to do anything but submit himself to her, and yet he could have stopped her at any time.

But he didn't want to. He finally understood what had passed between them that day and saw the stark beauty in it. And he understood that that was what Ali intended. In her own, very feminine way, she was showing him what she had felt.

In the exact moment that realization struck, Andre reared up, his hips jerking, a violent cry wrenched from him as Ali wrung the seed from his body with hers. In that exact moment, he realized what a truly fine present she had given him.

But in that moment he also knew he could never afford to return the gift of love.

Chapter 18

London was in full bloom, which Ali thought was particularly appropriate, since Hattie was to be married in only a week's time and would have all the beauty of April to surround her in her happiness.

Ali glanced over at her dear friend, who was picking over a selection of fabric, a frown of concentration on her face. She had a radiance about her that was unmistakable, and Ali suspected it was due to an equal combination of being in love and being relieved of her sensitivities, thanks to clever Andre.

Hattie had actually grown pretty, her eyes no longer puffy and irritated, her skin clear, her nose a delicate porcelain rather than red. It was extraordinary the difference it made, not only in the way she looked, but in her confidence.

Matthew walked about like a man in a daze, far more so than he ever had with her, and Ali was delighted to see it, for she knew that he truly was in love this time, and Matthew knew it too.

As happy as she was, Ali only wished that Andre would look at her with the same captivated, adoring expression. But she'd accepted her situation and would be an ungrateful fool to expect anything more.

"What do you think, Alexis?" Hattie said. "The blue or the green?"

"The green, by all means," Ali answered. "It picks up the lovely color of your eyes."

Hattie beamed. "It's so nice to have a color other than red. But I think you're right. Yes. The green it is."

She went back to her consultations with the dressmaker in the fitting room, and Ali gazed out the window, wondering when Andre would be finished with his business meeting. She knew he had little patience for this sort of female thing, but he was very nice about accommodating them anyway.

Actually, he was very nice about a number of things. Even London society said so, as if it had collectively thought him incapable of being pleasant or kind. Well, he'd shown them, hadn't he? He went everywhere with her, was amusing to her friends and attentive to her. Very attentive, Ali thought with a grin. Society talked about that too, and she hoped their ears burned, even if they had no way of knowing that he didn't truly love her.

Andre walked into the shop just at that moment. "What has you so amused?" he asked, slipping an arm around her waist.

"Nothing much," she replied, leaning into his weight. "I'm just happy you're here."

"Oh?" he said, giving her a very indecent stroke on her backside, although at least he took care to shield the gesture with his body. "Well, good. Then let's go home and I'll make you even happier."

"Andre, sometimes I wonder about you," Ali said with a smile, pushing his hand away.

"Sometimes I do too." And then he froze as the bell rang over the door, his back stiffening. Ali absorbed the thunderous expression on his face with trepidation and slowly turned.

Only to see the huge figure of Mrs. Herringer squeeze into the shop. Ali's hand slipped over her mouth as a thousand memories came rushing back. Mrs. Herringer yanking her arm out of its socket. Mrs. Herringer calling her awful, wicked names, Mrs. Herringer looking at her with unspeakable contempt. Ali felt ill, and a little moan inadvertently escaped her lips.

Andre instantly took her by the shoulders and turned her away. "Sit down," he murmured. "Keep your face averted. There's only one way to deal with this, and it's head-on."

Ali obeyed with alacrity, but she couldn't help watching Andre surreptitiously, for he instantly strode over to the counter where horrible Mrs. Herringer stood fingering the samples of cloth.

Andre picked up a long runner of black bombazine. "Contemptible," he said. "Beyond belief. If there's one thing I cannot abide, it is shabby goods that masquerade as something they are not."

Mrs. Herringer turned, her bosom swelling indignantly. "Do you address me, sir . . . oh!" Her eyes bulged. "Oh, my—Your Grace. What a happy coincidence!"

"Is it? I confess, I hadn't thought to see you again, Mrs. Herringer."

"Why no, indeed," she said, her pudgy hand fluttering at the neckline of her dress. "But of course everyone knows of your return and your marriage. My congratulations."

Andre gave her a wintry smile. "Thank you."

"Oh, my, yes," Mrs. Herringer said, encouraged. "Why, everyone speaks so fondly of your dear duchess."

Andre rubbed the corner of his mouth. "Do they? I suppose that's because my wife is socially adept as well as eminently likable."

"Well, naturally," Mrs. Herringer cooed, not seeing the trap directly in front of her. "A dear girl they say, and pretty as a picture."

"I wonder," Andre said contemplatively, "what 'everyone' would have said if I'd married a Turkish whore."

Ali nearly fell off her chair.

"I—ah . . . oh," Mrs. Herringer spluttered. "Oh, Your Grace, you tease."

"No. I don't tease, Mrs. Herringer. I am most sincere. Do you suppose only English people share your aversion to those from foreign lands, or is bigotry and cruelty a universal trait?"

Her mouth gaped open and she gasped like a landed fish. "If you refer to—"

"I assure you, it was merely a hypothetical question," Andre said as Hattie came out of the fitting room. "Hello, my dear. Are you ready to leave?" He held out his arm and Hattie took it, looking up at him with a puzzled expression.

"Where's A—" she started to say, but Andre cut her off.

"I thought we'd stop for a cream on the way home," he said, meeting Ali's eyes over Hattie's head. He nodded imperceptibly toward the door.

Ali saw precisely what Andre was up to, and she rose and walked quickly out of the shop while Mrs. Herringer stared Hattie up and down with her hideous bulging eyes.

"Come along then," Andre said. "I find I am impatient to be away, and the carriage is waiting. Good day, Mrs. Herringer."

"Good day, Your Grace," Mrs. Herringer said, watching the duke pull his bride out of the shop, a hand trembling at her ample bosom. She didn't know whether to be offended or thrilled, so she settled for the latter.

"Fancy that," she said gustily as the modiste's assistant appeared from the back. "I've finally seen the celebrated duchess. But no one said anything about her being a redhead."

"The Duchess of Montcrieff?" the assistant replied. "Good heavens no. That was her friend, Miss Charleton. The duchess has dark hair." She looked around, puzzled. "But where did Her Grace go? She was here only a moment ago."

Mrs. Herringer waddled to the window and peered out at the carriage that had pulled up. Sure enough, the duke was helping a young, dark-haired woman inside.

Mrs. Herringer ogled the lucky woman whom all of London talked about, but could see nothing but her back. She was desperate to get a look at the girl who had so quickly landed the black duke and stolen his heart in the process. She'd heard nothing else for months on end now.

And then the little duchess turned her head, smiling

up at her husband for one brief moment before disappearing inside, and a strangled gurgle emerged from Mrs. Herringer's throat.

"No ... No, it's not possible," she said as the carriage door closed and it rolled away. She sank down onto a chair, fanning herself wildly with her handkerchief.

"Madam? You look unwell," the assistant said. "May I bring you some water?"

"No. No, thank you. I just—it's nothing. I must have been mistaken. Yes. I'm sure I was mistaken. A momentary trick of the light." If there was one thing she was sure of, it was that Catholic dukes did not marry their heathen Turkish whores.

But on the other hand ... maybe this duke really had. He was queer enough, and it would explain the swift courtship. Maybe the brat had been pregnant after all when he sent her to England, and they had a love child tucked away somewhere. Oh, it was scandalous!

She really couldn't wait to spread the word. She'd be the envy of all her friends with such a deliciously ripe piece of gossip. And wouldn't *that* put the chit in her place?

The duke had some nerve, masquerading a Turkish savage as a decent God-fearing English duchess. Oh, indeed, she'd show him, wouldn't she just? Bigotry indeed.

Andre wondered what the buzz was about when he and Ali arrived at the Looleigh ball. He was accustomed by now to a general buzz accompanying them wherever they went, but this one was a little louder and a little more speculative than usual.

"What have you done now?" he murmured in Ali's ear as they were announced. "Is your dress the latest in Parisian designs?"

"It's the same one I wore two weeks ago," Ali replied with a mischievous smile. "Maybe that's what's causing such a stir."

"Ah, they must think me bankrupt," Andre said,

taking her arm and leading her down the stairs. "Poor sorry me, unable to afford to buy you a new dress."

But it was Matthew who finally clued Andre in. "My God, have you heard the gossip?" he whispered, finding him an hour later and drawing him to one side.

"No, and I'd like to know what in hell is going on," Andre said, thoroughly exasperated. "I've never had such sidelong looks cast my way. Ali seems oblivious, but something's up."

"It certainly is," Matthew said. "They're saying that you were—that you . . . that you and Ali were together in Turkey."

Andre's brow snapped down. "What do you mean?" he demanded.

"Oh, not the truth. They're saying that she was your Turkish doxy."

Andre stared at him in disbelief. "That damned Herringer woman . . ." he said, the light dawning.

"They're saying that she had your child years ago, and you've hidden it away somewhere in England."

Andre slowly shook his head. "What?"

"Yes," Matthew said despondently. "I've said it's all nonsense of course, but it's the talk of the moment."

"I can imagine," Andre said, a grin breaking out on his face. And then he threw his head back and roared with laughter, knowing full well everyone in the room was watching. "How perfectly wonderful. Ah, Matthew, how absolutely marvelous. The Herringer bitch couldn't have shot herself in the foot more successfully. Where's Ali?"

"She's talking with Shakelford and his wife. I don't think she has any idea."

Andre nodded. "Perfect. Shakelford's wife is ideal for my purposes. She'll have this new version out to everyone near and far with no time to spare."

He found Ali within a matter of moments. "I beg your pardon," he said, interrupting the conversation. "But I have just heard something of the utmost urgency, which I think my wife needs to know about instantly."

Lady Shakelford's eyes snapped to attention. Her

husband merely looked uncomfortable. "Alexis," he said, using the name he called her in public, "are you aware that we have had an illegitimate child ferreted away somewhere in England for the last five years or so?"

Ali's reaction was exactly what he had hoped for. She blinked, then burst into peals of laughter. "Oh?" she said. "Is that a variation on the story that I landed you by paying off a priest to invoke unholy rites?"

"Something like that," he said. "Better yet, though, did you know you were Turkish?"

Ali tilted her head. "Oh, but did I forget to tell you?" she said without missing a beat, and he liked her more than ever in that moment. "I was born in a harem, the child of a sultan."

"Well, you can't have stayed too terribly long in the harem, because according to local gossip I moved you into mine."

Ali's hand went to her mouth. "I forgot that too. Did I like it?"

"Naturally," he said easily, admiring her composure, although he could tell by a subtle little flash in the back of Ali's eyes that she was alarmed.

"Oh, good," she said. "But then how is it that we hid a child in England if we were so busy cavorting in Turkey?"

"I'm not entirely sure of the details myself. But we must have done an awfully good job, since neither of us knows anything about it." He smiled apologetically at the Shakelfords. "Obviously we're both terribly forgetful."

Lady Shakelford tittered. "Apparently so, Duke. One doesn't ordinarily misplace one's children. I suppose I should be shocked, but the two of you always do have the most extraordinary conversations."

"I suppose that's what comes of being a Turk," Ali said, looking at Andre innocently. "Do I make a good one?"

"Brilliant," Andre said with a tender smile. "If you'll excuse us, I'm going to ask my wife to dance."

"Oh, Andre," Ali whispered against his chest the

moment he'd pulled her into the waltz. "What has that awful woman gone and said?"

"The absolutely perfect thing if she had to say anything at all. Now smile, sweetheart. We have one hell of an evening to carry off."

And Ali did, Andre reflected later as he held her sleeping figure in his arms. But then, he was beginning to think that Ali could carry off just about anything.

"And there she was, Jo-Jean, as hideous as ever," Ali said, pouring him a cup of tea while she enthusiastically filled him in on all their news, "and just as stupid. Andre insulted her right and left, and most everything went straight over her horrible head. Unfortunately, she still made the connection somehow, for the story has been flying about since last week."

Jo-Jean stirred his spoon in his cup. "What does Andre say about all of this?"

"He's annoyed, but he's not really concerned," Ali said. "He just laughs it off publicly as the ravings of a demented old woman. Privately, I think he'd like to hang, draw, and quarter her."

"Hmm. And how are you handling it?"

"Oh, it doesn't bother me, not really. The story is so outrageous as to be ridiculous, especially the part about the child I've hidden away. It's her word against ours, and Mrs. Herringer has no influence, whereas Andre has a great deal." She shrugged. "Who is really going to believe I was Andre's Turkish whore?"

"No one in his right mind," Joseph-Jean said. "But it is a nuisance. Ah, well."

Ali grinned at him. "Can you imagine what would happen if I opened my mouth and let a stream of Turkish fly? I could probably bring half of London to its knees in one fell swoop."

Jo-Jean laughed. "From what I hear you've done that already. Andre says you're the toast of the town."

"Andre's prejudiced," she replied.

"Good. He should be. How is he, Ali?" Joseph-Jean leaned slightly forward, his gaze intent on her face.

"He's well. He's very well," Ali said softly. "I think

he's relatively happy, although he still won't discuss his parents, and I think he's still miserable about that underneath it all."

Joseph-Jean just shook his head. "Stubborn fool."

"It's so frustrating, Jo-Jean," Ali said, tucking her legs up under her. "I don't think he even realizes that I know them, that's how closed the topic is."

"I know they appreciate your letters," Joseph-Jean said quietly.

"I—I don't suppose you could tell me what—what happened between them? No one else will speak of it, and it might help me to understand." She looked at him pleadingly.

Jo-Jean looked down. "I'm sorry," he said after a long moment. "I really can't, Ali. It's not my place."

"What's not your place?" Andre asked, coming into the sitting room, and Ali turned around in surprise, praying Andre hadn't overheard anything more. But he seemed relaxed enough.

"Hello, sweetheart," he said, dropping a kiss on her head. "Well, Jo-Jean, when did you get in? And what are you doing closeted away with my wife, both of you looking as guilty as sin?"

"Oh, please," Joseph-Jean said, rising. "It's not as if Ali and I haven't spent months closeted away together, which exemplifies the point. She was just telling me about the current story that's circulating."

"Ah," Andre said, dismissing the subject. "That. It's no more than a tempest in a teapot, already yesterday's news. So. Are you looking forward to the lecture tomorrow?"

"I am. I'm also delighted that your new book has been received to such wide academic acclaim."

"Don't be modest. Your illustrations have received the same high praise, and you know it. It should be quite a turn-out."

"Indeed. Well. We shall see. In the meantime, tell me how Matthew and Hattie's wedding went?"

Ali launched into an enthusiastic recital, sparing Joseph-Jean no detail, and they were soon lost in laughter.

*   *   *

Ali listened with immense pride as Andre lectured the fellows and members of the British Museum, Joseph-Jean at his side with large illustrations.

Her smile widened as thunderous applause met his conclusion, and she watched him field questions from the audience with grace and good humor. Oh, he had come a long way from the days when she'd first known him, when he'd carried such a heavy burden in his heart.

He was so confident, so full of quiet enthusiasm for his subject, capable of making the dullest academic point sound fascinating. But best of all was the relaxed posture of his body, the brightness in his eyes, the smile that came and went like quicksilver. Yes, Andre's heart was definitely lighter.

Ali's own heart swelled with love. And then she heard a snide, murmured remark from behind her, the words spoken in Arabic.

"The damned man thinks he's God. Look at him, behaving as if he owns the British Museum and everything in it. Lord, what I'd give to see him brought down."

"One day, Allah be willing," came a second voice. "It is not right that you should be passed over like this. You have worked every bit as hard as he. Every bit. All this attention is only because he is now a duke."

Ali's spine stiffened and a fierce cold swept over her body. She knew those voices, had felt their sting before when she'd been a child dressed in *chalvars*. Dear heaven, it was the blond man Weselley and his awful Syrian, she was sure of it. She felt sick and terrified all at the same time, and she pressed her hands together hard, forcing them to cease trembling.

"Yes. A duke. With a duchess," Lord Weselley said sourly. "I wonder what his fine friend Claubert makes of that—although it doesn't look as if he's too concerned, given his self-satisfied expression."

"Why should be he?" Abraham said. "I'm sure he thinks their secret is safe."

Ali froze.

"Well, it will be my first priority to seek out Montcrieff's wife and satisfy my curiosity," Weselley replied. "I can't help but wonder why Montcrieff would take such a risk. Or perhaps he thinks no one would guess at the truth."

Abraham snorted. "Amusing, isn't it? If the truth were known, Montcrieff would be ruined. His reputation would be in shreds, and the British Museum would be forced to ostracize him."

"Maybe then they'd pay me some attention," Weselley said. "God knows I'm treated like dirt as it is."

"To cut your funding as they did—a vicious blow, delivered when you were not even in the country to defend yourself. It was probably the influence of that devil up there," Abraham replied.

"He's always had it in for me. Ah, well." Weselley snickered. "He's bound to slip up. And I'll be there when he does. Not with rumor or innuendo, but with concrete evidence."

Ali thought she really might be sick on the spot. The very evidence Weselley sought sat directly in front of him, if only he knew it. Dear heaven, they must have heard the rumors and guessed that Andre had married his servant boy. And if the word got out about that, Andre would be ruined. Society was not flexible when it came to the rules of correct behavior. Her mind raced furiously, trying to work out what to do next.

If either of them saw her, they would surely recognize her, and Andre's entire future could be compromised—no. *Would* be compromised, hopelessly and beyond retrieval.

Ali squeezed her eyes closed against an unbearable pain that stabbed suddenly through her heart. Andre. She had to protect Andre, no matter what it cost her.

For even if Weselley was a fool, he was also a peer, and his word carried influence. Mrs. Herringer's silly story was ridiculous, but Weselley had already guessed at the truth, and he obviously would stop at nothing to destroy Andre's reputation.

Not only would Andre be ruined, but Nicholas's and Georgia's reputations would be damaged by association. After all, they had fostered the deception for years, as had Matthew and the other members of the family. She couldn't be the cause of hurting so many people she loved. Especially Andre. Most especially Andre.

She pressed her fingers against her forehead, trying to think clearly through her panic. Weselley planned to seek her out. She couldn't let that happen, for then he'd have proof positive and wouldn't hesitate to use it.

But what could she do? What?

She couldn't go to Andre; he was overly protective of her as it was. He'd be sure to confront Weselley and bring himself down in the process. Andre had worked too long and too hard to have that happen, and Ali refused to be the source of his downfall, not when he had been kind enough to save her life and honorable enough to marry her. Not when she loved him more than life itself.

Her nails dug painfully into her palms and a cold sweat broke out on her brow as the only solution dawned on her with sickening clarity.

Without seeing her face, Weselley had nothing. No proof, no confirmation.

She would simply have to make sure that there was no possibility of his ever identifying her. And there was only one way to do that. She would have to disappear.

Ali ducked her head, unable to stifle her nausea. Murmuring an excuse, she moved out of her row, and keeping her head lowered and turned to the side, she managed to slip out the door undetected.

She found the water closet and was violently sick.

The carriage ride seemed to take forever, and Ali struggled against tears the entire way, trying not to think, not to feel until she'd reached the safety of her room. She forced a smile for the footman and another for the butler and swiftly went upstairs, refusing the aid of her maid to undress, desperately needing to be alone.

And in that aloneness, Ali sank onto her bed and cried as if her heart might physically break, for she knew that she had to sacrifice her beautiful dream in order that Andre might keep his.

It was God's will. It had to be. Only God could be so cruel.

Andre came to her later, but by then Ali was ready for him, her tears cried out, her mind made up. She'd even written the letter that he would find when she was gone.

She had this one remaining night with him, and she'd sworn to herself that she would make it last the rest of her life.

"You were brilliant," she said, greeting him with a warm smile that she hoped was convincing.

"They applauded, if that's any clue. Why did you leave early?" he asked, dropping a kiss on her cheek. "I looked for you in the crowd, but it was such a crush I just thought I'd missed you somehow, until I discovered you'd taken the carriage. You look pale. Are you feeling unwell?"

"I'm fine," she lied, relieved that he hadn't seen Weselley and wouldn't work out the problem. "I didn't want to distract you from all your admirers, so I left when you were answering questions."

Andre took off his camel-embroidered dressing gown and slipped into bed, pulling Ali gently into his arms. "What is it really, Ali? The truth this time."

"It's nothing," she insisted, wishing he would drop the subject, for she was about to burst into tears again, and that she couldn't afford. "If you really must know, I had a headache earlier."

"Ah," he said. "Benson mentioned you'd looked strained when you came home. Are you sure nothing happened to upset you?"

"Just a headache. I'm better now," she said, thinking that Andre always ferreted everything out of her with very little trouble, and if he carried on asking her questions, he'd have the whole story in minutes. "Andre? Could we not talk? Could we just hold each other, be together?" She had to fight hard to keep tears at bay. The effort nearly killed her.

He smiled at her then. "Be together?" he asked, smoothing his hands through her hair. "Oh, I think I might just be able to manage that. Are you sure you feel well enough, though?"

Ali simply nodded against his chest, suppressing a sob, thinking that death might be preferable to this agony. Never to feel Andre against her again, never to hear his voice? Never to have him love her ...

"Sweetheart? What is it?" he asked, looking down at her with concern. "Are you certain your headache is better? If it's not, tell me. I'll give you something for it."

She mutely shook her head. "Please," she whispered. "Please, just make love to me. That's all I want."

"Of course," he said, kissing her, stroking her hair, her face. "Of course I will." He kissed her again, softly at first, but quickly building it into something else, sensing her need, setting a deliberate fire between them.

"Andre," she whispered against his mouth. "Oh, Andre, don't stop. Don't stop tonight!"

"Whatever your heart desires," he murmured, pulling her even closer. "But goodness, maybe we should spend more evenings apart if this is the effect a little separation has on you."

Ali didn't reply. She couldn't. She pulled his head down and kissed him fiercely, forcing a groan from his throat.

Andre made slow, sweet love to her long into the night and she drank in every moment, every sensation, drowning in her love for him, giving him every last part of her, hoping that in the end it would be enough.

Because on the morrow she would be gone, and as angry as he would be, she wanted him at least to know that she had truly loved him.

Chapter 19

Pour yourself a drink," Andre said to Joseph-Jean the next evening, sticking his head out the sitting-room door. "Ali?" he called. "We're home."

He was surprised when Benson rather than Ali appeared. "What is it?" he asked impatiently.

"Her Grace took a train to the country this morning," Benson said. "She asked me to give you this as soon as you returned." Benson held out the silver salver with an envelope addressed in Ali's tidy hand.

"The devil she has," Andre said. Alarmed, he took it and dismissed Benson, ripping open the envelope.

My dearest Andre,
I know this is going to come as a shock to you, and I know you will be angry and confused. But what I do is for the best, you must believe me. I have left. I am not coming back.

Andre stared down at the page unable to believe his eyes. "Dear God no," he whispered, stunned.

It is not due to anything that you've done, you must believe that. It is only that the rumors have worked their toll, and I can't bear any longer to have people whisper behind your back and perhaps finally learn the truth.

I know that you are upset right now, but since you don't love me, you will recover soon enough. You must divorce me as soon as you can and marry someone else who will be able to give you children, since I haven't been any good at that either. I know Catholics aren't supposed to remarry, but you're not really

a Catholic, are you, since you don't believe in God?
You can say that I ran off with a lover if you like. I
won't mind.

It's not true, of course, for I could never be unfaith-
ful to you. I love you, Andre, and I always will, with
all my heart. More than anything I want you to have
a happy life. I know you felt obliged to marry me.
Maybe now you will find someone you can truly love,
someone without a past that can harm you.

I wish it could have been different. You will be in
my thoughts and prayers every day and night for the
rest of my life.

Ali

P.S. Please look after Sherifay for me. She'll be
lonely.

Andre shook his head back and forth in disbelief.
"Jo-Jean," he choked. "Jo-Jean. She's gone."

"Who's gone?" Joseph-Jean said, moving quickly to
his side. "Has someone died? Dear Lord, Andre," he
said, taking in his stricken expression, "what's happened? It's not your mother, is it?"

"Ali," he said almost inaudibly. "Ali's left me."

"I don't believe it," Jo-Jean said. "*Ali?* Ali can't
have left you—all she's ever wanted is to be with
you."

"Then read the damned thing!" Andre thrust out
the letter and Jo-Jean ripped it out of his hand. Andre
sank into a chair, trying to control his panic.

"Good God," Joseph-Jean said softly when he'd
finished. "What could have brought this on?"

"How in hell am I supposed to know?" He raked
his hands over his scalp. "Naturally she forgot to explain. She was fine last night. Well ... Actually not
fine. She seemed upset about something, but she said
it was a headache." He frowned, remembering Ali's
impassioned, almost desperate response to his lovemaking. "It has to have something to do with that
damned Herringer woman's absurd accusation. Look,
it says it right here, all this claptrap about the past."

"Yes, but the last time I talked to her, Ali didn't
seem to take it very seriously. You're sure she's not

upset that you're not in love with her? That's in there too."

Andre glanced up from rereading the letter. "No, of course not. We worked that out a long time ago. Ali's perfectly content with the way things are."

"Ah," Jo-Jean said. "I see. Well, perhaps someone said something to her last night, something that she thought might be damaging to you?"

"But what? And in any case, Ali's always told me everything. You know what she's like—she's an open book."

"Obviously not as open as you'd like to think," Joseph-Jean said mildly. "The last time she went running off was in Xanthos, and you couldn't work that out, either."

"What? Oh, that's right," he said, frowning. "She tore off that night I was telling her the Xanthian history for the tenth time. No, I never did find out what that was about."

"She also managed to hoodwink you into thinking she was a boy for six full months."

"Yes, all right, maybe so, but this is different," Andre said impatiently. "She's my wife, for the love of God. Wives don't generally take starts and go bolting off out of the blue, leaving ridiculous letters behind."

"It's not unheard of," Jo-Jean pointed out.

"But this is Ali. Ali's not like ordinary wives."

"No, she's not, is she?" Jo-Jean said with a smile that Andre found maddening. "Well, I suppose you'll have to go find her, won't you?"

"Find her ... why, of course," Andre said with a rush of relief. "Why didn't I think of that? All I have to do is fetch her back again. That can't be too difficult."

"I hope not," Jo-Jean said, scratching his ear.

"Oh, I imagine all I have to do is give her a good talking-to. Ali might be stubborn and overly emotional at times, but it generally doesn't take too much to bring her around."

"Do you suppose she went to Ravenswalk?" Jo-Jean asked. "After all, that's home to her."

"Don't be absurd," Andre said succinctly. "She's most likely gone to the farmhouse. It's her safe haven, and I gave it to her outright, so she would be fully within her rights."

"Isn't that a little obvious?" Jo-Jean asked. "Surely she'd know that would be the first place you'd look."

"Ali in her infinite wisdom obviously thinks I'll jump at her offer to divorce her, since she thinks it would be for my own good, the little idiot. It hasn't occurred to her that a divorce would cause a far bigger scandal than the truth."

Joseph-Jean gazed at the ceiling. "Whatever you say. You know Ali better than I. But for God's sake, get on with it—she has hours on you."

"Yes. I'd best take my carriage." He stuck his head out the door again. "Benson!" he bellowed. "Tell Hambley to pack me a case. I'm going to the country immediately. And summon the brougham."

Within a half hour, the horses were pounding toward the coast.

Andre arrived at Milford Farm shortly after dawn, exhausted, deeply worried for Ali, and furious that she had put him through a lot of unnecessary aggravation, even if she had convinced herself that it was on his behalf.

He went immediately inside and started straight upstairs to the bedroom. He pushed the door open, only to find the room empty and the bed neatly made.

The shock nearly undid him. He'd been so certain that this was where she'd be. "Damn!" he cried. "Where the hell are you, Ali?"

He shoved his hands on his hips and stared at the floor, his head spinning with questions. Hattie and Matthew were out of the country on their wedding trip, so they weren't a possibility. Anyway, he'd checked Raven's Close on his way out of Ravenswalk, and it had been shut up tight as a drum.

She wouldn't have gone to Sutherby—that wouldn't

be running away. A hotel, maybe? But Benson said she'd gone to the train station. And anyway, why in hell hadn't she taken the dog? She loved Sherifay. It didn't make sense that Ali would leave her in London.

"Oh—it's you, Mr. Saint-Simon."

He turned around to see Martha Lummus, her face wearing an expression of strong disapproval. "Mrs. Lummus, have you seen my wife by any chance?"

Her scowl deepened. "Indeed I have, only yesterday. Came on the train, she did. Packed up her things, crying her eyes out. Shame on you, I say, married only eight months to the sweetest girl in the world, and look at the state you've reduced her to." She crossed her arms. "And you two were always so happy when you came to stay. Never would have guessed you could have bungled it so badly."

"Never mind that, where is she now?" he said desperately. "Please, Mrs. Lummus, I must find her."

"My husband took her to Southampton yesterday afternoon. She said she was going home."

"Home?" he said with a rush of elation, thinking that Ali must have changed her mind at the last minute. "Excuse me," he said, "I have to get back to London immediately." He started to move past her, but Mrs. Lummus put out a hand.

"You won't find her there," she said, "not unless you can sail to your house. She took a ship."

"Oh, dear God," Andre said, his heart sinking further than he would have thought possible. "A *ship*? Are you sure?"

She nodded. "My husband was worried about her. He dropped her at a ticket agent and then he waited around the corner until she came out again and took a hansom cab away. Then he went inside and they said she'd bought passage for a ship that sailed last night." She gave him another mistrustful glare. "Said she was so upset she could hardly speak."

Andre rubbed a hand over his eyes. Ali. She'd taken a bloody ship. And there was only one place she would have taken it to.

"Mrs. Lummus. Martha," he said urgently, taking

her by the arms. "Please. Get your husband. I have to find out what ticket agent my wife used. Now. Quickly."

"I don't know as he should tell you. For all we know you've been beating the poor thing. Why else would she be running away?"

"I swear to you, it's nothing like that. My wife left the country because she is misguidedly trying to protect me. I knew nothing about it until yesterday evening or I would have come after her sooner."

"Oh," Martha Lummus said, but she didn't look terribly convinced. "You haven't been breaking the law, have you?"

'No," he said, wanting to tear his hair out. "I haven't been breaking anything, including my wife's head or heart. Please, Mrs. Lummus. I'd really like to get her back, but I can't do it standing here arguing with you."

"You can speak with Arnold, then," she said grudgingly. "But you'll have to wait until he's finished with the cows."

"I'll go to him," he said.

"No, you most certainly will not. In your state of mind you'll upset the beasts and sour the milk."

Andre was not sure when the role of master had been assumed by the servant, but he could see that Mrs. Lummus was not going to budge on the matter. In a way he couldn't really blame her. The situation did look highly suspicious. So he just nodded. "I'll be here."

He spent the half-hour wait going through Ali's things. He knew that she would have taken her passport from the London safe, and she had probably taken money as well to buy her ticket. He desperately hoped she'd taken enough to support herself until he could get to her. Knowing Ali, though, she probably hadn't wanted to deprive him of a single unnecessary shilling.

He looked inside the wardrobe. Her dresses were gone, and that was a relief, for it meant that she had no intention of cutting her hair and dashing around in *chalvars* again. He could only pray that she'd be sensible enough to use the protection of his name. But somehow he doubted she would. It would make her too easy to trace.

"Oh, Ali, why?" he groaned, sinking onto the bed and putting his head in his hands. "Why, for God's sake? What could possibly have chased you all the way back to Turkey?" He picked up a handkerchief lying on the bedside table. It smelled faintly of Ali's sweet, clean scent and a touch of jasmine.

The subtle perfume brought back a memory that had nothing faint about it. With a stab he remembered the evening only three weeks before that Ali had decided to explore the art of erotic massage here on this bed. It wasn't a night he was likely to forget.

But then the farmhouse held many extraordinary memories of various uninhibited hours they had spent here over the last eight months—the long winter nights, curled up against each other, reading or talking or making love. It was the first time in years he hadn't minded the cold, had enjoyed walking through the snow hand in hand with her, listening to her chatter.

And then had come the burgeoning spring days, when they'd had enough of London social life and taken a train to put it all behind them, if only for a day or two. God, the house felt hollow without her vital presence, he thought, feeling just as hollow himself.

But he'd find her. He'd find her and bring her home, back to where she belonged, firmly tucked at his side. He'd sworn to protect her and he would, with every fiber of his being, if he had to track her down to the ends of the earth.

"Mr. Saint-Simon?"

Andre looked up.

"Arnold's outside. He'll speak to you now."

Mrs. Lummus spoke far more gently than in their last exchange, and he wondered why. "Thank you, Mrs. Lummus," he said, rising and tucking Ali's handkerchief into his coat pocket.

He quickly went downstairs, immediately discovered

what he needed to know, and instructed his coachman to take him directly to Lloyd's ticket agency in Southampton.

"It's the worst of all bad luck," Andre said, accepting the glass of cognac that Jo-Jean had poured him, and throwing himself into a chair. "Not only did Ali get a fluke passage to Constantinople because someone canceled at the last minute, but there's also not another ship leaving for a fortnight." He took a long swallow of the badly needed drink. His nerves were in a terrible state, but he had no intention of falling apart. There was too much at stake.

"Someone has to have a boat going that direction. Can't we go to France or Italy and transfer?"

"We could, but all the schedules are conflicted. I checked. We'd be waiting for the same period of time. Damnation!"

"What about the Navy?" Jo-Jean asked. "Surely they'd accommodate two passengers on urgent business?"

"I don't have the flimsiest excuse to announce that I have to sail off to Turkey on an urgent mission, Jo-Jean. That and Ali's absence would only fuel the fire."

"Yes. Yes, I see. Whatever we do, it's imperative that everything be kept quiet on the home front. Well." He thought it over. "Suppose you announce that Ali's paying a visit to your parents, and you're staying behind on business until you can join her?"

Andre gave him a filthy look. "I think I can come up with something a little more useful than that," he said.

"Like what? You don't want your staff to know that Ali's fled the coop, so it's no good putting it about that she's at Sutherby or even Ravenswalk. Saint-Simon is perfect."

"Saint-Simon is ridiculous. People surely must be aware that I'm estranged from my parents. What would I be doing sending my wife there?"

"Andre, to the best of my knowledge the only people who know you're estranged from your parents, other than the entire village of Saint-Simon, are myself, your family, and the Daventry family. Oh, and Ali, of course, not that she knows any of the details," he added when Andre looked at him in sharp question. "We have all been careful to keep the situation quiet for your sake. So I see no logical reason not to use Saint-Simon as an excuse."

Andre's mood, already black, only turned blacker. "I won't hear of it."

"Why not? It's just a story after all, and you don't have anything better up your sleeve, have you?"

"Nothing at the moment, no," Andre admitted reluctantly.

"Well, then. I will write your parents informing them of the situation, and—"

"No! No, for God's sake don't do that," he said with a fresh surge of panic. "Please. If the word has to go out that Ali is in France, so be it. But it will damned well be left there."

Jo-Jean nodded. "A sensible decision. Very sensible. And if we have to wait a fortnight before leaving, then we might as well make the best use of our time."

Andre regarded him suspiciously, having already made what he considered an extraordinary concession. "What do you have in mind?"

"I think we should both be as visible as possible. After all, I'm the perfect person to help you suppress the story. If something was said that upset Ali badly enough to send her to Turkey, then some serious quashing is going to be in order."

Andre nodded. "Yes. That's wise, I suppose."

"And your job is to behave as casually as possible. If you suddenly revert to your previous behavior, people are going to make the correct assumption that Ali has bolted."

"What previous behavior?" Andre asked, puzzled.

Jo-Jean gazed at the ground, rubbing his forehead. Then he looked directly at Andre, and Andre couldn't read his expression to save his life. Probably because Jo-Jean's face was completely devoid of one.

"Just try to be your usual cheerful self," Jo-Jean said. "Now get some sleep. You look like a wreck."

"Thank you so much," Andre said dryly, but in all truth he felt like one.

"My pleasure," Jo-Jean said. "Good night."

Andre took his glass of cognac and headed straight upstairs. But as exhausted as he was, sleep didn't come. At four in the morning he finally gave in to sheer desperation and pulled Sherifay up from her position at his feet, curling her warm little body against his chest. But even that didn't soothe the gnawing ache that had taken up residence there.

"Oh, Ali," he whispered, succumbing to the fear that he'd been trying to keep at bay ever since he'd read her letter. "Please stay safe until I can bring you home. Please, sweetheart? Be careful. Don't do anything foolish."

All that answered him was the soft snuffle of Sherifay's breathing. Andre buried his face in her fur and concentrated on stilling the desperate pounding of his heart.

Andre stood near the stairs in Lord Umbersville's ballroom, grateful for a moment alone. The last two weeks had been sheer hell, between worrying about Ali and pretending he didn't have a care in the world.

On top of that, he missed her terribly. He missed the ring of her laughter, her spontaneity, the way she lit up a room when she walked into it. He missed her easy conviviality, the pleasure she took in everything and everyone about her, her whimsy, the sunny effect she had on people.

Now they constantly asked after her, and it was all he could do to keep a smile on his face and his posture relaxed as he forced an easy reply. He lied through his teeth, wanting to know exactly what they did—if she was well, when she was coming home.

But most of all he missed holding her in his arms, feeling her vibrant response to his touch, losing himself in their lovemaking.

Just like the first time, Ali had gone and taken the

sunshine with her, he thought with a heavy sigh. But this time it was a thousand times worse. Thank God they left for Turkey in the morning. At least he wouldn't feel quite so helpless.

His wandering gaze fell upon a familiar figure, and he looked again in disgust. So. Thomas Weselley had returned from his last disastrous expedition. He stood across the room, pontificating on something or other to someone who clearly didn't want to listen.

Well, Andre thought dryly, if he could find anything in his situation to be grateful for, he supposed it was that Ali happened to be out of the country at a most convenient time.

He wasn't particularly worried that either Weselley or his foul servant would recognize Ali, since the idea of a small, uneducated Turkish boy turning into the graceful, well-spoken, and attractive Duchess of Montcrieff would have been too enormous a leap for either of them to make. They had no way of knowing that Ali had ever left Turkey, let alone that she was female.

But on the heels of the stupid Herringer woman's story it was best that no connection be made at all, even though the rumor had all but been forgotten. Jo-Jean had been an enormous help with that, as had Nicholas and Georgia, who had come up to London to lend their support.

Weselley glanced up just at that moment and caught his eye, and to Andre's regret he instantly excused himself and swiftly crossed the room.

"Good evening, Montcrieff," he said, his pale gaze raking Andre up and down. "I didn't see you in the crush."

"Oh?" Andre said, thinking that his height made him hard to miss. "Were you looking for me?"

"Well . . ." Weselley said with a snide smile, "I understand congratulations are in order."

"I suppose you're referring to my marriage," Andre replied, in no mood to deal with Weselley's digs. "I doubt very much that you're referring to my latest book."

"See here, Montcrieff," Weselley said, his face flushing, "you might be the darling of the British Museum at the moment, but I assure you, your star will fall, and when it does, it will be fast and furious. You will be extinguished even more thoroughly than you might imagine."

"Really?" Andre replied indifferently. "And how is that going to happen?"

"Do you think you can hide your association with your friend Claubert forever?" he hissed under his breath. "I think not. People will begin to wonder."

"People will begin to wonder what?" Andre said, his own temper rising. "How fortunate I am to have a lifelong friend who has been invaluable to my work?"

Weselley sneered. "And how long do you think you can keep up that pretense? You may have married for appearances, Montcrieff, yet your wife is nowhere in sight and Claubert is seen everywhere with you. I suppose it didn't suit him very well, losing you to a wife." His eyes glittered. "Don't you think people will eventually begin to speculate?"

"People, my dear Weselley, are only speculating about whether I will die of loneliness before I meet up with my wife in France. You've obviously missed the point. But then you so often do."

Weselley stiffened, and Andre wondered for a brief moment if he was going to make a public spectacle of them both by knocking him to the floor.

Weselley managed to control himself, although the effort left him shaking. "You bloody bastard," he spat. "You've always thought yourself too good for everyone else. I ought to let the world know just what you and your pretty French friend are. And the minute I have proof, I'll do just that. I'd love to see you swing from the end of a rope and your friend alongside you."

Andre rubbed his forehead, resisting a strong temptation to ram his fist down Weselley's throat. "I'm sure you would," he said as evenly as he could manage, "but unfortunately, Weselley, your theory doesn't hold water. I know that you've pinned your ambitions on it, but what the world already knows is that I'm a man who is devoted to his wife."

Weselley's mouth drew into an ugly line. "So say you."

"And so say I, you damnable little weasel."

Andre jerked around. Jo-Jean stood there, his face black as thunder, and Andre realized with dismay that Jo-Jean had overheard at least part of their conversation. "Jo-Jean," he started to say, "I didn't realize you were—"

But Jo-Jean cut him off. "It's all right," he said, flicking Andre a quick glance. "I've known exactly what this excuse for a man has thought all these years." He turned back to Weselley. "And I've always thought you the scum of the earth, and your filthy servant with you. Furthermore, I've always thought you incredibly stupid and mean-spirited, not to mention completely lacking in ethics."

"What do you—how dare you," Weselley spluttered, his fists working at his sides. "Who do you think you are? You are nothing more than a hanger-on basking in reflected glory."

"I am Montcrieff's friend, and count myself fortunate to claim the privilege. Furthermore, I envy him his marriage. Not because, as you obviously assume, I am jealous, but because I hope to God one day I will be fortunate enough to find a wife I can love half as much."

Andre stared at his friend. He wasn't at all sure if Jo-Jean had just admitted to being in love with Ali or accused him of the same. Either way, it came as a shock.

"You, Weselley," Jo-Jean continued with a fire he rarely exhibited, "would benefit from some self-examination. Not that you'd like what you'd find. But it might at least keep you from judging people who are far superior to you."

"The—the devil, you say! How dare you speak to me in such a fashion?" Weselley looked as if he might fall into an apoplectic fit.

"I dare because it is the truth. And that, Lord Weselley, is something you know little about." He tapped his chin. "What do you think? Should I tell Montcrieff about the time that I saw you in Xanthos, rifling through his notes in the middle of the afternoon when you thought no one was about?"

Weselley turned a dull red. His mouth opened but no sound came out.

"I thought not. Although he already knows, of course. As he does about many of your other unfortunate . . . shall we say your 'misadventures'? Which, I might add, he has kept silent about. So far." Joseph-Jean smiled, but there was nothing amused in his eyes. "I think I've made my point." He turned on his heel and walked away.

Andre gave a faint nod of his head. "I don't think I could possibly have said it better. Good night, Weselley. And do us all a favor and vanish, won't you?" He followed after Jo-Jean, a smile hovering on the corners of his mouth.

Jo-Jean was full of surprises. Now if he could only work out what Jo-Jean had meant by his loaded comment about Ali. And how he felt about it, whichever way it had been directed. Andre left deep in thought, wondering if he'd developed a jealous streak, or if maybe he'd developed a heart.

Chapter 20

A li sat amid the ancient ruins, wondering for the hundredth time if it was possible to die of grief. She lifted her head from her knees as the light softened with the coming of dusk and gazed over the plain, not really seeing it, her thoughts turned inward.

It was here that she felt closest to Andre, as if he had left a small piece of himself behind, and sometimes she could feel an echo of him. But it didn't ease her heartbreak.

The thought that she would never see him again hadn't become easier to bear with time. Indeed, each day was more difficult than the one before as the grim finality of her life without Andre was brought home.

She gazed down at her wedding ring, the gold glinting in the sunlight, a tangible reminder of their bond. Her finger traced the warm circle. *Till death us do part ...* Well, she'd certainly love him until death took her, and probably beyond. She didn't have any choice in the matter.

Now she knew how Andre must have felt when his fairy-child had died. Now she knew why he had said that he had no heart, or one not worth anything, why he had been unable to love her—how could you love someone when your heart had been torn from your chest?

At least she had the comfort of knowing that Andre was still alive, that he was well and his life would go on without her. But Andre had no such solace. His true love lay cold in her grave, and he didn't even have the consolation of believing her to be in the hands of God and His angels.

Ali gazed down at the ground, her eyes dull with pain. She picked up a handful of dirt and let it trickle through her fingers. This was the very earth she had cared so much about, and yet it meant nothing to her without Andre. All the history, all the stories in the world, meant nothing to her without him to tell them. Nothing meant anything to her anymore.

But at least there was Umar. And what a good friend he was, instantly accepting her return, not balking at her sudden change of sex, insisting on sleeping outside her tent at night to protect her, and never going far from her side, save to tend the animals. And Muzaffer and Hatije and their children had also been very kind, giving her a tent to sleep in, feeding her, urging her to eat even though she had no appetite.

But she couldn't impose on their hospitality forever.

"Allah," she whispered, "since you've taken me away from Andre, could you maybe send me a sign of what You wish for me to do now? I can't stay with the Yourooks forever, for although they like me well enough, I'm even less one of them now than I was before. I don't even feel like a Turk anymore."

It was so strange being back in her country again. There were times that she felt as if she'd never left. And yet nothing was the same. She felt it from the moment she stepped off the boat into the bright sunlight of late May. It wasn't just the intervening years in another country, or that she was no longer a peasant girl but an educated and titled woman.

When she'd left, she'd been an angry, frightened child, forced away from the side of her beloved master. Now she was a woman who knew what it was to love a man with all of her heart and soul. She knew what it was to sacrifice that love. And she really didn't know if she could bear to go on.

"Allah, please," she begged. "Please—I desperately need Your help. Why have You abandoned me?"

There was no answer from heaven, just the sighing of the warm wind blowing across the plain.

Ali put her hands over her face, feeling more alone than she ever had in her life. But she refused to cry. She hadn't cried since leaving England and she wasn't going to start now. She couldn't. She knew she really would die if she gave in to the pain.

"Oh, Allah," she moaned. "Am I going to feel like this forever and ever?"

"Not forever and ever. Not for one more moment."

Ali's head shot up in shock. Her hands fell away from her face and she froze. For a moment she thought her anguish had finally driven her out of her mind, that she had conjured up a mirage, for Andre stood a few yards away, his posture still, watchful.

"Andre?" she whispered in disbelief. *"Andre?"*

"Certainly not Allah."

But despite his light words, she saw that his face held a mixture of uncertainty and infinite relief. And he looked tired, as if he hadn't slept in weeks.

"Oh, Andre!" Ali leapt to her feet as joy surged through her. Her knees almost buckled, but she tore across the three yards that separated them and flung herself into his arms. "Andre . . ."

"Ooph," he said, catching her up. "Hello, sweetheart. You seem to be happy to see me after all. I wasn't entirely sure what my reception would be."

She couldn't answer. She was too busy holding on to him for dear life, terrified that he might vanish as suddenly as he'd appeared. "Thank God," she said when she could breathe again, her voice muffled against his shirt. "Thank God . . ."

"Ali," he said unsteadily, "if you'd release your death grip, I might be able to kiss you. You would like to be kissed, wouldn't you?"

Ali raised her face to his, joyously drinking in the sight of him. "It's you. It's really, really you," she said, stroking his face, relishing the solid feel of him under her fingers, the scratch of his beard, the familiar outline of his cheekbones.

In answer his mouth came down hard on hers, his

kiss fierce and possessive, and she gave herself fully over to him, drinking him in like a person parched for life, shaking with love and infinite gratitude that Allah had heard her prayers and answered them.

He finally broke the kiss off, then took her by the shoulders and looked down at her, his expression anything but calm. "Now that we have that re-established," he said, breathing hard, "why don't you damned well explain yourself? By God, Ali, I should thrash you for giving me such a fright. Do you know how worried I've been, what hell it's been trying to find you?"

She swallowed hard, for she could see how upset he was. "I'm sorry," she said in a small voice. "How *did* you find me?"

"Do you want me to start at the part when I discovered you missing and nearly had heart failure? Or perhaps you'd like me to tell you about arriving a fortnight ago and being completely stymied," he said, rubbing his eyes. "The only place I could think you would have gone was to Kooník—you certainly wouldn't have gone anywhere near Dembre, where you might have run into Hadgi."

"No," she agreed, stroking his arm, his hand.

"And I knew you'd have to have gone by boat, since it would have been too dangerous for you to go by land. I reckoned even you weren't that foolhardy. But then I discovered that no one who fit your description had set sail south from Constantinole, that the only European woman who had departed was a grieving Italian widow who had reportedly taken a boat to Kastellorizo." He shook his head. "Italian, for the love of God. How was I supposed to know you spoke Italian?"

A smile flashed across Ali's face. "Nicholas taught me. He taught me Greek and Latin, too. And I taught myself Arabic," she added.

"Yes," Andre said. "I figured that out too, when the grieving Italian widow mysteriously disappeared in Kastellorizo, and a mysterious veiled Arab-speaking woman hired a boat to take her to Xanthos."

"I thought they were clever ruses, since I really was

grieving, and in both cases I could also wear a veil. How did you finally work it out?''

He sat down on a flat rock and took her hands, pulling her down next to him. "I didn't. I took a wild guess, since I'd run out of other possibilities.''

"I'm glad you did," she said softly. "I'm very happy to see you.''

"Umar was very pleased to see me too, I must say. He practically pushed me back on my horse and sent me up here, which led me to believe that you might be happy I'd come." He gave her a searching look. "But why did you go to such elaborate measures to cover your tracks, Ali? Why the devil did you find it necessary to run away at all, let alone to hide from me?''

"But I wasn't trying to hide from you," she said. "I was only trying to make sure that no one would ever connect me to you, just in case the story that I was here ever got back to England. That would have defeated the whole purpose of leaving.''

He sighed. "Why don't we just start there? I think you owe me an explanation after the last six weeks of hell you've put me through.''

"I really am sorry," she said. "I didn't think you'd come after me.''

"Don't be absurd," he said. "You're my *wife*, for God's sake.''

"Don't blaspheme," Ali said, delighted that he felt so strongly about it. "You didn't consider divorcing me?''

"No, I didn't consider divorcing you, and furthermore, I think I've earned the right to blaspheme all I want," Andre replied. "Now. Why did you run off?'' He pushed a strand of hair off her face. "Given how you reacted just now, I don't think I drove you away.''

"Oh, Andre," she said, "I've been so miserable. I couldn't bear living without you, but I couldn't bear the thought of your reputation being destroyed because of me, either ..." Her face fell as a terrible thought occurred to her. "But oh, Andre, nothing has changed. I still can't go home with you.''

"Ali!" he cried, shoving his hands through his hair. "For the love of God, *will* you tell me what the damned problem is?"

She hesitated. "It's Weselley and that awful Syrian," she said in a low voice.

"Were they talking about me?"

"Yes," she said. "They were."

He pounded his fist against his thigh. "Damn him! Did he recognize you? What happened?"

Ali bit her lip. "They didn't see me. But I overheard them talking. They know everything, Andre."

"What do you mean, they know everything? I don't see how, Ali."

"It's true. Weselley wants to destroy you." She twisted her hands together. "He was going to pay me a visit to confirm his suspicions, and then he was going to tell the whole story to the trustees."

Andre took her by the shoulders and looked into her face, hard. "What makes you think that? Tell me exactly, and I mean *exactly*, what you heard."

She repeated the conversation nearly verbatim. "And so you see," she said, finishing, "when he said that you were bound to slip up and when you did, he'd be there with concrete evidence, I knew there was only one thing to do."

Ali was astonished when Andre threw his head back and roared with laughter until tears streamed down his face. "What's so funny?" she said, shaking his arm, but got no reaction other than another wave of laughter.

"Andre," she said, growing annoyed. "I did not sacrifice my wonderful life with you to have you go falling about in hysterics. Surely you can see the gravity of the situation?"

"Ah . . . oh, sweetheart," he choked, wiping his eyes on his sleeve. "Only you. Oh, Christ." He looked at her then, the most enormous grin on his face. "I can see where you got hold of the wrong end of the stick easily enough, but *why* didn't you tell me about it that same night? You would have saved us both a great deal of trouble."

"Because," she said, furious that he wasn't taking the situation at all seriously, "I knew that you'd lose your temper and go straight to Weselley, and you'd hang yourself in no time flat."

He burst into laughter again. "Hanging is exactly what Weselley had in mind. God, I've missed you."

"I've missed you too, and you really must stop blaspheming. I wish you'd take the situation *and* God a little more seriously."

"Wish away," he said, still grinning. "Sweetheart. Oh, this is a comedy of errors."

"*Errors?*" she said, offended. "Andre, I'm not stupid, you know."

"You're anything but. However, you are innocent. You're perfectly safe from Weselley. Trust me, he doesn't have a clue about you, and he probably never will."

"But if he saw me . . ."

"In the first place, even if he saw you, he would never dream of putting the pieces together. Secondly, if he did and somehow managed to make the connection, he'd still keep his filthy mouth shut because he knows I could ruin *him* in no time flat, not that he isn't doing a fine job of that himself. And thirdly, not a soul would believe him."

"But why not?" she said, feeling completely confused.

"Because he already has a reputation as a liar and a cheat, and everyone knows he detests me. Believe me, my credibility is far above Weselley's. Furthermore, even if the story did come out, I don't think people would be overly outraged."

"Yes. Yes, they would," she said adamantly. "You know what society is, how easily reputations are ruined."

Andre shrugged. "Oh, I don't know. I'm sure I could find a way to explain to everyone's satisfaction, although I'd rather not have to." He grinned. "Anyway, if Weselley ever tries to cause trouble, I'll point Jo-Jean in his direction. That will take care of the problem fast enough. Jo-Jean is highly displeased with a certain assumption Weselley has made."

"But, Andre, you're not making any sense. What do you think Weselley and Abraham were talking about if it wasn't me?"

He took her hands. "This is a little difficult to explain, sweetheart. You see, Weselley and his nasty friend have harbored the impression that Jo-Jean and I have a . . . um." He scratched his cheek. "A *different* sort of friendship. He was hoping somehow to use that against me."

Ali stared at him. "Do you mean that Weselley and that awful Syrian think you and Jo-Jean are lovers? *That's* what they were talking about? Oh, Andre—how perfectly ridiculous!"

"You're aware of such things?" he said in surprise.

"Of course I am," she replied with exasperation. "You forget that I wasn't brought up as a hothouse flower. But why would he think anything so silly?"

"I suppose it has to do with the fact that I didn't show any interest toward women when I was at university," he said. "And then later, over here . . . well, Jo-Jean and I were constantly together, and women weren't part of the equation. So Weselley drew his own conclusions."

Ali nodded. "Of course," she said. "He wasn't to know that you were in love with Genevieve. He must have thought you simply preferred men."

It was Andre's turn to stare at her. "What?" he whispered, clearly shocked. "How do you—oh, God, Ali," he said, truly distressed. "How did you hear?"

"By mistake," she said, alarmed that she'd mentioned Genevieve without thinking. "No one meant for me to know. I suppose you were all trying to spare my feelings."

"What exactly do you know?" he asked, gazing down at her hand, running his thumb over her palm.

"Only that you loved her deeply from the time you were very young, and she died before you could be married. And that her death broke your heart."

Andre exhaled, then rubbed his forehead with one finger. "Yes. That's true."

"Andre," Ali said hesitantly, grateful the subject

had finally been broached and he hadn't bitten her head off, "I don't mind so much, not any longer. I understand better now why you can't love me. It took giving you up and feeling my own heart break, but I do understand." She stared down at the ground. "It's enough being with you."

"Ah, Ali," he said with a groan, pulling her close, holding her tightly against him. "Surely you have to know how much I care about you?"

Ali ran her tongue over her bottom lip, determined to have truthfulness between them, now that they had come this far. "Yes, of course I know that you care about me. But I'm not a fairy-child."

He leaned back and regarded her quizzically. "A fairy-child?"

"Yes," she said. "I'm not all golden and magical and good. I'm impossible and I enrage you sometimes and do stupid things—"

"Such as running away without consulting me first?" he asked, picking up her hand and kissing her fingers. "I'd have to agree. But, Ali, sweet, I never asked you to be a fairy-child, did I? You've filled your head with a lot of storybook nonsense if that's what you believe the case to be."

Ali bowed her head. "No," she whispered. "You don't understand."

"Don't I?" His voice was very quiet. "What is it that I don't understand?"

"That Genevieve was your fairy-child. I can never be like her," she said brokenly. "I can't be a moonbeam. Or fragile. Or even French. I can never belong to your life as she did."

He took her chin in his hand and raised her face, forcing her to meet his gaze. "Who has been talking to you to make you think these things?"

"No one," she said, pulling away. "You have said more by your silence than anyone could have given away in a single sentence."

He dropped his hand into his lap. "Then I'm sorry. I thought to safeguard your feelings, not hurt them."

"I don't need protection, Andre," she cried. "I need

honesty. I'm strong—I can take nearly anything, except for losing you," she said, looking down for a moment. "That I learned over these last weeks." She lifted her head and met his eyes. "But I won't be patronized. I'm not a child any longer, and I won't be treated as one. There's no need to keep Genevieve a secret."

Andre's silence beat into the air between them, heavy, stretched so taut that Ali thought she might break apart with tension.

"God knows you're not a child," he finally said. "And if I've patronized you, I swear it wasn't intentional. I only wanted to protect you."

"By keeping such an important thing from me? You didn't think I had a right to know?"

"No, Ali, it's not that," he said, his expression strained. "It's just that I've put that part of my life behind me. There are some things better left alone."

"I don't agree," she said. "You've dragged things out of me that I thought better left alone, and you never blinked an eye while doing it. Yet your previous life is a closed door?"

"My life is with you now. Please, sweetheart. Can't we take pleasure in seeing each other again, instead of doing a postmortem of the past?"

Ali was about to launch into an argument, but the genuine plea in his eyes told her that she'd gone far enough.

And sitting once more in the ruins of Xanthos with Andre at her side was more than she'd ever expected.

She turned into his arms. "All right," she whispered against his chest. "And thank you."

"For what?" he asked, brushing his mouth over her cheek.

"For saving me," she answered, her words unconsciously echoing the past, their very beginnings.

"Ali—" His voice caught. "I will never let anything happen to you. Never. Not if it's in my power to prevent it." He pushed her hair back off her shoulders. "But you have to help me out. No more disappearing acts? For any reason?"

"No more disappearing acts," she agreed, and wrapped her arms around his neck. "For any reason."

"Do you swear it?"

"I swear it," she said, and offered him her mouth. It was another form of surrender and just as gladly given.

"I thought the evening was never going to come to an end," Andre said, ducking his head as he entered the tent.

"We had a lot to celebrate," she answered, watching him from her position on the floor as he began to remove his clothes, her breath catching at the sight of his bare chest as he pulled his shirt off. Desire stabbed through her, making her ache for him. It had been so long, so unbearably long . . .

"Maybe," he said, mirroring her thoughts, "but six weeks away from you put things in my mind other than eating and dancing and telling stories into the small hours."

Ali smiled softly. "I could tell. So could everyone else. Did you see Umar's grin?"

"How could I miss it? I felt as if I were on exhibition—they all knew perfectly well that I was dying to get you into bed. And Jo-Jean was absolutely no help, grinning just as lewdly as Umar."

"It's wonderful to see him again. I'm glad he came with you." Ali shifted impatiently under the sheet, more than ready for him and wishing he'd hurry up.

"I don't think he trusted me to bring you back myself. Jo-Jean sometimes behaves as if I'm a small child with no sense." He tugged off his boots. "It's all because the extra year he has on me makes him feel superior," he added with a grin.

"Don't be ridiculous. He behaves that way because he loves you," she said. "He's always looked out for your best interests."

"He has indeed," Andre said softly. "Far beyond the call of friendship. Speaking of which, did you know that he loves you too?"

"Of course," Ali said, drawing a look of surprise from Andre.

"Oh?" he asked, frowning.

"Not like that, you idiot," she said, throwing a pillow at him. "He couldn't be happier for you—he's told me so any number of times."

"Well, that's a damned good thing," Andre said, stripping off his trousers, still looking annoyed. "Because I'd kill him if he said or did anything suggestive. He's made some comments in the past that lead me to believe he wishes he were in my position."

Ali burst into laughter. "*Jo-Jean?* Andre, he's like a big brother. He treats me exactly as he treats you, as if I need to be looked after."

"You do need to be looked after," Andre said, drawing back the sheet and coming down to her. "And I'm the only one who's going to do it." He pushed his hands through her hair and took her mouth in a heated kiss, his tongue playing wildly with hers, his teeth biting down on her bottom lip. "Is that understood?" he murmured against her mouth.

"Andre," she moaned. "Oh, I've missed you."

He raised his head and gazed down at her, the expression in his eyes fierce. "Don't you ever scare me like that again. Ever. Or I really will throttle you."

"No you won't," she said, her eyes shining with love. "You keep forgetting that you're not a violent man."

"Maybe not violent," he said raggedly, pulling her hard against him. "But definitely starved." He stroked his tongue down the delicate column of her neck, moving over her breast and finding her nipple, drawing it into his mouth as his tongue did extraordinary things to it and his hands did extraordinary things elsewhere.

They lifted and shaped the weight of her breasts, smoothed up and down her rib cage, over her back, restlessly cupping her buttocks, driving her beyond the brink of control. It was all so familiar, the pressure of his hard thighs parting hers, her legs falling open in helpless invitation, the feel of his stiff arousal pressing against her as his fingers slipped inside her, driving her into a frenzy.

And yet there was something new, something different about his lovemaking, as if he came to her not just to pleasure her, but for something much more important. She felt as if he was giving more to her of himself than he ever had before, freely and without reservation. She felt as if he were spinning pearls ...

"Ali," he whispered, his breath hot on her shoulder. "God, I was lonely without you ..." He moved down on the mattress, sliding his hands under her thighs and lifting them.

"Dear God, but you're beautiful," he said, gazing up at her for a moment, then lowered his head and took her with his mouth, his tongue sliding between her damp cleft, teasing, caressing, then setting the world on fire as he plunged deep, rhythmically moving in her.

Ali shook uncontrollably, inflamed by his erotic touch. Her fingers dug into his hair and she twisted beneath him, her hips pressing up against him as he pulled her even closer and used his mouth on her exquisitely sensitive flesh, bringing her to a shattering climax.

"Andre!" she cried, and he quickly came up to her, silencing her with his mouth, her taste on his tongue as he plundered her there too.

"Shh," he groaned. "We don't want Muzaffer and Hatije to think I'm murdering you." He kissed her again, hard, then nuzzled her breasts, suckling the erect peaks until Ali trembled and reached for him, wrapping her fingers around his erect shaft, his flesh blazing into hers.

"Now," she said, her voice choked. "I want you now, all of you ..."

"Oh, God," he managed to say, his breathing labored. "God, sweetheart, you can have it all, anything you want, but don't you damned well leave me again."

He rose over her and pushed between her silky folds, sheathing himself in her with a long inarticulate sound.

"I won't," she whispered as she took him into her as deeply as she could. "I swear it, Andre. I wouldn't survive."

He sank his teeth into her shoulder, struggling for control, then abandoning it. "Ali," he cried against her cheek, thrusting into her over and over in a primal act of possession. "Ali, come with me!"

Ali threw her head back, a long, keening sound escaping her throat as Andre took her beyond sentient thought into ecstatic release. She clutched at him, gasping for air, wave after wave of fulfillment washing through her, his body molten heat inside hers, driving her on.

He pushed into her hard and held, then suddenly stiffened, his back arching. "God!" he cried as a great shudder ran through him. "Ah, God," he moaned, throbbing deep within her, the spill of his seed scalding her, driving her back into another swell of glorious waves, and she clutched at his back with fierce little cries, losing herself to him once again.

Andre dropped his head onto her neck with a long groan. "I don't know," he said raggedly after a few minutes had passed and his breathing had calmed.

"What don't you know?" Ali murmured, thinking that it wasn't possible to have been in such terrible pain only hours before and now to feel so full and happy and complete. So blessed. Her hands smoothed over his back, slick with the sweat of spent passion.

"How you manage to undo me to such a degree," he said, nuzzling her ear. "I've never been reduced to such a pile of rubble as you bring me to."

"Not even with Genevieve?" she asked, then bit her lip hard as she heard the words she'd never intended to speak. "Oh . . ." she whispered, wishing desperately that she could take them back. "I'm sorry—I didn't mean that."

He pushed himself up on his forearms and gazed down at her, his eyes glittering silver.

Ali swallowed hard, wondering if she had ruined everything.

"Yes, you did mean it," he said, but to her surprise his tone was gentle.

"But you asked me not to mention her. And I cer-

tainly shouldn't have done it in bed," she said, morti-
fied that she could have been so insensitive.

"Listen to me, sweetheart." He brushed her cheek
with the palm of his hand. "Although it's true that I'd
rather not speak of the past, I don't blame you for
asking. And since you did, I might as well give you
an answer." He paused. "The truth of the matter is
that Genevieve and I never slept together."

"You didn't?" she said, a rush of joy flooding
through her at not just his reply, but also his willing-
ness to be honest, to broach the subject at all. "But
why not?"

He raised an eyebrow. "I don't usually make a habit
of compromising virgins, despite what you may think.
We were waiting to be married."

"Oh . . ." Ali said. "I hadn't thought of that."

"Naturally not. With your logic the cart very often
comes before the horse." He smiled down at her.
"Stop looking so contrite, sweetheart. It was a natural
enough question—but before you decide to query me
further on my sexual history, yes, I do have a basis
for comparison. And before you strike me over the
head, let me say that although you were not the first
woman in my bed, you will certainly be the last."

Ali couldn't help the small laugh that escaped. "By
choice, I hope, and not mere honor?"

Andre slid his thumbs over the smooth lines of her
jaw and drew them down the length of her neck. "Although I'd hate to have my honor called into question,
definitely by choice." He kissed her softly, then rolled
halfway onto his side, his arm flung over her waist.
He yawned loudly. "Sorry. I'll make love to you all
night long another time, but I haven't had much
sleep recently."

Within moments he'd fallen asleep. Ali settled into
his embrace, relishing the feel of his hard body against
hers, the heady scent of his masculinity, so long
missed, so much his essence. But it was the sound of
his soft, even breathing that cut through her, opened
all the doors of memory that stretched so far back.

Ali closed her eyes and finally allowed herself to
weep.

Chapter 21

Andre woke early the next morning and carefully moved Ali out of his arms. He dressed quietly, wanting to be sure he didn't wake her. He'd been alarmed by how pale and strained she'd appeared the day before, how much weight she'd lost, and he imagined she'd had as many sleepless nights as he had.

"Good morning," Umar said to him as he crossed the encampment. "You are up with the birds. Claubert is still snoring in my tent." He flashed him a smile. "Will you join me in a glass of tea? It is a pleasure to have your company again."

"Thank you. It's a pleasure to be here." Andre sat down by the little cooking fire and accepted the glass Umar handed him. "So, Umar. How have you been keeping in the last year? Any sign of a prospective bride?"

Umar shrugged. "I am young yet. It is you I am happy to see married. And to Ali. This came as a great surprise to us."

"I can imagine," Andre said, carefully sipping the hot liquid. "How did you and the others react to learning that Ali has been a female all along? I hope it didn't cause any offense that she violated all the rules of social interaction between men and women."

"It was a shock, but we understood," Umar said. "Especially when we heard the whole story." His brow drew down. "But we have worried for her. She reminded us all of how you were in the early days, mourning your first wife."

"My first—oh, that's right," he said, remembering Ali's original version of events that she'd littered about Kooník. "Actually, Umar, the story Ali told you isn't precisely accurate. I've actually never been married before this."

"Never been married?" Umar said, looking shocked to the marrow. "But what about your great tragedy, your terrible loss?"

"Well ... I did experience a terrible loss," Andre said, holding out his glass for more tea. "I loved Genevieve very much and it took me a long time to recover. But we weren't married, only promised to each other."

He realized with a vague sense of amazement that he hadn't given a second thought to bringing up the subject. Nor had it really bothered him yesterday; he'd been more concerned about sparing Ali's feelings than his own. It was an enormous relief, he discovered, to have it out in the open. And an enormous relief not to feel crippled at the mention of Genevieve's name.

"Ah," Umar said, nodding. "But now you are at peace with her death."

Andre gazed down at his glass, wondering if maybe he really was at peace with it. Was that possible? He wouldn't have thought so, but then why didn't he feel the old tug of pain?

"At least, it appears that way," Umar added when Andre didn't respond. "Or I do not think you would have come riding in here yesterday the way you did. And I do not think you would look at Ali as you do. As she looks at you." He rubbed his mustache. "It is good to see this kind of love between a man and his wife."

Andre's hand jerked, sending a wave of hot tea splashing onto his lap, but he didn't even feel it.

I'll never love anyone but you, I swear that to you on everything I hold sacred.

The words echoed around and around in his head, the vow he had made at the tender age of fourteen and never broken.

Or had he? Dear God, *had* he?

He put his glass down and swiftly rose. "Thank you

for the tea, Umar. If Ali asks for me, tell her I've gone up to the ruins. I'll be back later."

He didn't bother with a saddle, just threw the bridle on his horse and took off as if all the hounds of hell were on his heels, leaving Umar staring after him with astonishment.

Ali watched over the railing as the steamship began to chug out of the small harbor of Myra, or what as a child she had called Dembre. It seemed so odd to have come full circle, leaving for England from the same port her father had died trying to get her to. And now here she was, a young woman going home with a husband at her side.

It was amusing, the fuss they'd made at the pier over the great English duke and his wife. If they'd only known it was only little Ali, who years before had played in those very streets.

It all looked so familiar, the little town that she had once thought so huge. There, stretching above the trees, was the minaret that as a child she had heard the imam calling from. There was the market that she had shopped in with her foster parents. And there was . . .

"Andre," she said, grabbing his arm. "Andre, look!"

He turned from his conversation with Jo-Jean. "What is it, sweetheart?" he asked, alerted by the note of alarm in her voice. His gaze followed hers, landing on the bearded man standing on the pier, staring at them with his mouth hanging open.

"Good God," he said, putting his arm around her. "He must have come to see what all the commotion was about. What a piece of luck." He turned to Jo-Jean. "Do you have your pistol handy?"

"Naturally," Jo-Jean said, reaching inside his coat.

"Good," Andre said. "Do you see the watermelon that nasty-looking man on the dock is holding under his arm? I want you to shatter it."

"Andre, have you lost your mind?" Jo-Jean said,

regarding him with horror. "Since when do you want me to go around shooting at innocent people?"

"That, my good friend," he said very softly, "is Hadgi, Ali's foster uncle."

Joseph-Jean took aim.

Ali watched in spellbound horror as a loud crack reported in the air, mixed with Hadgi's scream of terror. The watermelon exploded, splattering everywhere. Hadgi dropped to his knees, sobbing, a large puddle spreading underneath him. It took him a moment to realize that the red, runny stuff all over him was not blood and pieces of his flesh, but watermelon pulp. A crowd quickly gathered around, laughing and pointing. Hadgi had never been a popular person in Myra. Now he was going to look like a fool as well, Ali thought with supreme satisfaction.

She couldn't help herself. She burst into gales of laughter, burying her face against Andre's coat. "Thank you. Oh, thank you," she said, wiping her eyes.

"My pleasure. Too bad Jo-Jean's such a crack shot. It would have been much more satisfying if he'd missed."

"For you, maybe," Jo-Jean replied. "You wouldn't have been the one languishing in a Turkish prison."

Andre didn't have a chance to answer. He was too busy answering the alarmed captain's questions.

Ali thought it very clever that Andre put the matter down to a simple wager made on impulse. Since the captain was a Turk, he naturally understood.

Ali rolled over in the narrow berth, stifling a moan against the pillow. She hadn't paid much attention to the dull nagging ache that had started in her abdomen the week before, since it came and went, and was only occasionally sharp enough to annoy her. Nor had she said anything to Andre, not wanting to worry him. He was preoccupied as it was, and that worried her far more than the pain did.

The only other time he'd behaved like this was when he'd taken her back to Sutherby after they were first married, when he thought he'd physically hurt her. And now she was certain he thought he'd hurt her again, because of Genevieve.

It was the only explanation. Why else would he have distanced himself from her ever since Xanthos? Oh, he was subtle, as he always was, but she still sensed his retreat. She'd just have to find the right time and place to bring the subject up. This was not it.

She rolled over again, her legs pulled up against the pain. It wasn't really so bad, she decided. And after all, what could anyone do? If it persisted, she'd see a doctor when they arrived in England in a week's time.

But Ali didn't have a week's time.

"Sweetheart?" Andre asked, surprised that Ali was still in bed. It wasn't like her to sleep in so late. "Ali? Wake up. It's nearly noon, you lazy girl." He bent down and shook her shoulder.

"Don't," Ali groaned.

"Oh, come," he said. "Since when do you . . ." He trailed off in sudden suspicion. Ali's hair appeared damp and he didn't like the way she was hunched up. He leaned into the confines of the bunk as best he could and put his hand on her forehead. It was cool, but clammy to the touch. "What is it, sweetheart? What's wrong?" he said, his alarm growing by the moment.

"Nothing really," she whispered. "Just a stomach upset. I was sick earlier. I'll be better soon."

"A stomach upset?" he asked, picking up her wrist and feeling her pulse. It was rapid and thready, not a good sign. "Roll over and let me have a look at you," he commanded.

Ali turned, but gave a sharp cry of pain, clutching at her abdomen.

He instantly dropped to his knees and pulled the covers back, prying her hands away. Then he pulled her nightdress up and carefully felt her abdomen, relieved to find that the right side was relaxed. But when he moved his hands, he found the lower left side was rigid, and Ali cried out again as he gently pressed down.

"How long has this been going on?" he asked.

"Since last week—but it was only a dull ache, Andre. It didn't really start hurting until this morning."

"And you've been nauseated, vomiting?"

She nodded, then gasped as another fiery stab of pain grabbed her.

"Is your monthly course late?" he asked, his heart contracting with cold fear.

"No. It was early. I'm sorry. I don't seem to conceive, do I?"

"Don't be silly," he said, feeling for any enlargement, terribly worried.

"Oh, Andre, don't! Please. It hurts so."

He took in the fine film of perspiration on her upper lip. Something was seriously wrong; he felt it in his gut, and he had a horrible premonition that he knew what it was. "I'll be right back," he said. "Don't worry. I'll be right back." He tore out the door.

Fortunately, Joseph-Jean happened to be coming down the corridor at that moment.

"Jo-Jean," he said, grabbing him by the arms. "There's something wrong with Ali—something very wrong. I feel it in my bones. I'm almost certain that she has an ectopic pregnancy."

"What?" Jo-Jean took in the expression of panic on Andre's face, and his hands went instantly to Andre's shoulders, steadying him. "Calm down. What's that?"

"It's a condition where the embryo develops in the fallopian tube instead of the uterus." He shoved his hands over his scalp. "God, I'm worried, Jo-Jean. I'm no doctor by any stretch of the imagination, but I know enough to know she has to get to one as soon as possible. A condition like this requires surgery."

"Surgery. My God. But how long can it wait?"

"It won't wait. I'd operate myself, but I have neither the instruments nor the skill. I think her fallopian tube might already have ruptured and she's bleeding internally."

"Good God," Jo-Jean said, paling.

"She said nothing." Andre beat his fist against the wall, feeling like taking the entire ship apart. "Nothing! She didn't think it serious. But then, I suppose it probably didn't bother her much until the damned thing ruptured. She'll die, Jo-Jean, if we don't get her to a surgeon, and maybe even then."

Jo-Jean thought quickly. "Perhaps we could have the boat make an unscheduled stop at Arachon. It's close enough to Bordeaux."

"Yes," Andre said. "Yes. Of course. Bordeaux. We can find a surgeon there." Good. Good, there was hope. Of course there was hope. Ali couldn't die. Not Ali.

"Andre," Joseph-Jean said gently. "Do you really want to take the chance of an unknown surgeon operating on her? You know the risks under the best of circumstances."

"What other choice do I have?" he snapped. "What else would you have me do?"

"I'd have you take the extra time and go by train to Beynac. From there it's not much of a distance to Saint-Simon."

Andre rubbed both hands over his face, then looked up. "I'm not taking Ali to Saint-Simon, and that's an end to it. We'll find her a doctor in Bordeaux. It's closer, and it will save her the journey."

Joseph-Jean lost his temper, something Andre had rarely seen him do. He shoved Andre up against the wall, half knocking the breath out of him.

"Have you lost your mind?" he shouted. "You have the one person who can get Ali through this. He can save her life, you idiot!"

"Oh? As he saved Genevieve's?" Andre shouted back, pushing Joseph-Jean away. "Maybe, if he's in the mood. Maybe—maybe, Jo-Jean, you're a gullible fool. Has that ever occurred to you?"

"The only thing that occurs to me, and has regularly occurred to me over this entire year, is that the only fool here is you."

"So. I was right. You are in love with her," Andre said furiously.

"No, I'm not in love with her, you blockhead," he said, pounding Andre back against the wall. "*You're* in love with her, although it would be nice if you could bring yourself to face the fact and tell her so."

The anger fled from Andre's face. "That's between Ali and me," he said, his voice very low.

Jo-Jean glared at him. "It's soon going to be a moot point unless you agree to be sensible. My God, Andre," he said, his voice breaking. "Ali might well die. What is more important to you? Your stupid, misplaced pride, or her life?"

Andre shuddered. "You know Ali's life counts above all else," he said hoarsely.

"Then damned well do something about it," Jo-Jean said, dropping his hands. "Give up this idiotic war of silence you've been waging the last nine years and help your wife. Take her to your father. She'll be safer with him than some butcher in Bordeaux, and you know it."

"Dear God." Andre felt sick, utterly confused, and deeply frightened for Ali. But Jo-Jean was right. She had to be his first—his only—consideration. His father be damned. At least he was skilled. The rest of it could wait till later.

Joseph-Jean gestured toward the ocean. "We're only a half hour away from shore. We can have Ali with your father in a matter of hours."

Andre ran his tongue over his dry mouth, then made his decision, even though it half killed him. "All right—I'll speak to the captain. And see if transport can be arranged. We'll go to Saint-Simon."

Joseph-Jean smoothed a cool cloth over Ali's face, his eyes clouded with concern.

"It's all right, Jo-Jean," Ali murmured. "It's all right."

From what she'd just overheard she knew she was sick, very sick. She knew that she would most probably die, and the idea of having to leave Andre hurt far more than the agonizing pain in her side. But she'd thought the situation through, and she'd made up her mind.

Jo-Jean took her hand. "How are you feeling?"

"Perfectly dreadful," Ali replied, attempting to smile. "Where's Andre?"

"He's speaking to the captain. He's going to ask him to change course so that we can get you to shore."

She drew in a shallow breath. "You want to take me to Saint-Simon, don't you? I heard you outside."

"Did you? I'm sorry. I suppose we became a little loud."

"Mmm, you were," she said after a moment. "I— I'm not going, Jo-Jean."

"Oh, yes," he said roughly, "you're going. You're going whether you like it or not, whether Andre likes it or not."

"Why? What good will it do? Why cause a catastrophe when there are other physicians?"

Jo-Jean sank to his knees, keeping her hand in his. "No, Ali. You don't understand." He covered the hand he held clasped with his other. "There are things the duke can do for you that other physicians can't."

"You only feel that way because he saved your life, Jo-Jean. But you're not thinking." She moistened her lips. "If we go to Saint-Simon, and Pascal can't help me, all it will do is create more damage between him and Andre."

"Ali, listen to me . . . you are very ill. You need the duke's help."

She shook her head. "I think I finally know what caused the rift between Andre and his father. It was what you said outside." Ali closed her eyes against a renewed stab of pain. "It was about Genevieve, wasn't it?" she said when it had passed. "Pascal couldn't help her, and Andre never forgave him."

"It's much more complicated than that. Even I don't know all the facts." He squeezed her hand. "But this is different, Ali. Please believe me."

"No, Jo-Jean. I won't be the cause of more trouble.

I won't. If I'm going to die, it's best if I do it under someone else's care."

"But suppose the duke could make you well?" he persisted.

"If I'm going to get well, then someone else can take the credit. It's too much of a risk. It will take a miracle to save me, Jo-Jean. Even I know that."

"That's the point!" he cried. He raised his eyes toward heaven, and muttered something she couldn't hear, but she had the distinct impression that he was saying a prayer of guidance. And maybe asking for patience, because he looked thoroughly frustrated.

"All right," he said. "All right then. I'm going to tell you something now, and I want you to listen to me very carefully, since this is not the sort of thing that the duke cares to have discussed. Ever." He took a deep breath. "You know that he saved my life. But what you don't know is that it wasn't in the ordinary sort of way that doctors save their patients." Jo-Jean gazed at her intently. "I tell you the story only because I think you need to hear it now, so that you understand why this is so important. And maybe you will understand why the duke never speaks of it." He paused. "I was born dead, Ali."

Her eyes widened. "What?"

"According to my mother, I was dead when the duke delivered me. He brought me back to life."

"Oh," she said, dismissing his statement, "well, of course he brought you back to life. Many babies don't breathe at the beginning. They need a little help." Ali turned her head to one side. "If you're trying to be persuasive, I already believe him to be competent," she said.

"Ali. He is more than competent. This had nothing to do with medicine, or with not taking my first breath. There was not a shred of life in me." He smiled down at her. "What I am trying to tell you," he said softly, "is that the duke can work miracles. And he worked one of those miracles on me."

"Miracles?" Ali whispered, thinking she must be delirious. *"Miracles?"*

"Yes," Joseph-Jean said. "Miracles. Do you understand now? And do you understand why no one has spoken of this to you?"

Ali closed her eyes, thinking of Pascal. So good, so gentle, so wise. She thought of his wonderful understanding of God and His angels, his easy acceptance of heaven, and how easy he had made it for her to accept it too. It was really not so hard to imagine his working miracles.

She thought of his love for Andre and his great sadness at their estrangement, his only child gone from him.

Andre has misplaced his faith in many things, Ali ...

She thought of lovely Lily, who missed Andre so terribly and suffered in silence.

And last, she thought of Andre, and knew that his real pain lay in the loss of his family, his true home, and his belief in God, and there was only one way for him finally to heal.

Ali's fingers crept to the angel Gabriel on its chain around her neck as a tear slid down her cheek. Of course. It was all suddenly so clear.

God was, as usual, working in His typically mysterious fashion. What was a little pain next to that?

She opened her eyes, a beatific smile on her face. "Take me to Saint-Simon."

Andre held Ali's unconscious body in his arms, his dark head bowed over hers. He wished the train would go faster. He wished she'd open her eyes. He wished a million things he couldn't have.

The fear was the hardest to bear, the heart-stopping, gut-wrenching fear. The idea of losing Ali was beyond him. He couldn't believe this could happen to him twice in a lifetime, to have someone he loved taken from him. But Ali was right: Genevieve had been like a moonbeam, delicate, fleeting, impossible to catch hold of. Ali was the exact opposite, a ray of sunshine, someone who lived life so ferociously, so fully, that is was impossible to imagine it being taken from her at all.

"Oh, God, sweetheart," he groaned, resting his cheek on her hair. "Please, Ali. Please hold on."

But there was no response to his anguished plea. He knew by the cold, damp feel of her skin and the rapid rate of her breathing that she was in shock.

Ali had very little time left.

She'd been drifting in and out of consciousness for hours now, and each time she was gone a little longer. "Sweetheart," he whispered. "You promised not to leave me again. Remember? You swore. Twice."

Ali's eyelashes fluttered. Her eyes half opened and she hazily focused on him. "I always keep my promises," she said groggily.

"Ali—oh, thank God. Thank God," he said, his voice cracking. "Please—try to stay with me. It's not much longer now. We're nearly at Beynac."

"Mmm," she said. "Good."

He smoothed her brow. "My father is very proficient. He'll have you better in no time."

"I know," she whispered. "You have to believe it too."

He swallowed hard against the knot in his throat. "I do," he said.

"No, I mean *really* believe it. I won't die, Andre. I promise. Your father will make me a miracle, I know he will."

A stab of pain ran through him at her words. He put his head back and blinked against the sudden sting of tears. "Now who's been telling you stories?" he said when he could speak again.

"Jo-Jean told me so that I would agree to go. Andre, whatever happens to me, you must make peace with him. Please."

"Ali, you don't know what this is all about."

She rested her cheek against his chest. "Yes. I do. He didn't make a miracle for Genevieve. That's it, isn't it?"

Andre brushed his hand over her hair. He'd have dropped the subject like a hot brick, but he'd do anything to keep her talking. And oddly, the thought of talking about it helped him to prepare himself to see his parents again.

"In a way," he said. "But to understand why he acted as he did, you have to understand that he and my mother opposed our marriage plans. Not vocally, but I knew nevertheless."

"Why?" she whispered.

"The same people who brought me up to believe that all people are equal privately were complete hypocrites. They believed that Genevieve wasn't highborn enough to marry me."

He gazed out the window, bitterly remembering his shock at their reaction to his announcement, politely enthusiastic, but laced with anything but enthusiasm beneath. "Naturally, I persisted. And then Genevieve became ill. My father didn't lift a finger to save her." He sighed. "The only miracle is that I didn't kill him."

He felt Ali's hand close on his with surprising strength. "You must find out the truth," she said. "You must."

"The truth? It's either that there is a God, and He and my father are both liars and thieves, or there is no God, and my father is still a liar, a fraud who allows people to believe that he lives in God's back pocket." He looked down at her. "Which is worse? I'm not sure."

Ali shook her head. "No, Andre. Something is wrong with the story. Something doesn't ring true."

"Jo-Jean really has been filling your head, hasn't he?" He glanced over at Joseph-Jean, who sat across from them, staring out of the window, clearly sick with worry. "Never mind," Andre said, trying to sound casual, "he can't help himself." He smiled at her and pushed a damp strand of hair off her forehead. "He believes the village legend that he was brought back from the dead. I think it makes him feel glamorous."

"Andre . . . you have to believe. You have to believe for me," she said. And then her eyes closed, and she was gone again.

Chapter 22

The carriage rattled along, the road becoming achingly familiar to Andre as they approached the village of Saint-Simon. Ali lay stretched out on one full seat, covered with blankets, her face stark white, her body trembling with the chill that came with fever and the onset of severe shock, her breathing rapid and shallow.

Andre hunched on the floor, cradling her head, torn by anguish. Joseph-Jean sat opposite in silence. Andre knew Jo-Jean shared his sense that Ali was very close to death.

He really didn't see what anyone, including his father, could do for her now.

The carriage made a gentle turn and he glanced up. Inadvertently, his eyes caught the towers and sloping roofs of the château sitting on its hill, and his heart did a somersault. Nine years. Nine long years since he'd seen his beloved home. And now he was returning as he had left. In grief.

They climbed the hill and crossed over the drawbridge, and finally the carriage came to a halt in the courtyard.

Andre swiftly picked Ali up and cradled her in his arms as Joseph-Jean opened the carriage door from the inside. She felt so light to him, so incredibly fragile.

"We're here, sweetheart," he murmured against her cheek. "We're home."

He started across the courtyard, wondering what the fastest way to find his father would be. It was approaching harvest, so he might still be out supervising in the vineyards. On the other hand, he might be down preparing the winery.

But incredibly enough, the huge front door of the château opened at that moment, and his father appeared, his head bent in conversation with someone Andre didn't know. Andre could only stare at him, a mass of conflicting emotions running through him. He couldn't even find his voice to hail him.

His father glanced up at that moment and froze, but only for a split second. "Andre," he said, taking in the situation instantly. "Dear Lord. Ali. What's happened?"

"She's dying, Papa," he said, his voice so choked that the words barely came out at all. "Please. Help her."

His father didn't hesitate, didn't for a moment behave as if any time had passed at all, that there was a bitter quarrel hanging between them. "Quickly, get her inside. Take her to the surgery. I'll be with you in a moment."

Andre didn't stop to think, to wonder how his father would even know it was Ali he held in his arms. He moved past him into the hall, feeling as if the matter had been taken out of his hands. And feeling unbelievable relief.

He gently placed Ali on the long table and arranged the blankets over her. "All's going to be well now, sweetheart. All's going to be well." He wished he believed it.

"I've sent Joseph-Jean to the winery for your mother," Pascal said, coming into the room behind him. "He told me everything." He bent over Ali, swiftly opening her clothing and moving his hands over her belly, an expression of intense concentration on his face.

Ali stirred and moaned under his touch.

"Andre. Call for hot water and get the sterile sheets." He lifted his head and met Andre's eyes. "I'm operating here and now. There's no time to wait for your mother to assist me."

Andre swallowed hard. "Do you want me to—"

"No. You'd be useless. I wouldn't ask that of my-self—it's your wife, for God's sake. Get the things I asked for."

Andre tore off, ordering an alarmed servant to send hot water, fetching the sheets, watching his father soap his hands and arms.

Pascal laid out the instruments, and Andre was sick-ened by the thought that they would be slicing into Ali's flesh at any moment.

"Maybe it's time for you to leave?" Pascal sug-gested, glancing up at him. "I know you have a strong stomach, but . . ."

"No. Not yet. I want to speak to Ali first." He bent down and smoothed her cheek with his hand. "Ali. Please. Fight for me, for both of us." He kissed her cold lips. "Remember your promise." Andre moved away.

Pascal touched his hands to the side of her head. "Listen, sweet girl. I want you to sleep now. Really sleep, deeply and quietly and peacefully. When you wake, you'll be much better."

As Andre watched, Ali's breathing slowed and be-came even. He released a deep breath of his own. At least some of the old magic was working. He knew she'd feel no pain.

"Go now." Pascal picked up the scalpel.

Andre swiftly left the room.

The little chapel that sat against the west boundary of the château's walls was cool, quiet. He didn't really know why he'd sought it out. He supposed it was be-cause it had given him comfort in the past, at a time when God had been his ally, not his enemy.

Andre sank into a pew and lowered his head onto his knees. Ali couldn't die. She couldn't.

For he finally understood that he loved her in a way that he'd never loved Genevieve. That had been the pure, idealistic love of childhood, which had carried over into his early manhood, never resolved, never fulfilled. It probably would have grown into something more mature had she lived, had they been given the chance.

But she hadn't lived. And Ali had come into his life in the most unexpected fashion, sneaking her way into his tightly guarded heart, lighting its darkened corners, bringing him unexpected joy, and finally—finally forcing him to realize what everyone had obviously been trying to tell him for the last year. He loved her with all of his heart.

It was a love that only a full-grown man could experience, born in the depths of suffering, nurtured in memory, fully sprung in marriage. And, blind, frightened fool that he was, he had never let her know how he felt. Now he might never have the chance.

Andre covered his face with his hands and wept.

And then he sank to his knees and he prayed with everything he had in him to the God he'd abandoned nine years before.

Ali had an extraordinary sensation of colors running through her, blue, pink, silver, and gold. She was floating, she discovered, somewhere very high. And the agonizing pain was gone, she realized. Now *that* was nice.

She could hear voices faintly talking from far away, and she strained to listen.

"Lily, thank God you've come ... quickly, hand me another clamp—she's bleeding heavily into the peritoneal cavity ... Suction as fast as you can ... No, not a pregnancy, a ruptured cyst ... Damn, what a mess."

Ali thought that it all sounded extremely dreary, but at least she knew where Andre had gotten his blaspheming from. She floated away, higher and higher, and then she found herself in the most beautiful garden she'd ever seen. There were orange trees in full blossom, and the air smelled of their sweet scent, mingled with ... jasmine. Yes, it was definitely jasmine. A waterfall cascaded into a pond, the color of the palest blue, so clear that she could see the pebbles on the bottom.

And flowers grew everywhere in the thick green

grass. She wiggled her bare toes in it, reveling in the feel of cool earth.

Then she noticed a shimmer of light off to one side, and she turned, the light growing so bright that she had to shade her eyes. As she watched, a magnificent figure walked out of the light toward her. With delight, Ali realized it was an angel, for it looked just like the angel on her necklace, with great golden wings and a golden halo to match. The very air seemed to fill with joy and love as the angel approached.

A low stone bench materialized, and the angel settled onto it and adjusted its wings. "Hello, Ali. How do you like my garden?"

"It's a very fine garden," Ali said, lowering herself to the grass at the angel's feet. The angel wasn't wearing shoes either, she noticed.

"Thank you. I'm fond of it myself."

"Am I dead?" Ali asked the angel.

"Oh, no. You're just here for a time while Pascal fixes your body. You were very sick."

"I know," Ali said. "I was awfully worried that I was going to be taken from Andre. And I'd only just been reunited with him after all that misery. But I'm not going to die after all?" she said, filled with a fresh rush of happiness that she would see Andre again.

"No. Ali. God wants you down on earth, loving Andre and the children who are waiting to be born to you."

Ali looked at the angel sadly. "But I haven't been able to conceive, angel, and it's been a whole year."

"Pascal will fix that too. Bringing Andre home to his parents wasn't the only reason for your illness." The angel smiled at her. "I can promise you, Ali, you will have a son in your arms by this time next year."

Ali clapped her hands together gleefully. "Then I will give Andre children after all? Oh, I've been so worried!"

"You will have sons and daughters to give you great joy."

"Angel ... I've been wondering. Why did Pascal and Lily have only Andre? Surely they would have liked lots of children. If there was something wrong with Lily, why didn't Pascal fix it?"

"There was nothing wrong. Andre was meant to be their only child, a special child," the angel said. "Pascal and Lily understood that."

"Oh ..." Ali said. "Well, he certainly is special. And I thank God for giving me to him."

The angel chuckled merrily. "It's been quite an adventure, hasn't it?"

Ali nodded. "Sometimes I really did wonder what Allah had in mind for me."

"You've been a good servant, Ali. Despite everything you went through, you never lost faith."

Ali sighed. "I just wish that Andre hadn't lost his."

"But he hasn't, beloved. I think you will find that he has come to a new understanding of his Heavenly Father, as well as his earthly one. He has learned the lessons put before him."

"I'm so glad. He's been very lonely all these years. Thank goodness he had Jo-Jean to look after him or I don't know what he would have done. Jo-Jean deserves a big reward."

The corners of the angel's mouth turned up in a mysterious smile. "Joseph-Jean has paid for his gift of life with his love. His reward is imminent."

Then the angel leaned forward and pressed a kiss that felt like the purest of light on Ali's forehead. "It is time for you to go now."

"Will I ever meet you again?" Ali asked anxiously.

"Of course. I am with you all the time, beloved. Who do you think has been attending to the details of your life?"

Ali grinned. "You certainly made them complicated."

"All in my work. But your pain is over, sweet one. And the only traces left are the ones lodged in your heart, those that have brought you wisdom."

The angel stood and moved away.

"Wait," Ali called. "Your name—what is your name?"

"Why, Gabriel, of course." The angel disappeared

back into the blinding light, but the sweet trill of its laughter lingered behind. When Ali looked down, she discovered that she was holding a lily in her hand.

Andre had no idea how much time had gone by. He didn't know if he had been praying for an eternity, or for only a moment. But when he opened his eyes, despite the acuity of his pain and worry, he felt as if an enormous burden had been lifted from him.

"Andre."

His head jerked up, his father's voice snapping him out of his daze. "Oh, God . . . Ali?" His heart began to pound in panic. "What happened? Is she—"

"She's fine. We'll have to watch her carefully for a week or so, but she's fine. Sleeping." Pascal sat down next to him.

Andre threw his head back. "Thank God! Oh, thank God." He didn't know whether to burst into tears or hysterical laughter. He settled on something in the middle, covering his face with his hands, not caring what his father thought.

Ali had made it through. That was all that mattered.

Pascal smiled at Andre. "You did well in assessing the severity of Ali's condition—she was very close to dying. I'm glad you brought her to me."

Andre gave his father a sidelong glance, unmoved by his approval. "Why? So you could perform a miracle?" he asked coolly. "Unlike the last time around?"

His father didn't answer, looking down at his hands.

"It's not that I'm ungrateful," Andre said. "I am, of course. But this changes nothing between us."

"Have you ever heard me say that I can perform miracles, Andre?" Pascal finally said, his voice very quiet.

"No, but I don't see what difference that makes. Are you saying you can't? Or are you saying that you can? It has to be one thing or the other."

The silence beat heavily in the little chapel as Andre waited for his answer. This was it, finally, the matter that had hung between them for all these years—a matter that could not possibly be reconciled by either the ways of man or heaven.

His father looked at him then. "The truth?"

"The truth. It's long past time for that, don't you agree?" He wasn't entirely sure that he really did want to hear it—it wasn't pleasant to hear any man condemn himself, especially not one's father. But then his father had condemned himself years before by his actions. What difference would words make now?

Pascal ran his thumb over his lower lip. "I wonder if you truly are finally ready to hear the truth," he said after another long pause, in an echo of Andre's thoughts.

"I'm as ready as I'll ever be," Andre said, steeling himself. "I'm just curious to see what your answer is going to be."

His father glanced up at the altar, then he looked back at Andre. "Yes," he said, and Andre could see the effort it cost him to speak. "Yes," he continued, his voice tight with strain. "If you really wish to know, the truth is that I can. Work miracles, that is."

"Dear God." Andre didn't know why, but hearing him admit to it came as a shock. He passed a shaking hand over his face. It didn't make sense. None of it made sense. Admitting to such a thing was as good as admitting to having murdered Genevieve, even if his father hadn't laid a hand on her—which was the point.

"Was that not the answer you wanted?" Pascal asked, his eyes intent on his son's face.

Andre swallowed, trying desperately to collect himself. "If that's the case," he managed to say through a tight throat, "then why didn't you save Genevieve? *Why?* How can you explain yourself? How can you offer up any defense against your actions? You *let* her die, damn you, without raising a finger to help her!"

"Andre, it is God who decides who lives and dies. I am only His instrument." Pascal sighed heavily. "I know this is hard for you to understand—God only knows it's next to impossible to explain. But I swear to you, there was nothing I could do for Genevieve. It was her time. Please try to understand?"

"Understand?" Andre asked furiously. "It wasn't your decision to make! You just said you weren't God!"

"No," Pascal said with an ironic smile. "Nothing like, I'm afraid. But nevertheless, I knew from the day Genevieve was born that she was always more God's than ours."

Andre frowned heavily. "What do you mean by that?"

"Genevieve was born with a malformed heart," Pascal said gently.

"What?" Andre said, shaken to the core. "A malformed heart? What kind of an excuse is that? She was perfectly healthy, you know she was!"

"No. She wasn't. Surely you must have seen that she became ill more often than the average person, that she didn't grow as she might have done. I was surprised she lived as long as she did, but I imagine her love for you fed her will."

Andre slowly shook his head in flat denial. "No. No, I don't believe it. I can't. If that were the truth, Genevieve would have told me. We told each other everything."

"But she didn't know about her condition. No one did, save for your mother. What good would it have done for her to live with a death sentence hanging over her when there was no treatment?" He exhaled. "So I kept my peace and tried to keep her as healthy as I could for as long as I could."

"And her last illness?" Andre asked curtly, examining his father's face for the lie which he was convinced had to be there. "Why did you choose not to help her? It was a simple case of lung congestion—I've seen you cure scores of people with the same problem. Explain that."

"In Genevieve's case, it put too much of a strain on her heart. As I said, it was her time, Andre. All I could do was to help her go in peace. There seemed no point in prolonging her suffering." Pascal touched his arm, and Andre flinched. "I'm sorry," he said, taking his hand away. "If there is one thing I regret it's that you weren't there, but there was no way of knowing when you'd arrive."

Andre covered his eyes with one hand. "No," he said, shaking his head back and forth, his entire world spinning as his father's words rewove the fabric of everything he'd believed for so long. What of the last nine years? If what his father said was true, they had been a travesty, his isolation, much of his pain unnecessary. And that thought he couldn't bear to entertain. "No," he said. "No. It's too easy. There has to be more to it than that. What about your opposition to our marriage? You may have held your peace, but I felt it. God, how I felt it."

"I know you think your mother and I disapproved of your wanting to marry Genevieve, but that wasn't the case at all. We were simply concerned for both of you, given her condition."

"I would rather have had a little happiness than none at all," Andre said tightly, looking over at him.

"And how would you have felt if Genevieve had become pregnant? She would never have survived. Her death would have been on your conscience always."

"What?" he said in total confusion.

"I planned to caution you against conception if you had married. I didn't want you to live with the burden of Genevieve's death, which was inevitable anyway. But given your nature, had her death been in any way on your account, you would have suffered for a very long time. It seems you found a way to do that anyway."

Andre couldn't reply. There was something in his father's flat statement, in the compassion in his eyes, that spoke of truth. And with an agonizing wrench of finality, Andre knew in his heart that his father did speak the truth, that he had spoken the truth all along. It was he who had refused to hear it. He felt suddenly, violently sick.

He laid his folded palms sideways against his mouth, pressing back the taste of bile. Then he pushed them flat against his thighs with a deep, shuddering breath. "I didn't know. God help me, I didn't know."

"I would have told you all of this that night, but

there was no talking to you. Still, I'm glad that you trusted me enough to bring Ali here. At least that was a life that could be saved."

Andre turned to his father, tears shimmering in his eyes. "I don't know what to say," he said, his voice breaking. "All these years ... all these long years away, all because of a serious misconception on my part. Ah, Papa—I feel such a fool. Such a damn stubborn fool." His body shook from head to toe as it finally released the burden it had carried for so long, as he let the barriers down, allowed love to rush in and suffuse his spirit, nurture him, heal him. And it hurt like hell.

Pascal reached out and pulled him into his arms, holding him close as if he were still a small child in need of comforting and absorbed his wrenching sobs until they finally subsided.

"Do you know," he said, releasing Andre and wiping away his own tears, "there was a time before you were born that I was laboring under some misconceptions myself, and I was extremely angry with God. I remember wondering if He was next going to demand the sacrifice of my firstborn son." He was silent for a long moment. "Well ... at least it was only for nine years and not a lifetime."

"Oh, Papa," Andre cried, his heart breaking over what he had done to the parents he loved so deeply, for the suffering he had caused them so needlessly. "What have I done?"

"You've finally learned to face pain, instead of suffering interminably trying to avoid it," Pascal said simply.

"God—all this time, trying to push everything away, using my anger with you to justify my actions." His voice dropped to a whisper. "I thought that if I let myself feel I'd break apart. I was even terrified to love Ali, for fear of the same thing."

"But now you know that you can't avoid love any more than you can avoid pain," Pascal said. "And that's a valuable lesson, especially for people like you and me."

Andre looked at him in hard question through the blur in his eyes.

"Andre. I know how it is to feel things so deeply that you want to die. It's as if we don't have a buffer against the world. But you can't create one. And isolating yourself is a waste of time." He smiled sadly. "I tried that too by retreating into monasteries. It didn't work, any more than your leaving your home and your family worked for you. In the end, the only solution is to submit to God's will." He smiled. "And to swear a lot. And to find a woman to love as much as I love your mother and you clearly love Ali."

Andre wiped his streaming eyes and nose. "How did God ever make anyone so understanding, so good?"

Pascal snorted. "Don't fool yourself. He may have saddled me with a gift that can be a complete headache at times, but I'm no saint. Ask your mother."

"Where is she?" Andre asked, suddenly desperate to see her.

"She's sitting with Ali," he said with a smile. "She's very happy you're home. Overjoyed is a better word."

"Papa—Ali? She's really going to be all right?"

"She's really going to be all right," he replied, and Andre could see that he had no doubt of it. Pascal stood. "Why don't you come and see for yourself? Your mother is probably growing impatient to lay her eyes on you."

"Tell her I'll be up in a little while. There's something important I have to do first."

Pascal gazed at him, his eyes searching. "A good idea," he said. "I'll see you back at the house when you're finished."

Andre watched his father go, thinking that apparently he read minds as well as he worked miracles.

"Oh. And by the way," Pascal said over his shoulder as he pushed the chapel door open. "Just so you know, not every medical marvel involves a miracle. And not every miracle involves medicine. Welcome home, Andre."

The cemetery felt peaceful, the only sound the gentle whisper of the wind through the trees. Andre knelt by Genevieve's grave, running his hands over the face of the cool headstone.

"Genevieve, my dear girl. I've come to say goodbye." He rested his forehead on his hands. "I will never forget you, or the time we had together, everything that we shared. Thank you for your gentleness, your innocence, your sweetness. Thank you for your love."

He stood, wiping his blurred vision with one hand, and he placed the flowers that he'd brought on the pebbles that covered her grave. "And now it's time for me to let go of you. Rest well, dear one. Be happy in God's arms."

He felt a rush of peace, the kiss of the breeze on his cheek.

He turned, looking up toward the château. Toward life. Toward Ali.

And then he walked out of the enclosed cemetery, softly shutting the wood door behind him as finally as he shut the door on the past.

Andre's gaze fell on his mother, who sat by the bed holding Ali's hand in her own. She looked tired, slightly strained around the eyes, but beautiful as ever. God, she was a welcome sight. "Hello, Mama," he said softly.

"Andre! Oh, Andre—I don't believe it ..." Lily rose from her chair and rushed toward him, arms outstretched, her eyes flooding with sudden tears.

He pulled her tightly to him, trying to hold his own tears in check. "Don't cry, Mama. Please don't cry. It's all right. Everything is all right now."

She pressed her forehead against his chest, hard. "I should paddle you, you know."

"You should. But I'm bigger than you are."

Lily gave a choked laugh and looked up into his face. "You always were too impudent for your own good." Her fingers lovingly stroked his cheek. "Andre. How I've missed you."

"I've missed you too," he whispered, covering her fingers with his own. "More than I can possibly say. How is Ali?"

"Come," she said, taking his hand. "Look." She drew him over to the bed.

He gazed down at Ali. Her face was tranquil, relaxed, her breathing soft and even, although her color was still very pale. He touched her hair, his hand shaking slightly. She looked so vulnerable, but oh, so alive. So alive. Even now he could feel the life force emanating from her, and he was infinitely grateful for it.

He glanced up at his mother. "Papa truly did save her, didn't he?"

"Yes," she said bluntly. "He did."

"He told me," Andre said equally bluntly. "About all of it. About the miracles, about Genevieve, about what really happened."

"Yes, I know," she said. "I gather you've come to your senses. And high time too. Although I can't hold you entirely at fault, Andre."

She sank into the chair next to the bed, and Andre carefully settled himself on the edge of the bed, taking Ali's hand into his, relishing its warmth. "You can't?" he said. "I don't see how you can think me anything but a hotheaded, stubborn idiot."

"No," Lily said. "Well, perhaps partially," she added, "but you can't help yourself. That's breeding from my side, and nothing will change it but experience. What I meant," she said at his look of surprise, "is that your father and I are also to blame for what happened."

"What do you mean? Papa said that none of it could be avoided." He frowned, wondering if his father had not told him the full truth. Had they disapproved of Genevieve, after all?

She folded her hands together and placed them in her lap. "I don't refer to Genevieve," she said, answering his silent question. "I refer to you, Andre. The truth of the matter is that you grew up in idyllic circumstances. Your life was entirely happy—nothing tragic happened around you, and you were surrounded by love everywhere you went."

"Yes," he said. "It's true. But what more could you

have wanted? What more could any parent want for a child?"

"I don't know," she answered. "Maybe a larger dose of reality. I suppose we wanted to protect you from all the sad things in the world, from all the pain we had been through. But as a result you went into manhood unprepared for pain, for disappointment, for disillusionment."

"Mama," he said, deeply touched, loving her even more for her incredible generosity. "Please don't take my stupidity upon yourself. Please. No one could have asked for a happier childhood." He smiled at her. "I just needed some sense knocked into my head—and I needed Ali."

Lily looked down at Ali. "You are fortunate in your wife, Andre."

"I know," he said quietly. "Oh, I do know. I've learned more from Ali about bravery in the face of suffering, about love given without condition, about ..." He had to stop and swallow against the hard lump in his throat. "About strength," he managed to finish.

"And you can take hope in all the strength Ali has. And in her love for you."

"You're going to love her too," he said, wiping his eyes again. "She's a wonderful girl. Unique."

"Actually," Lily said with a broad smile, "I've loved Ali for years. So has your father."

Andre stared at her, stunned. "No. Oh, no ..."

"Yes," Lily said, laughing. "Come now, you can't think just because you chose to turn your back on everything and everyone that the rest of us would do the same? Ali has given us great pleasure over the years. We all knew you were going to marry her years before you did, you know. Or at least we hoped you'd have the good sense."

"So *that's* why Jo-Jean said that you approved of our marriage," he said, enlightened at last. "And I thought it was her pedigree you liked."

"Andre," Lily said gently. "All we have ever wanted is your happiness. Pedigrees mean nothing to either of us, and you really ought to know that. It was clear to us from the beginning that you and Ali were meant to be together." She smiled. "It appears we were right."

Andre just shook his head. "The brat," he said. "The little brat. She never said a word. Not one word."

"And why would she have? Ali, no doubt, was protecting you. We all seem to have a bad habit of wanting to do that. But I imagine she's brought you great happiness."

"Yes. She has." He arched an eyebrow. "She's even managed to turn Sutherby into a happy place. Imagine that. Mrs. Grimes walks around with a smile on her wrinkled old face—and Pennyswell looks as if he's in his second childhood."

Lily nodded. "Well, that's good. They all deserve a little happiness. God knows your grandfather made their lives a misery." She looked up as Pascal came into the room. "Hello, darling. Have you been out killing the fatted calf? Oh—I suppose that will have to be my job," she said, with another smile. "You and Andre are hopeless."

"Pity, isn't it?" Pascal said, amused. "It must be dreadful for you to be saddled with squeamish men." He walked over to the bed and looked down at Ali, checking her pulse, then pulled the covers back and cast a glance at the white bandage that covered her abdomen, Andre watching him anxiously.

"Good," he said. "Perfectly clean." He covered her up, then smoothed a hand over her brow. "Hello, Ali," he said. "I think it's time to wake up. Andre looks as if he's about to expire from worry."

Her eyelids fluttered slightly, and her tongue flickered over her lips. And then her eyes slowly opened and she blinked. "Andre?" she whispered.

"Right here, sweetheart," he said, squeezing her hand, relief and thankfulness nearly overwhelming him.

"Do you believe now?" she asked, and he had to lean down to hear her. "Do you?"

He placed a gentle kiss on her cheek. "Yes, I believe now," he murmured hoarsely. "I believe. Thank God, Ali. Thank God."

"I did," she said, a mischievous smile playing around the corners of her mouth. Then she turned her head. "Pascal. You're here. You fixed me, didn't you? Thank you."

Pascal brushed a hand over her hair. "You made a most dramatic entrance as usual," he said. "Although this time you managed to scare me half to death."

"I'm sorry," she said, attempting a smile. She lifted her gaze. "And Lily," she said. "You're here too. How wonderful."

"Hello, my darling. How do you feel?"

"Happy," Ali said softly, sleepily. "So happy to be here. And happy too because I had the most beautiful dream imaginable."

"What was that?" Pascal asked, stroking her hair again.

"Do you know the little angel Gabriel you sent with Jo-Jean for my wedding day?"

Andre glanced at his father in surprise. He'd had no idea that the necklace Ali always wore had been a wedding present from him. He felt even more ashamed of himself, if that was possible.

"Yes, of course," Pascal said.

She moistened her lips. "Well, I dreamed I was in heaven, and I met Gabriel, who gave me a lily."

Pascal smiled softly. "Did you?"

"Pascal, did you ... will I ever be able to have a child?" she asked, her brow furrowing.

"I don't see any reason why not. As a matter of fact, I found some adhesions which might have made it difficult for you to conceive before this, but that's all sorted out now."

Ali's face lit up in a brilliant smile. "Thank you. Oh, thank you. My angel told me you would fix it all." She sighed. "I think I have to sleep again." She moved her fingers in Andre's hand. "Will you stay with me for a while, Andre?"

"Of course I will," he said, his heart nearly breaking with love. Ali. Sweet, sweet Ali. He was so damned lucky. And so very, very grateful.

He waited until she'd fallen into a deep sleep, then

went straight to the chapel to offer up a fervent prayer of thanks.

Believe? he thought, kneeling at the little altar, bowing his head. *Oh, yes. He believed. He believed as he'd never believed before. He believed in grace. In forgiveness. And most of all, he believed in the power of love.*

Andre lifted his head and gazed at the Cross. "Thank you," he whispered. "Thank you for healing Ali. And thank you for healing me."

Ali thought a month had been entirely too long to have to wait to be with Andre, but she planned to make up for that tonight, now that Pascal had told her it was safe. She hugged Pascal in sheer glee at the news, causing him to make a ribald comment about his son's apparent prowess.

Andre still had no idea, she thought wickedly, watching him celebrate the successful harvest in the annual fête in the village square. Wouldn't he be surprised?

He'd had a wonderful time, taking pleasure in simply being home again, helping to bring in the harvest, reacquainting himself with his friends, spending hours with his parents trying to make up for lost time. He was a far cry from the Andre of old, even from the one she had married, or the one who had come to Turkey to bring her home.

There was something different about this Andre, she thought, laughing as he and Jo-Jean danced a wild country jig on top of one of the long tables. It was as if he had grown wings and taken flight. She loved seeing the light in his eyes, the softening of his face when he spoke to his father or mother, the laughter that echoed from one end of the château to the other and out into the fields. And interestingly enough, he no longer felt the cold.

It was obvious to anyone who watched that Andre was where he belonged, that he loved Saint-Simon and its people with everything in him, that he belonged to them as much as they belonged to him, that his heart was wide open.

It saddened her that she would never belong in his

heart in the same way. But at least she could give him children who would, children born into the same heritage. And tonight she planned to try.

"Ali? What has put such a dreamy look on your face?" Andre asked, coming into the bedroom to say good night, as he did every night. "You've been wearing it since this afternoon."

Ali smiled at him from under the covers. "Would you like to see my scar?" she asked. She lifted the sheets.

"Your *scar*? If you'd like, but what the devil would . . ." A wicked grin flashed across his face. "Yes," he said. "I think I'd like to see your scar very, very much."

"It's not terribly impressive," she said. "Your father was very neat."

"I don't mind," he said, falling onto the bed and pulling her into his arms, then sitting up and tucking her back against his chest. He inched her nightdress up over her thighs, his fingers lightly caressing her skin as he went. "Now where is this magnificent piece of work?" he asked.

"Higher," she said with a laugh. "You'll never find it if you stop there."

"I wouldn't mind," he said, brushing his fingers over her downy curls. But he pulled the linen up to her waist obligingly enough and peered down at the thin red line. "Hmm. Very handy." He brushed a finger over it. "Do you have anything else you'd like to show me?"

Ali shifted her weight on the hard bulge that pressed against her buttocks. "Yes," she whispered.

"Thank God," he said, his hands cupping her breasts, his thumbs toying with her nipples through the thin fabric. "Celibacy has been torture. But are you sure it's all right, sweetheart?"

Ali tilted her head back against his hard shoulder in answer, and he accepted her invitation, bringing his mouth down to hers, stroking his tongue over her lips. "Mmm. Sweet," he said, then deepened his kiss. And then he twisted her around to face him, settling her naked flesh over his hips. He pulled her nightdress over her head and tossed it on the floor.

"It's been hell sleeping in the next room too, thinking of you, all alone in this big bed." He bent his head to her breast, pulling it into his mouth, milking her rosy nipple until she writhed against him, rubbing her hips against his erection.

"That's enough of that, or it will all be over before we've even started," he said, rolling her off him. "I'm determined to take this very slowly and carefully." But despite his words, it took him only a minute to strip and come back to her.

He lay down on his side, his full length stretched out next to her and he cupped her face between his hands. "Do you have any idea how much I've missed you? I mean really, really missed you? You've been busy lying about recovering in luxury while I've been in a fully healthy state of rampant desire, having to lust for you from afar."

"Trust me, you haven't been the only one," she said, stroking her mouth against his warm cheek, her hands exploring the hard curves of his back, the valley of his spine.

"Mmm," he murmured, cupping her buttocks, his erection pressing against her belly. "It occurred to me in one black moment that my father was paying me back for my idiocy by putting a prohibition on you."

Ali smiled and nipped his shoulder with her teeth. "It would have served you right. You can't imagine what happiness it gives me to see you with them, to see you here."

Andre rolled her onto her back and gazed down at her, his hands smoothing the hair off her face. "Ali." He kissed her again, his mouth caressing, gentle, but his control didn't last long, and the intensity with which he kissed left her breathless.

She shuddered as he ran his mouth down her neck, over her breasts, tracing the underswelling with his tongue, his hands smoothing over her ribs, her hips, stroking the delicate flesh of her inner thighs as his thumbs found her cleft and moved on it.

"Andre," she moaned, rising up to meet his intimate touch. And then she felt the blunt pressure of his erection pushing against her entrance, and she opened to welcome him, reveling in the feel of him sliding into her, filling her with his length.

"God, that's good," he whispered, his breath hot against her cheek. He began to move in her, each smooth stroke gentle and controlled, yet powerful. "Ali ... you're so full of life. You are life. My life."

She opened her eyes to find him gazing down at her, and she caught her breath, astonished by what she saw. His eyes, the color of pure smoke, blazed into hers, and his face was filled with a fierce joy she'd never seen before. She felt as if he were looking inside her, straight into her heart, as if each thrust he made in her body was directed toward the same place.

She felt as if they were one entity, one thought, one heartbeat. She felt as if she were back in heaven. And in that moment, heaven came down to her as his body erupted in hers, and hers shattered around his, one life, one shared piece of eternity.

When her heart finally stopped pounding, she realized that warm tears were sliding down her cheeks. She wasn't sure if they were her own or Andre's, for when she opened her eyes, she saw that his face was streaked with tears too. She reached up to wipe them away.

"How I love you," he whispered. "Oh, *God* how I love you."

Ali's hand stilled in shock. "Andre ..."

"I've been wanting to tell you all this last month, but I knew that if I tried, I'd probably end up doing things I shouldn't. So I waited," he said, kissing her forehead. "And I'm glad. It wouldn't have been the same without showing you how damned much."

"But I—but I thought ..."

"Sweetheart. As much of an idiot as I was about my parents, I was even a bigger one about you. I love you with everything I have in me, and maybe more than that."

She mutely shook her head, unable to believe her ears, that he was actually speaking the words she had thought she'd never hear. "I can't . . ." She stopped, knowing there were no words for the enormity of what she was feeling.

"I've loved you for a long time," he said. "A very long time, even if I couldn't admit it to myself."

"But what about Genevieve?" she asked in a small voice.

"Oh, Ali," he said tenderly, stroking her face, "there's a part of me that will always love Genevieve. But I'm no longer that same boy who fell in love one fine spring, or even the young man who grieved her death. I'm a man deeply and irrevocably in love with his extraordinary wife."

"But Genevieve was your fairy-child," Ali said, blinking away a fresh rush of tears.

He smiled and stroked his thumbs over her eyes. "No. She was *your* fairy-child. I don't want a fairy-child, my love. I want you, just as you are. Exactly as you are in every way."

Ali smiled up at him mistily. "Are you sure? Really, really sure?"

"Perfectly. If I hadn't been so damned frightened of the depth of my feelings for you, I would have realized the truth a long time ago." He exhaled. "I'm sorry. I know I hurt you."

Ali pulled his face down to hers and kissed him. "No. Don't be sorry. Please don't be sorry. There isn't any room for sorrow in all this happiness."

"You know," he said, "if I had never loved Genevieve, I don't think I'd have known how to love you so well. Does that make sense?"

Ali nodded. "Yes," she said, her heart aching with her limitless love for him. "I understand. I really do understand."

He has learned the lessons put before him.

Joy joined the love in her heart.

"Good. And I intend to prove it to you every single day for the rest of my life. In England, in France, in Turkey, wherever we happen to be, you're going to be the most adored wife ever."

"Oh, I do like the sound of that," Ali said, wrapping

her arms around him and pressing her cheek to his bare chest. "I really, really do."

He chuckled. "And now I'm going to give you a nice wash. Standard procedure for recuperating patients, not to mention thoroughly ravished and beloved wives." Andre kissed her again, then slipped out of bed, going across the room to fetch a basin of water and a cloth.

Ali smiled to herself in incredible happiness. Andre loved her. Had always loved her. It was a dream finally come true. And she had the most extraordinary feeling that there was another dream that had finally come true as well.

She rolled onto her side, her hands pressed low against her abdomen, not in pain, but in wonder, for she felt certain that they had just conceived a child.

She felt Andre's weight on the mattress, and the sound of water dripping as he wrung the cloth out in the basin. And then she heard the slow intake of his breath.

"Ali," he said, and she heard quiet astonishment in his voice.

"What?" she asked lazily.

"The scars . . . the scars on your back. Where the hell have they gone to?"

"What do you mean?" she asked, puzzled.

"I mean they've damned well disappeared. There's not a trace of them! Scars just don't disappear. Dear God . . ."

She reached her hand around and felt, her fingers moving over her skin. He was right. The ridges were gone. "But how . . . ?" she started to say.

"I don't bloody well know. You don't think it was my father working one of his miracles, do you? But what else could it be?"

Ali shook her head, a huge smile on her face, as the faint echo of the angel's words came back to her.

Your pain is over, sweet one. The only traces are the ones lodged in your heart, those that have brought you widsom.

She turned over and looked up at Andre, her eyes

shining. "No. I don't think that particular miracle was your father's doing. But what I do think is that every last one of my dreams has been made into truth," she said, smoothing her hands over his cheeks. "And I also think I'm the luckiest woman alive."

"And I the luckiest man," he said, enfolding her in his embrace. "Truly the luckiest man."

She tucked herself into his shoulder. "Thank you, God and Gabriel," she whispered. "Thank you."

Author's Note

The country Türkiye, or Turkey, as it is called in the West, did not exist as a nation until 1922 when Mustafa Kemal Atatürk formed the republic from what remained of the decimated Ottoman Empire after the First World War.

The majority of the land on which Turkey now sits has been known since ancient times as Anatolia, a word taken from the Greek *anatole,* "sunrise." Home to known civilizations since 7000 B.C., Anatolia has been ruled by the Hittites, the Greeks, the Persians, the Romans, and the Byzantines, among others. In the eleventh century it was invaded by the Turkoman, who founded the Seljuk Empire and introduced Islam to a country that had been Christian since the time of Constantine nearly a thousand years before. In the fourteenth century, when the emirate of Osmanli took over the quarreling factions created by the constant warring between the Mongols and the Seljuks, Anatolia became known as the Ottoman Empire. Although at its height the Empire extended as far north as Hungary and parts of Russia, as far south as Egypt and parts of Arabia, and as far west as Algeria, the term *Turk* was only ever applied to the people who lived in Anatolia.

In the time that Ali and Andre would have been there, Anatolia was caught in the grip of the last dark years of Ottoman rule. The language Ali would have spoken as an Anatolian Turk was known as Osmanlica, a complicated, flowery mixture of Persian, Arabic, and Turkish that bears little resemblance to the language you hear in Turkey today.